MW01088003

WITH A
VENGEANCE

ALSO BY RILEY SAGER

Final Girls

The Last Time I Lied

Lock Every Door

Home Before Dark

Survive the Night

The House Across the Lake

The Only One Left

Middle of the Night

WITH A VENGEANCE

A NOVEL

RILEY SAGER

DUTTON

DUTTON

An imprint of Penguin Random House LLC
1745 Broadway, New York, NY 10019
penguinrandomhouse.com

Copyright © 2025 by Todd Ritter
Penguin Random House values and supports copyright. Copyright fuels creativity, encourages
diverse voices, promotes free speech, and creates a vibrant culture. Thank you for buying an
authorized edition of this book and for complying with copyright laws by not reproducing,
scanning, or distributing any part of it in any form without permission. You are supporting writers
and allowing Penguin Random House to continue to publish books for every reader. Please note
that no part of this book may be used or reproduced in any manner for the purpose of training
artificial intelligence technologies or systems.

DUTTON and the D colophon are registered trademarks of Penguin Random House LLC.

BOOK DESIGN BY GEORGE TOWNE

LIBRARY OF CONGRESS CATALOGING-IN-PUBLICATION DATA

Names: Sager, Riley, author.
Title: With a vengeance : a novel / Riley Sager.
Description: New York, NY : Dutton, 2025.
Identifiers: LCCN 2024056777 | ISBN 9780593472408 (hardcover) |
ISBN 9780593472415 (ebook)
Subjects: LCGFT: Thrillers (Fiction) | Novels.
Classification: LCC PS3618.I79 W58 2025 | DDC 813/.6—dc23/eng/20250103
LC record available at https://lccn.loc.gov/2024056777

ISBN 9798217046379 (export)

Printed in the United States of America
1 3 5 7 9 10 8 6 4 2

The authorized representative in the EU for product safety and compliance is
Penguin Random House Ireland, Morrison Chambers, 32 Nassau Street,
Dublin D02 YH68, Ireland, https://eu-contact.penguin.ie.

For my family

WITH A
VENGEANCE

DEPARTURE

THE TRAIN ISN'T empty, although it certainly feels that way. Whole sections currently sit unused. Coach cars. Dining car. Sleeper. All are vacant and silent save for the echo of the train itself clickety-clacking over the tracks. This train that can hold dozens, even hundreds, is occupied by only eight people.

Seven are alive.

One is dead.

That wasn't the case a minute ago, when the whole lot of them were very much alive. But unexpected things happen when traveling by train, and this, apparently, is one of them. It certainly took Anna Matheson off guard. Her reaction makes it clear this isn't the plan at all. She seems honestly distressed by the body now splayed flat-backed on the floor of the first-class lounge.

A strange reaction.

Anna has every reason to want the others dead.

Those others, by the way, are the six people aboard this train at her invitation. One that, had they known who was doing the inviting, all would have declined.

Your singular presence is requested on an overnight
rail journey from Philadelphia to Chicago
beginning the evening of December 14
aboard the Philadelphia Phoenix

Departing Philadelphia at 7 P.M. EST
Arriving in Chicago at 7 A.M. CST

Not particularly compelling, as invitations go. It's 1954, after all. No one wants to spend thirteen hours on a train when United Air Lines can get you to Chicago in just under three. Anna knew this, of course, which was why she added a handwritten message on the back, specific to each recipient. Although their misdeeds are the same, their secrets are different.

Those individualized notes were all it took to get the six of them here. They didn't care that they had no idea who the invitation came from or why it was extended to them. Nor were they bothered by the lack of a way to RSVP. They all showed up at the scheduled departure time, invitation in hand. Now here they are— five guests, one hostess, her accomplice, and a corpse.

Not enough time has passed for color to drain from the dead person's face. Their eyes are wide open and aimed at the ceiling, and flecks of crimson stain the foam still bubbling at the edges of their mouth.

This, it's clear, was not a natural death.

Nor was it painless.

At least it was quick, the time between the first sign that something was amiss and sudden death totaling less than a minute. The victim didn't even have a chance to let go of the white linen yanked off a cocktail table as they fell. One end of the tablecloth remains gripped in lifeless fingers. The rest of it still clings to the table, soaked through with gin spilled from an overturned martini glass.

In another minute, someone will have the good sense to use a dry tablecloth to cover the corpse. Until then, everyone stares at it in combinations of shock and disbelief, none more so than Anna, over whose face ripple a thousand emotions. The biggest of them, though, is fear.

Because now that one of the passengers has been murdered—by someone else in that very car—she fears it's only a matter of time before it happens again.

7 P.M.

THIRTEEN HOURS
TO CHICAGO

ONE

ANNA MATHESON CLEARS her throat, straightens her spine, and steadies her trembling hands. She pictures herself as a statue, rigid and impenetrable. Anything to make her look like she's not afraid, when in truth she's been scared for so long that fear has seeped into her marrow.

Still, when she begins to speak, her voice is firm and clear.

"You know who I am. Just as you know why I've gathered you here. If you haven't figured it out yet, you will very soon."

Anna pauses, just as she'd rehearsed, the length timed to the millisecond to allow any unlikely stragglers to catch up.

"By now, you've recognized each other. Maybe you've even had a chance to chat a bit. Likely long enough to suspect that you've been brought here under false pretenses. That suspicion is correct. The reason for this journey is simple. I'm here to—"

Just then, the train lurches, sending Anna off balance. In the tiny bathroom of her room, she watches her reflection sway in the equally tiny mirror. The first time she'd been on the Philadelphia Phoenix, everything had felt enormous. Not just the room, but the train itself. Every car seemed endless, as if walking the entire length of the train constituted a journey of miles.

Then again, Anna had been eleven at the time, and trains loomed large in her life. Especially ones run by the Union Atlantic Railroad. Unlike most rail lines of the day, Union Atlantic had been privately owned. Her father had inherited the family business when her grandfather passed away. In another bit of unconventionality, it hadn't relied on an outside company like Pullman to build its cars and locomotives. Union Atlantic designed and manufactured its own in-house at a facility in Philadelphia, including the Phoenix. Anna's mother had even designed the interiors, filling them with her favorite fabrics and colors. Velvet drapes, chenille upholstery, damask walls. All in shades of peacock blue, emerald green, and rich ivory surrounded by walnut and gold leaf and bronze.

After her mother, her brother, and Anna herself, the Philadelphia Phoenix had been her father's pride and joy. Debuting in 1937, it wasn't the first streamliner train, nor was it the fastest or the most famous. But those superlatives didn't matter. The Phoenix was still a gleaming marvel that offered both jaw-dropping speed and unparalleled luxury.

Plus, her father loved it, which is the main reason Anna chose it for the night's journey. It serves as a reminder to the others of all that had been taken from her.

The train lurches again, this time with purpose. A moment later, someone raps four times on the door.

Seamus.

Here to tell her what she already knows.

The train is in motion.

There's no turning back now.

Anna hurries to the door, feeling the train picking up speed beneath her bare feet. A strange sensation that, for a second, wreaks havoc on her balance and makes her reach for the wall to steady herself. No matter how many times she travels by train, it always takes Anna a moment to navigate that unwieldy combination of standing on solid ground while also being in motion. "Train legs," her father had called them.

Removing her hand from the wall, she stands in the middle of the room, waiting for her legs to learn how to absorb the gentle rocking of the train. Once they do, she's able to reach for the door, unlock it, and pull it open.

As expected, Seamus is on the other side, filling the narrow corridor that runs the length of the car. The windows behind him show nothing but blackness. They are now in the tunnel on their way out of the city.

"Everything going as planned?" Anna asks, unconcerned that she's standing at the door wearing only her slip. Seamus has seen her in far less.

"So far."

"And the engineer? Is it still Burt Chapman at the controls?"

Seamus responds with a nod. "Yeah. Watched him climb into the locomotive myself."

A relief. Burt Chapman has been guiding the Phoenix since the very start. He is, Anna knows, a good man. He sent a condolence card when her father died. It was the only one Anna and her mother had received. That act of kindness made her think Burt could be trusted to take them to Chicago without any hiccups. The massive amount of money she paid him certainly helped.

"You're certain he's capable of doing it by himself?" Seamus says. "Thirteen hours is a long shift without any breaks."

"Burt will be fine. He's run this route so many times that he could probably do it with one hand tied behind his back. What about the rest of the crew?"

"They've been taken care of," Seamus says. "Every conductor, cook, porter, and brakeman. Here's hoping they still have jobs after this."

Anna lets the comment pass. Seamus had made clear his

concerns that the night might ruin the livelihoods of the innocent men who work on the train. Anna had considered it, too. Concluding that there was no other choice, she provided all of them with ample compensation. Three months' salary, in cash, with a little extra going to those most vulnerable to punishment from their boss.

But the fates of the train's workers are the least of Anna's worries. She's more concerned about its passengers.

"And the others?" she says. "Did everyone come?"

Seamus scowls, which worries Anna. Although he rarely smiles, Seamus's scowl is equally elusive. Without it, she would have assumed the answer was yes. She knows these people. She knows what they can and cannot resist. But the look on Seamus's face suggests something has already gone wrong.

And this is a journey during which nothing can go wrong.

"Yeah," Seamus says, hedging. "But there's a wrinkle."

"What kind of wrinkle?"

Just then, a voice rises from the door at the end of the car. A man. Clearly impatient and self-important. Jack Lapsford, Anna guesses.

"Can I get some goddamn help over here?"

Anna ducks back into her room. He can't see her. None of them can. Not yet. She nods to a still-scowling Seamus, reminding him that, for now, he needs to keep pretending he works for the railroad.

"Coming, sir," he says, forcing an obsequious smile.

Anna closes the door and presses her ear against it, listening to Seamus make his way to the end of the car.

"How may I be of assistance?"

"You can start by telling me where all the damn porters went."

With that comment, Anna knows with certainty that the man is Lapsford. The entitled cretin.

She locks the door, this time also using the dead bolt. She

needs to be extra cautious now that she knows everyone is on-board. When she returns to the center of the room, her legs remain unsteady. This time, the culprit is Jack Lapsford's voice. Hearing it reminds Anna of the enormity of this journey. What she intends to do. What she *needs* to do. How, after so much planning, it is now underway.

Anna picks up the manifest sitting atop the bed, reviewing the names and assigned room numbers of the six passengers invited onboard.

Sal Lawrence, Car 12, Room A
Lt. Col. Jack Lapsford, Car 12, Room B
Kenneth Wentworth, Car 12, Room C
Herb Pulaski, Car 13, Room A
Edith Gerhardt, Car 13, Room B
Judd Dodge, Car 13, Room C

Each name ignites a flare of rage in Anna's chest. These people—these six rotten, repulsive, *evil* people—are on this train at this very moment. If she wanted to, Anna could go down the line, moving from door to door, killing them all one by one.

And she very much wants to.

Which is why she and Seamus occupy Rooms A and B in the train's eleventh car, leaving the third room there vacant. It serves as a buffer of sorts, protecting everyone from her worst instincts.

Anna drops the page and looks to the window, surprised to realize they're out of the tunnel and moving steadily away from the city. For so long, she'd thought this night would never come. Now that it has, it seems to be going by faster than she ever expected.

The lights in the room flicker out for a moment. Not an un-common occurrence on the Phoenix, which requires more power than most trains because of its luxurious trappings. Still, the moment of darkness is a concern, especially when it provides Anna with a clearer view out the window. The train now moves under a dark sky punctuated by large flecks of snow.

Anna had followed the weather reports and knew they'd likely be encountering snow. She just didn't expect it to be so early, assuming instead that the first flakes wouldn't be seen until the train was halfway across Pennsylvania. Now she worries about how large a storm awaits them as they move west—and if it will be enough to stop the Phoenix.

Because under no circumstances can the train stop.

To do so, even for thirty seconds, could completely ruin Anna's plan.

The lights flash back on, obscuring the view out the window. Forcing her legs into motion, Anna dresses quickly, assembling the look she'd worked so hard to cultivate.

Red dress.

Demure yet curve-hugging. Tailored to fit her like a suit of armor but with just enough give that she can run in it, if it comes to that. She suspects it might.

Red mules.

A necessary evil. The advantage is that the heels make her look taller, more formidable. The downside is that they could become a problem if she does need to start running.

Red lipstick.

Just because.

Blond hair pinned into a vaguely unflattering bun, a choice made with function and not fashion in mind. Anna doesn't want her shoulder-length hair getting in the way. It's the same with her jewelry. That means no necklaces, bracelets, or anything else that someone could latch onto. Other than diamond studs in her ears, the only accessory she wears is a single lapel pin that belonged to her father.

A tiny silver train engine pinned at her bodice, closest to her heart.

Then there's the knife. Flat-handled and boasting a four-inch blade, it's hidden beneath her dress, slid into a sheath strapped to her upper thigh. Anna thought it necessary, just in case she reaches a point when running isn't even an option.

As she studies her ensemble in the bathroom mirror, Aunt Retta's voice rings through her thoughts, bright with satisfaction.

Now that, my darling, is how you dress for revenge.

That was always Anna's intention. But even she's surprised by her appearance. She looks resplendent. One of her mother's favorite words, probably because it described her perfectly. Margaret Matheson had possessed an elegant grace most women only dream about, Anna included. Her mother had that magical ability to make everything—from the most expensive of gowns to jeans and a flannel work shirt—look like it was fresh off the Paris runway, designed specifically for her.

Her parents' courtship had been brief but intense, with a mere two weeks between first meeting and being wed by a justice of the peace. The speed in which it happened prompted rumors of a shotgun marriage. Tommy's birth eight months later did nothing to quell them. The reason it didn't become a society scandal was twofold. Most of Main Line Philadelphia didn't openly engage in such gossip, and the few who did could see how besotted Arthur Matheson was with his new bride.

Oh, how Anna's father had gazed at her mother. Everyone did, of course. They couldn't help it. Anna, in particular, found herself frequently awestruck by her mother's sheer loveliness. But no one looked at his wife quite like Arthur Matheson. Every time he saw her, his face would go slack for a moment before lighting up with joy. And her mother would beam right back.

For a few months when she was very young, Anna had become

convinced her mother was a movie star, for only people in the movies glowed that same way. Her friends' mothers certainly didn't. More often than not, they just looked dour and sad. But her mother? She positively shimmered. Which is why every time Anna went to the movies, she expected to see her mother's face flickering across that silver screen.

Even when that childish notion left her, Anna still believed her mother could have been a star, had she chosen to pursue it. Tommy, too, who had inherited her good looks and dazzling smile. He carried himself with the ease of a matinee idol.

It never bothered Anna that she took after her father, a man of unremarkable appearance. She grew up pretty but plain, displaying none of the sparkle her mother and brother possessed. To Anna, it didn't matter. She knew her family shared a charmed life.

For a little bit anyway.

Soon it was all gone. Tommy first. Then her father. Then her mother, whose light at that point had long been extinguished.

Anna forces herself not to think about all of that. She knew the journey would dredge up all those awful memories. She just didn't think it would happen this quickly. There'll be plenty of time to dwell on the past later. For now, she has to finish getting ready for her grand entrance, an act she anticipates and dreads in equal measure. In the mirror, she flicks her gaze to the reflection of the open bathroom door behind her and the room beyond it. A chair sits by the night-shrouded window, designed to swivel so the passenger sitting in it can properly take in the passing scenery. Right now, though, the chair is turned to the bathroom, holding not a passenger but a black leather briefcase.

Inside it is Anna's past.

And, she hopes, her future.

Turning back to her own reflection, Anna quickly applies a second coat of lipstick. As her lips gleam crimson, she mouths the part of her speech that had been cut off by the train's sudden lurch into motion.

"The reason for this journey is simple," she says, staring into the mirror but picturing the men and women she has lured onto the train. "I'm here to get justice. Because I have irrefutable proof that the six of you are responsible for destroying my family."

TWO

INCLUDING THE LOCOMOTIVE, the Philadelphia Phoenix consists of fourteen cars. Judd Dodge counted them as he paced the platform, debating if he should board. It's the same number of cars the Phoenix had during its heyday, when folks clamored to ride the most luxurious train this side of the 20th Century Limited. Thirteen cars of unlimited comfort, all pulled by an engine that could handle twice that many.

Judd knows because he designed it that way.

That was his job, once upon a time. Building engines for the Union Atlantic Railroad, which was peanuts compared to some of the other train lines in the nation. Its reach was small, limited to places in close proximity to Philadelphia. One line to New York City, another to Washington, D.C., a third shuttling riders to Atlantic City. The Philadelphia Phoenix was built with expansion in mind. A gleaming streamliner that traveled nonstop to Chicago.

Judd had beamed with pride the first time he saw the Phoenix gliding down the tracks. Sleek as a silver bullet, it moved fast, appearing speedier thanks to a flame-orange racing stripe that ran the length of the train on both sides. Not being a parent himself, Judd imagined it was the same feeling as watching your child take their very first steps. Something stationary had been put into motion, and he'd made it happen.

While every car on a train is valuable in its own way, with each one serving a distinct purpose, Judd knows that none are more important than the locomotive. Without one, the rest of those cars would remain useless atop a set of rails, on their way to nowhere. A train can only fulfill its destiny with a sturdy engine at the helm.

Judd made sure that his engines were sturdy.

Until the one time he was told to do the opposite.

After that, he no longer had the stomach for the job, so he quit and became a professor. He certainly looks the part, with his tall, rigid posture and wire-rimmed eyeglasses. Those glasses now slip down Judd's nose as he leaves his assigned room.

Because of the spaciousness of the first-class rooms, the corridor that leads to them is especially narrow. Standing in that cramped strip of hallway, Judd finds himself face-to-face with a wall sconce that has a loose bulb. It buzzes like a housefly while casting an unnerving flicker over that end of the corridor.

The cramped hall, the strobing bulb, even the car he's been placed in—unlucky number 13—makes Judd reconsider the wisdom of boarding. Fifty-three years old, he'd always been considered intelligent. A genius, some said, especially with machines. Yet he didn't need to be a rocket scientist to know this wasn't going to be a leisurely journey. The handwritten note scrawled on the back of the invitation said as much.

I know what you did.
If you don't come, others will know, too.

That message, alarming enough to get him to the station, also kept Judd from immediately boarding the Phoenix. While the note was clearly a threat, he remained uncertain about its seriousness. It could be nothing but a cruel trick by someone who thinks they know what happened. Or it could be a reminder to keep quiet from someone who does know the truth. Either way, Judd understood that he couldn't simply ignore it, which is why he eventually hopped onto the train at the last minute. He preferred to face the threat amid the hustle and bustle of the Phoenix. After all, no harm could come to him when there were others around.

"Ticket?" a gray-haired conductor asked as Judd moved deeper into the first of the train's two coach cars.

"I-I don't have one." Judd showed the invitation, making sure the conductor could only see the front of it. "Just this."

The conductor nodded. "Of course. But you're all the way on the other end of the train. In first class."

A porter was summoned. One whose smile faltered slightly as he took Judd's overnight bag and began to lead him to the back of the train. Because of his familiarity with the Phoenix—and because of his preboarding tally—Judd knew exactly what lay both ahead of and behind them. First, naturally, was the locomotive, which had once been his pride and joy. When he saw it for the first time in more than a decade, it felt like being reunited with a long-lost love. He couldn't help but admire his handiwork. The train, despite running for many years over many more miles, was still a beaut.

Behind the locomotive was the baggage car, followed by two coach cars. Back in the day, the Phoenix had the best coach seats in the country. Wide and comfortable, they reclined farther than most, allowing for easier sleeping on overnight trips.

Because of this, the coach cars were usually the most crowded on the train. That night, though, Judd saw few passengers occupying them. Those who did either gave him a cold stare as he passed or avoided eye contact altogether.

The next car was a sleeper, designed for those who wanted more than the bare minimum. It consisted of bench seating during the day that got converted into rows of curtained bunks at night. There were even fewer people in that car, which caused a nervous flip-flop in Judd's stomach. He'd been counting on safety in numbers.

His stomach did another somersault in the lounge, which sat completely empty. While it was nothing fancy, there were normally at least a couple people from the coach and sleeper cars inside stretching their legs or flipping through one of the newspapers and magazines fanned out across the end tables.

"Please keep up, sir," the porter said when he noticed Judd pausing to take in the vacant room. "We need to get to your room before the train departs."

Judd quickened his pace, following the porter into the club car, the first of four on the Phoenix devoted to food service. Like the lounge, the club car was also empty, save for a bored-looking cashier manning the counter where coach passengers should have been lined up to buy sandwiches, soda, and beer. With no one to serve, the cashier eyed Judd warily and asked the porter, "You're taking him through the galley?"

"It's faster this way," the porter said before pushing into the galley car, where all food aboard the Phoenix was prepared on-site. But instead of cooking, those inside the galley stood before empty counters and unlit stovetops, as if waiting to be told to begin. None of them looked at Judd and the porter as they carefully picked their way through.

The galley, Judd knew, was the line of demarcation between the haves and the have-nots. After it, the rest of the train was the domain of first-class passengers, starting with the dining car, where passengers who could afford it normally feasted on prime rib, lobster thermidor, beef Wellington, and the Philadelphia Phoenix's world-famous red velvet cake. When Judd entered with the porter, he saw workers in formal attire setting the tables with white linen, china from Villeroy & Boch, and Chambly silverware.

The extravagance continued in the adjoining first-class lounge. Only top-shelf alcohol sat behind the oak bar, poured into Baccarat crystal glassware. The white-jacketed bartender gave the porter a single nod as he hurried Judd past plush seats and cocktail tables to the rear of the train.

After the lounge came three cars of first-class accommodation, each containing three spacious rooms. *A hotel on wheels!*, ads proclaimed when the Phoenix first went into service. A boast to be sure, but one that contained some truth, for the rooms on the Phoenix were among the biggest on rails. Judd's own room boasted a full bed, a swiveled easy chair in addition to a love seat, a closet, and a private bathroom.

The porter pointed it all out before hurrying away so quickly that Judd didn't even have time to give him a tip. The fifty-cent piece remained gripped in his hand as he surveyed the room. Who, Judd wondered, had summoned him here? When his gaze landed on a vellum card sitting atop the bed's pillow, he hoped it would provide at least a partial answer. Instead, it was only another invitation.

Your presence is requested at a cocktail reception
in the first-class lounge at 8 P.M.
Please be on time.

Judd reached into his jacket for the pocket watch he always carried with him. Snapping it open, he checked the time. Seven o'clock. Right on schedule, the train lurched into motion. And so the mysterious journey began.

Too nervous to wait in his room for longer than fifteen minutes, Judd moved to the narrow hallway, where he now stands. As the loose bulb still buzzes in the wall sconce and the snow-dappled sky passes outside the window next to it, Judd thinks about the strangeness of that journey from the front of the train. It seemed both fraught and frantic, almost as if everyone he encountered was eager to leave.

As for the first-class cars, he's seen or heard no one since the porter's abrupt departure—a realization that roils Judd's already dyspeptic stomach. While certainly not the most crowded part of the train, he expected to see *someone* else around, even if it was only a conductor making sure no one from coach snuck into the train's more elegant back half.

He turns to his left, facing the entrance to the observation car at the very back of the train.

A sleek cylinder of glass and steel, it boasts floor-to-ceiling windows that offer a panoramic view of the passing scenery. Overhead is a glass window that provides an equally grand view of the sky. One journalist aboard the Phoenix's maiden journey had likened the observation car to "being in a fantastical spaceship where the outdoors feel like they're indoors and nothing but thin panes of glass separate you from earth and sky."

The observation car delighted those who could afford access to it, and over the years it had attained an almost mythical status. It was even rumored that Clark Gable and Carole Lombard, riding the Phoenix to a Chicago movie premiere in 1940, became so enamored with the observation car that they asked to spend the night there.

Because of its popularity, Judd assumes the observation car will be the place to spot a fellow passenger. But when he peeks inside, he sees that it, too, is empty.

Odd.

And, Judd has to admit, more than a little unnerving.

Through the observation car's yawning windows, he sees the

outskirts of the city. Dingy one-story homes, empty factories with broken windows, crooked fences with gaps in the pickets. He'd grown up in a place just like this, his family crammed into a shotgun shack so close to the tracks that the whole house shook when a train rumbled past. As a boy, he stared out the window as they went by, marveling at how those iron behemoths could be propelled over a set of rails by something as simple as steam and human ingenuity. He wondered about the men who made it happen. He wondered what it felt like to harness such power.

Judd eventually learned, building and tinkering first in his backyard, then in a garage when his family moved to a slightly bigger house. His education continued at a series of factories similar to the ones zipping by the observation car in decrepit streaks. Despite never having gone to college, he was a smart young man. A quick learner, too, and not just about train engines. He was a whiz at chemistry, math, even magic, using his long, narrow fingers to perform sleights of hand that amazed his co-workers. Ultimately, he got a job at the Union Atlantic Railroad, doing well enough to catch the eye of its owner, Arthur Matheson.

The two hit it off immediately. They were, Judd liked to think, cut from the same cloth. Just two big kids playing with the ultimate model train, eager to make it bigger, faster, stronger. Not to mention sleeker.

"I want a train that looks and moves like liquid mercury," Art told Judd one day over lunch. "Think you can make that happen?"

"Yeah," Judd replied. "I think I can."

And he did.

That, Judd realizes now, is when the trouble began, ultimately leading him to do the unthinkable. Even now, he can't quite believe he played a key role in something so horrible. Nor can he shake the feeling this train ride is all about paying the price for his past sins.

As he stands in the empty observation car he helped design, Judd longs to be anywhere but here. He wants to be sitting in coach, enjoying the comfort of strangers, knowing they have no idea what he's done—or what he's capable of.

He leaves the observation car, gripped by a feeling of apprehension he can't shake no matter how much he tries. Moving through the narrow hallways of the first-class section, Judd notes how the Phoenix's interior has grown shabby since he'd last been onboard. In addition to the buzzing wall sconce, he spots tears in the upholstery and a threadbare streak in the blue carpet where hundreds of passengers have trod.

Maybe that explains the noticeable lack of riders. Word has gotten out that the vaunted Philadelphia Phoenix is now a shell of its former self. More likely, the sparse ridership is the result of changes taking place outside the formerly grand train. Interstate highways have spread like ooze across the country, choking a once-pristine landscape with traffic. Meanwhile, the sky is quickly filling with planes. If a major city doesn't yet have an air terminal, it will soon. With options like that, no wonder few people choose to ride by rail.

Yet Judd sees no one as he rushes toward the front of the train. Each car he traverses contains the ghostly chill of something recently abandoned.

In the first-class lounge, the bartender is nowhere to be found.

In the dining car, there's nary a waiter around, even though all the tables are set for passengers who haven't yet materialized.

In the galley, pots sit on cold stovetops and knives glisten from racks on the wall. His footfalls rise from the tiled floor, echoing off the appliances, impossibly loud. When Judd accidentally elbows the handle of a pan, sending it clattering to the floor, it sounds like a gunshot.

The eerie emptiness continues into the coach quarters. The club car's tables are bare, its banquette seats empty. Coffee cups sit neatly stacked next to a silver samovar on the counter, with no one behind it to fill them.

And so it goes with each car he enters. In the coach lounge, issues of that day's late edition of *The Philadelphia Inquirer* lie neatly fanned out across end tables, untouched. In the sleeper and coach cars, every seat is vacant. No one dozes in their chairs. Or gazes out their windows. Or shuffles to the lavatories in the back of each car.

As Judd moves through them, his worry hardens into outright fear.

Every single person he saw earlier—from conductors to porters to passengers—is now gone, leaving the Philadelphia Phoenix completely empty.

THREE

FOR THE JOURNEY, Herb Pulaski chose a dark green Brioni suit that—like Herb himself—has seen better days. Both man and clothes are frayed at the seams, although for different reasons. The suit's condition is Herb's fault. He wears it all the time. Having grown up in his big brother's hand-me-downs, he enjoys showing off in a pricey suit.

As for his own wear and tear, Herb chalks that up to bum luck. Some men are born lucky, and he's not one of them. Even when fate does sometimes smile on him, it comes with a catch.

And it never lasts very long.

That's why Herb arrives at the first-class lounge twenty minutes early, clutching both the card he'd found in his room and the original invitation he received in the mail. He worries he won't be let in without them. He's accustomed to not being allowed into places, both before he had money and after. Now that he's on the verge of having no money again, Herb thinks it's important to not just be present but to be the first to arrive. That way, everyone who comes in after will see him and know he belongs here.

If anyone else shows up.

The lounge is empty when Herb enters, making him feel foolish about bringing along the invitation. No need to worry about being let in when no one else is there to stop him. There's not even anyone behind the semicircular bar at the rear of the car. Just a gleaming oak bar top and, behind it, several mirrored shelves cluttered with liquor bottles. Herb considers hopping behind the bar and pouring himself a drink to steady his nerves, but he fears someone else might enter at last and mistake him for the bartender. Determined to avoid such indignity, he sits in one of the plush armchairs scattered throughout the car, lights a cigarette, and looks around.

The lounge reminds Herb of his suit. Fancy but faded. Between the chairs are small round tables covered with white linen frayed at the edges. The curtains at the windows are blue velvet, similar to those in Herb's room, but so long they brush the floor. Catty-corner from the bar, at the front of the car, sits a baby grand piano.

Herb continues to wait in solitude as his cigarette becomes a smoldering butt in the ashtray and a thin sheen of sweat has formed on his brow. Nerves, he knows. He needs to make a good impression.

He examines that first invitation, fixating on the note written across the back.

It will be to your financial benefit if you come.

Herb doesn't know anything more than that, but he's eager to find out. It's probably an investment opportunity. Not that he has any money to invest with. Not anymore. But he'll find some, if necessary. He just hopes that this time it's on the level.

That wishful notion leaves Herb's head the moment the door at the front of the car swings open and someone else finally enters the lounge.

Someone, it turns out, Herb used to work with.

He feels a fresh sheen of sweat on his brow as Judd Dodge stares him down and says, "Are you behind all this?"

"What do you mean?" Herb asks while using a handkerchief to mop his brow. "Behind what?"

"There's no one else on the train," Judd says. "There used to be, but they're all gone now. No conductors. No porters. Even the goddamn passengers are gone. Yet here you are, sitting in the very lounge where I was instructed to be by eight."

"But ain't you the one who invited me here?"

"No, *I am not*," Judd says, overenunciating his words to make it clear he's smarter than Herb. A rude move, Herb thinks. Snobbish, too. He knows they both come from identically humble roots.

And it's likely the reason both of them agreed to do something terrible.

The two hadn't been close when they both worked for the Union Atlantic Railroad. Judd had headed up the design team, located in a section of the company jokingly known as the Brain Train. Herb spent his time in the manufacturing plant, the factory foreman who made sure the engines Judd designed got built, including the one pulling the very train they are on.

Their paths collided one fateful day when Herb received Judd's design for a train commissioned by the U.S. Army. An old-fashioned workhorse of a steam engine. While it was intended to be built quickly and cheaply, Herb saw immediately that the design was flawed. Things were out of balance, with the engine too big for the train and too powerful for the kind of iron Judd wanted to use to build it.

Herb took the plans back to him and said, "Something about this isn't right. This engine won't last a single trip."

"I didn't come up with it," Judd replied. "The boss man did. And he demanded it be built this way."

Herb knew he was lying, and not just because there was no way Arthur Matheson could have designed an engine by himself. That was Judd's job, and everyone knew it. No, what tipped Herb off was the fact that his boss would never in a million years cut corners like this, even with a war going on.

"This stinks to high heaven," he told Judd. "And I think you know what's causing the smell. So, this engine of yours won't get built until you tell me what it is—and what's in it for me."

Judd indeed told him everything, bringing Herb into a deal that would have disgusted him if he hadn't been in desperate need of money. He'd grown up with nothing, a trait that followed him into adulthood, even though he'd spent years working at Union Atlantic. It was a job he hated, although Herb knew he should have been grateful. He could have been overseas, dodging bullets on the front lines. A fate he'd avoided only because his work was considered valuable enough to snag him a Selective Service deferment.

That hadn't made the work any easier. It didn't cool the plant, which got hotter than a furnace. It didn't make his muscles ache less or keep the stink of grease from following him home. When he slept, clanging machinery and white-hot steel filled his nightmares.

Herb agreed to take part, ethics be damned. And for the first time in his life, he felt like a winner. Finally, he had all the money he needed. More than enough to pay off his debts, quit his job, move out of his crummy apartment, and find a house in a well-to-do development outside the city. He bought a new car, new clothes, new everything. He even got himself a wife—no small feat for someone like Herb, who didn't have much in the looks department. With his thick arms, squat frame, and embarrassingly hairy knuckles, he looked half-gorilla. His wife didn't mind as long as she had money to spend. She liked the finer things even more than he did.

Which, it turned out, was too much.

Now the money is all but gone. Herb knows that only another big-time score will keep his wife from leaving and him from being forced back to the heat, noise, and stink of the manufacturing plant.

"Wait," he says. "You got an invitation, too?"

"I did," Judd says.

"What do you think it's about?"

"Beats me." Judd starts anxiously pacing the car, which makes Herb feel a little jumpy himself. "But something's not right here. Those people I saw when I boarded. Where'd they go?"

"They probably got off the train," Herb says.

"But why? Someone had to tell them to do it." Judd suddenly stops pacing. "And the only person I can think of with that much power is the man who owns this train."

God, Herb hopes not. He doesn't want to be forced to think about what they'd done. How innocent men had died, including that Matheson boy. How their charred, mangled bodies have replaced noise and steel in his nightmares.

"Do you think he has something else planned?"

"If he does," Judd says, "I don't want any part of it."

"Maybe it's something on the level," Herb says hopefully. Because even if it's not, he knows he'll still go along with it. He has no other choice. Desperate times and all that. "Or maybe it wasn't him who brought us here."

Judd resumes pacing, crossing the car twice, a finger pressed to his chin. It makes Herb wonder if this is how he came up with the design for the Philadelphia Phoenix. Even more, he wonders with a shudder if it's also how Judd thought up the train engine that enriched their lives while destroying so many others.

"Of course it's him," Judd says. "Even so, something's not right. Do you have the invitation on you?"

Herb does, having slipped it into a jacket pocket when Judd entered the lounge.

"Take a look at it," Judd tells him. "See anything strange?"

Herb examines the invitation, noticing nothing out of the ordinary. There's a starting point, a destination, and the assumed time it will take to get between them. Thirteen hours. At first, Herb thinks Judd is confused about the listed arrival of seven A.M. because he forgets they'll be changing time zones somewhere in Indiana, thereby gaining an hour. Only after staring at the card a few seconds longer does he realize what Judd's referring to.

The invitation only details the trip to Chicago.

There's no mention of how they're supposed to get back home.

FOUR

SALLY LAWRENCE *HAD* noticed the lack of information regarding the return to Philadelphia. She came anyway. She knows
a shakedown when she sees one. And the note on the back of the
invitation made it clear this one would be foolish to ignore.

Remember the old you? I do.

Sally now stares at the handwritten message, thinking not
about who sent it—she'll find that out soon enough—but the answer to the question it poses.

Yeah, she remembers.

Despite all the great lengths she's taken to forget.

The first big change was her name. She goes by Sally now,
abandoning the nickname used by everyone from her sister to her
boss to her dates.

Sal.

As in "Keep your expectations low, Sal. That way you won't be
disappointed." And "Fetch me another cup of coffee, Sal, and close
the door behind you." And "Gee, you're a great gal, Sal, but I'm
looking for someone different."

Well, someone different is what she became. The moment she was officially rich, Sally marched into the city's ritziest beauty parlor and said, "Turn me into Veronica Lake." The beauticians tried their best. After hours of bleaching and plucking and spackling her face with makeup, Sally looked in the mirror and hardly recognized herself.

The transformation had continued. She whittled down her figure through a combination of crash diets, pills, and calisthenics. She bought new clothes to wrap around her new body. Gone were the frumpy knits and tweeds that made her look twice her age. Sally now wears only the latest, most expensive fashions. Her current outfit is an ivory wool bouclé suit with mother-of-pearl buttons and a matching handbag. Even though the salesgirl who sold her the ensemble swore it makes her look younger, Sally begs to differ. She thinks she looks like a rich spinster, which is closer to the truth than she cares to admit.

Sally now studies herself in the mirror, wondering if she should change. The options are plentiful. Because she'll be winging it once she reaches Chicago, she packed for every occasion. Two suitcases, one trunk, and a makeup case.

She roots through one of the suitcases, finding a flask glinting like a polished nickel at the bottom of the bag. She uncaps the top, tips it back, and takes a deep swallow. The sweet burn of whiskey spreading through her chest brings with it a sigh of relief.

God, she needed that.

Not just to get through whatever the journey is going to bring but to help her deal with being on the train itself. She has a lot of memories of the Phoenix, all of them tainted by what happened. Before boarding, she feared they would come back to haunt her. Dozens of memories, spinning around her like phantoms and eating away at her conscience until she could no longer take it.

When she eventually did step onto the train—after steeling

herself with a stiff drink at the station bar, of course—Sally felt . . . nothing. No memories, good or bad, and definitely no guilt. She hopes it will stay that way—and that the journey won't be something she later regrets.

Looking back on it, Sally sees her life as a long series of regrets, starting with the night she entered that bar twelve years ago. She'd been so young then. So foolish. Just a woman searching for something primal and forbidden. She'd found it all right, leading to still more regrets.

She remembers staring at the photographs of that night, wanting to both weep and throw up and flat-out murder the unctuous man showing them to her.

"I can make these go away," he said. "In exchange for a favor."

Sally told him yes, that she'd do anything, just please end this.

Another regret, for he'd made her go through with it. Still, he kept his word—and made Sally ridiculously wealthy in the process.

And that's her biggest regret of all.

Sure, she's rich, but it came at the expense of so many others. All those boys dead. A family ruined. One that, if she dares to think about it, had treated her better than her own.

A memory arrives, sudden and uninvited. Her riding the Phoenix on its maiden voyage, in a room just like the one she currently occupies. It might even be the same room. They look identical. Bed. Chair. Bathroom. Curtains at windows that can be slid open by pulling down on them. There are two windows in the room, one by the swivel chair and the other by the bed. Only the window by the chair is open in her memory, letting in spring air that cools her and the girl next to her as they pass a crowd gathered along the tracks.

Wave to all the people, Annie.

Sally washes the memory away with more whiskey, noticing her watch as she tips back the flask. Almost eight.

She needs to be in the first-class lounge, presumably to find out who the hell invited her here.

Sally drops the flask into her handbag and leaves the room. Outside, she sways from one side of the corridor to the other. While she wants to think it's from the rocking of the train, she knows the cause are the sips of whiskey and the drink—okay, *drinks*—she'd consumed before boarding. Still swaying, she vows to drink less while in Chicago. But seeing how she's not there yet, there's no harm in taking one last sip from the flask.

One sip turns into two as Sally moves through the accordion-like tunnel connecting her car with the one in front of it. After drifting down another tight corridor—and one final gulp of whiskey—she returns the flask to her handbag, squeezes through another accordion, and pushes into the first-class lounge.

Two men are inside, both of whom she once knew—and had no desire to ever see again.

"Well, shit," she says.

Judd Dodge gives her a sarcastic nod. "Nice to see you, too, Sal."

In that moment, Sally realizes all her attempts at transformation were for nothing. Even though she lost thirty pounds, elevated her style, and went from mousy brunette to cool blond, there are still people who see her for who she truly is.

Rotten to the core.

FIVE

IN CAR 13, Edith Gerhardt leaves Room B and is stopped short by what she sees in the thin strip of corridor. There, directly opposite her door, is a wide window darkened by the nighttime landscape passing outside. And in that darkness, she sees her own grim reflection.

Gray dress under a gray coat. Gray hat atop gray hair. Even Edith's skin is an ashen shade, her pink lipstick its only spot of color.

I look like a ghost, she thinks with alarm, suddenly recalling her grandmother's tales of the grand estate that had once been in the family but was lost long before Edith was born. According to her grandmother, it had been haunted by a spirit known as Grauer Geist.

Gray Ghost.

Family lore was that his presence foretold impending doom, making Edith even more perturbed by her spectral appearance. Is she the doomed one or merely the messenger? She suspects it's a little of both, considering how everyone she had ever loved is now dead. Yet she keeps on living, a fact she acknowledges with a slight nod to her ghostly reflection, which nods back in unison.

Edith continues to the end of the car, feeling slightly foolish for interacting with her reflection. Almost as foolish as she feels for being on the train in the first place. She shouldn't be here, she thinks. No good will come of it.

The invitation had almost gone into the trash. Edith had no idea who sent it, after all. Nor did she have any desire to travel, even just for a day or so. Born in Bonn, raised in Munich, and widowed in Berlin, she immigrated to the United States in 1936. That was enough travel, as far as she was concerned. But when she saw the note on the back of the invitation, Edith understood that this was a journey she had to take.

How much will you pay to keep your secret?

The answer, Edith has already decided, is as much as necessary, even though she abhors spending money. She'd grown up poor and remained that way through her marriage and beyond, scraping by right up until she reached America. Now sixty-nine and wealthy beyond her wildest dreams, Edith treats money as something delicate that must be preserved. She lives frugally, spending little, giving less. Her biggest expense is tithing to her church. Ten percent, as the Bible instructs.

Wasting money, she thinks, is a distinctly American trait. And despite living in the United States for almost twenty years, she remains resolutely German. For example, her outfit for the journey—gray wool dress, matching coat and pillbox hat, sensible shoes—is the same one she wears to church each Sunday. If it's good enough for God, she thinks, it's good enough for a train trip.

Especially one she fears will end up costing her so much.

While Edith doesn't know who's behind this obvious case of blackmail, she has her suspicions. As for what she's being black-mailed about, well, it could be one of two things—and both have to do with her life in Germany.

Edith hadn't wanted to leave her homeland. Unlike many German émigrés, she didn't flee to escape Hitler's rise. No, she left because her husband died, as had the rest of her family. Faced with building a new life without them, Edith realized it was better to do it elsewhere. She was pragmatic that way. She knew that Hitler sought too much, too fast. His ambition would ultimately lead to Germany's ruin, especially once the United States got involved. America, she understood, would be the inevitable victor, and so she moved there.

Edith loved Germany, yes, but she loved survival even more.

Survive she did. She even thrived, quickly getting a job as a housekeeper for a rich Philadelphia family. Her employers treated her well, but with indifference. She was just a worker to them. One of many. Their children, however, were a different story. They adored her, and she adored them right back. They were, in many ways, the children she never got to have, and she showered them with affection.

Still, Edith understood it wouldn't last. She never let emotion cloud her thinking, especially as Hitler's quest for world domination started playing out exactly as she predicted. She knew a moment would come in which she'd have to choose between her new home and her old one.

The moment to finally pick a side came in 1942.

Edith did—and is now rich because of it.

But that doesn't keep her from expecting to see Grauer Geist at any moment. If family history is any indication, his appearance is inevitable. That's why Edith keeps giving fleeting glances to the windows as she moves through the train. Satisfied that it's her ghostlike reflection keeping pace with her and not a different, more dangerous specter, she pushes into the first-class lounge.

Three other people are there. Two men—one in a garish green suit made for someone half his age and half his weight, the other in more appropriate black—and a woman in ivory. Despite their clashing styles, Edith assumes they know each other. They stand close together next to the piano, whispering, oblivious to her presence.

"Edith Gerhardt," she announces in a German accent all her years in America have done nothing to tame. "I am expected."

The three others stop whispering and look her way. To Edith's surprise, she recognizes all of them. They do the same with her. And if Judd Dodge, Herb Pulaski, and Sally Lawrence aren't happy to see her, Edith is even more displeased to see them.

Because there, right in front of her, is another ghost.

But it's not Grauer Geist coming to haunt her.

It's her past.

SIX

LT. COL. JACK Lapsford gets things done.

That's his specialty.

A military man through and through, he ascended to his current rank by demanding answers, making tough decisions, getting results. Now seventy-two and retired, he heads to the first-class lounge ready to get this—whatever it is—over with.

Along the way, he thinks of the questions he plans to ask whoever summoned him here. The first concerns not just this train but all of them. Why do they make the passageways so narrow? Lapsford isn't a small man by any means. But he certainly isn't the largest. He's seen bigger in his day, which makes him wonder how those fellows navigate trains. Because he's having a terrible time of it, proceeding slowly, both shoulders brushing the sides of the corridor. If someone were to approach in the opposite direction, there'd be no room to let them pass.

Not that Lapsford has seen another passenger since boarding. That's his second question: Where is everyone? The only other person he's seen is the conductor, which makes Lapsford uneasy. Normal trains—embarking on normal trips—are filled with riders, porters, waitstaff. This train seemingly has no one.

Minutes after departing Philadelphia, he'd gone to the dining car, hoping to at least get a decent meal out of the trip. No such luck. All nine tables—one for each first-class room—were set for dinner, but no one was seated at them. Nor were there any waiters working the car. On the way back to his room, he saw it was the same in the lounge. Empty seats. Empty bar. Empty car.

While Lapsford has no desire to bump into someone in the train's cramped passages, it would at least put him slightly more at ease. At that moment, he feels like the only person onboard. A preposterous notion, yet there it is.

Next to that in Lapsford's thoughts is a third question—*Why am I here?*

Technically, he understands why. Someone knows something about him that they shouldn't. Now he needs to mitigate the damage, monetarily if necessary. At least that's his interpretation of the message scribbled on the back of the invitation.

How does it feel to have blood on your hands?

What continues to bedevil Lapsford are the logistics surrounding the situation. Who, exactly, is privy to this information they shouldn't have? How did they acquire it? What do they want from him, other than money?

The one question he doesn't have is what it's regarding.

This is about what happened twelve years ago.

Of that, he has no doubt.

Lapsford was still in Washington at the time, part of a group charged with the logistics of warfare. Getting troops and equipment where they needed to be, when they needed to be there. And to do that, the military needed trains. Big ones. Powerful ones. Which is how Lapsford found himself having a steak and scotch dinner with a man connected to an entire railroad.

Only the man wasn't lobbying for a big military contract. He wanted Lapsford to give one to someone else—for the most nefarious of reasons.

"What you're suggesting is sabotage," Lapsford said then, red-faced and flustered. "Why do you think I'd go along with such a scheme?"

"Just hear me out," the man said. "Look what happened after Pearl Harbor. America finally woke up. It sure as hell got FDR's attention. Support for the war skyrocketed. Thousands of men enlisted. But that was six months ago, and we're still playing catch-up to Hitler even though we're now in the thick of the fight. You know that better than anyone. The only way to get the military up to speed is by giving the country another reason to rally around Uncle Sam."

Lapsford knew the man was right. Roosevelt's foot-dragging had cost them greatly. America should have been readying for war months before actually joining it. Now they needed more men, more resources, more everything. Even though a smaller version of Pearl Harbor might be just the kick in the pants the country needed, there were ramifications to consider.

"But men are going to die," he said. "Innocent ones."

"They'll probably die anyway."

Although a cruel reply, Lapsford appreciated the man's bluntness, for that was indeed the likely outcome. That's all war was, really. Masses of innocent, expendable men being tossed into the meat grinder of battle. The key to victory was to lose fewer than your enemy.

"But those men are needed elsewhere."

"If it finally gets America truly ready for war, then their sacrifice will not be in vain."

"And as an added bonus, you get to destroy the competition," Lapsford said.

His dinner companion leaned back in his booth, a glass of Macallan in one hand and a Davidoff cigar in the other. "That's not why I'm doing this. But since you brought it up, if this goes according to plan, I will be reaping the financial rewards. As will you. From what I hear, Jack, it wouldn't be the first time."

At that moment, Lapsford knew that the choice presented to him wasn't really a choice at all. So he made it happen, because getting things done was what he was good at. And he doesn't regret it. Regrets are for the weak. The strong never look back. They only stare forward.

Lapsford does just that as he enters the lounge. Eyes on the door, chest puffed so much it strains his shirt, heart thrumming in anticipation just beneath the fabric. But once he pushes his way inside and Lapsford's gaze lands on the four other people in the lounge, his chest deflates and his heart briefly stops.

He recognizes these people.

And he's not pleased to see them.

"What the hell are you doing here?" he says to the two men and two women, who clearly don't have an answer.

"We could ask you the same thing," says the younger of the women. Lapsford can't remember her name. They'd only met briefly, passing each other on their way to and from giving testimony that damned the reputation of an already dead man.

"One of you didn't organize all this?"

"No," says the taller of the two men. This time, Lapsford can place a name to the face. Dodge. Judd Dodge.

"Then why are we all here?" he says, adding the biggest question of them all: "Who's responsible for this?"

SEVEN

UNLIKE THOSE GATHERED in the lounge, Dante Wentworth knows without a doubt who's behind the trip.

Ironic, considering how he's not even supposed to be on the train.

The invitation had been addressed to his father, Kenneth Wentworth, along with a handwritten message on the back that was as vague as it was ominous.

You and I have unfinished business.

That note is what piqued Dante's interest when he spotted it on his father's desk. Even after twelve years, he still recognized the handwriting. Those elegant curves and swoops were impossible to forget. Seeing them again after all this time compelled Dante to pocket the invitation and attend in his father's place.

Not the first time he's shown up uninvited. In fact, it's a bit of a habit for Dante. One he always gets away with. He's young, handsome, charming, and rich—four characteristics that allow those who possess them to do practically whatever they please.

In this instance, it also doesn't hurt that his father owns the

Philadelphia Phoenix. Not originally, mind you. A dozen years ago, the Phoenix—and the company that had built it—belonged to Arthur Matheson. But it's now his father's property, and Dante suspects he could drive the train all the way to Chicago if he wanted to. His father does it all the time. Never one to resist playing with his toys, he likes to climb into the front of the locomotive whenever he rides the Phoenix, taking over the controls and guiding it into the station.

Dante isn't inclined to do the same. Unlike his father, he has no interest in the trains and railroad lines that built his family's wealth. At thirty, he's still young enough to see the future, and it sure as hell doesn't involve trains. Dante knows they will soon become dinosaurs, replaced by fast cars, jet engines, and whatever new technology everyone but his father is developing.

But for now, the Phoenix still rumbles down the tracks, and he's one of the few people on it. By Dante's count, there are at least five others onboard, not including the shifty-looking conductor he spotted skulking around earlier. In the past thirty minutes, he's heard people exit the two other rooms in his car and listened to the footfalls of three others as they passed on their way to the first-class lounge.

Before heading there himself, Dante studies the invitation that had arrived exactly two weeks ago. While intended for his father, the message on the back could also extend to him. He and his hostess definitely have unfinished business. And Dante, for one, is very much looking forward to seeing how it plays out.

He slips on his jacket, adjusts his tie and pocket square in the bathroom mirror, and leaves the room. As he makes his way through the car, he practices how he'll greet his hostess after such a long absence.

It's good to see you, Anna.

No, Dante thinks. That's too weak.

I'm pleased to see you, Anna.

Dante shakes his head. Too formal.

I've missed you, Annie.

Now, that might work. It all depends on the way he says it. Too much emphasis will make him sound desperate. Not enough might make it seem like he doesn't mean it, when he absolutely does.

No matter what he says, Dante has the feeling it will be lost in the shock surrounding his presence. After all, Anna is expecting his father. Dante hopes she'll eventually forgive the intrusion.

When he at last bursts into the first-class lounge, Dante expects all eyes to turn his way. That's normally what happens when he enters a room. Part of it stems from his reputation as Philadelphia's most eligible bachelor. Dante Wentworth, dashing heir to a railroad fortune. The rest has to do with his formidable good looks, which are routinely admired by women and envied by men.

That hadn't always been the case. As a boy, Dante was gangly and ungainly, with a chin too sharp for his cherubic face and eyes that were too large, too wide. He eventually grew into his features, puberty righting all those physical wrongs. The rest of his body caught up with his too-long limbs, and his face lost its baby fat, revealing a square jaw that was just right. As for his eyes, they became sapphire pools so arresting it prompted his mother to say, "You're going to break a hundred hearts, Dante. Be gentle about it."

She was right. Between then and now, Dante has broken many hearts. And he has been gentle with all of them except one.

Rather than stop everything when he enters, the five other people clustered inside the lounge are too busy speaking in hushed tones to notice his presence. Dante uses the rare moment of anonymity to size them up. To his surprise, he recognizes all of them. Judd Dodge and Herb Pulaski. Sally Lawrence and the dour Edith Gerhardt. And, of course, the esteemed Lt. Col. Jack Lapsford, who's as much of a blowhard as Dante's own father. Seeing them all together like this gives Dante a kick of excitement. Anna is definitely up to something.

"I'm telling you, it's not a coincidence," Judd Dodge says, hissing the word.

Lapsford scoffs. "So you *do* know why all of us are here."

"I know why," Dante says.

This finally gets their attention. All eyes turn to Dante, who reacts with a satisfied nod. Now *that* is what he's accustomed to.

The others recognize him as well, of course, and most of them seem surprised by his presence. Apparently, they also expected his father.

"Dante Wentworth," Sally Lawrence says. "Is this your father's doing?"

"I'm afraid not." He continues deeper into the car, passing the others on his way to the piano. There, he sits and starts aimlessly tickling the ivories. "But I know who *is* behind it."

Jack Lapsford steps toward him, impatient. "Then what's this all about? If you know who brought us here, tell us."

"This is the work," Dante says as he bangs out a fanfare on the piano, "of someone none of us—especially me—thought we'd ever see again."

What Dante doesn't say is that, other than himself, no one is going to enjoy seeing Anna Matheson again. This, he's certain, won't be a happy reunion.

8 P.M.

TWELVE HOURS TO CHICAGO

EIGHT

ANNA WAITS IN her room, watching the clock, her muscles coiled in both anticipation and dread. For the thousandth time, she tells herself she's doing the right thing, that nothing will go wrong, that in twelve hours this will all be worth it. But then a nagging, negative part of her brain tells her—also for the thousandth time—that she's not, that something will, that there's no guarantee justice awaits at the end of the line.

But then Seamus knocks on her door and Anna stops thinking altogether. Instinct takes over.

"It's time," Seamus announces when she opens the door.

"Is everyone else off the train?"

Anna knew none of the invitees would willingly board an empty train, so she arranged for the crew members she'd paid off to act like they were going about their business until a minute before departure. As for the passengers, they were friends and family members of the crew. Anna made a point of throwing a little money their way as well.

"They are," Seamus says. "I swept the train from front to back myself. It's just you, me, and the six people in the lounge."

Anna smooths her dress before doing the same to her hair. As she lifts the briefcase from the chair by the window, she says, "What about the wrinkle?"

"You'll find out soon enough."

The interior lights of the train flicker again as they leave the room, spilling into a corridor that alternates between darkness and light. Anna spends each millisecond of darkness to monitor the snowfall outside. Slow, but steady.

"Everything will be fine," Seamus says. When the lights return to full brightness, he adds, "See?"

The first-class lounge is the car directly in front of theirs. So close that Anna can hear a murmur of voices and the unexpected sound of the piano. Knowing all six of them are inside, mere feet away, makes her suddenly queasy. When the train sways, she moves with it, practically swooning.

"You okay?" Seamus asks as he takes the briefcase from her hands.

Anna shakes her head. "Not in the least."

But she needs to be. She can't let nerves get the best of her. Not now. Not after so much planning and so much expense. Still outside the lounge, Anna pauses and closes her eyes, not yet ready to see the others through the circular window in the door.

In that darkness, she can only think of her father, her mother, Tommy. She even spares a thought for Aunt Retta, her father's only sister, who'd loved him so much his fate had driven her insane.

They're gone now.

All because of the six people on the other side of that door.

Anna inhales, exhales, opens her eyes. Through the window, she sees five of the six. Three have their backs turned to her. The other two are in profile. The sixth remains hidden behind them, seated at the piano, playing an inappropriately jaunty tune.

She'd often wondered how it would feel to see them again. Long, sleepless nights in which every possible scenario from hurt to hate to rage stormed her thoughts. But nothing conjured up by her imagination came remotely close to the reality of finally laying eyes on the people who had destroyed her life.

That hollow thudding in her chest? A surprise. As is the heat coursing through her veins. A fiery burn hotter than any fever. But the real shock is the memories that suddenly appear, many of them not unpleasant. She knows these people, some better than others. A few are practically strangers, met once or twice. Others she had considered family. After years of rage, Anna assumed any trace of fondness she'd once felt for them was long gone. Yet a small bit apparently remains, and now it rises to the surface, bubbling up among the anger and grief.

When she spots Edith Gerhardt, for instance, all Anna can think about is how, when she was younger, Edith had called her Schatzi.

Her little treasure.

Spoken when she woke Anna in the mornings and when she kissed her forehead at bedtime. Edith, who had fed Anna, doted on her, put Band-Aids on her skinned knees, and once even threatened to break the arm of Matty Bernard, who had been picking on her at school. A sign, Anna now knows, that despite her grandmotherly appearance, a darkness lurked within Edith.

As for Sally Lawrence, who in Anna's mind will always remain Sal, there was no such darkness. Not even a hint of it. In her view, Sal was perfect from the moment she became her father's secretary at age eighteen. As a girl, Anna had loved visiting her father at the office because it meant spending time with Sal. When she grew older, precariously walking that tightrope between child and teenager, Anna considered Sal a surrogate older sister, confiding in her about things she'd never tell her mother. Boys, puberty, bras.

To young Anna, Sal was everything her mother was not. Independent, opinionated, seemingly in no hurry to settle down or settle for less. Even though Anna had adored her mother, Sal proved to her there was more to life than gowns and glamour and being a perfect hostess. If there was any darkness evident in Sal's behavior, Anna had completely missed it.

She assumes that's why Sal's and Edith's betrayals hurt more than the others. She had once loved both women, which makes her subsequent hatred all the more acute.

Make no mistake, though. Anna hates everyone in that lounge, even those she doesn't know well or only in passing. Her experiences with Judd Dodge and Herb Pulaski, for instance, were limited to the annual Christmas party her father threw for employees. God, he loved those parties. Anna did, too, because it brought out the best in her parents. Her father spent weeks planning them, going all out to make sure everyone got into the holiday spirit. He'd spike the punch bowl and hang mistletoe and hire a big band to play jazzed-up versions of carols.

Each year, Anna's mother bought a new dress for the occasion. Something satiny and sparkling that caught the light when she inevitably got up to dance. Anna would watch, rapt, as she put on lipstick, rouged her cheeks, applied perfume to her neck and wrists. She'd then offer Anna a single spritz before taking her and her brother downstairs for the festivities. Some of Anna's fondest memories were of Edith tucking her into bed as the party continued downstairs. Snug under the covers, she'd fall asleep to the sounds of swing music and clinking champagne glasses, the lingering scent of Chanel No. 5 still on her wrist.

When Anna first met Judd Dodge at one such party, he proclaimed he was a bit of an amateur magician and proceeded to make a candy cane suddenly appear in his previously empty right hand. A dazzled Anna accepted it in awe. From that point on, Judd insisted on calling her Candy Cane whenever they met, and Anna insisted on seeing another magic trick, even after she should have outgrown such things. Judd always obliged. His last trick, at the final Christmas party, was to turn a sprig of holly into a rose at full bloom, which he presented to Anna with a chivalrous bow.

Herb Pulaski was equally memorable—for all the wrong reasons. Anna always felt a shiver of apprehension when he entered the party, brought on by the way he took in the surroundings with envy so palpable it bordered on disgust.

At that last-but-no-one-knew-it-yet party, Herb had backed Anna into a corner, his breath hot and stinking of scotch. "You have no idea how lucky you are," he said. "No idea at all. Nice house. Nice clothes. But without your rich daddy, you'd have nothing. Just like me." It was Tommy who'd eventually come to the rescue, guiding Herb away with delicate tact.

As for Lt. Col. Jack Lapsford, Anna knows him the least, having only met the man once. When he came to dinner to discuss the railroad's importance to the war effort with her father, she had found him haughty, self-important, and dreadfully dull. Ironic, considering how that dinner set the stage for everything that came after.

Then again, maybe it didn't. Anna suspects that, had that dinner not taken place, her family's downfall would have happened anyway.

Kenneth Wentworth would have seen to it.

His father's chief competitor was, after all, the man behind everything. The one who made all the plans and pulled all the strings. It's why, of all the people involved, Anna hates him the most. And it's why she's relieved that Kenneth Wentworth, still seated at the piano behind the others, is the one person she can't yet see. She fears what she might do once he comes into view.

The cluster of five starts to break up. Sal moves to one of the plush chairs near the bar, looking startlingly different than Anna remembers. The unadorned realness she had admired as a girl has been replaced by cool elegance. Fancy dress, blond updo. Sal wears neither comfortably, looking instead like someone hiding behind a disguise.

Edith, on the other hand, hasn't changed a bit. Watching her drift to the opposite side of the car, Anna is struck by a memory from her childhood. Shopping at Gimbels and getting lost in the holiday crowd, prompting several minutes of panic. But then she heard her name being called, turned around, and saw Edith across the sales floor. Anna beamed, then, because she knew she was lost no more.

Anna pushes the memory aside, focusing on the three men whose backs had been turned to the door. Lapsford, Pulaski, and Dodge. They part, finally revealing the man at the piano.

Anna freezes at the sight of him. In that stillness, she chokes out a gasp.

Instead of Kenneth Wentworth, the man idly playing the piano is his son.

Dante.

Even though Anna despises the others, she had at least prepared to face them. Dante is a different story. She never thought she'd see him again, nor did she have any desire to. Yet here he is, his unexpected presence more than a wrinkle, which is how Seamus had put it. This is a goddamn fold.

"What's he doing here?" Anna hisses to Seamus.

"I was going to ask you the same thing," he says. "I thought you invited him."

Anna hears a hint of distrust in his voice, as if he suspects her of diverting from their plan. His tone holds other notes as well, including anger on her behalf. Seamus knows everything about her history with Dante Wentworth, and judges him accordingly. But running alongside the anger is a thin streak of something else.

Anna can't be sure, but it sounds like jealousy. Unwarranted. Seamus has no need to be jealous of Dante, for a multitude of reasons.

"I invited his father," she says. "Where is he?"

"Beats me," Seamus says. "All I know is that he's not on this train."

Anna curses under her breath. This is a terrible development. Their whole plan hinges on Kenneth Wentworth being here. Not his son, for whom Anna harbors a different kind of contempt. Dante's crimes weren't nearly as heinous as those of his father or the others. In fact, he had committed no crime at all, unless you consider breaking a girl's heart criminal, which Anna certainly does.

Just like with the others, seeing Dante again unlocks a thousand memories, none of which Anna longs to dwell upon. To keep from being overwhelmed by them, she forces herself into action, flinging open the door to the lounge and stepping inside.

Dante is the first to notice her, his piano playing ceasing in a crash of discordant notes. Silence falls over the car as the others turn her way, either surprised or confused or both. Anna peers at them through narrowed eyes, her gaze cool, calm, and piercing. Inside, however, is a vastly different reaction. Her heart thunders and her stomach clenches and her brain roars with violent thoughts.

God, she hates these people.

Hates them with the fiery heat of a thousand suns.

Facing them again, she's overcome by the urge to kill each one in a hundred vicious ways. Shooting them in the head. Stabbing them in their cold hearts. Ripping them from limb to limb. The thoughts are so bad—so ferociously violent—that she almost flees the car out of fear she might attempt some of them.

And that would be the worst thing to do.

So Anna forces the violent thoughts from her mind, stiffens her body, hardens her heart. She opens her mouth to speak, but no words come out. Something she hadn't planned for. And she thought she had prepared for everything. Yet there she stands, speechless, astonished she ever thought she'd be able to talk.

What can she say to the people who took everything from her? What words will even come close to conveying the depths of her pain, her grief, her primal rage? Certainly not this speech, rehearsed so much she can now recite it in her sleep. What had once seemed so forceful now feels puny and weak when facing her enemies.

Anna forces out the words anyway. She has to say *something*.

"You know who I am. Just as you know why I've gathered you here. If you haven't figured it out yet, you will very soon."

She takes the practiced pause, measuring its length in her head. As she does, something else nudges into her thoughts. Something unrehearsed, unexpected, and unwelcome.

Aunt Retta on the evening Anna came to live with her at her mansion in upstate New York. She didn't know her only living relative well. When Anna was a girl, her father's older sister visited so infrequently that she seemed more myth than person. Every few years she blew through the house like a frigid wind, staying only an hour or so before gusting back out again.

All Anna knew about her aunt Henrietta—Retta for short— was that she had married a much-older iron magnate at eighteen, been widowed at nineteen, and inherited her husband's millions at twenty. Never having children herself, she was utterly incurious about her niece and nephew. What little love Aunt Retta had in her heart was reserved for Anna's father. There was no room for anyone else. And when he died, that heart became so prickly it might as well have been surrounded by barbed wire.

Anna was sixteen when she went to live with Aunt Retta, too old to be coddled in her sadness yet still too young to handle it all with the stoicism and grace expected of adults. Alone and walloped with grief, she stood in front of the aunt she barely knew, hoping in vain that the gray-haired woman with the pinched face and red-rimmed eyes would say something—anything—to make her feel better.

"I wish there was someone else to take you," Aunt Retta said instead, a statement that would have been breathtaking in its cruelty if Anna hadn't felt the same way. She wanted to be with anyone other than her widowed aunt. But her brother was dead. As was her father and, as of the day before, her mother.

"But seeing how there isn't," her aunt continued, "you are now my burden to bear."

"I'm sorry," Anna said.

That was when Aunt Retta slapped her. A stinging backhand as sharp and sudden as a snakebite.

Anna stood there, aghast, taken aback not just by the pain of the slap but its surrealness. *Did that really happen?* she thought. *Is this just a nightmare?*

And for a second, she wished it were. Because that meant when it was over she'd wake up in her old bed, in her old room, in her old house, and that her mother and father would be waiting at the breakfast table with Tommy, who'd tease her about being a sleepyhead while eating French toast. But as her cheek throbbed and her aunt—who'd literally just slapped her—continued to stare, Anna realized that it was indeed a nightmare, but one from which she would never, ever wake.

Not knowing how to react, she began to cry, although it ended up being more of a wail than anything else. High-pitched. Tearfilled. Earsplitting. Full of rage and despair and utter hopelessness. Instead of comforting her, Aunt Retta simply watched Anna until her emotional tempest calmed to regular-grade grief.

"Finished?" she eventually said.

Rather than wipe the tears away, Anna left them on her face, wet, salty, and hot. "Why did you hit me?"

"To see what kind of girl I'm dealing with," Aunt Retta said. "The answer, it seems, is a weak one."

Her aunt moved across the parlor to a massive wingback armchair, which she settled into like royalty on a throne.

"You should know by now that we live in a brutal, cruel world populated by brutal, cruel people," she said. "Those who react the way you just did—all that crying, all that begging for pity—are doomed. The only way to survive is to accept life's blows and not even flinch. If you can do that, the world will know you're a woman to be reckoned with."

In the weeks that followed, Aunt Retta would test her mettle several times, slapping Anna at random moments. First thing in the morning. Right after dinner. While the two engaged in tensely silent strolls over the estate grounds.

Very quickly, Anna learned not to flinch.

And when that happened, the slapping stopped. Anna never asked why, because deep down she already knew. She had won Aunt Retta's respect, if not her affection.

Anna also eventually realized that those intermittent slaps, so hard they left welts for days, weren't born of cruelty. They were Aunt Retta's way of teaching her a valuable lesson.

Absorb your pain.

Control your hatred.

Hone your stillness until it becomes dagger sharp.

The people who flail and rage rarely accomplish anything. But those who control their emotions even in the most fraught of situations?

They get results.

So Anna pushes the memories away and refocuses on the task at hand.

"By now, you've recognized each other," she continues. "Maybe you've even had a chance to chat a bit. Likely long enough to suspect that you've been brought here under false pretenses. That suspicion is correct. The reason for this journey is simple. I'm here to get justice. Because I have irrefutable proof that the six of you are responsible for destroying my family."

Indignant murmurs rise from the crowd, muted by the rattle-clack of the train in motion and a forlorn toot of the locomotive's horn as they approach a strip of highway. The crossing is heralded by a clanging train signal that flashes red as it slides past the lounge windows. The lights and the noise feel to Anna like an alarm, warning her that there's no predicting how others in the car will react to her announcement. They might be furious. They might try to fight. They might even try to kill her. Maybe in the next second or two. She drops her hand to her side, ready to reach for the knife under her dress.

Once they clear the crossing, Anna takes a deep breath and continues.

"On June seventeenth, 1942, a troop transport train left Philadelphia on its way to Fort Benning in Georgia. The train, from locomotive to caboose, was brand new, manufactured by my father's company specifically to transport troops and supplies. Onboard were more than two hundred American soldiers off to fight in the war, including my brother, Thomas Adam Matheson."

Saying her brother's full name wallops Anna with another memory. She and her parents on the platform, clinging to Tommy, silently begging him not to go, even though they knew he would. He enlisted the day he turned eighteen, eager to be on the right side of history. No amount of crying and pleading would have kept him from getting on that train.

"Be good, Annie," he whispered in Anna's ear after kissing her on the cheek. "Take care of Mom and Dad for me."

Then he was off, leaping onto the train as it lurched into motion with a steam-filled gasp. Before disappearing inside, Tommy lingered in the doorway to wave good-bye. Even though she assumes her memory is colored by what happened later, Anna can't recall a moment when her brother had looked more handsome, more dashing, more *alive*.

It was the last time she saw him.

Anna swallows hard, bracing herself for what comes next, forcing out the words she needs to say.

"What no one on that train knew was that the engine in the locomotive had been designed to fail. Its construction was purposefully shoddy, the materials it was made of weak. The iron couldn't contain the sustained force it took to pull a fully loaded train hundreds of miles. In short, it was a bomb. And outside Raleigh, North Carolina, it went off."

Anna pauses, overwhelmed by images of the resulting disaster. The charred earth, the derailed train, the rail cars ripped open like sardine cans. For a time, pictures of the tragedy were everywhere, inescapable. A cruel reminder of what she had lost.

"Thirty-seven men were killed in that explosion," she says. "Including my brother. All that remained of him was a piece of charred uniform. Investigators believe the impact of the explosion ripped it from his body."

A sob bubbles up from deep in Anna's chest. Thinking about Tommy still does that to her. Every damn time. He was so young, so kind, so vibrant. Even when they were young, at ages when most brothers and sisters battled for their parents' attention, he never once let her feel less than extraordinary.

On Anna's birthday, Tommy would make her a bouquet of paper flowers, each one more elaborate than the year before. When she was six and fell from a tree and broke her arm, Tommy wore a makeshift sling so she wouldn't feel like an outcast. He took her to movies, taught her how to drive, always took the smaller piece of dessert so she could have the bigger.

Growing up, Anna had tried to repay him with kindnesses of her own, often coming up short. Tommy never seemed to mind, which made the last thing he asked of her all the more gutting.

Take care of Mom and Dad for me.

Anna promised that she would—and then she had failed spectacularly.

"I loved my brother," she says. "I miss him every day. He was good to me. He was good to several of you."

She gives Sal and Edith pointed looks. Other than Anna, they're the only two people in the lounge who knew Tommy well, who had watched him grow and flourish. They'd been the ones to comfort Anna during his funeral, her parents too shell-shocked by grief to pay attention to their now-only child. She remembers standing between Sal and Edith, weeping, as an empty coffin was lowered into the ground. Now she stares at the women, wondering if they remember, too.

If they do, they don't show it. Edith looks past her, focused on the door behind Anna, her expression stoic. Sal, on the other hand, stares at the floor.

"Immediately following the tragedy, blame fell to my father." Anna absently touches the silver locomotive pinned to her dress. Because it's one of the few things that remains of her father, she treats it like a talisman. Touched rarely, and only when she needs extra strength.

"You all know what happened after that."

She skips the reminder because she doesn't want to be reminded herself. Not that she could ever forget the events that occurred two weeks after Tommy was laid to rest. First, both federal and military authorities came to the house to question her father. They did the same the next day with all his employees. The day after *that*, they raided the house for evidence, leaving with an armful of incriminating documents and her father in handcuffs.

Anna will never forget how bedraggled he looked. Hair askew, graying stubble on his chin, his bare feet shoved into the first pair of shoes he could find. Polished black loafers, the patent leather shining in the morning sunlight as he was hauled away. Nor will she forget his last, desperate words.

"It wasn't me, Annie. I would never hurt you like this."

The seized papers and the testimony of others painted Arthur Matheson as a Nazi sympathizer who tried to aid the enemy by hindering the U.S. war effort. Anna's father was eventually hit with dozens of federal charges, ranging from sabotage to treason to thirty-seven counts of murder, including that of his own son. Denied bail, he was sent to federal prison to await trial.

It never happened.

On his second day there, an inmate stabbed Anna's father thirty-seven times.

Once for every person killed in the explosion.

Edith and Sal didn't come to her father's funeral. No one did. It was just Anna, her mother, and Aunt Retta standing in front of a blessedly closed casket as a pastor-for-hire gave the briefest of prayers. In that moment, Anna consoled herself with the assumption that it would be the lowest point of her life. That things couldn't possibly get worse.

Until they did.

The absence of a trial didn't keep her father's reputation from being posthumously destroyed. A Senate hearing took care of that. During the proceedings, broadcast on every radio station and exhaustively detailed in every newspaper, five star witnesses gave sworn testimony about how and why Arthur Matheson committed sabotage.

Lt. Col. Jack Lapsford said Anna's father approached him about manufacturing trains expressly for troop transport.

Judd Dodge described several meetings in which he tried to convince Arthur that his locomotive design was doomed to failure.

Herb Pulaski swore that Arthur had ordered him to cut corners as much as possible in the building of that locomotive.

Sally Lawrence provided notes detailing those conversations, along with dozens of memos signed by her father backing them up.

Edith Gerhardt testified about how Arthur seemed highly interested in the Third Reich and even insinuated he'd hired her simply because she was German.

By the time it was all over, not a single person in America besides Anna, her mother, and her aunt believed that Arthur Matheson was innocent. Her father's company, now worth a fraction of its value, was sold to his chief competitor. And her mother retired to her room, escaping her grief with a steady diet of booze and pills, and leaving Anna utterly, entirely alone.

This lasted a full two months before her mother, bursting out of her bedroom, suggested a picnic. A sudden, surprising treat. They drove outside the city, to a grassy hill that overlooked the Delaware River. There, high above the water, Anna reverted to childhood, doing cartwheels in the grass and making daisy chains for their hair. The one she'd given her mother sat crookedly atop her head as she sat on the hood of the car, smoking one Pall Mall after the other.

"My girl," her mother said. "My beautiful girl. One day, you'll forgive me."

Then she got into the car, started the engine, and drove off the cliff into the river.

Twelve years later, on a train her father used to own, Anna struggles to keep that particular memory at bay. She assumes that if she closes her eyes, the image on the backs of her eyelids will be of her mother sitting calmly behind the wheel as the car sails toward certain doom. And that if not for the white-noise clatter of the train, she'd hear her mother's car crashing into the river below. Even so, she catches the faintest hint of it—like the echo of an echo. A horrible crunch-splash that she still sometimes hears in her nightmares.

It makes Anna unexpectedly relieved when someone else in the lounge finally speaks.

"What does any of this have to do with us?"

It's said by Dante, the only person on the train ignorant enough to get away with such a question. He poses it with enough sincere curiosity to make Anna wonder just how much he knows about what happened back then—and his father's role in all of it. She herself had known so little.

At the time, Anna never gave much thought to why Edith suddenly quit, why Sal made herself invisible, why her father's once-devoted employees distanced themselves. She assumed it was because they, like everyone else, thought her father had blood on his hands. People naturally pull away from those who've suffered a great loss out of fear that their bad luck is transferable and will soon upend their own placid lives.

It didn't matter to Anna that these same people had testified against her father. She continued to give them the benefit of the doubt, thinking them mistaken, misguided, or simply confused about what had happened. Never did she consider that all of them were part of a concerted effort to destroy her father, everything he worked for, and everything she loved.

She'd learned that only a year ago, when Aunt Retta was on her deathbed. By then her aunt's body was riddled with cancer, the disease eating away at her. Anna dutifully sat by her bedside all day and into the night, although her aunt by then was asleep more often than not, thanks to the morphine.

But on that day, she jerked to life, startling Anna from her own fitful sleep in the chair beside the bed.

"Anna." At first, her aunt's voice was just a whisper, but it grew more forceful with every word. "Your father didn't do it."

She tried to quiet Aunt Retta, who'd said something similar a thousand times in the eleven years they'd lived together. That her father was innocent. That he couldn't have done all the horrible things he'd been accused of. That he was framed.

Anna, of course, believed her, just as she believed her father when the police carted him away in handcuffs. It didn't matter that everyone else—the cops, the military, the U.S. government, even his own employees—thought him guilty. Anna knew in her heart that her father was telling the truth when he swore his innocence.

But she also knew it was too late to do anything about it. She didn't want her aunt to waste her final words speaking about a past that couldn't be undone. But Aunt Retta insisted on talking. She tried to sit up, the exertion of it making her wince in pain. Anna forced her back against the pillow, where her aunt stared at her with fire in her eyes.

"I have proof," she said.

NINE

THE MEMORY OF that moment makes Anna's heart skip, just as it had back then. Staring at her soon-to-be-dead aunt, she'd leaned in close and said, "What kind of proof?"

"Documents. Dozens. Showing he had nothing to do with it." Although Aunt Retta had begun to fade, she mustered a wicked smile. "And showing who did."

"Where are they?" Anna said.

Aunt Retta's head lolled across the pillow. "Not here. Somewhere safe."

"How can I find them?"

"They'll find you," her aunt said, in a voice that the approach of death had reduced to a murmur. "When they do, make the people responsible pay. Make all of them pay."

Those were the last words Aunt Retta ever uttered. Within the hour, she was dead.

The proof found Anna soon enough, as did Seamus. Now both are on this train, intent on fulfilling Aunt Retta's last request.

She's going to make all of them pay.

"Contrary to his testimony, it was Jack Lapsford who approached my father about manufacturing a train to transport troops, and not the other way around," Anna says, making sure to direct her gaze at the former military man. He stands in a self-important way familiar to anyone who witnessed his testimony at the Senate hearing that all but buried the reputation of Anna's father. He's filled out since then, Anna notices. Turned soft by wealth and a shocking lack of remorse about his role in what transpired. "He did so with the full knowledge that the engine would be designed to fail, causing mass loss of life."

"That's preposterous," Lapsford huffs.

"Is it?" Anna says, turning her attention to Judd Dodge. He sits slumped in one of the lounge's chairs, looking dejected, his long body folded in on itself. A man with no more tricks up his sleeve. "Mr. Dodge was the man who designed that ticking time bomb of an engine, although he had shown my father a far different set of plans."

"That's a lie," Judd mutters so weakly it's clear that not even he believes it.

Anna swings her gaze to Herb Pulaski, seated next to Judd. He twitches in his chair, his face slick with guilt sweat. He avoids eye contact with Anna, looking everywhere but at her.

"Mr. Pulaski oversaw the building of the faulty locomotive, following the plans hidden from my father," Anna continues. "Even though, as the man who monitored the construction of every locomotive at the company, including the one at the front of this train, he knew it was doomed to failure."

Herb opens his mouth, as if about to defend himself, before snapping his jaws shut and staring shamefully at the floor.

Seated on the other side of the car is Sal Lawrence, making Anna avert her gaze. She can't bear to look into Sal's eyes.

"While all that was happening," she says, "the women were doing their part. Sally Lawrence, my father's devoted secretary, spent her time writing false correspondence, creating fake memos, and forging my father's name, all in an effort to incriminate him."

Anna turns her attention to where Edith sits, her posture perfect, her hands folded primly in her lap.

"Some of those documents were kept in his office, while others were planted inside his home by his housekeeper, Edith Gerhardt," Anna says. "When later asked about them, Edith told the authorities she wasn't surprised by their presence, seeing how she suspected my father of being a Nazi sympathizer."

It's a dizzying set of accusations, made worse by how Anna imagines all of them enacting their misdeeds. A movie montage of treachery.

Jack Lapsford, smug in his uniform, telling Congress how her father had begged to build a troop train, his bottom lip quivering as he claims that never in a million years did he think it would lead to sabotage.

Judd Dodge bent over his drafting table, calculating the exact weaknesses he'd need to add to the engine to make it look like it was running fine while also ensuring its eventual failure.

Herb Pulaski on the factory floor, looking on as men in welding helmets and leather aprons built a locomotive to Judd's specifications. "Don't worry, fellas," Herb says amid the sparks and clanging. "I've been assured this engine will be as solid as all the others."

Sal Lawrence typing away in the middle of the night, her bent desk lamp a spotlight on her fingers as they fly over the keys. Appearing across the page is a fake memo with fake dates and fake details. After ripping it out of the typewriter, Sal forges Arthur Matheson's signature.

Edith Gerhardt creeping upstairs while no one else is home, the pages clutched to her chest. In the office of Anna's father, she places them in desk drawers, hiding them beneath ledgers and stationery. Places where no one but the police would think to look.

"It was a six-person conspiracy," Anna says, wiping the images from her mind because she fears she might do something rash if she doesn't. "Jack Lapsford, Sally Lawrence, Judd Dodge, Edith Gerhardt, and Herb Pulaski all helped frame my father. They lied to the authorities. They covered up their own crimes. And it was done at the behest and instigation of my father's biggest business rival, Kenneth Wentworth."

Anna stares directly at Dante as she says it, taking great pleasure in the way his features freeze in shock. She doesn't know what he expected by coming here, but she's certain it's not this. She hadn't expected it, either, when she finally examined the evidence her aunt had gathered, all of it pointing to Kenneth Wentworth as the plot's mastermind. Once she did, though, it all made sense.

"Your father's just as bad as the rest of them," Anna tells Dante. "No, I take that back. He's worse. Which is why he should be here instead of you."

Dante remains frozen for ten, twenty, thirty seconds. After what she'd told him finally sinks in, he does the unthinkable.

He smiles.

It's a wide smile. Slightly crooked and blindingly bright. The kind of smile that had once made Anna melt whenever she saw it. Now it only leaves her frustrated, for it means he doesn't believe anything she just said.

"You really think *my* father was behind all of this?" Dante says. "Why would he do that? He's as patriotic as they come."

"This wasn't about devotion to America. In fact, it had nothing to do with the war. This was greed, pure and simple. Your father wanted to expand his holdings and grow his wealth while not spending too much money in the process. My father's railroad was the easiest target. Did you know your father had tried to buy my father's company? Twice?"

"I didn't," Dante says, his lips still curved.

"Both times, my father's answer was an outright no."

Dante's smile falters. "And *my* father doesn't take no for an answer."

"Exactly," Anna says with a nod. "Angered by my father's refusal to sell, he created an act of sabotage, framed my father, devalued the company, and bought it dirt cheap. As a bonus, he was awarded the lucrative military contract my father received. Millions of dollars that flowed directly to your father, who then divided it up and gave it to the five other people in this lounge tonight. A reward for doing his bidding, betraying my father, and betraying their country."

Dante's gaze floats around the lounge, briefly alighting on each of the others gathered there. His stare contains a mix of confusion and amusement, like he still thinks all of it is simply some elaborate prank.

"But why? Why would any of them take part in something like that?"

Anna doesn't know. That's one of the reasons she brought them all together like this. She needs to learn why each of them did it. Now she watches them, her breath lodged in her throat, waiting to see if one of them has the guts to answer.

No one does.

Weaklings, Anna thinks as she gestures to Seamus to bring her the briefcase. Once it's in her hands, she raises it so the others can see.

"In the past year, I have obtained dozens of documents detailing the plot against my father. Not the ones you forged," she says, glancing toward Sal. "Or that you planted in our home," she adds, shooting a harsh look Edith's way. "Real ones. Taken together, they tie all of you and Kenneth Wentworth to the deaths of thirty-seven people and the cover-up that happened afterward."

"You're bluffing," Lapsford says.

"I can assure you, Mr. Lapsford, that I'm not." Anna holds out the case. "Would you like to see for yourself?"

"*I* would," Sal says as she marches toward Anna, grabs the briefcase, and takes it back to her chair. There, she sets the case atop a small cocktail table and opens it up.

Anna and Seamus watch from the back of the car as the others draw closer to Sal. Judd Dodge stands behind her, adjusting his glasses. Herb Pulaski pulls a handkerchief from his jacket pocket and wipes his glistening brow while Edith Gerhardt blinks several times, as if preparing to see a ghost. Even Dante, still pitched somewhere between shock and incredulity, cranes his neck from his spot at the piano, straining for a glimpse.

By now Sal has the lid fully lifted. Inside the briefcase is a large sheet of paper folded into quarters. Sal opens it to full size, revealing a blueprint.

"What is this?" she asks everyone and no one.

Judd Dodge reaches over her shoulder and snatches the blueprint from her hands. "It's my design. For the locomotive. The real one. The one that—"

"Don't say another word," Lapsford warns.

Judd ignores him and turns to Anna, his face paler than the white lines curving over the blue paper in his hands. "How did you get this?"

Anna honestly doesn't know. By the time all the evidence was presented to her, it was too late to ask Aunt Retta when or how she had gathered it.

"What else is in there?" Lapsford asks while lunging for the briefcase.

"Nothing," Sally says, which is the truth. Other than the blueprint held in Dodge's trembling hands, the briefcase is empty.

"Told you she was bluffing," Lapsford says. "She only has dirt on Judd."

Judd Dodge gulps. "And that's enough to hang me."

Lapsford rips the blueprint from Judd's hands, leaving behind only a corner scrap that remains pinched between Judd's thumb and forefinger. Lapsford keeps tearing, shredding the blueprint into ragged pieces that he tosses onto the floor.

"Now she has nothing," he says.

"On the contrary, I have dirt on all of you," Anna says. "This was just a hint of what's in my possession. And I have copies of everything."

Lapsford, less certain than he was a second ago, storms up to her. "Where's the rest? Is it on this train?"

"By now, I hope I strike you as being smarter than that."

"Then what's this all about?" Sal asks. "Why the hell are we here?"

"To blackmail us," Edith says with disapproval, as if she herself isn't guilty of far worse.

Herb mops his brow again. "If it's money you want, I don't have any."

"Even if you did, I wouldn't take a penny of your blood money," Anna says.

"Then what do you want?" Lapsford says.

"She wants to kill us."

Judd Dodge is the one to say it, his words bringing instant silence to the car. Standing with the scrap of blueprint still between his fingers, he rotates slowly, facing the others. "Don't you see? She brought us here to murder us. This trip—this *night*—is her chance for revenge, and it's been a long time coming."

"I have no desire to kill you," Anna says, leaving out how she had certainly considered it. As she pored over the evidence gathered by her aunt, her brain filled with violent thoughts. Of strangling them with her bare hands. Of holding them underwater until their eyes bulge and their faces turn blue. Of stabbing them, shooting them, stomping them to pulp.

Even now, she scans the lounge, looking for weapons, seeking out things that could inflict the most pain. A corkscrew, for instance, that could pluck out Sal's eyes. Or a wine bottle that, when broken, could be plunged into Lapsford's meaty neck. The knife at her thigh pulses coldly against her skin.

But killing them isn't enough. Anna realized that early on. While a flash of righteous violence would feel glorious in the moment, it wouldn't satisfy, it wouldn't *linger*. What she needs is something longer. Something drawn out to a torturous degree. What Anna wants is for each of them to lose the will to live—and then be forced to keep on living. Only then will she be satisfied.

Revenge is fleeting.

Vengeance lasts a lifetime.

"Death," she tells Judd, "would be a mercy for you all. And considering what you did to my family, I'm *not* in a merciful mood."

She spreads her arms wide, gesturing to the lounge's walls and the windows through which nothing can be seen but dark sky, an even darker landscape, and whirling flakes of snow.

"This train is expected to reach Chicago at seven tomorrow morning. Roughly two hours ago, the head of the FBI's Chicago field office received a package containing the rest of the evidence I have against you. With it was a letter alerting them to our arrival time and a suggestion that they be waiting for us on the platform, arrest warrants in hand. If you're lucky, maybe J. Edgar Hoover will be there to greet you. He loves being in the spotlight, and this is going to shine a bright, blinding light onto your crimes."

As Anna talks, it feels like a fire is growing in her gut, the flames leaping through her rib cage, setting her heart ablaze. Intense heat courses through her limbs. If her eyes start to glow orange, she won't be surprised. Such is the strength of her fury.

"All of you will be arrested, tried, and, I'm certain, convicted by both the judicial system and the court of public opinion. You will become the most hated people in America, just like my father was. You will lose everything, just like I did. You will go to prison—and you will die there. Maybe as quickly and as violently as my father. Or maybe you'll end up like the Rosenbergs."

Anna pauses, allowing all of them to think about Julius and Ethel Rosenberg, who'd been electrocuted the previous year. She assumes they're imagining a fatal current coursing through their own pained bodies. At least, she hopes they are.

"It's my personal goal for all of you to have long, healthy lives. And when you do eventually die, broken, miserable, and alone, no one—absolutely no one—will mourn you."

Anna had spent almost a year on that speech, honing every word, rehearsing it so much it has settled into her bones and become a part of her. In all that time, she thought she'd feel all-powerful after finally speaking it to those who had wronged her. A goddess of vengeance cursing her enemies.

But now that her intentions have been revealed, uttered aloud and therefore unable to be taken back, Anna feels not euphoria or relief but exhaustion. The fire inside her is now a faint flicker, allowing sadness to creep in at the edges. She misses her family. She misses her old life, not to mention her old self. And she's tired. So very tired. It had taken such a long time to get here—and there's still so much further to go. Eleven hours, to be precise. And she needs to be alert for all of it.

"Now," she says, "are there any questions?"

Lapsford speaks first. "Do you seriously expect us to just sit here and wait to be taken directly into the hands of the FBI?"

"Yes," Anna says, when the truth is she assumes very few of them will go down without a fight. All the more reason for her to be on guard until the very end of the journey.

"Well, you are sorely mistaken about that," Lapsford says. "Because I will be getting off this train at the very next stop."

Anna remains silent, knowing something Lapsford doesn't. In the previous month, she and Seamus had taken the Phoenix from Philadelphia to Chicago a total of ten times. Sometimes they had rooms in first class. Others were long journeys spent sitting up in coach. No matter their accommodations, they used each trip to take copious notes. Now Anna knows where the Phoenix will be located at all times, what other trains pass it and when, and what stations dot the entire route.

Right on schedule, a toot of the horn and a slight slowing of the train heralds their approach to one of those stations.

Harrisburg, Pennsylvania.

But instead of stopping, the Phoenix keeps moving. Past the platform where several nighttime passengers linger. Past the bored porters and empty newsstand. Past another train idling on the opposite track. At the window, Lapsford watches it all go by. "Why didn't we stop?" he asks, panic setting in as the Phoenix clears the station and begins to pick up speed.

"Because this is an express train," Anna says. "There are no other stops, no delays. Just a straight shot to Union Station in Chicago."

Lapsford remains at the window, fixed on the station receding in the distance, as if trying to will the train to reverse course. "But it has to stop at some point, right? To refuel?"

"It's a diesel-electric locomotive," Judd says from the other side of the car. "Fast. Efficient. It can easily make it to Chicago without refueling. With only one man at the controls, if need be."

"Well, I refuse to stay here a second longer," Lapsford says, peeling himself away from the window and puffing out his chest. "I demand you stop this train and let us off."

"I'm afraid that's not possible," Anna says.

"If you don't do it, I will."

Lapsford looks past her, and Anna knows exactly what's caught his attention.

The emergency brake.

A flat rod of bronze ending in a looped handle, it hangs discreetly in the corner of the car, opposite the piano. The others notice it, too, and Anna watches as they tense, preparing to spring for it.

Before she can warn them not to, three of the six make a dash for the brake. Lapsford, Herb Pulaski, and Sal. They elbow each other, jostling for position as they scramble across the lounge. Almost caught in the melee, Anna feels herself being pulled out of the way by Seamus.

By then, Lapsford has beaten the others to the brake, surprisingly nimble for someone his size. With a smug look of satisfaction, he hooks his fingers around the handle.

Then he pulls.

9 P.M.

ELEVEN HOURS TO CHICAGO

TEN

NOTHING HAPPENS WHEN Jack Lapsford yanks the emergency brake. Not even after he pulls on it a second and third time. The train keeps barreling down the tracks, moving closer to Chicago with each passing second.

This isn't a surprise to Judd Dodge, who knows better than most how the emergency brake works. While the others had braced themselves for a sudden, screeching halt, he remained standing in the center of the car, knowing a lurching stop would never come.

"Why the hell isn't anything happening?" Lapsford asks as he frantically pulls the brake a fourth time.

Judd shakes his head and sighs. "Because pulling the emergency brake doesn't stop the train. It just alerts the conductors that something is wrong. If it's determined the train does need to be stopped, they alert the engineers in the cab, who engage the brakes."

Next to him, Lapsford looks around the lounge. "But the only conductor is—"

"Me," says the large man who's been hovering behind Anna Matheson the whole time. Now he pushes his way into the center of the car, commanding everyone's attention. "Only I'm not really a conductor."

"Allow me to introduce you to Seamus Callahan," Anna says. "His older brother was Sean Callahan. If that name is familiar to you, it's because Sean Callahan was one of the thirty-six men who died alongside my brother. What you caused didn't just hurt my family. It hurt scores of families."

The man glares at them, lingering a moment on Judd in a way that makes him nervous. All coiled muscles and dark eyes under hooded lids. Even though Anna swears she has no intention of killing them, Seamus Callahan looks like he wouldn't mind at all if they were dead—and that he'd happily do the honors.

"I know a dozen men who would gladly be here instead of me," he tells them. "Unlucky for you, I'm here. And I'm sure as hell not about to tell the engineer to stop this train."

"Then I'll tell him myself."

This comes from Lapsford. The idiot. Still fooling himself into thinking they can get away with what they'd done. Judd, on the other hand, knows it's hopeless. Even if Lapsford does manage to stop the train, there's nowhere for them to run. Outside is nothing but dairy farms and fallow hayfields. And now that the FBI has proof of their crimes, it will only be a matter of time before they swoop in and round them up.

"Be my guest," Anna says, another sign to Judd that any attempt to stop the train will be useless.

He'd underestimated her, that much was certain. Honestly, Judd hadn't given Art Matheson's daughter much thought at all over the years. Whenever the guilt did weigh on him, it usually was reserved for Tommy Matheson, the men killed with him, or even Art himself. But Anna rarely crossed his mind. A mistake, Judd now knows. For the girl he used to call Candy Cane turned out to have many tricks up her sleeve.

"I will," Lapsford says, still oblivious.

He storms out of the first-class lounge, followed quickly by Herb and Sally. Even Edith Gerhardt, the calmest and quietest of the group, joins them. Together, they rush out of the car like a herd of caged animals just set free.

Judd leaves, too, although not because he thinks they'll succeed. He just wants to get away from Anna and her thug. Which, he soon understands, isn't going to happen. Because as they move from the lounge to the dining car, Judd hears Anna say, "Seamus, you know what to do if they get out of hand."

"I certainly do," Seamus says, which gives Judd another nervous twinge. He has no idea what Seamus will do if one of them—likely Lapsford—becomes unruly. All he knows is that he doesn't want to find out.

Although Judd is tall himself, it feels like Seamus looms over him as they join the others midway through the dining car. At the front of the pack, Lapsford continues to lead the charge, taking them single file through the galley, then the club car, then the lounge in coach. Their progress slows in increments with each car they pass. By the time they reach the sleeper car, Judd realizes the others are just now learning what he already knows—that the rest of the train is completely empty.

"Where is everyone?" Sally says.

"Gone," says Seamus, who'd been silent for so long that the sudden sound of his voice startles Judd.

Herb Pulaski, directly ahead of Judd, says, "Where?"

"Does it matter?" Seamus says.

No, Judd thinks. It doesn't. Right now, what matters is that they're the only people on a train that will bring them right into the hands of the FBI. He looks down at the scrap of blueprint still in his hand. It sticks to his clammy palm. A mark of his guilt. Even if Anna's lying and doesn't have a single other piece of proof, he knows that this bit of paper is enough to send him to prison for the rest of his life.

How Anna got her hands on it, Judd has no idea. He'd been assured by Kenneth Wentworth that it was destroyed along with everything else that linked them to the train explosion. Clearly a lie. Judd suspects Wentworth kept everything, just in case he needed to use it against them. He should have known better than to trust him. Then again, Judd hadn't been thinking clearly when Wentworth sidled up next to him at the annual Matheson Christmas party.

"Art Matheson sure knows how to show off," he said casually between sips of his scotch.

Judd turned to him. "What do you mean?"

"This party," Wentworth said. "It's all for show. Art wants everyone to see his beautiful house and his beautiful wife and his perfect children. Why don't you have any of that, Judd? From what I hear, you're the one who does all the work."

Wentworth was spot on, especially in regard to the Philadelphia Phoenix. On paper, the train looked like a collaboration between two equals. The natural culmination of a meeting of the minds. Arthur Matheson imagined it and Judd made it a reality. In truth, Judd had done most of the imagining and designing. But during the Phoenix's much-heralded debut, it was only Art who spoke to the press, who was photographed wearing an engineer's cap in the cab of the locomotive, who acted like the whole damn train had been built with his two bare hands.

Even years after the train's debut, nothing had changed. The only man anyone associated with the Phoenix was Arthur Matheson, a Philly blue blood who had inherited the Union Atlantic Railroad from his father. No one knew about Judd, the dirt-poor boy who grew up to be a genius capable of building the greatest train in the country.

That's the reason he continued listening to Kenneth Wentworth that night at the party. And it's why Judd ultimately agreed to take part in the nefarious plot Wentworth proposed to him the following Monday. He didn't give any thought to the collateral damage. The lives that would be lost and the families left devastated. He only focused on what he wanted.

No, what he *deserved*.

Judd was owed all the things Art Matheson had. The big house and beautiful wife and plucky kids who would inevitably glide through life as if they were on rails. Most of all, he deserved Art's reputation. Since he was the brains behind it all, then the credit should be his as well.

He's about to get credit, all right. Anna has seen to that. Soon everyone will know exactly what he did.

Judd follows the others into the baggage car, where the bulk of passengers' luggage is usually stored. What should be packed from floor to ceiling with trunks, suitcases, and boxes now sits empty. The car has become nothing more than a stainless-steel echo chamber they must pass through on the way to the locomotive.

Standing between them and the locomotive proper is a door reinforced with steel. Beyond it, Judd knows, is the engine. Beyond that, at the very front of the train, is the cab where the engineers sit. While one could technically man the controls all by himself, two is the standard number for an overnight trip of this duration. Despite being romanticized in novels and movies, toiling on a train is often boring work, especially in the locomotive. All one sees is a pair of rails stretching to the horizon, with hundreds of miles more ahead. Men falling asleep at the controls is not unheard of.

On most streamliners, there is no access to the cab from within the train. The engine blocks the way, forcing engineers to board directly into the cab using a ladder. That's not the case with the

Phoenix. Because it was built to be an express train going nonstop for long distances, Judd added a narrow passage that skirted around the engine to allow engineers to enter and exit the cab during shift changes without stopping the train.

A passage that starts just on the other side of the locomotive door.

The five of them gather around it as Jack Lapsford grasps the handle. The door doesn't budge. That it's always locked for security reasons is another thing Judd could have told them if only they bothered to listen.

Lapsford knocks on the door, the sound so loud in the empty car that Judd can feel it in his chest. Back in the lounge, he'd all but accepted defeat. Anna had bested them, and he was prepared to face the terrible repercussions of his actions. But now that he's mere inches from the engine, Judd realizes he's not ready for that yet. He'll never be ready. He doesn't want to be arrested. He doesn't want to go to prison. And he certainly doesn't want to die there.

Judd's panic ticks higher, prompting him to shove Lapsford away from the door. Rather than knock, Judd pounds on it. More than the rest of them, he needs to stop the train, even if it means breaking into the locomotive and shutting down the engine himself. He can do it, too. The Phoenix is his baby, and he knows how to stop it. He'd even destroy it if necessary.

But first, he has to get the attention of the engineers. What happens next depends on them. Steeling himself for confrontation, Judd continues to pound on the door, waiting for whoever's on the other side to open it and decide his fate.

ELEVEN

EIGHT CARS AWAY, Anna faces the only other person who remains in the first-class lounge, desperately wishing he'd also leave. More than that, she wishes Dante Wentworth had never boarded the train to begin with. It's his father she wants here, trapped with the others in her meticulously woven web.

That Dante crashed the party shouldn't surprise her. After all, it's how they first met.

"I must admit, I'm impressed," he says. "This is quite a plan you've cooked up, Annie."

It takes all of Anna's strength to not gasp. No one has called her that in a very long time. Hearing it again after such a long absence makes it feel like time has bent back on itself, shuttling her into the past.

"One you shouldn't be a part of," she says. "If you think taking your father's place tonight will spare him, I can assure you it won't. You're only delaying the inevitable."

Dante sits back down at the piano. "I'm not here to spare anyone. Least of all him."

"Then why are you here?"

"Because I wanted to see you," Dante says with such sincerity that it would have made sixteen-year-old Anna swoon. He always knew exactly what to say. He still does. But Anna has learned a few things herself over the years, including how to resist the charms of Dante Wentworth.

"What made you think I would be here?"

"The invitation," Dante says. "When I found it on my father's desk and read the message on the back, I knew you were behind it. You should have had someone else do that part, you know. I'd recognize your handwriting anywhere."

Anna briefly closes her eyes, mad at Dante for noticing and mad at herself because he's right. They'd written to each other so much back then. Letters filled with swooning declarations of love that will make Anna die of embarrassment if she gives them too much thought.

So she doesn't give them any thought at all. That was a long time ago. In another life. And the lovestruck teenager who spent all those late-night letter-writing sessions searching her brain for words to describe how her heart felt is dead. In her place is a different Anna now.

Dante, on the other hand, seems exactly the same. He's older, of course, the hard living of his twenties giving him a touch of raggedness that somehow only makes him more handsome. Especially when he starts playing the piano again, his face scrunched in concentration as his nimble fingers trip across the keys. This time, Anna recognizes the tune. "You Made Me Love You."

That had been her favorite song, back when she was in love with *him*. A time in which they were supposed to hate each other.

No one had explicitly told them that. Things didn't work that way on Philadelphia's Main Line. People who lived where they lived and were as rich as they were didn't have enemies. There, everyone smiled and air-kissed in public while trying to tear each other to shreds behind closed doors. But their fathers were business rivals, so it was silently decreed that the two of them should have nothing to do with each other.

Anna knew who Dante was, of course. They moved in social circles close enough for her to hear all about the charming rapscallion son of Kenneth Wentworth. Enough for Anna to know that she'd probably hate him. At sixteen, she was a hopeless romantic, raised on love sonnets and Shakespeare. She had no time for the spoiled sons of local captains of industry. It didn't matter that she was the spoiled daughter of one. Anna swooned over Laurence Olivier and harbored dreams of being an actress herself. She'd even been cast as Juliet in her prep school's upcoming production of *Romeo and Juliet*.

Then came her parents' annual Christmas party, in which their house was flooded with strangers in formal attire, including a boy in a sharp navy suit and red silk tie. Halfway through the party, he slid next to Anna and introduced himself only as Dante, either because he didn't want to share his last name or because he knew he didn't need to. In Philadelphia, there was only one Dante worth knowing.

"I'm—" Anna started to say, but Dante cut her off.

"Oh, I know everything about you, Anna Matheson."

Anna blushed, although she had no idea why. Maybe it was the knowing way Dante said it, as if he had peered into her thoughts and seen her deepest, darkest secrets and yearnings. More likely, it was because Dante was undeniably gorgeous. Even though she'd been told he was handsome, Anna was still unprepared for the sight of the boy standing in front of her. Those blue eyes. That swoop of dark hair that couldn't quite be tamed. The slightly crooked smile that alternated between awkward, devilish, and seductive. Her beloved Olivier had nothing on Dante Wentworth.

Thankfully, Anna kept enough of her wits about her to say, "Surely not everything, Mr. Wentworth."

"I know that we're not supposed to mingle."

"Our fathers definitely wouldn't like that," Anna said.

"Which makes the idea seem deliciously appealing."

Dante took a step closer, and Anna's world narrowed until it was just the two of them. It didn't matter that they were in a crowded house filled with holiday revelers. All she could see was the beautiful boy standing before her.

As soon as she was fully under Dante's spell, it was broken by the sound of Anna's mother shouting across the room.

"You get away from him!"

A hush fell over the party as Anna's mother stomped to a corner of the room where her brother, Tommy, was talking to a man she'd never seen before.

"I said get away from him!" her mother bellowed. "Don't you dare talk to my son!"

Tommy, now the center of attention, tugged at his shirt collar as his cheeks turned crimson. "We're just chatting, Mom."

"I don't care," her mother snapped. "Go to your room."

The focus of her mother's wrath raised his hands in innocence. "I was just being friendly, Maggie."

"That's Mrs. Matheson to you. And nothing you do is friendly, Mr. Wentworth."

Anna looked to Dante, noting the resemblance between him and the man being yelled at by her mother. Both were roguishly handsome. They even shared the same crooked smile. When Dante flashed his, Anna understood something she should have known all along. The man was his father—and neither of them had been invited.

Dante gave a blithe shrug and said, "I suppose I should have mentioned that earlier."

Anna said nothing in response. She was too upset by her mother's reaction to Kenneth Wentworth's presence. Margaret Matheson never got angry. Ever. Yet Dante's father made her absolutely livid. Anna searched the crowd for her father, finding him standing in the shadow of the staircase, watching the argument over the rim of a raised rocks glass.

"You need to go," Anna told Dante. "Right now. Both of you."

Dante bowed and said, "It was a pleasure, Miss Matheson. May our paths cross again soon."

In the weeks that followed, Anna tried hard not to think about Dante. But then in late January, during the first scene of her final performance as Juliet, Anna spotted Dante in the front row. His presence threw her so much she momentarily forgot her entrance line and had to be prompted by the classmate playing the nurse. In those first, fraught moments of her performance, Dante was an unwanted distraction, and not just because she knew he was watching. It was the way he watched that Anna found disconcerting. Completely still, his attention rapt, yet always sporting that crooked grin. Like he was imagining Anna saying her lines directly to him. And when she took her final bow, no one in the audience applauded louder than Dante.

After the show, he appeared backstage with a bouquet of roses. Presenting them to her, he said, "That which we call a rose by any other name would smell as sweet." Despite all reservations, Anna was smitten.

Now she's anything but as Dante continues to play the piano. "Are you going to do this all the way to Chicago?"

"Would you like me to, Annie?"

That nickname again. Her heart thrummed like a plucked piano string each time he said it.

"That's Miss Matheson to you."

"I remember when you used to call me Danny."

"That was a long time ago," Anna says, pausing to add a caustic "Mr. Wentworth."

Dante beams, pleased by how easily they've fallen into that old familiar rhythm. While certainly *not* pleased, Anna isn't surprised. He always managed to coax out her sharp wit, no matter how serious she tried to be.

"I assume that, despite Jack Lapsford's blustering efforts, this train won't be stopping until we reach Chicago," Dante says.

Anna looks out the window, seeing that the train is running parallel to a river, hugging the curve of the shoreline. Several houses sit on the other side of the water, their lit windows reflecting off the surface in golden shimmers. They're smack-dab in the middle of Pennsylvania now, Anna knows, moving steadily northwest until they reach the Ohio border. From there the train will head due west, taking them across Ohio, through Indiana, into Illinois and, finally, Chicago.

"No," she says. "It won't."

The wrong thing to say, because it allows Dante to continue playing. Anna sits, resigned, as he starts a new song. "Someone to Watch Over Me."

"At first, I wondered why you were doing this," Dante says. "It all seemed so complicated. The train. The journey. The—"

He pauses, searching for the right word, which prompts Anna to offer "Dramatics?"

"Exactly," Dante says. "All the dramatics. When it would have been so much simpler to let the FBI do the work of tracking everyone down, rounding them up, and arresting them."

"Like what will soon happen to your father? If it hasn't happened already."

Dante ignores the remark. "Instead, you chose to do this. Don't get me wrong, I applaud the effort. The fake conductor was an especially nice touch. What's his name again?"

"Seamus."

"That's right. Seamus." Dante's playing softens until only the lightest of notes rise from the piano. It sounds intimate. Like a whisper. Talking over it, he adds, "Are the two of you lovers?"

"That's none of your business."

Dante shrugs, and Anna takes it to mean he assumes the answer to be yes.

"As for the train's legitimate workers, I imagine you paid them off."

"I did," Anna says.

"My father won't be happy about that."

"I think he'll soon have more important matters to worry about."

The music stops as Dante leans against the piano edge and rests his chin atop a closed fist. "Do you really think my father was behind all of that?"

"I know he was," Anna says. "Honestly, you should, too. I have it on good authority that you work for him now."

"So it says on my business card," Dante replies. "But you can hardly describe what I do as work. My father barely speaks to me, and when he does, it's to shoot down one of my suggestions. Honestly, I spend most of my day sitting at my desk and shuffling paper from one side to the other."

"Come now. I'm sure you carve out plenty of time to flirt with the secretaries."

"Only the ones that remind me of you," Dante says, giving Anna a look of such acute longing that her breath catches in her throat.

"Regardless of what you do or don't do for your father," she manages to say, "it's obvious he was up to no good back then. How do you think he got his hands on my father's company? Or this very train?"

"I assumed he was doing your family a favor."

Anna doesn't know whether to laugh or be insulted. "A favor?

My family lost everything in the process. And lest you forget, our fathers hated each other."

"They did," Dante says. "But I always thought that, like all good rivalries, there was some mutual respect involved."

The comment finally makes up Anna's mind. Insulted it is. Not to mention enraged.

"If your father had one ounce of respect for mine, he wouldn't have organized an entire conspiracy to destroy him. Sal, Lapsford, the others, they did the dirty work, but your father was behind it all. You're forgetting I have proof."

"About this evidence. What, exactly, is it?"

"Memos, correspondence, more blueprints, even photographs."

Dante leans forward, the look on his face turning from blithe to troubled. "And you think it's enough to prove my father organized it?"

"Without a doubt," Anna says. "The most damning evidence is the financial records. In 1942, your father transferred massive amounts of money to five numbered bank accounts in Switzerland. Care to guess who those accounts belonged to?"

"I think I already know," Dante says.

"It's foolproof," Anna tells him. "I wouldn't have gone to all this trouble if it wasn't. Your father's going to pay for what he did. All of them will. Their lives are ostensibly over the moment we reach Chicago."

"That's another thing I wondered about," Dante says. "Why Chicago? I mean, I understand the symbolism behind taking the Phoenix. That's unmissable. But a train to Washington or New York would have been faster—not to mention easier. I knew there had to be another reason. And I've finally figured it out. Would you like me to tell you?"

Anna stands and stretches. "By all means, explain my motivations to me."

"You want to watch us squirm," Dante says.

"And is it working?"

"Do you see me squirming?"

"No," Anna says as she starts toward the door, on her way into the dining car. "Fortunately, the night is still young. Now, if you'll excuse me, I'm going to see what the others are up to."

Dante rises from the piano to follow her. "Probably beating down the door to the locomotive at this point."

"It won't work."

Anna walks briskly through the dining car and galley, forcing Dante to scramble to keep pace. In the sleeper car, he says, "I've been meaning to ask you. How did you make it so there'd be no other passengers?"

"I have my ways. After all, the train needed to be empty. I didn't want to offer anyone a single means of escape." Anna gestures to the doors at each end of the car. "On a crowded train, with people bustling to get on and off, it would be easy for someone to slip away in the crowd."

"And it avoids having innocent bystanders onboard when things get ugly," Dante adds. "Now that they know they're trapped on this train, it's only a matter of time before these people start to turn on each other."

Anna doesn't think so, despite already assuming things will get heated once desperation sets in. She predicts accusations, confessions, blame being lobbed from one person to the next. And while she knows there's a chance they'll go after her and Seamus—hence her knife and his own form of protection—she doesn't think any of them will resort to targeting each other.

Still, as she and Dante enter the baggage car, Anna immediately clocks their manic mood. Judd Dodge stands at the door to the locomotive, slamming his fist against it to no avail. That doesn't keep Jack Lapsford from also trying. Trading places with Judd, he tries the door himself, first pulling the handle, then pushing it, then pulling again. When neither motion causes it to budge, he resorts to pounding on the door and yelling, "Hello? Whoever's in there, open up at once!"

Sal joins in, punctuating her words with sharp raps against the door. "This! Is! An! Emergency!"

Anna pictures Burt Chapman at the front of the locomotive, oblivious to the racket. Even if he can hear them, she knows he'll ignore it.

"I told him one of you would probably say that," Anna says, announcing her presence in the baggage car.

Judd gives her a desperate look. "Then why isn't he answering?"

"Because I knew we'd end up here eventually," Anna says. "So I told him not to open the door. After paying him handsomely, of course."

"Whatever she's paying you," Sal says with another bang on the door, "we'll offer double!"

Anna puts a hand on her hip, impatient. "I told him you'd say that, too."

"A million dollars!" Lapsford shouts, an amount that makes Herb Pulaski gasp. The others, too, give him looks of stupefied shock. The only person not surprised is Anna.

"He knew that was coming, too," she says. "There's literally nothing you can say or do that will get him to stop this train."

"But *you* can stop it, right?" Judd asks.

"On the contrary, not even I can do that. Because I assumed one of you would try to imitate me—or, God forbid, coerce me through violence—I instructed the engineer to not obey a word anyone said. Even me."

"You're nuts," Sal says. "Truly insane."

Lapsford affirms that sentiment with a nod. "Why would he agree to that?"

"Because everyone who normally works on this train, from the dishwasher to the chief engineer, knows the purpose of this journey," Anna says. "And they were all too happy to step aside or, in the engineer's case, provide assistance. Workers also died because of your scheme. The engineers. A conductor. Two porters. On the railroad, devotion runs deep. They want justice as much as Seamus and I do."

Lapsford either doesn't understand or doesn't care. Pounding his fists against the door, he yells, "I am a high-ranking member of the United States Army, and I command you to stop this train."

"*Retired* high-ranking member," Dante says, coming to Anna's side. "Which doesn't give you any authority at all. In fact, since this train belongs to my father—and since it will someday be mine—I think I'm the one who has the ultimate say over where it goes and when it stops, don't you?"

"Then stop it and let all of us off," Lapsford demands.

Anna goes rigid as Dante approaches the door. Before boarding, back when she still expected Kenneth Wentworth, she told Burt Chapman his boss would be on the train—and that he'd likely do anything to stop it. Burt assured her she had nothing to worry about, especially once she told him what Wentworth had done. It didn't hurt that she'd paid him twice as much as the rest of the train's crew.

But Dante isn't his father. Charm and persuasion are his specialties. If anyone can sweet-talk his way into stopping the Phoenix, it's him.

He knocks on the door and clears his throat. "My name is Dante Wentworth. My father owns this railroad, including the train you're controlling. As you've heard, there are some people out here desperate for you to stop it so they can disembark. Considering these circumstances, I think it's best that—"

Dante turns to give Anna a look she finds unreadable. For a

second, she can't breathe, certain he's about to single-handedly stop the train and ruin her plan. All that work gone. All that plotting for nothing. All that expense wasted.

But then that crooked grin spreads across his face, and Anna exhales.

"I think it's best that you keep this train moving," Dante continues. "Ignore what anyone out here says, just as Miss Matheson instructed. Do not stop for any reason until we reach Chicago."

He raps twice on the door and waits. A moment later, two more raps rise from the other side. Burt has received his message.

The train will not be stopping.

TWELVE

DANTE WHIRLS AROUND to face the others and, with a clap of his hands, says, "Now, who's up for a drink?"

He makes it two steps before the others swarm him, furious.

"Are you crazy?" Judd yells while, at the exact same time, Sal says, "Why did you do that?"

"You've just doomed us all!" Lapsford then bellows, his face crimson. "Including your father."

"Maybe he deserves it," Dante says. "In fact, I'm starting to think all of you do."

Lapsford glowers at him. "This isn't over. There's plenty of time between here and Chicago."

"More than ten hours," Judd adds as he pulls a pocket watch from inside his jacket. Too flustered to open it, he puts it away without checking to see if he's right.

"And I *will* find a way off this train, even if it means killing you and her." Lapsford jerks a thumb in Anna's direction. "In fact, there's nothing to prevent us from doing just that and ending this whole charade."

Anna nods to Seamus, who takes a step forward while simultaneously removing a revolver from his pocket. Someone—either Sal or Edith, Anna isn't sure—lets out a shocked cry. A few of the men gasp. Even Dante gives Anna a wide-eyed look, as if he suddenly thinks she's crazy.

He's wrong there. In that moment, Anna is absolutely, utterly sane.

Next to her, Seamus aims the revolver not at Lapsford but at the car in general, his meaning clear. He can shoot any one of them if he wants to, a realization that makes Lapsford back away with his hands raised.

Seamus glares at the group, and for a second Anna, too, fears he might abandon their plan and shoot them all dead. There are enough bullets in his six-shooter. One for each person.

"I told you she planned to kill us," Judd says.

Anna steps in front of Seamus, blocking everyone's view of the revolver. She'd been reluctant to let him bring it, knowing the situation was fraught enough without adding a gun to the mix. But, just like with the knife strapped to her thigh, she ultimately deemed it a necessary precaution.

"No one is going to kill anyone," Anna says. "I meant it when I said I want you all alive. Seamus has the gun to ensure that all of you remain calm."

"And what if we don't?" Lapsford says.

Seamus pokes his head out from behind Anna. "Then you get a bullet in you. That'll calm you down. You want to wait a little bit, Lieutenant Colonel? Or should I just shoot you now?"

Herb Pulaski breaks away from the group and heads for the set of double doors in the center of the car. "The rest of you can stay here. But I'm not waiting around to get arrested or shot."

He unlatches the doors and yanks them open. Wide enough for large trunks and pieces of luggage to fit through, their opening creates a gaping hole in the side of the train. Cold air blasts through the car, bringing with it a scattering of thick snowflakes that spiral to the floor. Riding the air with them is the noise of the train itself. A loud clattering of steel wheels on iron rails that echoes off the car's barren walls. Buffeted by the wind and noise, Herb moves closer to the opening.

"What are you doing?" Judd says, shouting to be heard over the racket.

"What do you think? I'm gonna jump off this goddamn train. I suggest the rest of you do the same."

Herb stands in the doorway and grips both sides of the frame, preparing to leap. Anna sweeps up behind him, panicked he'll go through with it. Over his shoulder, she sees that the train is still following the path of the river. There are no longer any houses on the opposite shore, however. Just a dark, rugged expanse of water and woods dusted with falling snow.

"The average speed of this train is sixty-five miles an hour," she tells Herb. "If you jump, there's a fifty-fifty chance you'll be killed instantly. Especially if you get pulled under the wheels. They'll slice you faster than a knife through butter."

Herb leans into the empty space beyond the doorway. "I'll risk it."

"Suit yourself," Anna says, changing tactics. "But even if you are lucky enough to survive the jump, you won't emerge unscathed. There *will* be injuries. Broken bones. Cuts and abrasions. You certainly won't be able to run. You probably won't even be able to walk. And if, by some miracle you can, there's nowhere for you to go. Not much of an escape plan, is it?"

Herb turns away from the opening to look at her. Anna searches his face, pleased to notice that hesitation has begun to settle over his features.

"I'm waiting, Mr. Pulaski," she says. "Do you intend to jump or not?"

Herb looks back outside and Anna can tell he's doing the calculations in his head, deciding if it's ultimately worth the risk.

"Would you like me to push you?" she says.

"No!"

Herb leaps away from the door, not stopping until his back is flattened against the opposite wall. Anna takes his place at the doors, slamming them shut. The wind instantly ceases as the noise of the train quiets to a steady clickety-clack.

"Now that you've come to your senses and realized there's no getting off this train until Chicago, I recommend all of you make your way back to the first-class lounge," she says.

No one disagrees with her. Not even Jack Lapsford, the most contentious of the bunch. All five of them shuffle out of the baggage car, overseen by Seamus. Anna and Dante follow a short distance behind.

"Why didn't you try to stop the train?" Anna says softly once they reach the second coach car and are filing down the aisle.

"I have my reasons," Dante replies. "Ones that have nothing to do with you."

He says nothing after that. No one does. Passing row upon row of empty seats, the group becomes a grim parade, struck silent by the lack of people. When they return to the first-class lounge, Judd Dodge says, "I think I could use that drink now."

Dante steps behind the bar. "Pick your poison."

"Gin," Judd says.

"Works for me," Sal announces as she drops her handbag onto the bar and pulls out a tube of lipstick.

"I'll take one, too," Herb says. "Seeing how this might be my last chance for a stiff drink."

Lapsford chimes in with "Make mine a double."

Dante gathers the necessities with the same dexterity he applied to the piano. Within seconds the bar top is crowded with martini glasses, a cocktail shaker, and a bottle of Tanqueray.

"Anything for you, Edith?"

Edith, sitting primly at a distance, shakes her head. "Alcohol dulls the senses."

"Yeah," Sal says while applying the lipstick, outlining her mouth in a shade of red as bright as blood. "That's the point."

Dante fills the cocktail shaker with ice, gin, and two splashes of vermouth. After giving it a good stir, he lines up four glasses and runs the upturned shaker back and forth over the row until each one has the same amount. He then spreads his arms wide above the finished cocktails and says, "Come and get 'em."

Already at the bar, Sal hovers a hand over the glasses before choosing one on the end of the row. Herb is next, snagging the one now in the center without thought. After him comes Lapsford, who reaches for one glass, changes his mind, takes the other. Turning away from the bar, he brushes against Judd, who picks up the remaining glass with his right hand and carries it to the center of the car, where he stands alone.

For a moment, they drink in silence, letting the gravity of the situation sink in. Herb takes the tiniest of sips, grimacing at the martini's strength. On the opposite end of the spectrum is Sal, who tips the glass back, her fresh lipstick leaving a crimson stain on its rim. Lapsford keeps his glass at his lips, glaring over the drink at Anna, while Judd, in no hurry to take a sip, checks his pocket watch and stifles a yawn.

Another horn toot rises from the front of the train, long and languid in the dark night. It's followed by a similar one from farther away. Another train is in the vicinity, roaring in the opposite direction on the set of tracks running parallel to their own.

Within seconds, the train is beside them, rattling by with a car-rocking whoosh. The lit windows of the other train pass their own in flashbulb bursts. Bright. Fleeting. Blinding in their intensity. The blink-quick glimpses of people on the other train filling coach seats, mingling in the club car, and eating in the dining car make those trapped on the Phoenix lean closer to watch with palpable envy.

Then the other train is gone, leaving them with nothing but a view of the snow-studded landscape. Anna hopes all of them are thinking about how this is their last moment of comfort before it's taken away from them forever—and that this knowledge makes it all the more painful.

She looks to Seamus, who'd noticed the same thing and flashes her a half smile. Rare for him. A sign that, despite a few hiccups and Dante's presence, their plan is working.

But then someone in the car coughs.

Then moans.

Then emits a sickly combination of the two.

All eyes turn to the afflicted party—Lt. Col. Jack Lapsford, who at that moment is collapsing into the nearest chair, martini sloshing. He sets it down and uses that now-free hand to clutch his chest.

"Help," he gasps. "I think I'm having a heart attack."

Those nearest him—Sal and Herb—are by his side in an instant, uncertain how to help. By the time Anna pushes herself between them, Lapsford's face has turned bright red.

"Can you breathe?" she asks as she kneels before him.

Lapsford's head lolls back, neither shake nor nod. Anna grasps his free hand in both of her own. She places two fingers against his wrist, feeling his pulse. While Anna is certainly no doctor, it seems normal to her. She suspects her own heart is beating twice as fast.

"I don't think it's his heart," she says. "Maybe a stroke?"

Anna stands and steadies Lapsford's head between her hands. His eyes are open, and she stares into them, searching for signs of stroke, of seizure, of brain hemorrhage. Not that she knows what those signs are. Anna assumes something will reveal itself. But as she gazes into Lapsford's eyes, there's nothing obviously wrong with them.

"We need a doctor!" someone shouts.

"What we need is to stop this damn train!" someone else yells even louder.

"No!" Anna whirls around to face them, the tone of her voice and the ferocity of her words silencing the rest of the car. "This train stops for no one."

"But this is an emergency," Herb says.

Anna is no longer so sure of that. There are no signs that anything is wrong with Lapsford other than his dramatic appearance. Which, now that Anna thinks about it, seems too dramatic, especially for someone with a normal pulse and no obvious affliction.

She turns back to Lapsford, whose breathing instantly calms. His expression, too, changes from panic to one of defiance, with a touch of amusement thrown in for good measure. In that moment, Anna knows her suspicion is correct.

Nothing is wrong with Jack Lapsford. He had simply faked a heart attack to get her to stop the train.

"I had to give it a shot," he says when it's clear he's been caught once again trying to stop the train.

Anna can only shake her head in disgust. What a weak, cowardly man.

"You're probably the worst person on this train," she tells him. "Considering your fellow passengers, that's—"

She's cut off by the sound of a martini glass being slammed against a cocktail table. Pivoting toward the sound, she sees Judd Dodge, now empty-handed, staring into the middle distance. Mouth open and eyes wide, he looks like a man currently glimpsing some indescribable horror at the end of the car.

But there's nothing there. Just the bar with Dante still behind it and the mirrored shelves in back of him reflecting the scene unfolding in the center of the car.

Anna, having just been duped by Lapsford, makes no move to help. No one does.

Judd lists to the right, grasping the tablecloth of the cocktail table as if that alone can keep him upright. The cloth instead slithers across the table, toppling the martini glass and causing Judd to lose his balance entirely. He hits the floor with a sickening thud, the sound muting the single, agonized moan escaping his lips.

In a flash, Anna is at his side, kneeling over him, trying to steady him the same way she'd done with Lapsford moments earlier. As Judd writhes on his back, a slick of foam bubbles out of his mouth. Like someone afflicted. Someone rabid. Flecks of red stain the foam. A bloody, viscous mess gurgles past his lips and oozes down his chin.

Anna gapes at it, helpless and horrified. "Judd, can you talk? Tell me what's wrong."

Speechless, Judd only shudders.

Then, with a groan and a rattle, he goes still.

Anna slaps his face, lightly at first, then with increased force. She continues slapping, panic underscoring every strike, until Seamus gently pulls her away.

"No," Anna whimpers. "He can't be."

With a trembling hand, Seamus places two fingers against Judd's neck. He looks at Anna and shakes his head. After quickly crossing himself in silent prayer, Seamus removes Judd's glasses, places the same fingers he'd just used to seek out a pulse atop his eyelids, and gently slides them closed.

To the others in the lounge, that's the moment it becomes real. When all of them understand that this isn't a blatant attempt to stop the train or another part of Anna's plan.

Judd Dodge is dead.

10 P.M.

TEN HOURS
TO CHICAGO

THIRTEEN

FOR A FULL minute after Judd Dodge is declared dead, no one speaks. At least not loud enough for anyone else to hear. Plopped into a chair, Edith Gerhardt whispers a near-silent prayer. Next to her, Herb Pulaski moves his lips but no words come out.

As for Anna, she can't even breathe. If she does, she's not cognizant of it. It feels to her as if she's the dead one. Considering where she is and who she's with, that would have been less surprising than *this*.

Still on the floor, she looks across the car to Dante, and their eyes meet in a silent exchange of worry. He was right. They have turned on each other. In a way she never expected.

Anna risks another glance at Judd, struck by how undignified he appears in death. His eyes are closed, yes, but that's the only thing resembling a peaceful repose. The rest of him, from the blood-flecked foam on his lips to the tablecloth still in his grip to the odd, angular bend of his right leg, looks like a man still suffering. It makes Anna shudder. She'd wanted him to suffer, but not like this.

It's a relief when Seamus gently straightens Judd's legs and removes the tablecloth from his fingers. It's even more of a relief when he places a dry cloth from a neighboring table over the corpse, shielding it from view.

"Is he really dead?" Herb says.

Seamus nods. "Yes."

"We need to contact the police," Edith says.

"What we need," Lapsford says, "is to stop this goddamn train!"

"No!" Anna says from her spot on the floor. "This train isn't stopping."

Sal stares at her, bug-eyed. "Not even for *this*? You're nuts."

The others nod and mutter in agreement. Even Seamus, standing next to Judd's body, seems torn about it. "What should we do, Anna? This wasn't part of the plan."

"I don't know," she says. "I need to—"

Think.

That's what she needs to do, when all she wants is to cry. Not for Judd Dodge himself. He doesn't deserve her tears. What he *had* deserved was to pay for his sins. And while that might currently be happening if there is a heaven, a hell, and judgment in the afterlife, Anna isn't able to witness it.

And that's what *she* deserves. It's what her whole family deserves. What she owes them as their last surviving member.

Make all of them pay, Aunt Retta had told her, and Anna vowed that she would. But now it's impossible to make that happen. That's why Anna feels the tears burning at the corners of her eyes. Judd's death denies her the chance to see *all* of them brought to justice.

Her plan now feels like water pooled in her cupped hands, slipping between her fingers and draining away. All that work for nothing. All that wasted money, not to mention opportunity. She could have made it easier on herself, as Dante pointed out. Summoned the FBI, handed over the evidence, watched the arrests happen. But that hadn't been enough for her. Not after what these people had done to her family. Like a queen bee hunting those who destroyed the hive, she wanted them to feel her sting.

But someone else had struck first, and the pain she feels keeps the tears welling. She thinks of what Aunt Retta would say in this moment. Don't cry. Don't show emotion. And for God's sake, don't flinch.

Anna stops the tears from falling through sheer force of will and climbs to her feet. She needs to focus, to concentrate, to figure out what to do next.

The others are right. The best course of action *would* be to notify the authorities. But that means stopping the train, and she'd gone to great lengths to ensure that that couldn't happen, not ever thinking there might come a moment in which the train *needed* to stop. With that scenario unlikely at best, Anna can think of only one other option—identify the killer herself.

Rotating slowly in the center of the car, she says, "Which one of you did this? You're all going to prison anyway, so you might as well confess now and save the police a lot of time and effort."

"What makes you think it was one of us?" Lapsford asks.

"Well, it had to be someone on this train," Anna says. "And since we're the only people on it, that means it was one of you."

"Or one of *you*," Lapsford says, pointing to Anna and Seamus. "I think Judd was right. You *are* trying to kill us."

Anna's not surprised by being pegged a murderer. In fact, she expected it. And even though she knows none of them will believe her, she says, "I already told you my plans. If I intended to kill all of you, I would have done it by now."

The statement—as blunt as it is unnerving—quiets the car. A few seconds of silence follows, broken only when Herb gestures at Seamus and says, "What about him?"

"What about *you?*" Seamus says back. "Anna and I aren't the only ones capable of murder. Considering what the rest of you have done, you're all more suspicious than the two of us. If Mr. Dodge was murdered—"

"If?" Sal says with a roll of her eyes. "What else could have killed him?"

Anna approaches Judd's body, carefully tiptoeing past it to reach the cocktail table he'd stood next to before hitting the floor. While some of the tablecloth is on the floor beside him, a martini-soaked portion still clings to the table's surface. Resting on its side atop it is the martini glass Judd had drunk from. Anna swipes an index finger along the inside of the glass, feeling a gritty residue.

She lifts the glass to her nose and sniffs, detecting a sharp, unpleasant chemical scent.

"He was poisoned," she announces.

"You sure about that?" Seamus says.

"Not a hundred percent. But I've drunk enough martinis in my life to know they don't smell like this. Someone put something toxic in Judd's drink."

"Told you it was murder," Lapsford says with smug satisfaction.

While that fact is now obvious, Anna still doesn't understand the motive behind it. Why would someone want to kill Judd Dodge? If anyone on this train is a target for murder, it's her, followed closely by Seamus. Yet someone killed Judd instead.

"Did any of you have a grudge against Judd?" she asks, not expecting an honest answer.

Edith shakes her head, while Lapsford says, "I barely knew the man."

"Not me," Herb says. "But he did seem a bit jumpy when he first got here."

"Jumpy how?" Anna says.

Looking jumpy himself, Herb wipes his brow with a handkerchief and then starts twisting it in his hands. "Nervous. Like he had a bad feeling about this night."

"As well he should have," Sal says. "Seeing how one of you offed him."

On the other side of the car, Jack Lapsford looks her up and down. "Excluding yourself, I see. In my mind, that makes you the prime suspect."

"The feeling's mutual," Sal says.

"I had no reason to kill him," Lapsford says. "Even though he all but confessed to treason and sabotage when he saw that blueprint."

Whether intentional or not, Lapsford's response provides Anna with a prime motive for murder. Judd *did* say he drafted the blueprint that had been in the briefcase, even clarifying that it was for the locomotive that had been designed to explode. That's as close to an admission of guilt as she could hope for.

Maybe one of the others, worried he'd easily confess to everything they'd done, resorted to murder to keep Judd quiet. But who? And when?

Anna tries to summon details from minutes earlier. Whoever did it had to have slipped the poison into Judd's glass without anyone else noticing. But not much time had passed between Dante making the drinks and Judd's sudden collapse to the floor. And Anna had been too distracted by the passing train—not to mention tending to Lapsford during his faked heart attack—to notice much of anything else.

"Who was standing next to Judd when he died?" she says.

"No one," Seamus says. "He was alone."

"And no one got near him after he grabbed his drink from the bar?"

"No."

Seamus turns to the bar itself. Dante remains behind it, not having budged since pouring the martinis. Aware of the suspicious way everyone is looking at him, he says, "You don't seriously think I did it, do you?"

"A man did just die while drinking a martini *you* mixed," Seamus says.

"But why would I kill him?" Dante said. "*When* could I have killed him? You all saw me mix those martinis right in front of you. I made everyone's drinks at the same time, in the same shaker. If I poisoned Judd's, then Sal, Herb, and the lieutenant colonel here would also be dead."

Sal stares at the glass still in her hand and, seeing that it's mostly empty, lets it go with a gasp. The glass hits the floor, its stem snapping at her feet. Herb and Lapsford, both of whom had set their half-consumed drinks aside earlier, exchange stricken looks.

"But you're not dead," Dante adds. "Which means I didn't poison Judd's drink. How could I? I didn't know who'd be taking which glass. I let them pick."

"It's true," Anna says, recalling how Dante, as he did with everything, presented the drinks with a charming flourish. "He set out the glasses and poured the drinks, but the rest of it was random."

"And Judd took the last glass that was left," Dante says.

"Who took the first?"

"Sally," Edith says, piping up from her chair by the window. "She chose first."

Sal whirls on her. "So you're saying I did it?"

"I'm simply pointing out that you had the opportunity," Edith says.

"As did Herb." Sal grabs her handbag from the bar and uses it to gesture at the man next to Edith. "And Lapsford. And everyone else in this car. Including you, Edith. Speaking of which, you've been suspiciously quiet throughout all of this."

Edith sighs. "I see no point in raising a fuss. Especially when you and the others are all too happy to do it for me."

"Or maybe you've been plotting something this whole time and hoping no one would notice."

Now that Sal's mentioned it, Anna realizes Edith has been silent for most of the night. Following, never leading. Usually speaking only when spoken to. A far cry from the gregarious woman who'd once regaled Anna with stories from German folklore.

"I've done nothing wrong," Edith says. "I've barely moved since we returned to this car."

"Who took the second drink?" Anna asks.

Herb raises his hand. "That was me."

"And I took the third," Lapsford announces. "Anyone who watched me do it saw that I didn't tamper with the remaining glass."

"But you *did* change your mind," Dante says, drifting back to the bar top and placing his hands where the final two drinks had been. "I saw you reach for one glass, decide against it, and grab the other. What made you change your mind? And don't say it's because one had more in it than the other. I poured the same amount into each glass."

Anna approaches Lapsford, curious. "Was there something wrong with the other drink? Is that why you left it for Judd?"

"Not the drink itself," he says. "Both looked exactly the same. It was the glass that prompted me to choose the other drink."

"The glass? What was wrong with it?"

"There was a smudge on the inside rim." Lapsford holds up an index finger. "Like a fingerprint. So I took the glass that was cleaner."

Anna rushes back to the table beside Judd's corpse. The martini glass is still there, now sitting upright after she found the residue inside. Turning it over in her hands, she sees several fingerprints, including a lengthy smear left by her own index finger when she swiped the inside rim. If Lapsford had seen a print mark there, it's now indistinguishable from the rest.

"Dante," she says, returning to the bar. "Which direction were the martini glasses facing when you grabbed them? Up or down?"

"Up," Dante says before ducking behind the bar to double-check. "Just like all the others."

"Did you examine any of them before putting them on the bar?"

"I barely even looked at them." Dante pauses, awestruck. "Wait, I know what you're thinking."

There's a gleam in his eyes that Anna remembers well from her youth. It revealed itself whenever Dante was excited about something, whether it was her agreeing to go on a first date with him or that time he suggested they go skinny-dipping in his backyard pool. Every time, Anna found herself eagerly going along with it. Including, to her shame and eventual regret, the skinny-dipping.

Now, many years later and under very different circumstances, she realizes how easy it would be to get swept up in that old, familiar rhythm with Dante. Tearing her gaze away from his sparkling eyes, Anna reminds herself who Dante is, what he did to her, and what his father did to her family.

"And what am I thinking, Mr. Wentworth?"

If Dante notices her change of tone, he doesn't show it. "That it was the glass, and not the drink, that was poisoned."

"It's possible," Anna admits, countering his enthusiasm with a frown. This is nothing to be excited about. A man is dead, her plan has been reduced to rubble, and they're not even close to reaching Chicago. Then there's the fact that, if poison had been placed in that glass, it means Judd might not have been the intended target—and that the killer could have put it there *before* they'd all gathered in the lounge.

"So it wasn't one of us," Sal says, thinking the same thing.

"I didn't say that," Anna snaps.

Yet she's certainly considering it. If her theory is correct, the killer might not even be among them. Yes, they're currently the only people aboard the Phoenix, but that hadn't been the case earlier that evening. Anna thinks about the dozens of workers and pretend passengers who were aboard the train minutes before its departure. Any one of them could have slipped behind the bar of the first-class lounge and coated the inside of a single glass with poison.

Why someone would do that is beyond Anna. It makes absolutely no sense, which is why, in her mind, it remains likely that it was the work of someone in this very car at this very minute. After all, the car had been empty at some point immediately after the Phoenix left the station.

"Mr. Pulaski," Anna says.

Herb, still gripping his handkerchief so tightly his knuckles are white, looks up, startled to hear his name. "Yes?"

"You said you and Mr. Dodge were alone in this lounge before the others arrived. Is that true?"

"Yeah."

"I can confirm that," Sal says. "They were the only ones inside when I got here."

"And which one of you was here first?"

"Me," Herb says after a nervous swallow and another dab of his brow. "But I didn't do anything to any of the glasses. I swear. You can even search me."

That, Anna realizes, isn't a bad idea. If the killer is someone in this car who dropped the poison directly into Judd's drink, then whoever did it still has the container that held it. A vial or pillbox or small bottle.

"I'll take you up on that offer," Anna says. "In fact, everyone needs to empty their pockets and purses. Starting with you, Mr. Pulaski."

Herb does as he's told, slowly emptying his pockets and revealing the contents. Two invitations—one for the lounge, the other for the train journey itself—a thin billfold, a pack of Lucky Strikes, and a silver lighter. Anna examines all of it. The billfold is empty except for a five-dollar bill, there are eight cigarettes left in the pack, and the lighter produces a flame with a single flick.

Before handing everything back to Herb, she nods toward Seamus. "Pat him down. Just to be sure."

"Now you wait just a goddamn minute," Lapsford says as, five feet away, Seamus frisks Herb from feet to shoulders. "This is a free country. You have no right to search me or anyone else without just cause."

Anna gestures to the cloth-covered corpse at the far end of the car. "I think that's cause enough, don't you? If you're innocent, you have nothing to worry about. But if you refuse to be searched, we'll all just assume you're the killer. The choice is yours."

Lapsford thinks it over before turning his pockets inside out. There's nothing in them but a Baby Ruth candy bar partially melted by body heat. When Seamus swoops in to pat him down, Lapsford expresses his disapproval with several annoyed huffs.

"I'll go next," Dante says as he steps from behind the bar. He removes his suit coat and passes it to Anna, who roots through the pockets, finding only a striped breath mint in a cellophane wrapper. As Seamus approaches to search him, Dante grins and says, "You sure you don't want to do the honors, Annie?"

Anna cringes at another use of his nickname for her. Although several threats currently exist on this train, failing to resist Dante's charms is among the biggest.

"I'm certain," she says before motioning for Seamus to frisk him. The ensuing search is rougher than the others, with Seamus spinning Dante around and shoving him against the bar. The pat-down is even worse, leaving Dante looking rumpled by the time it's over.

Anna tosses his jacket back to him as she and Seamus turn to Sal.

"I suppose you should search the women," Seamus says.

An impossible task, Anna realizes as she faces Sal. She can endure Sal's presence when she's among the others, in the thick of the group. But being one on one with her is too much for Anna to bear. Her anger is too great, Sal's betrayal too painful, her memories too raw.

Like the year Sal spent Thanksgiving with her family and they stayed up late painting each other's toenails, giggling so hard they woke Tommy in the next room. Or during the Phoenix's maiden voyage, when Sal slid open the window and told her to wave at all the people who'd gathered to watch the train go by. Or when she was sixteen and had told Sal her biggest secret—that she was in love with Dante Wentworth.

"Be careful," Sal had warned. "Boys will break your heart without a second thought."

Dante did indeed break her heart, but not nearly as much as Sal had. Anna would rather touch the cooling corpse of Judd Dodge than lay hands on Sally Lawrence.

"You do it," she tells Seamus. "I'll check her bag."

"Don't get any ideas," Sal warns Seamus as he comes in for the frisk. "You're not my type."

Seamus starts patting her down. "Good. Because if I were, I might have to throw myself off this train."

Anna turns to the bar and grabs Sal's handbag. Sorting through it, she finds a compact, lipstick, a small bottle of nail polish, and a silver flask with a bit of liquid sloshing inside. Uncapping the flask, Anna smells what's inside. Whiskey. Not poison.

"She's clean," Seamus says.

Anna drops the flask back into the handbag before returning it to Sal. "So is her bag."

That leaves only Edith, who remains in her seat, arms

stubbornly folded across her chest. "I refuse to take part in this indignity," she says. "You should be ashamed of yourself for treating ladies this way."

"Ask me if I care," Seamus tells her. "Now get up so I can search you."

"My purse is in my room, and I have no pockets. There's no place for me to hide anything."

Desperation has crept into Edith's voice. With it is a tinge of fear that Anna wants to enjoy but can't. She's too busy thinking about all the times Edith had awakened her from childhood nightmares, kissing her forehead while whispering, "It's just a bad dream, Schatzi. Nothing will hurt you while I'm here."

"Let me do it," Anna says, surprising everyone, including herself. Just like with Sal, she has no desire to engage with Edith on an individual level. But it's clear Edith isn't going to let Seamus pat her down without a fight. Anna's willing to push her distaste aside and do it herself if it means speeding things up.

Standing before Edith, she says, "Come on. Let's get this over with."

Edith slowly rises to her feet. "Schatzi," she says, not without warmth.

The word unlocks something in Anna. Not mere anger, although she's plenty angry. It's more complex than that. Anna *hates* this woman. She hates who Edith is and what she's done. Yet Anna also still loves her. At least the memory of loving her, which is made more complicated by knowing that she once thought Edith had loved her in return.

"Don't call me that," Anna says, her tone a warning.

She begins her search at Edith's feet. That she wears sensible shoes doesn't surprise Anna in the least. She'd always valued comfort over style, and these black flats, polished to a shine, are no different. Anna moves her hands quickly up Edith's sturdy legs, barely skimming the hose she wears like a second skin.

"You look well," Edith says as Anna begins patting her thighs, her hips, her waist. "So grown-up now."

Anna refuses to look at her. She focuses only on Edith's dress. The drab shade of gray. The scruff of the wool beneath her palms. How, within seconds, those same palms will have to travel to more intimate places.

"Your mother and father would be proud of how beautiful you've turned out," Edith says, perhaps to make what's coming next less awkward. Anna doesn't think so. There's a sly edge to her voice that feels to her like Edith is needling.

"Don't talk about my parents," Anna snaps.

She's at Edith's bosom now, patting it down quickly, before moving on to her upper arms and shoulders.

Edith shakes her head. "They'd be proud, but they would also weep at the person you've become."

Hearing that unleashes in Anna a rage so ferocious it literally blinds her. Stars dot her vision, blocking out Edith's face. The anger is all-consuming, filling Anna's ears with the sound of her pounding heart and making her hands go numb. For a moment, she sees nothing, hears nothing, feels nothing.

Sound is the first sense that returns, in the form of ragged, pained croaks that Anna can't quite identify. Next comes sight, the stars fading just enough for Anna to see her hands wrapped around Edith's throat. A second later, she feels the bunching of skin beneath her palms as she squeezes Edith's neck.

Anna drops her hands, shocked. By now Seamus is upon her, dragging her away from Edith while hissing in her ear, "Get a goddamn hold of yourself."

Seamus guides her to the nearest chair and Anna falls into it.

Across the lounge, Edith also returns to her seat, taking in air with great, heaving gasps. With a trembling hand, she massages the spot on her neck where Anna's own hands just were. Seeing the twin red marks she left behind makes Anna angry at Edith for egging her on but even more mad at herself for falling for it and entirely losing control.

"Pull yourself together," Seamus tells her. "She's not worth going to prison over. None of them are."

"I'm s—"

Anna stops herself from saying the word.

Sorry.

Because she's not. Of all the emotions colliding inside her, sorry definitely isn't one of them.

"It won't happen again," she tells Seamus.

He nods. "Good. I'm assuming you didn't find anything."

"Nothing," Anna says. "Just like the others."

"Because none of us did it," Sal says from the opposite end of the car, making Anna realize they've all been listening—and watching—this whole time.

Anna stands and smooths out her dress, trying to signal strength and composure. But it's too late. They've all seen how easily she can snap. Forget her parents. It's Aunt Retta who'd be disappointed. Her actions were a flinch writ large.

"One of you killed Judd Dodge. There's no one else here who could have done it. And none of us are leaving this car until the killer confesses."

No one does, which isn't a surprise to Anna. She didn't expect anyone to come forward—yet. Clinging to the hope that it's only a matter of time before one of them cracks, she decides to wait them out.

Five minutes pass.

Then ten.

Then fifteen.

As they near twenty minutes of unbearable silence, Anna finally hears something. But the sound doesn't come from inside the lounge. It's on the outside, just beyond the door at the front of the car.

Footsteps, followed by a single, desperate "Hello?"

Hearing it, Anna swings her gaze to the door, watching in astonishment as it opens.

A man stands on the other side, peering into the car. His gray flannel suit and light blue shirt make it clear he's not an engineer, and the shocked look on his face suggests he wasn't expecting to find anyone in the lounge. Those inside it stare right back, equally stunned.

Because it turns out there aren't only eight passengers aboard the Philadelphia Phoenix.

In truth, the number is nine.

11 P.M.

NINE HOURS TO CHICAGO

FOURTEEN

"THANK GOODNESS," THE surprise ninth person says as he surveys the crowd in the lounge. "I was starting to worry I was the only one on this train."

He flashes a cautious half smile that vanishes when he spots the cloth-covered corpse of Judd Dodge.

"I—" He says nothing more after that, his body language speaking volumes as he starts to back through the door.

Anna, until now frozen in shock by the presence of another person on the train, suddenly springs from her chair before the stranger can escape. "Wait!"

Blocking the closing door with an elbow, she latches onto the man's sleeve and pulls him through the door, steering him to the nearest chair. The stranger drops willingly into it, allowing Anna to get a good look at him. He appears to be in his late twenties and plain in every regard. Sandy hair, brown eyes, a face that would likely pass for handsome in different lighting and under more relaxed circumstances. Everything about him, from his suit to his wingtips, seems to strive for a conventionality that borders on the invisible.

"Why are you on this train?" Anna demands.

The stranger shoots another quick glance at the corpse on the floor. "That man. Is he—"

"Dead?" Anna says. "Yes."

The man lurches forward, and for a moment Anna thinks he's going to throw up. Or faint. Or both. Feeling very much the same way, Anna nudges him upright again and says, "Were you working with him?"

Confused ripples form across the man's forehead. "What? No, I—"

"Then who are you with?"

"Myself."

Anna gestures to the others in the car. "None of them brought you?"

"No," the man says, defensive now. "I brought myself."

"You couldn't have," Anna tells him. "There's no room on this train."

The stranger looks around the half-full lounge, no doubt thinking about the rest of the train and trying to make sense of it all. "But it's empty."

"That doesn't matter. So I'm going to ask you again, and this time you're going to tell me the truth. Why are you on this train?"

"Because I made a mistake." The man sighs and stares at the spot of floor between his well-polished shoes. "I got mixed up on the platform and boarded the wrong train."

Anna blinks in agitation. Having an innocent bystander on-board is the last thing she needs right now. "The wrong train?"

"I'm supposed to be heading to Baltimore right now," the man says. "Once I realized what happened, it was too late. This train was already moving. Where's it headed?"

"Chicago."

"Wow." The man widens his eyes before grimacing. "I really botched up this time. I guess I'll get off at the next stop and, uh, try to backtrack to where I need to be."

"There isn't a next stop," Anna says.

"What do you mean?"

"This train is an express going straight to Chicago."

"My boss is going to kill me." The stranger, realizing the inappropriateness of the phrase, takes on a stricken look. With another darting glance at Judd's body, he says, "I'm sorry. I'm just really, um, nervous."

Anna backs herself to the other side of the car, settling on the armrest of the chair across from the man. "Nervous or scared?"

"Both," he admits. "But more scared?"

Anna feels more than a little frightened herself. This is bad, she thinks. Very bad. Practically catastrophic. Yet another thing threatens to ruin her plans. All because some idiot stepped onto the wrong train.

If he's telling the truth, of course. Anna knows there's a very good chance this man is lying.

"Tell me your name," she says.

"Reginald," the man says. "Reginald Davis. My friends call me Reggie."

Anna considers this, wondering if it's an alias. She replays the way he said it in her mind, searching for signs of hesitation, of performance, of untruth. There's nothing that stands out, which makes her doubly suspicious.

Seamus must feel the same way, because he takes a step toward them and says, "You got proof of that, Reggie?"

"A driver's license?" Anna suggests. "Or a passport? Anything to let us know you're who you say you are."

"How about my word?"

Anna chuckles dryly. "That means nothing here."

"My wallet's in my overnight bag. Which is still in coach." The man dips a hand into his jacket pocket. "But I have my ticket. See?"

He holds out a slip of paper so that Anna can see both the station of departure—Philadelphia—and his original destination of Baltimore. She eyes it with suspicion. Just because he bought a ticket doesn't mean he intended to use it.

"Why didn't we see you earlier?" Seamus says. "All of us went to the front of the train and back again more than an hour ago. Yet you were nowhere to be seen."

Reggie hesitates, his face turning an embarrassed pink. "I was in the lavatory."

"That entire time?" Anna says.

"I was sick. My nerves, you see. When I realized I'd boarded the wrong train, they got the best of me. While I was holed up in the lavatory, I heard you all going back and forth. It was a relief. That's why I entered the first-class section. To find you."

"A move you're probably regretting right now," Seamus says, signaling that he might believe Reggie.

Anna finds herself doing the same. Thanks to his dazed look and timid bearing, it's easy to imagine Reggie Davis having a nervous stomach.

"Do you regret coming back here?" Anna asks.

"Yes," Reggie says. "A little. I mean, I needed to understand what was going on. Why is no one else on this train?"

"Because I bought all the tickets."

Reggie reacts with a look of bug-eyed consternation. "*All* the tickets?"

Anna nods.

"How much did that cost?"

"Everything I had," Anna says. "This is a private journey. Arranged by me for my special guests."

"So, it's a party?" Reggie says.

"Not in the least."

Reggie, now seemingly more uncertain than ever, tugs his shirt collar and gives one last look at the corpse on the floor. "Well, I'm sorry to barge in like this. If you all don't mind, I'll just go back to coach and stay there until we reach Chicago."

He stands and makes for the door again. This time, Anna is ready for it and blocks his escape. Reggie is part of this now, whether he wants to be or not. She certainly can't have him bopping around the empty train on his own.

"I'm afraid that's no longer an option, Reggie."

"Listen," he says. "Whatever's going on here, I don't want any part of it. I'm just an insurance salesman from Lansdale. Unlike you, I'm not standing around doing nothing while there's a dead man in the car. Now, it's time you start answering some of my questions, starting with who *you* are and what the hell is going on here."

Anna realizes she has no choice but to tell Reggie the truth. Innocent bystander or not, he deserves to know as much as everyone else onboard.

"My name is Anna Matheson."

"Matheson?"

Anna's not surprised the name rings a bell. Even twelve years later, her father remains infamous throughout America.

"Daughter of Arthur Matheson," she says before giving him a truncated version of who she is, who the others are, why they're all on an empty train barreling toward Chicago, and why it's unlikely to stop until they get there.

Reggie listens intently, every so often repeating a key word, as if trying to underscore its importance in his mind. "Framed." "Conspiracy." "Justice." When Anna finishes, he points to Seamus and says, "So he's with you?"

"Yes."

"And the others are . . . ?"

"Guilty," Anna says.

"Not me," Dante announces from behind the bar. "I want to make that clear."

"Nor me," adds Lapsford, a lie Reggie doesn't acknowledge because he's too busy taking fleeting glances at Judd Dodge's corpse. "How did he die?" he says.

"He was murdered," Anna says, seeing no reason to shield the stranger from something he's already surmised.

Reggie lets that sink in a moment before asking the inevitable follow-up question. "Did you do it?"

"If I say no, will you believe me?"

"Not sure."

Anna can't help but smile. The man might be lying about everything else, but at least she knows he's being honest about that. "Well, please believe me when I say I did not murder him. But someone in this car did."

Reggie looks around the lounge, aghast. "Why?"

"I'm still trying to figure that out."

"Was—" Reggie gulps. "Was he one of the people who—"

"Yes," Anna says, less to spare him from speaking the obvious end of the sentence than to prevent her from hearing it. "But I didn't want him dead. You must believe me about that, too, since many of the others in this car don't."

Reggie spends a moment trying to process all of this, looking not at Anna but at the bar in the corner of the car. "Could—" His voice is a harsh scratch. He swallows, licks his lips, and tries again. "Could I trouble someone for a drink?"

Sal lets loose with an inappropriate laugh. "Trust me, pal. That's the last thing you want."

"Why?"

"Because his drink was poisoned," Anna says. "That much we do know."

"But not by me," Sal says.

"Or me," Lapsford is quick to add.

Reggie looks again to the bar, which Dante currently leans against as if he works there. "What about him?"

"I'm just an innocent bystander like you," Dante says.

"A bystander? Yes." Anna pauses, narrowing her eyes at Dante. "Innocent? Not at all."

"But someone here killed him?" Reggie says.

"Correct. And now that you know the situation, you can understand why it's impossible to let you return to coach. Since you know a murderer is aboard this train, it's vital that you stay with us. For your own protection."

Exhaustion nudges Anna from all sides. She's now responsible for keeping this stranger alive for the rest of the trip. For keeping all of them alive. A burden she never considered when planning this night. The realization makes her so tired she's forced to leave the doorway and sink into the nearest chair, hoping Reggie doesn't again try to make a run for it. She doesn't possess the energy to chase after him if he does.

She's relieved when, instead of retreating, Reggie moves deeper into the lounge. He looks again at the body of Judd Dodge. This time, it's not a fleeting glance but a full-on stare.

"Is it possible he could have done it himself?"

"Impossible," Herb Pulaski says, piping up for the first time since being searched. "Judd would never poison himself."

"Never?" Reggie looks to Anna. "These people who framed your father. You said this train's taking them straight into the hands of the FBI, right?"

"It is," Anna says, wondering where he's going with this. Wherever it is, she's perked up considerably. Her earlier exhaustion is gone, replaced with throbbing curiosity.

"So, he knew that once this train reaches Chicago, he'll likely be going to prison."

"That's where they're all headed," Anna says, reminding the four remaining conspirators in their midst.

"When faced with the prospect of spending the rest of his life behind bars, what if he chose to die instead?"

Anna studies Reggie, still wondering if he is indeed who he claims to be. His suggestion seems too shrewd for someone foolish enough to not know he'd boarded the wrong train. Then again, maybe he's simply read a lot of mystery novels and watched too many detective movies. Anna herself is the same way. One of the reasons they're aboard this train is because she was inspired by all the films she'd seen that were set on one. *Strangers on a Train. The Narrow Margin. The Lady Vanishes.*

Now that she finds herself trapped in a real-life murder mystery, Anna understands she must think and act like the characters in those movies. Which normally would mean not trusting the seemingly innocent stranger who just happens to be in the wrong place at the wrong time.

Yet there's undeniable logic behind Reggie's suggestion. Anna thinks about Judd's location when he died. Standing alone. Distanced from the others. That relative isolation is the main reason she's struggled to identify the person who poisoned him. No one was near him once he took his drink from the bar. Taking all of that into consideration, it becomes more and more likely that Judd Dodge poisoned himself.

And Anna can think of only one way to find out for certain.

"We should search him, too," she says. "If Mr. Davis is correct and Judd did poison himself, the proof would be in his pockets."

She approaches the corpse, followed closely by Seamus. The others move in as well, surrounding Judd's body while maintaining a respectful distance. Only Reggie stays at the other end of the car, as if he now regrets bringing up the possibility that it was suicide instead of murder. Still, he makes no move to exit the lounge and run back to coach. A sign to Anna that he's as invested in this as the rest of them.

Anna hesitates before lifting the tablecloth, daunted by the task at hand. She's about to search a dead man, and there's not a single thing she can do to make it seem less terrible than it is.

"I can do it," Seamus says as he kneels on the other side of the body. "After all, I searched the others."

Not all of them, Anna thinks, shamed by the memory of her hands around Edith's neck, of the way she squeezed her throat, blind with rage. It dawns on her that Seamus is likely thinking about it, too, and that his offer has less to do with her hesitation and more with her flash of violence.

"Be my guest," Anna says.

Seamus lifts the tablecloth as far as Judd's shoulders, keeping his face blessedly covered. He then quickly shoves his hands inside all of Judd's pockets, retrieving only a single item—a pocket watch.

"That's all there is," Seamus says, holding out the watch. After everyone gets a look, he returns it to the appropriate pocket and pulls the tablecloth back over Judd's body.

Anna stands, frustrated and disappointed in equal measure. Knowing Judd was responsible for his own death, Anna thinks grimly, would have made things easier for her. Now she's forced to once again face the fact that someone else in this car is a murderer.

And that they might strike again if given the chance.

She has no proof of that, of course. Just a sticky, uneasy hunch, mostly based on Dante's earlier warning. *It's only a matter of time before these people start to turn on each other.* If someone did turn on Judd, nothing is stopping them from doing the same to the others.

And to her and Seamus.

"It's late," she announces. "In light of what happened to Mr. Dodge, I think it's wise if we all retreat to our rooms and remain there until we reach Chicago."

"What about me?" Reggie says, looking truly worried that he'll be forced to sleep in the lounge with a corpse present.

"There's an empty room in the next car," Anna says. "You can stay there."

"Can I fetch my overnight bag from coach?"

"Of course. When you return, Seamus will take you to your room."

Reggie hurries out of the lounge, perhaps never planning to return. And maybe, Anna thinks, that's for the best. He's likely better off spending the rest of the trip locked in a lavatory in coach than casting his lot with the likes of them.

"Since you're so convinced this is our last night of freedom," Sal says, "maybe we don't want to spend it locked in our rooms."

"I don't give a damn about what you want," Anna says. "But if I were you, I'd enjoy the space and privacy while you still can. From what I hear, prison cells can get awfully cramped—and crowded."

"Well, I'm not going anywhere just yet," Lapsford says, his bluster returning in full force. "Not until the two of you have been searched."

"Yeah," Herb adds. "You searched us. We should be allowed to do the same to you."

Seated next to him, Edith brings a fluttering hand to her neck and says, "It's only fair."

"As you can see, I have no pockets in which to hide anything," Anna says.

"How do we know you're not hiding something under your dress?" Lapsford says.

Anna gives him an icy stare. "I'm not going to strip naked in front of you, if that's what you're suggesting."

"No, but someone should at least pat you down."

That, Anna thinks, is better than being forced to strip naked. She nods for Seamus to do it. Although two people in the car have previously used their hands to roam the most intimate parts of her body, he's the only one she trusts.

"Not him," Lapsford says. "One of us needs to do it."

He takes a step toward Anna, who stops him with an outstretched hand.

"If you lay even a finger on me," she warns, "I guarantee you'll walk away with a broken hand."

"And I'll break the other," Seamus says, resuming his place at Anna's side.

Anna can't stand the thought of anyone else touching her. Especially Edith, who might feel the urge to reciprocate what Anna had done to her. And the very idea of Lapsford or Herb doing it makes her nauseous.

That leaves Dante, who happens to be the other man in the car whose hands she's felt on her body. And from the smug grin spreading across his face, it's clear he remembers it as well as Anna does.

"I'm game if you are," he says, reading her thoughts. "It'll be just like old times."

Anna hates the idea, but she also doesn't have much of a choice.

Just as she's about to agree to it, another option presents itself, in the form of Reggie Davis returning with a compact suitcase.

"Mr. Davis should search me," she says.

Reggie drops the suitcase, dumbfounded. "Me? Search *you*?"

"In order to prove that I'm not the culprit, someone needs to pat me down," Anna says. "And I trust you more than I trust any of them."

"But I'm a stranger."

"Which is exactly why I trust you over them. I know what they're capable of. You're an unknown quantity."

"But—"

"No more buts," Anna says, her arms raised at her sides. "Let's just get on with it, please."

Reggie approaches, and Anna braces herself to be frisked by a stranger. Because she knows the others are watching, including Dante, she looks only at Reggie. That's another reason she requested he pat her down. She wants to again get him in close proximity, where she can study his features, searching for signs he's been telling the truth. So far, all she sees is an apologetic look on his face as his hands roam her body, starting with the shoulders. When he slides them past her breasts, his face reddens.

"I'm so sorry," he whispers.

Anna nods for him to continue. He does, quickly patting down her stomach and hips. The moment he touches her upper thigh, Anna realizes she has more than modesty to worry about. During all the shock and suspicion surrounding Judd's death and Reggie's arrival, she'd completely forgotten about the knife strapped to her leg. No one else knows about it. Not even Seamus. Anna intended to tell him, days earlier when she decided the knife would be a good idea, but it slipped her mind amid all the last-minute preparations for the trip.

Now Reggie's hand is a millimeter away from it.

Anna goes rigid, waiting for him to discover it. There's no way he won't. While flat enough to remain unnoticed to those merely *looking* at her dress, the knife is all but certain to be felt beneath it.

Sure enough, Reggie's hand stills at the spot where the knife is sheathed. Anna sucks in a breath, knowing he can feel it beneath the fabric and dreading a second from now when he tells the others she has a weapon.

She waits for it.

Frozen.

Fearful.

The second she was dreading never arrives, stretching into two, three, four. Then Reggie's hand moves past the knife, joining his other hand in a quick skim of her knees and ankles. Anna watches, buzzing with anxiety.

But then Reggie stands and says, "She's not concealing anything."

Anna's dread tilts into confusion, which smooths into relief. She exhales, confident that Reggie isn't going to tell the others about the knife. She doesn't understand why or how long it will last. All she knows is that, for now, her secret is safe.

"Thank you, Mr. Davis," she says, outwardly displaying the composure missing from her internal thoughts. With a nod toward Seamus, she adds, "Now him, if you don't mind."

"I mind it," Seamus says. Still, knowing the alternative, he removes his conductor's coat and turns out the pockets, showing they're empty save for a gold watch attached to a chain and, of course, his revolver.

"I'll hold that for you," Anna offers.

Reggie stares at the gun, wide-eyed and horrified. "Why does he have that?"

"Protection," Seamus says as he shrugs the jacket back on and returns the revolver to an inside pocket.

"Considering the purpose of this trip, I thought it necessary," Anna adds.

"And considering what happened to *him*," Reggie says with a nod toward the corpse of Judd Dodge, "maybe having a gun on this train is a very bad idea."

"I agree," Jack Lapsford pipes up from the other side of the lounge.

Anna glares at him. "That's not for you to decide."

"What about me?" Reggie says. "I'm not one of them. I didn't do anything wrong. Don't I get a say in this?"

"I'm afraid not." Fully aware that his very public objection to Seamus's gun could also extend to her knife, Anna softens her tone. "This plan—and its rules—were set long before we knew you were on the train. Now that you're here, they still apply to everyone."

Reggie raises his hands, as if it's he and not Seamus who's supposed to be frisked next. "Then I don't want any part of this. I'm going to go back to coach and sit there until we reach Chicago. In the meantime, you can kill each other for all I care. Just leave me out of it."

"I already told you why that's not an option," Anna says. "You're a part of this now, whether you like it or not."

"Can you guarantee my safety?"

Anna can't, so she doesn't even try. "I can promise you that Seamus and I will do everything in our power to keep you safe. Seamus will take you to your room now. Lock the door and stay inside until we reach Chicago. Seamus and I will check on you every so often, just to make sure you're fine."

Reggie's hesitation makes it clear he still doesn't like the idea. Neither does Anna. Her preference would be to not have him on this train at all. But since she can't stop the train and let Reggie off, the next best option is to put him in an empty first-class room and hope he stays there.

"Go on," Anna says gently, even though she wants to say something else.

Why didn't you tell the others about the knife? Are you really who you say you are? And, most pressing of all, *Are you also hiding something?*

FIFTEEN

FROM THE MOMENT Reggie's hand passed over Anna's thigh, he knew she was hiding a knife. He also understood why she had it, which is why he remained silent. If he were her, he'd want a weapon, too, in a crowd like this.

But a knife is different than a gun. Sure, knives can kill, but not as easily. To hurt someone with a blade, you need to get close to the person you're attacking. Close enough to know who they are. A bullet needs no such thing. It can strike from a distance, hitting anyone unlucky enough to be in its path.

Following Seamus down the corridor of the next car, Reggie wonders how much experience he has with guns. Probably plenty, from the looks of him. Reggie estimates he's about thirty-five, give or take a couple of years. Old enough to have likely seen combat during the war. Seamus has the same gruff weariness as other veterans Reggie has come into contact with. Men who saw too much horror to forget about it.

Seamus stops at the last room in the car and throws open the door. "Here it is."

Reggie peers inside like an animal facing a cage. "Are you sure I'll be safe in here?"

"If you do what Anna says, you should have no problem."

"And is she safe?" Reggie asks.

Seamus nods. "Yeah. As long as I'm around."

"Have you thought about what might happen if that's no longer the case?"

He means no offense by the question, and Seamus seems not to take any. Both men know it's entirely possible that whoever killed Judd Dodge might try it again. And that Seamus, thanks to the gun, is a prime target.

"I'll be fine," Seamus says before lumbering back the way they came.

Alone in the room, Reggie takes a long, wide look at the space. It's bigger than he expected. Fancy, too. Far nicer than what he's used to. Hell, there's even a bed. He's never had a room on a train with a bed that doesn't fold up into the wall.

He sits on the edge of the mattress, testing its firmness. Soft as a feather. It's a shame he's not going to be able to use it to get a little shut-eye. He needs to be awake and alert for the entire trip.

Boss's orders.

Reggie stands and examines the room's other surprise amenity— the bathroom. Although smaller than a broom closet, it's better than those stinking, shared lavatories in coach. He crinkles his nose at the memory of hiding in the one located in the second coach car, flinging himself inside the moment he heard people stomping through the sleeper car. He barely made it, closing the door behind him just as the others entered the car. Pressed against it, he listened to the group make their way to the front of the train, wondering which of them were on the list of names he'd been given. All of them, from the sound of it.

He stayed locked in the lavatory for what felt like an hour before the group passed by again. Just to be safe, he waited an additional hour before deciding to join them in the back half of the train.

Now he's here, in a place he never, ever expected to be.

Reggie reaches for his overnight case. He didn't pack much. There wasn't time to add anything more than a shaving kit, an extra shirt, and a ham sandwich wrapped in wax paper in case he got hungry. Although the sight of the sandwich makes his empty stomach rumble, eating will have to wait a few more minutes. There's another task he must do first.

From an inside pocket of his suit coat, Reggie removes the wallet he'd told Anna was in his suitcase and the ticket he'd quickly purchased to lend credence to his lie about boarding the wrong train. Philly to Baltimore. The cheapest one available. He drops both into the small suitcase and pushes them aside along with the shirt and sandwich, reaching for something else.

A list of six names in alphabetical order, last name first.

He looks it over, matching the names to the people on the train. All present and accounted for except for one—Kenneth Wentworth. A possible transcription error, considering the presence of Wentworth's son.

Outside his door, Reggie hears footsteps in the hallway. The others making their way to their own rooms. He waits until they pass, still listening closely once they're gone. There could be a straggler coming by. Or, worse, a lurker who doesn't want to be heard. Sure enough, after five minutes of intense listening, Reggie hears a single set of footsteps.

Only these don't pass by his door.

They stop there.

Soon there's a quiet knock on the door, followed closely by the voice of Anna Matheson. "Mr. Davis? May I speak with you a moment?"

Reggie goes to the door, opening it just a crack. "Can I help you with something?"

"I just wanted to thank you." Anna pauses to look up and down the car. Satisfied there's no one else around who can hear her, she adds, "For not mentioning the—"

"Yes," Reggie says, cutting her off. "Of course."

Anna bites her bottom lip, the obvious question hovering between them. Why didn't he mention she had a knife? Again, Reggie doesn't force her to say it.

"I thought it was a good idea to keep quiet," he says. "Considering the circumstances, you have every reason to want to protect yourself."

Anna exhales, relieved. "Yes, that's exactly why I have it. And I appreciate your discretion."

"Your secret's safe with me," Reggie says. "Was there anything else you wanted to tell me?"

"Just that, despite the rather tense situation you've been thrust into, I assure you that Seamus and I won't let anything happen to you. Just lock your door and stay in your room. If you do that, you should be perfectly safe."

Reggie acknowledges the advice with a nod. "Thank you. I'll do exactly that. Hopefully, you won't see or hear me again until we reach Chicago."

After Anna leaves, he follows orders and locks the door. As for Anna's other piece of advice—staying put—well, that one will go unheeded. Because Reggie will need to leave his room very shortly.

Back at his overnight case, he removes a red pen and presses its tip to the first name on the list.

Judd Dodge.

Then he drags the pen across the page, crossing out the name in a single, quick stroke.

When that's done, he reaches back into the suitcase, running his hand beneath the extra shirt until his fingers touch cold steel.

There it is.

The biggest tool of his trade.

Reggie isn't sure if he'll take it with him when he leaves the room. On one hand, it's better to be safe than sorry. On the other, it's more exciting to go without it. He decides to play it by ear, depending on his mood. For the moment, he's content simply knowing it's there if he needs it.

And that there's now another gun on this train.

SIXTEEN

OUTSIDE ROOM C of the train's thirteenth car, the sconce with the loose bulb continues to flicker and hum, casting an intermittent glow over the corpse of Judd Dodge. Still shrouded beneath a tablecloth, the body is carried by Seamus and Dante. Neither man wants to be doing it, but they have little choice. They can't just leave him on the floor of the lounge.

Anna follows them, watching from the doorway as Seamus and Dante place the body onto the mattress and swap the tablecloth that covers it for a sheet. It feels more reverent that way.

"Does anyone want to say anything?" Dante asks.

"Only that I'm sorry he didn't suffer more," Anna says before walking away.

She returns to her own room, leaving the door unlocked for Seamus, who she knows will join her there soon. Until he arrives, she stretches out on the bed. God, she's exhausted, and it's not even midnight. She'll be positively catatonic by the time the train reaches Chicago.

Her eyes refuse to stay open, so Anna doesn't fight them. She simply lies there, eyelids shut tight, even as Seamus enters the room, his presence as familiar as her own.

"We failed," she says.

"I know."

Seamus climbs onto the bed and lies down next to Anna, their bodies inches apart yet comfortably close. Theirs is an unusual bond, forged through unimaginable grief and the strangest of circumstances. Lying beside Seamus now, Anna thinks about their first meeting. That cold, gray day in the cemetery after she had buried Aunt Retta. Few people showed up to pay their respects, which made Seamus easy to notice in the sparse crowd. He had the look of a brawler. Big, and clearly well-built, but with a lithe physicality to him. He was graceful for someone so large, moving toward her with catlike precision once the funeral was over and everyone else had dispersed.

"Your aunt sent me" was all he said.

"How did you know her?"

Seamus looked to the open grave and the coffin that had just recently been lowered into it. "I didn't. We never met in person. But she wrote to me a few times."

He didn't explain the nature of the letters, nor did he need to. Anna knew that, in a quest to clear her father's name, Aunt Retta wrote letters to all the families of the train explosion's victims, trying to convince them someone other than Arthur Matheson was responsible. Anna had always assumed no one wrote back. Clearly, she was wrong. At least one person had.

"Who did you lose?"

"My brother. Sean Callahan."

Anna knew the name. She'd made sure to memorize the identities of all the victims. They were, after all, the men who had died alongside her brother.

"I'm sorry for your loss," she said. "It was kind of you to pay your respects."

"That's not why I'm here. There's something I need to show you."

They trudged to a black Buick parked at the edge of the ceme-tery. "A gift," Seamus said, opening the trunk. "From your late aunt."

Six boxes sat inside the trunk. When Anna saw them, she un-derstood not only what they contained but that Aunt Retta was right. The proof had indeed found her.

Seamus followed Anna to the mansion that had once been Aunt Retta's but now belonged to her. Together, they spent the next twenty-four hours sorting through all the information con-tained in those boxes—a painful, painstaking process.

The evidence left Anna feeling stunned, not just by the breadth of the plot but by the people involved. People she knew. People her father had trusted. People they both had loved. Sal and Edith, Herb Pulaski and Judd Dodge. Seeing their names, their deeds, and their outright treachery had left her so raw and betrayed and furious that there was no question in her mind that vengeance had to be enacted.

"Do you think we should kill them?" she said.

"Yes," Seamus replied. "All of them need to die. And I want to be the one to do it."

Anna ultimately decided that death wasn't enough punishment for everyone involved. It was too easy, too quick. Short of kidnap-ping and torturing them over an extended period of time—an idea she and Seamus discussed at length—the only way to guarantee an adequate amount of suffering was to bring all of them to justice. Something that's now impossible.

"Which one of those bastards do you think did it?" Anna says.

Beside her, Seamus shrugs. "Honestly? Any of them. Including Reggie Davis. You think he's lying?"

"If so, he's very good at it."

Anna knows that from experience. When he told the others she wasn't carrying a weapon, Reggie had sounded so convinc-ing that even she almost believed him. Although grateful for that particular lie, Anna wonders if it's not the only one he's told them. While it's certainly possible he boarded the wrong train, it's also not very probable. Because of that, Anna can't shake the feeling he's here for a reason.

"Either he really is an insurance salesman who got on the wrong train—or he's a plant sent by Kenneth Wentworth."

"My money's on insurance salesman," Seamus says. "The plant sent by Wentworth is clearly his son."

Anna sits up, surprised. "Dante? He's here for a different reason. Or so he says."

"And what's that?"

"To see me."

"You really believe that?" Seamus asks.

"Maybe. I get the feeling he's trying to help us."

A few hours ago, Anna thought she'd never see Dante Wentworth again, let alone trust him. But the fact that he didn't stop the train when he had the chance tells Anna there's more to Dante's presence than he's letting on.

"Or maybe he's lying through his teeth," Seamus says.

There it is. Another flare of jealousy.

What happened between them occurred only once. An unplanned tumbling into bed when the burdens they both carried had become too heavy to bear. Fueled by wine and grief, they tossed those burdens aside, along with their clothes and inhibitions. Anna was surprised by the intensity of the encounter. How eager they were to escape their pain, if only just for a night.

One night was all they got. When they woke the next morning, their limbs still entwined, Anna felt not embarrassment but another, worse emotion: resignation.

"We can never do this again," she said.

"It's too sad," Seamus added in agreement.

And while that had seemed to be the end of it for Anna, perhaps it wasn't for Seamus, who's more sensitive than his hulking appearance suggests. The possibility that he might still have feelings for her worries Anna. The night has already been disrupted enough. She can't have emotions—Seamus's or anyone else's—messing things up even more.

"For me, the biggest suspect is Jack Lapsford," Anna says, even though she has nothing to back the claim. Just a stirring in her gut that tells her Lapsford's up to something. He's certainly the most vocal of the bunch. The most desperate, too.

While he wasn't close enough to slip poison into Judd's drink when no one was looking, that doesn't mean he couldn't have done it another way. It's possible he poisoned the martini glass in the first hour of the trip when no one had yet entered the lounge. Or he could have spiked Judd's drink unnoticed when he went to the bar to collect his own.

"But why would he kill Judd?" Seamus says. "Why would any of them?"

Anna understands what he's getting at. If anyone on the Phoenix has justifiable reason to commit murder, it's her and Seamus. Which means the two of them also have the biggest targets on their backs. She can't fathom why one of the others would, as Dante had predicted, turn on their own.

But turn they did. And Anna can't shake the feeling that one of them, in a desperate bid to appear innocent, has decided to get rid of those who know the most about their guilt—their fellow conspirators.

"Because the dead can't tattle," she says.

"You think whoever killed Judd is planning to do it again?"

"Possibly," Anna says. "To avoid that happening, we need to keep an eye on everyone for the rest of the trip. That means checking on them once an hour, maybe more."

Seamus nods. "To make sure one of them isn't up to something."

"And to make sure the others remain alive."

The irony isn't lost on Anna. In order to destroy their enemies, they must first protect them.

But she also knows monitoring their every move isn't enough. They can't just hope Judd's killer doesn't strike again. They need to stop whoever did it before they get the chance.

"I still don't understand the poison. Why did the killer have it? I mean, who brings poison onto a train?"

"Someone who intended to use it," Seamus says.

"That's what's strange," Anna says. "I don't think anyone knew who else was going to be aboard the Phoenix. That makes it highly unlikely this was premeditated murder. I think the killer decided to do it *after* realizing what this trip is all about. That means it's someone who always carries poison with them or else—"

Seamus sits up. "They found it on the train."

"Exactly. And if we can also locate it, that might give us a good idea of who used it." Anna slides off the bed, her eyes bright. "Find the poison, find the killer."

SEVENTEEN

ANNA ASKS SEAMUS if she can take the first watch, and he agrees. By now he knows that when she asks something of him, it's really an order.

One he obeys every time.

Almost.

It's not that Seamus doesn't have his own opinions about what to do. He certainly does. But when he disagrees, he willingly defers to Anna. Yes, he lost a brother, but Anna lost her entire family. If it were possible to weigh their individual grief, hers would surely tip the scales.

He was at least able to properly bury his brother, laying him to rest next to their parents in the meager family plot. According to Anna, nothing lies beside the graves of Arthur and Margaret Matheson. Just an empty coffin. The different ways in which their brothers died—his from internal injuries, Anna's completely obliterated—makes it clear they were in different parts of the train when it exploded, and likely never met.

Seamus also knows it doesn't matter.

Both are gone and never coming back.

Alone in his room, he goes to his suitcase on the bed, untouched since he boarded the Phoenix. He didn't pack much. Just a shaving kit, a change of clothes for when he's finally allowed to shed his conductor's uniform, and his wallet.

Seamus's hand shakes as he reaches for the wallet. Damn this trembling. It's gotten worse in the past few hours. So bad he could barely check Judd's neck for a pulse he knew no longer existed. In that moment, he was certain everyone noticed. Especially Anna, who rarely missed a single detail.

Now his hand positively vibrates as he removes a photograph from his wallet, its edges ragged from a dozen years of similarly tremulous viewings. Seamus looks at the uniformed young man in the picture and his heart clenches.

Sean.

His big brother.

The Callahans were not a happy family. His father drank too much. His mother spoke too little. Both were quick to use their fists. As a result, Seamus and his brother grew up in tense silence that lasted until their parents died within a year of each other. After that, Sean became his north star, guiding him into adulthood through the power of example. Whatever Sean did, Seamus followed, whether it was joining the high school football team or enlisting in the Army.

Then Sean was killed, and Seamus, having no one to emulate, lost his way.

Until he found Anna.

He didn't know what to expect when he approached her in the cemetery a little over a year ago. Her aunt had given him Anna's name but no picture or description. "You'll know her when you see her" was all he was told.

And he did.

The only person left in the cemetery, Anna was easy to identify. But even if she had been surrounded by dozens of people, Seamus would have known it was her. Loss recognizes loss. He approached her and said, "Your aunt sent me."

Anna turned to him, giving him a look unlike anything Seamus had seen before. Instead of grief, her eyes blazed with purpose, as if she sensed exactly who he was and why he was there. He's been by her side ever since. Whether that will still be the case when they reach Chicago is unknown. They haven't discussed what comes after their plan.

If there is an after.

He slips his brother's picture back into his wallet, which is returned to the suitcase. Then he stretches, trying to release the tension of a long night that's not even halfway over. As he moves, something deep in the pocket of his uniform vest knocks against his rib cage.

Seamus reaches into the pocket and removes a small pillbox Reggie Davis never got the chance to find after being spooked by his revolver. For that Seamus is grateful, because it spared him a lot of explaining.

With still-trembling hands, he lifts the box's lid and peers inside.

Resting on the bottom are several pills, chalky and white.

Seamus counts them. Right now, there are five. Satisfied by the amount, he snaps the box shut and returns it to his pocket.

He knows that earlier in the night, the number of pills had been six.

MIDNIGHT

EIGHT HOURS TO CHICAGO

EIGHTEEN

AN EMPTY TRAIN is a quiet one. Disconcertingly so.

On a sold-out voyage, it's never quiet, even in the dead of night. There are always people whispering in the darkness, snores rising from berths in the sleeper car, men playing cards in the club car until the sun peeks over the eastern horizon. Underneath it all is the sound of the train rushing inexorably forward. A constant click-hum of steel wheels on iron tracks that soothes some, irritates others. Now, though, that calming, maddening, unceasing sound of the train is all there is.

That's especially true in the first-class lounge, where a man recently died and where Anna now carefully steps over the spot where it happened. She's checked the other first-class cars to make sure everyone is in their rooms. They are, their doors closed and, hopefully, locked.

Anna knows she should do the same thing, but the itch to find the poison that killed Judd Dodge is too strong to resist. Based on its odor, she suspects a cleaning product. And on the Phoenix, there are only two places where those reside—the galley and the janitor's closet tucked into a corner of the club car.

For the first hour of the train ride, the entire lounge had been unattended, giving anyone a chance to sneak into both places. But that's not when Anna suspects the poison was obtained. That would have required premeditation, and she doubts anyone quite knew what they were in for before she appeared in the lounge. No, she thinks whoever killed Judd grabbed the poison when everyone moved through the train in their futile attempt to stop it. By then Judd had all but confessed to his role in the scheme, giving one of the others the idea to kill him before he could implicate anyone else.

Continuing across the lounge, she looks to the window to check the weather conditions outside. It's snowing harder now, the flakes whooshing by the size of dimes. But this is still the eastern edge of the storm—and Anna's well aware it will get worse the farther west they travel. By now the train has left Pennsylvania and is just beginning the long trek across Ohio. She sighs thinking about that timetable. Five hours into the trip, and they have so much left to go.

She pushes into the dining car, which feels haunted by its emptiness. It unnerves her to be moving through these cars alone. She chalks it up to their size, their opulence. These are spaces intended to hold dozens in a luxurious embrace. When they are devoid of that, it makes Anna feel like a trespasser.

And she's not the only one.

As she enters the dining car, Anna spots someone else moving through the door at the opposite end, heading into the galley.

She hurries across the car, determined to catch whoever it is before they get a chance to move entirely through the galley. But when she passes from one car to the other, she realizes that's not their plan. The person has stopped at the icebox in the center of the galley and now stands partially obscured behind the open door. A man, Anna realizes. Beneath the door she can see trousers and black leather shoes.

"Who are you?" Anna says. "What are you doing here?"

"My name is hunger and I'm desperately looking to be sated."

Anna groans. It's Dante. Of course. Now peering around the icebox door to flash her that all-too-familiar grin.

"You could have at least ordered something for us to eat before you kicked the staff off the train."

"I paid them off," Anna says. "There's a difference. And food was the least of my concerns when planning this voyage."

"Obviously. The only thing in here are cold cuts." He removes a slab of roast beef wrapped in butcher paper and drops it on the counter. "Is there any bread?"

Anna moves to the other end of the galley, where a breadbox sits next to an eight-slice toaster. Once upon a time she knew every inch of this car. She and Tommy were constantly here, cajoling the cooks into giving them treats. Their favorite was Stella, who made a mean fried chicken and the best sticky buns on Earth. Anna could devour one in three bites.

She thinks of Stella as she opens the breadbox and pulls out a loaf for Dante. He claps in delight and grabs a nearby knife.

"Would you like a sandwich?"

"I refuse to eat anything you prepare," Anna says. "Or have you forgotten what happened in the lounge?"

Dante pushes the knife through the loaf, cutting off two thick slices. "Come on, Annie. You know I had nothing to do with that. But at least you got your wish. Everyone's definitely squirming now."

"If you think I'm happy that Judd Dodge is dead, then you're quite mistaken. I didn't want any of this."

"Maybe not consciously," Dante says. "But deep down, hidden in a dark place you don't like to think about, part of you wanted this to happen. And that same dark part of you wishes it would happen to all of them. That's why I think you planned this trip. You were secretly hoping it would end this way."

"I told you why I planned it."

"And I don't buy that excuse one bit. If you wanted to watch my father and the others squirm, you could have done it in court."

Anna knows it would have been easier—not to mention far less expensive—to give the FBI the evidence and let them arrest everyone. It also would have been deeply unsatisfying.

"Seeing them in court isn't enough," she says. "I wanted to see their faces when they realized they were cornered on this train. I wanted them to know they'd been trapped—by me."

"What did you think would happen then?" Dante asks. "That they'd all confess and tell you why they did it?"

Yes, Anna had indeed hoped for that, and still plans to get at least some of them to admit what they'd done—and why. Sal. Edith. Even Herb Pulaski. Even though learning the reasons for their betrayal won't bring her family back, Anna suspects it might bring some closure.

Still, that's not the main reason she planned this trip. For her, it's not about the journey but the destination.

"I had to watch my father be handcuffed and dragged from our home," Anna says. "Now I need to see the same thing happen to all of them. I need to be there when they're taken into custody. I need to witness their public disgrace. I need to see, with my own eyes, the moment their lives and reputations are ruined. Then they can have their day in court, which my father was never given, and rot in prison for the rest of their lives."

"Including my father," Dante says.

"Especially him. Which is why I'm still mad at you for taking his place."

"I remember when you were happy to see me."

"That was a long time ago," Anna says.

Not so long, though, that she forgets every moment spent with Dante. She remembers everything, especially when he showed up with those roses to her final performance as Juliet. Even then, she resisted, likely for the same reason he pursued her. It was forbidden. So Dante pushed harder, making it a point to show up at events where he knew Anna would be. Parties and picnics and debutante balls. Even when he wasn't invited, he found a way in. In Philadelphia society, the Wentworth name opened many doors.

Each encounter was a dance, the steps of which included flirtation, banter, some light verbal sparring. Eventually, Anna's defenses lowered bit by bit, while at the same time his boldness grew. A brief touch of her hand. A featherlight kiss on her cheek. Finally, after one such occasion, he offered to walk her home. Instead of answering yes, all Anna said was, "Our parents can never know."

They walked in silence, their steps slow and their pace languid. At one point, Dante's hand brushed Anna's, and, much to his surprise, she clasped it. As they neared her house, Anna drew closer. The clasp became an embrace, which turned into a clinch. Pressed against her, Dante leaned in for a kiss.

"We shouldn't be doing this," Anna whispered, even as her mouth rose to meet his. "It will only end in heartbreak."

Dante swore that she was wrong.

She wasn't.

"Why did you pursue me?" she says now. "Back then? You could have had your pick of girls, yet you chose me."

Dante opens the nearest cupboard, revealing shelves neatly stacked with bowls and plates. He moves to the drawer below it. Inside are rolls of tinfoil and plastic wrap. "Because none of the girls were as special as you."

"I'm serious."

"As am I," Dante says. "Very early on, I realized how amazing you were. That's why I pursued you. Even though I knew my father would be furious if he ever found out."

"Your father's a terrible person."

"I see. So what does that make me?"

"A heartless cad," Anna says, making sure to inject the words with extra sting. Because only heartless cads are capable of doing what Dante did to her. The flirting, the wooing, the charm. By the time they shared their first kiss, she'd already been head over heels, although she made a point of trying not to show it.

After that kiss—that glorious, head-spinning, shudder-inducing kiss—it became impossible to hide her feelings from him. She was sixteen, madly in love, and mistakenly thought Dante felt the same about her. That's why she behaved so foolishly for months. Sneaking out in the middle of the night. Meeting Dante in secret. Kissing him so intensely that her lips grew raw and her body ached with yearning.

Looking back on it, Anna realizes it was her own damn fault for falling so hard. That having playacted Juliet on the stage, she wanted to experience her own forbidden romance. One that should have been over when Dante, then eighteen, enlisted in the Army but ended up at Princeton by way of a previously undetected heart murmur. Instead of stopping things, Anna prolonged them by writing to Dante almost every day. Florid letters in which she bared her soul—and her desires.

She finally succumbed to them when Dante returned home on fall break. She remembers everything about that night in shivery detail. Alone outside his house on an unseasonably warm October night. His impish suggestion that they go skinny-dipping in the pool. The way his expression turned lustful when she agreed. And then everything that followed.

The pleasure.

The guilt.

The utter heartbreak when she never heard from him again, not even in the weeks that followed, when tragedy upon tragedy befell her family. The boy she loved had abandoned her when she needed him most, taking her innocence with him. By the time her mother was dead and buried, Anna assumed she'd never see Dante again. Nor did she want to. She knew she was better off without him. Now he's back, bantering with her as if none of that had ever happened.

"I've never forgiven you, you know," she says.

"I noticed."

"You just vanished. If I was so special, why did you disappear like that?"

Dante leans against the counter and looks at her in a way he never did when they were younger. Back then, his gaze always held mischief, lust, or a combination of the two. Now, though, he stares at her with clear-eyed understanding and, Anna hopes, regret.

"The way I treated you was truly awful, and I'm sorry," he says.

Anna stiffens in surprise. She never expected an apology. Not from Dante Wentworth. "I don't know what to say."

"You don't need to say anything. It's me who needs to explain why I behaved so atrociously. When your brother was killed, I wanted to go to the funeral, but my father wouldn't allow it. I told him that you and I had been meeting in secret. That I was falling in love with you. My father didn't care. He forbade me from seeing you again. He told me I couldn't have anything to do with you or your family. And when your father was arrested, I started to think that maybe he was right, no matter how much I wanted him to be wrong. Only now do I know the real reason he made me stay away."

"Because your father is the guilty one," Anna says.

"Apparently so," Dante says. "I know you'll never be able to forgive him, with good reason. But I hope you'll eventually find some way to forgive me."

Anna thought she'd hate Dante for a very long time. Likely forever. But now that he's here looking and acting the way he did all those years ago, she barely recalls the hatred. All she can remember are the times when she thought she loved Dante. Whether it was really love or merely a teenage infatuation she eventually would have gotten past, well, Anna never got the chance to find out. Now her mind races with *what if*s. What if Dante had said this a dozen years ago? Would that have changed things? Would it have made her life slightly more bearable? She'll never know, which is why all she can manage to say is "Maybe. Someday."

That seems to be enough for Dante, who nods and says, "Right. Good. Until then, help me find some mustard. No man, no matter how hungry, should be forced to consume a dry sandwich."

"Find it yourself," Anna says. "I came here to look for something else."

They switch sides of the car, where Dante opens the door to the pantry and scans the shelves. The top one holds baking supplies. Flour, sugar, and baking soda, not to mention the food dye used in the Phoenix's justly famous red velvet cake. The favorite dessert of Anna's father, it's still served in both the club car and the dining room. The shelf below it bears other tricks of the trade. Salt and spices, distilled vinegar and canola oil. And, yes, a jar of mustard.

"Sweet nectar of the gods," Dante says before spreading some on the bread. He quickly adds a few slices of roast beef and takes a mighty bite. With his mouth still full, he adds, "What are you looking for?"

Anna, now on her knees, opens the door to the cabinet beneath the sink. "Poison."

Dante swallows with an audible gulp. "That's not funny."

"Good. Because I'm not joking."

Anna peers into the dark and musty recesses of the cabinet. In the back, sitting behind a bucket and next to a canister of drain cleaner, is a box of rat poison. Its presence isn't a surprise. She suspects every train with a galley car has some.

She grabs the box and looks inside. The poison itself is a white powder that's roughly the size and consistency of table salt. Bringing the box to her nose, she gets a whiff of the same chemical smell she detected in Judd Dodge's martini glass.

Dante, his sandwich completely forgotten, stands behind her. "Is that—"

"Yes," Anna says before he can finish the question. "This is what killed Judd."

NINETEEN

ANNA STANDS IN the middle of the observation car, the box of rat poison at her feet. She shifts nervously from one leg to the other as, in the preceding three cars, Seamus rouses everyone from their rooms. Not that anyone requires rousing. As the others file into the observation car, Anna sees they're all dressed in the same clothes they wore in the lounge. No one, it seems, is willing to risk falling asleep.

"Why are we here?" Lapsford grumbles as he enters the observation car.

The reason Anna chose this and not the lounge is because bringing the poison into the same car where a man died from ingesting it struck her as being in poor taste. The observation car, with its row of seats that circle the entire room, is the next-best gathering spot.

But that's not what Lapsford is asking, Anna knows. She waits until everyone else has arrived before answering it.

"I found this in the galley," she says.

"*We* found it," Dante adds.

Anna wishes he hadn't, because it prompts Seamus to ask, "Why were you in the galley with him?"

"We weren't together," Anna adds.

Dante nods. "I was making a sandwich."

"And I was looking for this." She nudges the rat poison with her foot. "The murder weapon. Now, who's been in the galley tonight?"

"We all were," Sal says. "All of us passed through it on our way to the locomotive and back."

"Did anyone linger there?"

"Not on the way there," Seamus says. "I was in the back of the pack, so if someone did, I would have seen it."

"And we took up the rear on the way back," Dante says.

They're right, much to Anna's disappointment. That narrows it down to before everyone gathered in the lounge.

"Was anyone in the galley between seven and eight?" she asks.

"I was not," Edith says.

Herb chimes in with "Me neither."

"Nor me," Sal says.

"If I was," Lapsford says, "I wouldn't tell you."

Anna crosses her arms. "So that's a yes?"

"It's a definite no," Lapsford says. "For me and for everyone else. The only people who were on this train before us were you and your thug."

Seamus shoots him an angry look from across the car. "Watch the name-calling. There's a few choice words I could use about you."

"What about him?" Sal says, pointing to Reggie Davis. "He could have spent hours in there and no one would have been any wiser."

"Me?" Reggie looks around, his eyes wider than those of an animal about to become roadkill. "I was in the lavatory most of the time."

"Mr. Davis has nothing to do with this," Anna says, even though she's still not entirely sure about that. While she doesn't think he poisoned Judd, there remains something slightly suspect about his presence. Ever since he stumbled into the lounge, she's sensed that he's more interested in what's happening than he lets on.

Lapsford turns and lumbers toward the door. "I've had enough of this. You've already searched us. None of us had any poison. I'm going back to my room."

"As am I," Sal says, trailing him out the door.

The others do the same, leaving just Seamus and Anna. Before she can ask, he sighs and says, "I'll follow them to make sure everyone is where they're supposed to be."

Anna remains in the observation car, feeling stupid for thinking this would go anywhere. What did she expect? A confession? As Judd's death already proved, those on this train who confess get killed.

Now alone in the observation car, she looks through the curved window to the receding length of track they've already traveled, cleared of snow by the train's wheels. The parallel rails narrow before vanishing over the dark horizon. All those miles. All those events that brought her to this car, on this night, at this moment. Looking backward, Anna imagines her entire life stretching behind the train. As if it were possible to hop off and start the long journey into her past, reversing time. And that if she walked long enough and far enough, she'd eventually reach the place where her family was still alive and she was still happy and nothing about her current life existed.

It's a lovely thought. Foolish, too. Because Anna knows that life, just like the train she's on, can only surge forward.

The things Edith said about her parents earlier stick in her mind like a bad memory. If they could see her, right this very minute, what would they think? Anna hopes they'd understand that she's doing this for them and for Tommy and for all those other people lost that dreadful day. She hopes they'd approve of her relentless determination.

Yet a small part of her suspects Edith is right. That her parents and Tommy would indeed weep at what she's turned into. That instead of shutting herself away with Aunt Retta, they would have wanted her to meet someone, fall in love, get married. More than anything, she thinks they'd all want her to be happy. Something Anna hasn't been in a very long time.

She drops into one of the observation car chairs. Like the ones in the first-class rooms, they swivel to face the windows. Her father's innovation. He was so proud of it that he spent most of the Phoenix's maiden voyage in the chair where she now sits.

Anna remembers finding him here in the wee hours of the morning. Eleven at the time and too excited by the festivities to sleep, she left the room still dressed in her pajamas. After padding through the rest of first class, she joined her father in the observation car. Like Anna, he was too buzzed by the night's activity to sleep. But he also wasn't completely awake. To Anna, it seemed like he was dreaming with his eyes open and a smile on his face.

"Hey, Annie," he said. "Come sit next to me a while."

They sat in silence for a long time, her father eventually breaking it to say, "Do you know what we're on, Annie?"

Anna had rolled her eyes. Of course she knew. "A train."

"Yes, but it's more than that." Her father paused, still wearing that far-off look. "You know how sometimes you travel in your dreams? You fall asleep and are whisked someplace far away? That's what this train is. A dream on wheels. But in this dream, people really do travel. They board the Phoenix, have a nice conversation, maybe something from the club car, and then, after some time looking out the window and watching the miles fly by, they fall asleep. And in the morning, they're somewhere else. Somewhere exciting."

He held out his hand then and said, "Do you want to dream with me, Annie?"

The sound of the train's whistle echoes through the night, tugging Anna from her reverie. Sitting up, she looks around, half expecting to see her father beside her, fast asleep.

Instead, she sees Tommy.

He occupies the seat next to her, more skeleton than flesh and blood. Skin drips from his bones like wet paper and a massive hole sits in the center of his chest. Inside that dark hollow, Anna can see the curve of his ribs and his still-beating heart. She looks away, to his face, which has melted into a bloody ooze. A sick, gurgling sound emerges when he opens what used to be his mouth.

"Take care of Mom and Dad for me," he says.

Anna wakes up, this time for real, snapping out of the nightmare with a full-body spasm. Frantic, she checks the seat next to her. Not that she thinks Tommy will still be there. Not looking like that. More of him exists in her nightmares than what was left after he died.

Still, she's relieved to see the seat empty. It tells her she's awake. How long she was asleep, she has no idea. Five minutes? Ten? It was at least long enough for the storm outside to gain intensity, the flakes now bigger and faster.

In that blur of snow, she notices something else. Reflected in the window's curved glass is the silhouette of someone entering the observation car. Startled, Anna spins the chair around to see who it is.

Edith Gerhardt.

Anna immediately tenses but says nothing. What can she say to the woman who was supposed to take care of her? Who had given her so much comfort yet also caused so much pain?

"I'm glad you're still here," Edith says, absently touching her neck. A silent reminder of what Anna had done little more than an hour ago. If Edith intends the gesture to make her feel bad, it does, although not because she's sorry she caused the woman pain. Anna only feels bad that she lost control, however briefly. She vows not to let it happen again, even as her blood begins to boil at the unexpected sight of Edith.

"I'm not," she says.

Edith ignores the jab. "I saw someone exiting the galley. I didn't want to mention it in front of the others. I didn't want anyone to think I was making accusations. But not long after the train left the station, I went to the dining car, hoping to get a cup of tea. Finding no one there, I left. But as I was heading back to my room, I spotted someone else leaving the dining car. Since he wasn't in there when I peeked in, I can only assume he came from the galley."

"Who was it?"

"The lieutenant colonel."

Lapsford. So he lied about not being there before everyone gathered in the lounge. Anna stands, eager to confront him about it. In order to leave, though, she must squeeze by Edith, who reaches out as she passes, uttering a beseeching "Schatzi."

Anna evades the touch and makes it to the door, but not before thinking of something else she can say to Edith. Something she *needs* to say, even though she knows what she should be doing is running away as fast as she can.

"Was any of it real?" she asks, unable to keep her voice from cracking with pain. "The hugs. The comforting. The love and care and devotion for me and Tommy. Did you mean any of it? Or was that all just an act?"

Edith steps toward her. "No, Schatzi, I—"

"Stop calling me that!" Anna snaps. "Don't you *ever* call me that again."

"You have every right to be angry. You have suffered terribly."

Edith shakes her head, as if she wasn't one of the causes of that suffering. "But what happened, it was not personal. You must understand that."

Anna recoils in disbelief, astonished Edith could say such a thing. Her brother wasn't just killed, he was erased, leaving no trace, as if he never existed. Her father was murdered so violently that Anna still can't comprehend it. Her mother chose to join them in death rather than stay alive with Anna. All because of something Edith was a part of. That made it *very* personal.

"My entire family is gone," she says.

Edith gives a curt nod. "As is mine."

"But I didn't cause that. No one in my family did. Yet they're dead. Because of you."

It takes Anna every ounce of self-control to not wrap her hands around Edith's neck. She keeps them clenched at her sides, aching to experience the sensation a second time. A finger twitches when she notices a slight bob in Edith's throat as she says, "I never wanted to hurt you or your family."

"But you did."

"Because there was a war going on," Edith says, as if that excuses it. "That's the cruelty of war. It makes good people do terrible things for their country."

"But you weren't in Germany. You were here. In America. With us."

"Just because someone leaves their home doesn't mean they no longer love it. Nor does it mean they won't do anything to help it."

"That's what you thought you were doing?" Anna says as she absently touches the tiny silver locomotive pinned to her chest, reminding her of everything she has lost. "Helping your homeland?"

"Of course that's what I was doing."

Anna's entire body goes rigid when she realizes what's just happened.

Edith has confessed.

Not that Anna had any doubt she was involved. Aunt Retta's boxes of proof made sure of that. But it's more shocking when coming from Edith herself. More painful, too. Especially the part about why Edith had betrayed her family.

"You testified under oath that you thought my father was a German sympathizer." Anna's hands continue to clench, all but begging her to reach out, encircle Edith's neck, squeeze. "But it turns out you were merely talking about yourself."

"I refuse to apologize for my beliefs," Edith says.

"But you're still going to pay for them. And you should be afraid of what's coming."

"Perhaps," Edith says with a resigned sigh. "But when you reach my age, you find that things you once feared don't scare you anymore."

"Not even death?"

Edith fixes Anna with an enigmatic smile and says, "There's no reason to fear what's inevitable."

To Anna, that cryptic grin seems like an invitation. As if Edith, knowing what's coming, wants to be put out of her misery just like Judd Dodge was. And Anna's tempted to oblige her. So very tempted that she thrusts her still-twitching hands behind her, fingers intertwined.

She needs to leave.

Right now.

Before she loses all control again.

"Killing my brother and framing my father helped *nothing*," she says. "I hope you eventually understand that. In the last moments of your life, I hope you realize it was a mistake. That everything you did was a waste. And when you take your final breath, I hope the only things you feel are pain, fear, and regret. Because that's all you deserve."

Anna turns and hurries out of the observation car before Edith can respond. She refuses to give her the last word.

In Car 13, the light fixture that had been flickering across from Room C has gone out, casting that end of the corridor in thick shadow. Standing in the gloom, Anna sees someone exiting through the door at the front of the car.

A man. All she catches is the back of his head and the breadth of his shoulders. Enough for her to think that his frame doesn't match anyone else on the train. Seamus, Lapsford, and Herb Pulaski are broader, Dante and Reggie narrower.

Now it's too late to see more. Whoever it was is gone.

Worried by the prospect of someone else roaming the train, Anna surges through the otherwise silent hall. The door to Room A opens a crack as she passes, giving Anna a glimpse of Herb Pulaski peering nervously into the corridor.

"Stay in your room," she tells him. "Keep your door locked."

She keeps moving, pleased to see that no doors are open in Car 12. Hopefully everyone is where they should be.

Locked in their rooms.

Alone.

Safe.

When Anna enters Car 11, she again sees the door at the opposite end just beginning to shut. This time, she runs through the car, trying to catch up to the man in the lounge.

It turns out to be completely empty. Yet the car feels only recently vacated. As if someone had just been there seconds earlier. So Anna moves on, into the dining car, which despite being fully lit contains a similar shiver of another person's recent presence.

It goes on like this as Anna progresses to the front of the train, pushing through car after car. Galley. Club car. Coach lounge. Each one is empty. By the time she reaches the coach cars, all hope that she might be following someone is gone. No one is here, a fact

Anna realizes when she reaches the cavernous luggage car. She even tries the door to the locomotive, thinking the person she saw might have been Burt Chapman, the engineer.

It wasn't. The door is still locked.

And whoever it was has completely vanished.

Anna backtracks, returning to the second half of the train. When she enters the dining car, she comes to a stop just beyond the door. The car, which had been lit when she passed through minutes earlier, is now pitch dark. And while she considers the idea of an electrical malfunction of some sort, Anna knows in her gut that someone turned the lights off on purpose.

Someone just now moving through the door at the back of the car. Through the quickly closing gap, Anna spots the same person she half saw leaving Car 13. It's only a partial glimpse. A sliver of a second in which the man looks to the side, revealing his profile before slipping from view.

Anna stops in her tracks, overcome by a sudden, startling chill.

She recognizes the man, even though his presence on the train is impossible.

He's been dead for a dozen years.

And while she knows it could be a trick of the light or exhaustion clouding her vision or even a lingering scrap of nightmare, Anna can't shake the feeling that—despite all logic and reason and laws of nature—she's just seen her brother.

TWENTY

STILL IN THE observation car, Edith Gerhardt stares up at the snow-filled sky through the window in the ceiling and thinks about the past. Looking at the snowfall always had that effect on her, even when she was a little girl on the rooftop of her family's ramshackle apartment building, her eyes aimed skyward.

Watching the snow now makes her think of her childhood, her parents, her husband, and a hundred other things. Friends and pets she'd completely forgotten about now appear so vivid in her mind it's as if she'd seen them minutes earlier.

And she thinks about Anna and Tommy, the closest thing she's ever had to a son and daughter. They were good children. Well-behaved. So devoted to each other that they couldn't see how different they were. Anna took after her father. Smart, astute, prone to bouts of quiet, but always with a dreamy look in her eyes. Tommy was clearly his mother's child. How handsome he'd been. How effortlessly charming.

For six years, she cared for them, even though she'd been hired as a housekeeper and not a nanny. She couldn't help herself. She'd always wanted to be a mother, but it never worked out while her husband was still alive. So Edith had transferred all that untapped maternal longing onto the Matheson children. Making Anna breakfast, sneaking Tommy chocolate, tending to their skinned knees, frostbitten cheeks, foreheads hot with fever.

All of it had been real.

Of that, Edith is certain. Yet it didn't stop her from choosing Germany over them when the time came to pick a side.

Kenneth Wentworth had a lot do with that. Edith always referred to him as Der Spinne. The spider. Always skittering into places he didn't belong, often at the worst possible time. And she was just a mere fly who got caught in his web the day he came to the Matheson residence when she was the only one home.

"Mr. and Mrs. Matheson aren't here," she said, which didn't seem to surprise Mr. Wentworth.

"I'm here to see you," he said. "You might not remember me. We've only met once or twice. Kenneth Wentworth."

Of course Edith remembered him. Mr. Wentworth was hard to forget in many ways. He was handsome, for one thing. He and his son had also shown up uninvited to the annual Matheson Christmas party, an incident that had upset Mrs. Matheson greatly. She'd made quite a scene. A reaction that left Edith with a sense that Kenneth Wentworth was not a man to be trusted.

The feeling grew even stronger that afternoon, when he said, "I wanted to talk to you about the war."

The question made Edith uneasy. From her accent, it was clear where she was from, and as Hitler's mighty grip spread across Europe, she'd noticed the way reactions to her had changed. Formerly friendly shopkeepers grew curt. Housekeepers from neighboring homes stopped waving to her when she passed. Distrust of Germans, she realized, was everywhere.

"What about it?" she said.

"Surely you have an opinion."

Edith certainly did, but that was none of Kenneth Wentworth's business. She started to close the door, mumbling an apologetic "Excuse me, but I must get back to work."

Before she could completely shut the door, Mr. Wentworth blurted out the question that would change her life—and destroy the lives of her employers.

"Where do your loyalties lie, Miss Gerhardt?"

"Mrs.," Edith said, quickly correcting him. "And they lie with my adopted country, of course."

"Then would you care to explain this?"

Kenneth Wentworth removed a photograph from his jacket pocket and showed it to Edith. She seized up at the sight of her younger self smiling for the camera, so proud of her crisp brown uniform and the swastika armband wrapped around its sleeve. Her husband stood next to her, dressed the same, giving a stiff-armed salute.

Edith remembered the occasion. It was 1934, and her husband had just been made a ranking member of the Kreisleitung, the district level of the Nazi Party. How proud she had been then. After years of decline, Hitler and the Third Reich were changing Germany for the better. And she and her husband were doing their part.

Years later, as Edith looked at the photo, all sense of pride was gone. She felt then—and still feels now—that Hitler was correct about the German race being superior to all others. Just look at their accomplishments over the centuries. All that art and music and technological advancement. But Edith also knew what it meant if her past was revealed, especially with the war in full swing.

"Where did you get this?" she said.

Kenneth Wentworth flashed a reassuring smile. "Don't worry, Mrs. Gerhardt. I have no intention of causing you any trouble."

"Then why are you here? Why are you showing me this?"

"Because I have a proposition for you."

Edith knew even then that it was less of a proposition and more of a demand. He'd give her the photo—plus a heart-stopping amount of money—in exchange for her hiding business files throughout Mr. Matheson's office.

"What if I refuse?" she asked.

"Then things could get very unpleasant for you, very quickly."

"These files, what are they? Does it have something to do with the war?"

"Yes," Kenneth Wentworth said. "Although it's more personal than political."

Edith's knees weakened, for she knew this had something to do with Mr. and Mrs. Matheson. "Which side will benefit?"

"Your side, of course," Mr. Wentworth said, adding with a wink, "The real one."

"Isn't this a disservice to your country?"

Kenneth Wentworth smiled again, this one more sinister than reassuring. "The only allegiance I have is to myself. But you, on the other hand, strike me as a person devoted to her homeland. Think about how this might help them."

"Then I'll do it," Edith told him. "For Germany."

What she hadn't known at the time was the personal toll it would take. She didn't know that the plan involved a train exploding and Tommy Matheson torn to pieces and Arthur Matheson's arrest, public shaming, murder. But there was no backing out. Edith, by that point rich beyond her wildest dreams, had no choice but to keep up the ruse.

Now she stares up at the falling snow, slightly dizzy when she realizes that Anna was right. Nothing she'd done has helped anyone but her and her co-conspirators. Soldiers died and lives were destroyed for absolutely no reason. Germany still lost the war, becoming a shell of its former self. And Edith has never gone back there, which is more telling than she cares to think about. If she loves her homeland so much, shouldn't she be there and not on this train, being inexorably pulled to her ruin?

Yes, she realizes. She should. Yet she never considered going back. And now she understands it's because, deep down, she knew that returning to Germany and seeing how much it had changed would have made the futility of her actions clear.

The realization hits her like a lightning bolt. A single, sizzling thought exploding in her brain as the rest of her seizes up.

It was a mistake.

All of it.

Betraying her employer, destroying his family, and covering it up had been a complete waste.

And now she regrets everything.

Edith tears her gaze from the observation car roof. As she looks at the snow-swept landscape outside, she becomes aware of someone approaching her from behind.

Slowly.

Silently.

Edith spots them in the observation car's windows, which distorts the person's reflection like a fun-house mirror. It takes her a moment to recognize the figure in the glass. When she does, Edith whirls around with a shocked gasp.

"Grauer Geist," she says.

TWENTY-ONE

ANNA DOESN'T IMMEDIATELY follow Tommy.

Because it's not him. It can't be. He's dead and ghosts don't exist. Come to think of it, she's starting to doubt she saw anyone at all. It's late, she's exhausted, and she's spent hours subsisting only on adrenaline and rage. It wouldn't be a surprise if she started to see things and sense people who aren't there.

Or maybe it's just memories that Anna senses, swirling like the snow outside. She and her family spent so much time aboard the Phoenix that every car has them. Giggling with Tommy in an upper berth of the sleeper car. Playing penny poker with a group of traveling salesmen in the club car. The dining room is especially full of them, Anna realizes as she moves through it on her way to the rear of the train. She'd sat at every table and likely eaten off every plate. Looking at one spot, she remembers being there with her parents and Tommy on the Phoenix's maiden voyage, when her overjoyed father offered her a sip of champagne. Its bubbling fizz tickled her nose.

At the table next to it sits the memory of playing Go Fish with Tommy and her mother. Then there's the booth in the corner, where they all ate dinner on what was to be their final trip aboard the Phoenix as a family. The whole time, Anna had tried to muster the courage to tell them about Dante. That they'd been dating in secret. That she loved him. That nothing they could say would make her feel differently.

She never could bring herself to do it. A few weeks later, there was no need.

Anna shakes her head, pushing away the memories. They didn't cause her to see things. Nor was it her imagination or a trick of the light or anything else people use to explain things away.

Someone is moving around this train.

And she's going to find out who it is.

Walking with renewed purpose, she passes through the lounge and into Car 11. At Room B, she knocks on the door until Seamus answers. Peering at her in confusion, he says, "What's wrong?"

Everything, Anna thinks. "Nothing," she says. "Just making the hourly rounds."

"I can do it, if you want."

"No. I've got it."

Anna continues down the car, rapping on Reggie's door until he answers. "Making sure everything is okay," she says.

In Car 12, she no longer bothers trying to explain herself. She simply knocks on all three doors in the car. Sal, then Lapsford, then Dante. When she sees that each one is in their room, she moves on.

It's the same in Car 13 and Room A, where Herb gives another nervous peek through the cracked door. Anna sidesteps to Room B. Edith's room.

She knocks.

There's no answer.

She knocks again.

Still nothing.

Anna twists the knob and the door clicks open. She steps into the room, thinking that Edith might have fallen asleep.

The room is empty.

Back in the hallway, Anna looks to the last place she saw Edith. The observation car. In the center of the door is a round window that resembles a submarine portal. Fitting, for it feels to Anna like she's just been thrust underwater as she approaches it.

Breathless. Panicked. Swept up in a dangerous current that takes her through the door against her will, unable to stop despite knowing what waits on the other side.

Edith.

Anna finds the woman on her back in the middle of the observation car, her arms flopped at her sides and both legs slightly bent at the knees. Edith's eyes remain wide open, as if she's staring at the night sky above, even though there's no life behind them.

Wrapped around her neck is a cord from one of the drapes, which someone had used to strangle her.

The scene is so horrible that Anna's forced to look away. A flinch that even Aunt Retta would understand. She turns her gaze to the car's windows instead, seeing nothing but a curtain of snow, rustled by wind that whistles against the side of the train.

They've entered the heart of the storm.

1 A.M.

SEVEN HOURS
TO CHICAGO

TWENTY-TWO

A MINUTE PASSES before Anna is able to look again at the corpse of Edith Gerhardt. Unlike after Judd's death, she doesn't cry or rage. All she can do is gaze at Edith's body and try to summon a bit of the hatred she'd felt for the woman. It should be easy. She'd despised Edith for so long that it became second nature to her. Something ingrained. But, much to her surprise, all Anna can think of is Edith's warmth beside her as she woke her in the mornings. And the sound of her footsteps, so light for such a sturdy woman, in the hallway outside her room. And the way the entire house smelled when Edith made her apple strudel. A rare treat reserved for her and Tommy's birthdays.

Whatever anger Anna feels is reserved for the person who took Edith's life.

And for herself.

No, she's not the person who killed Edith, but she is responsible for her death. Judd's, too. Both would still be alive if she hadn't tricked them into getting onto this train. It doesn't matter that each of them came of their own accord. Or that this trip wouldn't have been necessary had they not betrayed her father twelve years earlier. This was all her doing, and now a second person will be denied the justice she so craves.

Anna hears movement in the preceding car, followed by the low hum of voices. She must have screamed, although she has no memory of it. Based on the sound rising behind her, she had to have done something to draw the others' attention.

Sure enough, when she turns around, she sees the Phoenix's remaining six passengers huddled around the doorway. All display various states of shock. None more so than poor Reggie Davis, who Anna is certain didn't expect one murder when he boarded the wrong train. Now there have been two. And someone currently standing in front of her is responsible.

"Which one of you did this?" she says, needing to ask the question even though she doesn't expect an answer.

"If I had to guess," Lapsford says, "I'd say it was you."

The accusation isn't a surprise. Lapsford saw Anna put her hands around Edith's throat. They all did. They'd watched her knuckles clench as she squeezed.

"I didn't do it," she says. "I found her like this. I swear."

Seamus pushes past Lapsford. "Did you leave this car after the rest of us?"

"She did," Herb says. "I saw her go by."

Anna had all but forgotten Herb cracking open the door to his room and watching as she passed. She wishes she'd remembered, for it now makes her look more suspicious than she already does.

"Yes, I stayed here," she says. "There's no reason to lie about it because, one, Mr. Pulaski saw me and, two, I have nothing to hide."

"Was Edith here with you?" Sal asks.

Again, Herb plays the part of tattletale. "She was. I heard them arguing."

"We weren't arguing," Anna says, knowing it's just a matter of semantics. She thinks of it as a confrontation, which is different from an argument, though not by much.

"It sounded like one to me," Herb says. "'You should be afraid of what's coming.' That's what she said. I heard it with my own ears."

"That doesn't mean I killed her."

"What did it mean?" Sal says.

"That she—and all of you—should fear what's going to happen once we reach Chicago."

Sal honks out a derisive snort. "Like you plan on letting us get there."

"Getting you there is my only plan," Anna says.

Exhaustion settles over her as she wonders just how that plan has gone so awry. Yes, she assumed there'd be hiccups, but nothing she and Seamus hadn't prepared for. Never did Anna think she'd be forced to plead her innocence to the likes of Sally Lawrence, Jack Lapsford, and Herb Pulaski. They're the guilty ones. Not her.

"Did you see anyone else go by?" she asks Herb.

"Only you," he says.

Anna's heart sinks into the pit of her stomach. She was hoping Herb had seen the man she glimpsed roaming the train, ideally as he snuck back into the observation car after she'd passed.

"Did *you* see someone?" Seamus says.

Yes, Anna thinks. *My brother.*

"No," she says, because it's safer that way. Not to mention more logical than what she's thinking. Tommy is gone. No part of him exists. "But Edith was still alive when I left. I didn't strangle her."

"She wasn't strangled."

This comes from Reggie Davis, who had slipped into the observation car unnoticed while the rest of them cast accusations. Through the open door between the cars, Anna sees him kneeling next to Edith's body, looking but not touching.

"How do you know that?"

Anna drifts closer, rapt, as Reggie points to Edith's neck, where unblemished skin is visible beneath the drapery cord. "There aren't any ligature marks. If she had been strangled with this cord, we'd see abrasions on her skin."

By then, Seamus has joined them. Standing on the other side of Edith's body, he says, "Then how did she die?"

"I'm thinking suffocation. See how her lipstick is smeared?"

Reggie sidles next to Anna and points to a pale pink smudge on the edge of Edith's mouth. Anna knows the color well. It was Edith's preferred shade.

"Was it like that when the two of you were in here?" Reggie asks.

"No," Anna says.

"My guess is she was smothered. It would have to be something within easy reach yet also unobtrusive."

Anna looks around, settling her gaze on one of the swiveled chairs facing the windows. "Like a cushion?"

"Exactly," Reggie says as he begins moving from chair to chair, removing their cushions and flipping them over. He makes it almost completely around the car before stopping and exclaiming, "Found it!"

He shows Anna and Seamus the underside of the cushion. There, centered in the gray fabric, is a streak of pale pink.

"The killer likely snuck up on Mrs. Gerhardt, forced her to the floor, grabbed this cushion, and held it over her nose and mouth."

"Then what's the point of the cord?" Seamus says. "Why make it look like she was strangled?"

Anna knows why. "Because it makes me look guilty."

"Bingo," Reggie says.

She studies him as he stands there gripping the murder weapon, framed by the snow-studded window behind him. "You're not an insurance salesman, are you?"

"No, I am not," Reggie says, casting his eyes downward.

"And you didn't board the wrong train."

"I did not."

"Then who are you?"

Reggie returns the pillow to the chair and reaches into an interior pocket of his jacket, producing a copper-colored badge.

"Special Agent Reginald Davis," he says. "Federal Bureau of Investigation."

TWENTY-THREE

REGGIE KNOWS HE'S only on the train because he stayed late at the office. He stuck around after everyone else left because he had a date with Katie, a girl he'd only recently started dating. They had tickets to see *South Pacific* at the Forrest Theatre. His idea. Katie, as far as he could tell, had no opinion on Rodgers and Hammerstein, whereas Reggie loved them.

It turned out that drinks and a show weren't in the cards that night. Not after Reggie heard his name being called as he had one foot out the door. It was his boss, Ed Vesper, the only person in the dim and otherwise empty office.

"Yes, sir?" Reggie said.

"Get to the 30th Street Station," Vesper barked. "It's your unlucky day."

"What's going on?"

Vesper explained that he'd just gotten off the phone with the chief of the Chicago bureau. They'd received an interesting package from the daughter of Arthur Matheson. He didn't need to explain who Matheson was. Reggie knew all about the man who'd become the shame of Philadelphia.

"What did she send them?"

"Six boxes of so-called evidence that Matheson's daughter says proves he didn't do it."

Reggie's heart started playing hopscotch in his chest. "Art Matheson is innocent?"

"According to his daughter, he is," Vesper said. "Claims there was a conspiracy against him. And because that's not crazy enough, she included a note saying that she'll be bringing the six people who really blew that train to smithereens to Chicago aboard the Philadelphia Phoenix."

"Who are they?"

"The very same people who testified against her father."

Stunned, Reggie grabbed a pen and wrote down the names. Being a Philadelphia boy, he was familiar with all of them. Kenneth Wentworth was still a railroad bigwig in the city. The others he remembers from their testimony. Matheson's secretary, his housekeeper, two employees, and a military man. Reggie was in high school when it all went down, and he'll never forget skipping class so he could listen to the hearings on the radio.

"Do you think she's telling the truth?"

"From what little of the evidence they've seen so far, the folks at the Chicago bureau think she could be."

Reggie got a tingle of anticipation that shimmied all the way down to his tailbone. It was soon followed by a far different feeling—dread.

"Once word gets out about this, half of America is going to want to kill these guys."

"I know," Vesper said. "Which is why you need to be on that train."

"When does it leave?"

"Seven."

Reggie checked his watch. That was in ten minutes.

"Why don't I just arrest them?" he said.

"Because the Chicago bureau won't know for certain if any of them did anything wrong until they sort through all of this evidence. That's going to take all night. Just get on that train and make sure none of those six people get off it before Chicago."

"And that's it?"

"That's it," Vesper said. "Don't get involved. Don't interfere. Just stay out of the way and observe."

Reggie bolted for the door, coming to a stop right on the threshold as doubt crept in. He shouldn't be the one doing this. Another, more experienced agent should go in his place.

"Sir, are you sure I'm the right man for this job?" he said.

Vesper surveyed the empty desks and corner offices with their lights out and blinds drawn. "Right now, you're the only man here."

"But—"

"Just get on that damn train," Vesper snapped.

As Reggie grabbed his things and hustled out the door, his boss shouted one last order at his back.

"Oh, and don't let anyone know who you really are. If word gets out there's a fed onboard, all hell is going to break loose."

It's broken loose anyway, despite Reggie following his orders. Now he has no choice but to come clean, especially to the woman who organized the chaos. And she appears none too happy to be told the truth.

"You're with the FBI?" she says after closing the door between the cars so that it's just her, Reggie, Seamus, and the dead body of Edith Gerhardt.

"I am."

"And yet you said nothing. You did nothing. Even after someone was murdered."

Reggie feels a twinge of irritation on the back of his neck. An angry itch. "One, I didn't know what the hell I was walking into. All I knew is that there was a dead body on the floor and a bunch of people who might try to off me next if they knew I was a fed. Two, my orders are only to make sure they arrive in Chicago. I was told not to get involved or interfere."

"Well, you didn't," Anna says. "And now another person is dead."

"Don't try and pin this on me, lady," Reggie says, getting even more annoyed. The irritated flush has spread to his face. He feels its heat on his cheeks. "None of this is my fault. I'm not the one who had the bright idea to invite a group of killers on a thirteen-hour train ride. This plan of yours mucked things up big-time. If these people are as nefarious as you say—"

"They are," Anna says.

"Then you should have come directly to the FBI. We would have taken care of things for you."

Anna Matheson crosses her arms, indignant. "The last time the authorities took care of things, my father was unjustly arrested and murdered in prison."

"I get that," Reggie says. "It still doesn't mean you should have taken matters into your own hands. I mean, what if one of them somehow managed to get off this train and escape?"

"I made sure that wouldn't happen."

"No, instead they're killing each other. Which a lot of folks would have no problem with. Most people would say them being murdered is the perfect form of justice."

"Not me," Anna says.

"Why do you get to decide that? What about the families of those soldiers killed alongside your brother? Shouldn't they have a say in all this? I'm sure some of them would gladly murder the likes of Sally Lawrence or Jack Lapsford with their bare hands."

"As would I," Anna says, her sharp tone making Reggie flinch. "But I haven't. And I won't. All I care about is keeping them alive. I need—"

"To bring them to justice. I know. But a lot of people would take issue with your definition of that."

"Including you?"

"Yes," Reggie says. "You're not the only person who lost someone during the war, you know."

"You did, too?" Seamus chimes in.

"My father."

Reggie looks away, annoyed at himself for revealing even that much about his past. He hates talking about it, which is why he never does. People love a good sob story, and his is a doozy. Lucky for him, Anna Matheson and Seamus Callahan know what that's like.

"I'm sorry for your loss" is all Seamus says. Anna responds with "Likewise."

Reggie drops into the nearest chair, suddenly exhausted. "Even though I understand your reasons, what you're doing here is dangerous. Not to mention borderline preposterous."

"There's nothing borderline about it," Anna says. "It's crazy that I thought I could do it. I assumed one, if not all, of them would threaten me."

"Hence his gun," Reggie adds, jabbing a thumb toward Seamus.

"Are you armed?" Seamus says.

Reggie pats his jacket pocket, where he stashed his gun before leaving his room. "Better to be safe than sorry," he says. "Hopefully we'll have no need to use it."

Anna starts pacing the room, moving back and forth in front of the wide windows, casting occasional looks outside. There's nothing to see there. Just streaks of white as the train hurtles through the blizzard.

"What do we do now?" she says. "We can't just wait for whoever's doing this to kill again."

"Who do you think is the killer?"

"Lapsford," Anna says.

At the same time, Seamus replies, "Dante Wentworth."

Reggie clocks the wary look that passes between the two of them. It's the first crack he's noticed in their otherwise unified front. "A difference of opinion, I see. I guess the only way to find out who's right is to interrogate everyone on this train to find out where they were when Edith Gerhardt was killed—and if any of them had a reason to want her dead."

He stands, makes his way out of the car, and faces the others still clustered in the hallway of Car 13. To say they look confused would be an understatement. All of them strike Reggie as downright befuddled.

"I'm Special Agent Reginald Davis," he says. "Starting right now, I'm in charge of escorting all of you to Chicago."

The reactions of those in the corridor are as predictable as the sunrise. Herb Pulaski's face goes pale. Sally Lawrence gasps. Lt. Col. Jack Lapsford, just accused of murder, huffs in annoyance. And Dante Wentworth, also accused and also annoyed, says, "Are you arresting us?"

"No," Reggie says. "Not yet anyway."

He regrets the words as soon as he says them. Now there's a target on his back—and any one of them might try to take a shot. Reggie realizes he's going to have to be extra careful around this crew.

Staying out of the way is no longer an option.

TWENTY-FOUR

HERB PULASKI NERVOUSLY stuffs a cigarette between his lips.

"Mind if I smoke?" he says, even though he shouldn't have to. It's his room, after all. The only reason Anna Matheson and this FBI guy are here is because they forced their way in. They told him they need to talk to everyone on the train and that he's first. Now they perch side by side on the bench seat while Herb squirms in the chair by the window.

"Not at all," Agent Davis says.

Herb lights up and lowers the window an inch, letting in a whistling gust of icy wind. A few snowflakes ride in with it and pinwheel across the room. Herb doesn't mind. He's been sweating like a pig all night, with good reason. Anyone finding out they were tricked the way he's been would do the same. He should have known this wasn't a get-rich-quick scheme the moment he opened that damn invitation. But he was desperate—and that always leads to poor decisions. He knows that from experience.

The only consolation is the fact that everyone but Kenneth Wentworth was also tricked onto this damn train. Of course the richest of the bunch would know enough to avoid getting caught.

If he had any money to wager, Herb would bet it all that Ken Wentworth is at this very minute hightailing it out of the country. Mexico, maybe. Hitting one of those fancy Acapulco beaches with a fake passport in hand and a wallet thick with pesos. Herb wishes he were that lucky.

Still, he's luckier than Judd Dodge and Edith Gerhardt. The poor bastards. Five minutes ago, Herb had watched Seamus Callahan and Agent Davis carry Edith's body to the room next door. Knowing her corpse is now lying there makes him take an extra-long drag off his Lucky Strike.

"Where have you been for the past hour?" Agent Davis says.

Herb blows out a stream of smoke. "Right here."

"The whole time?"

"Yes, sir. After what happened to Judd, I figured it was best to stay put."

The FBI agent arches a brow. "Did you assume there'd be another murder?"

"No, I—" Herb can't finish the thought. He doesn't know what he assumed. He was too busy panicking about going to prison to dwell on anything else. "I just had a bad feeling, that's all."

"So you're scared," Anna says.

"Of course I am."

Herb's answer seems to please her. The corners of her mouth twitch into a half smirk. This is what she wants, Herb realizes. To turn up the heat and see them sweat. Well, she succeeded. He's now sweating buckets.

"Did you have any animosity toward Judd Dodge or Edith Gerhardt?" Agent Davis says.

"Not really," Herb says. "Judd always acted like he was smarter than everybody else, but I didn't mind it too much. Some guys are like that. And, in his case, he was probably right."

"And Edith?" Anna says.

"I barely knew her."

"So you didn't wish them dead?" Agent Davis asks.

Herb inhales, shakes his head, exhales.

"What about my father?" Anna says, leaning forward. "Did you wish him dead? Or my brother? Or my mother?"

"I didn't."

Anna stares at him, her gaze so piercing it makes Herb squirm. "Then why'd you do it?"

Good question, Herb thinks. He did it because he's not smart like Judd Dodge is. *Was,* Herb reminds himself. Judd is dead like Edith. Just a corpse laid out in a room down the hall.

"I was in a jam," he says, when in truth he was stuck in something far more serious. Financial quicksand.

Like a lot of guys, Herb needed some way to blow off steam at the end of the day. Rather than booze, which he didn't have much taste for, or women, who didn't have much taste for him, Herb liked to gamble. Little stuff at first. A couple of trips to Saratoga. Card games in smoke-filled backrooms. He wasn't looking to get rich. Not really. It was just a hobby. A way for a lonely man like himself to pass the time. But each morning, when he returned to the heat and the noise of the manufacturing plant, he couldn't help but dream of changing his fate.

Knowing all it would take was one big-time score, Herb increased his gambling, winning some and losing some until soon all he did was lose. But he believed that men made their own luck, so he kept at it, always waiting for that single, life-changing win. After burning through his meager savings, he started borrowing money. First from his folks, then from his friends, then from the kind of guys who demand speedy repayment and take drastic measures when you fail to provide it.

Like his life.

It was those guys Herb was thinking about when Judd told him the truth behind the faulty engine design. And paying them off was the reason he said yes.

Now here he is, on a train being shuttled to the feds, sharing a car with two dead bodies. Herb pictures them stone-still in their rooms, their dead eyes wide open. An image so horribly distracting that he misses what Agent Davis is saying now.

"Mr. Pulaski? Did you hear what I said?"

"Yes," Herb says. "I mean, no. I was—"

Thinking about Judd and Edith. That's what he was doing. Wondering what they felt when they were dying.

"I asked if you heard anyone else in the car after you saw Miss Matheson."

"No. Just her."

"So there was no one else in this car but you?"

"No," Herb says, still distracted. He can't stop thinking of Car 13 as a coffin. They're the same shape, after all, and now share the same purpose. Long narrow boxes in which the dead are laid to rest. And Herb feels like he's trapped inside this coffin on wheels, about to be buried alive.

Or killed.

Because Herb's starting to realize that's the pattern. Judd was the first, followed by Edith. Respectively, they occupied the last room on the train and the second-to-last. If the killer continues working his way down the train, room by room, his is next.

The idea sends so much panic streaking through him that Herb can scarcely breathe. He stubs out the cigarette, suddenly craving nothing but fresh air in his lungs.

"Am I going to die tonight?"

"Not if I can help it," Anna says.

Herb feels tightness growing in his chest. That last cigarette was a bad idea. Just like getting on this train was a bad idea. And now he's terrified he's about to pay the ultimate price.

"I don't want to be here anymore," he whimpers.

"You should have thought of that before ruining dozens of lives," Anna says.

"But what if I get killed?"

Herb becomes aware of the way Agent Davis and Anna Matheson look at him. Not with scorn and definitely not with pity. Their expressions are something in between. A potent disgust.

"I've made it very clear that I want you alive when we reach Chicago."

"How long will that be?"

"A little under seven hours."

That's a long time trapped in a room, with two dead people elsewhere in the car, and a killer on the loose. Herb swallows hard. Anna notices and softens, just a tiny bit. A kindness Herb knows he doesn't deserve.

"Just keep your door locked," she says. "Don't let anyone in. Either Seamus, Agent Davis, or I will come by to check on you every hour."

While nice to hear, it doesn't halt the panic spiking through Herb's thoughts or ease the aching tightness in his chest. He still can't breathe properly—an affliction that'll likely last the rest of the trip.

As Anna and Agent Davis leave, Herb opens the window all the way. Buffeted by snow and howling wind, he sticks his head out the window and takes a couple of deep breaths. Inhaling and exhaling as the frigid air stings his face, Herb can think of only one thing.

He should have jumped when he had the chance.

TWENTY-FIVE

IF THERE'S ONE lesson Lt. Col. Jack Lapsford learned from his time in the military, it's to always have a battle plan. And make no mistake, this *is* a battle. War has broken out on this train. It's him against Anna. Lapsford cares nothing for the others onboard. They're just cannon fodder. Likely as doomed as Judd Dodge and Edith Gerhardt.

So Lapsford says nothing.

Silence is the best defense. Another lesson from his military days. When in a bind, just clam up. Don't say a word. Don't implicate yourself, like Judd did. The fool got himself killed the moment he admitted that blueprint was his handiwork. He'd served his confession to Anna on a silver platter and got what was coming to him.

Lapsford doesn't know how that bastard Kenneth Wentworth roped Judd and the others into his goddamn scheme. Probably the same way Lapsford was forced to get involved—good old-fashioned blackmail. Sometimes, on nights when sleep doesn't come easily, Lapsford replays that dinner in his mind. The way Ken Wentworth stared at him over his fifty-dollar scotch as he said, "From what I hear, Jack, it wouldn't be the first time."

"I don't know what you're talking about," Lapsford said, even though he knew exactly what Wentworth was getting at.

"Don't play dumb, Jack. You're no good at it. I know all about your deal with Barnett Aeronautical."

Lapsford went cold then. He thought no one knew about his arrangement with Barnett. In order to secure a massive government contract, they promised to cut a few corners, provide airplane engines for the military at below cost, and let Lapsford pocket the cash that was left.

"That's different," he said, talking when he should have said nothing. "That's just good business."

"It's war profiteering. Lucky for you, I don't look down on such a thing." Wentworth sucked on his cigar, blowing out smoke before adding, "But imagine, for a moment, that I did. It would be my duty as a patriotic American to alert your commanding officer about your little agreement with Barnett. Think about what would happen then, Jack. A court-martial. A dishonorable discharge. Definitely jail time. You can go through all that or you can help me out and make ten times as much as your deal with Barnett."

Cowed by that prospect, Lapsford realized there was no way out of the situation. He had to go along with Wentworth's scheme, as despicable as it was. It was either that or the destruction of his career, his reputation, his whole goddamn life.

"You're a ruthless bastard," he said.

Wentworth bowed his head, as if he'd just been paid the ultimate compliment. "Thank you."

"Why are you so hell-bent on doing this?" Lapsford asked. "And don't tell me again that it's to rally the country around the war effort. That's a crock, and we both know it. So what's your real reason?"

"I hate Arthur Matheson," Wentworth said. "And I want to destroy him."

"There are other ways of doing that."

"But this will guarantee it."

"What did he do that makes you hate him so much?"

Wentworth swirled the scotch in his glass, staring at the amber liquid. "He took something from me. And now he's going to pay for it. With your help, of course. And your reward will be more money than you'll know what to do with."

Kenneth Wentworth was right in that regard. Lapsford ended up making a fortune. But now all the things Wentworth threatened him with that night are literally staring him in the face. Lapsford stares back, sizing up Agent Reginald Davis and finding him lacking. As a military man, he has little respect for the FBI. Despite both being on the same side, Lapsford finds them too flashy, too full of themselves. Especially that J. Edgar Hoover. Agent Davis is no different, sporting a smug look as he says, "Did you murder Judd Dodge and Edith Gerhardt?"

Lapsford doesn't respond.

"If you did, you might as well admit it," Anna Matheson says. "You're going to prison regardless."

Lapsford looks at her, wondering if she knows what her father took from Kenneth Wentworth. He suspects not. She's probably just as oblivious as he is. Wentworth never gave him more details, even after Art Matheson was long dead.

"My attorney will beg to differ."

"He's not here right now," Agent Davis says. "So how about I ask you some questions I know you can answer. How well did you know the deceased?"

"I didn't know them at all, really. Just a few brief encounters."

"What were your opinions of them?"

"You're assuming I had opinions of them," Lapsford says.

"You didn't?" Agent Davis asks. "Why not?"

Lapsford yawns, feigning boredom. "It wasn't worth my time."

"Speaking of time," the agent says, using a segue so awkward it makes Lapsford audibly groan. "Where were you between our gathering in the observation car and Edith being found dead there?"

"Right here," Lapsford says.

"The whole time?"

"Of course."

"How do we know you're telling the truth?" Anna leans forward, a glint in her eye that Lapsford doesn't like one bit. "After all, you lied earlier about being in the galley not long after the train left the station."

"Who told you that?" Lapsford says, to his instant regret. It almost sounds like a confirmation, which it isn't. Even though he was in the galley shortly after seven, he'd never admit it.

"Edith," Anna says. "Is that why you killed her?"

"I won't be saying another word until I have a lawyer present."

Lapsford knows that this, too, makes him sound guilty. A simple no would have sufficed. But, fearing he's already said too much, he reverts to saying nothing at all. Agent Davis and Anna Matheson continue to pepper him with questions, none of which he answers. He's gone mute, which is how he should have been all along.

After five more minutes and a few last, desperate attempts at getting him to talk, Agent Davis and Anna leave his room.

A temporary victory, Lapsford knows.

This battle is far from over.

TWENTY-SIX

"WELL, THAT WAS pointless," Reggie says as they stand in the corridor outside Lapsford's room.

Anna turns to face the door to Room B. "You should go back in there and arrest him."

Even though Lapsford said next to nothing, a far cry from Herb Pulaski's torrent of words, she remains convinced he's the killer. He was in the galley shortly after the train departed, meaning he could have found the rat poison and gathered enough to kill Judd Dodge. When he found out Edith saw him, Lapsford decided to kill her, too.

Still unknown is how he knew Judd would implicate himself after seeing his blueprint in the lounge. Or how Lapsford managed to slip the poison into Judd's drink. Or how he found out Edith had told Anna about seeing him in the galley.

"On what grounds?" Reggie says.

"Murder. Conspiracy. Sabotage. Treason. He's guilty of it all."

Reggie shakes his head, dashing her hopes. "To arrest him, I'd need some evidence of that. And, thanks to you, that's in Chicago. Until this train stops at Union Station, Jack Lapsford is a free man."

"Even if he kills again?" Anna says.

"Without proof, one of the few ways I can arrest someone for murder is if I catch them in the act."

"And what's another way?"

"Get them to confess." Prepared for another round of questioning, Reggie drifts down the corridor, stopping in front of Room A. Before knocking on the door, he turns to Anna and says, "You coming?"

Anna doesn't budge. She knows whose room it is, and just like with Edith earlier, she has no idea what to say to Sal Lawrence.

"No," she tells Reggie. "You do this one on your own."

As he knocks on Sal's door, Anna moves into Car 11 and stops at the window. The view outside hasn't changed. A full whiteout. Anna can barely glimpse the night sky through the skein of snow.

She continues to the center of the car and raps once on the door to Seamus's room. After a pause, she does it three more times, putting extra strength on the final knock. The secret code so he knows it's her. Thirty seconds pass between the last knock and Seamus opening the door—a stretch of time that Anna would have found worrisome if not for the slather of shaving cream on his cheeks and the straight razor in his hand.

"You're shaving?" she says as she steps into the room and closes the door behind her.

"Have to pass the time somehow, don't I?" Seamus ducks into the bathroom. "Has anyone confessed yet?"

"No such luck."

Anna stands in the bathroom doorway and watches Seamus slowly scrape the razor down his cheek. A strangely intimate act between a man and woman who aren't married, aren't lovers, aren't even related. But they are bonded, Anna knows, in a way that few people will ever experience or understand.

That's why Seamus, catching her eyes in the mirror, says, "Are you okay?"

"Of course. Why wouldn't I be?"

Seamus flings a bit of foam from the razor and starts on the other cheek. "Because Edith is dead. And, unlike Judd Dodge, you knew her well."

Anna thought she did. A long time ago. The end result is that she both loved and hated Edith, the emotions feeding off each other until she couldn't tell them apart. It's made the night far more difficult than she ever expected. The hate, she was prepared for. It was the slivers of love that were a surprise. Now Edith is dead, and Anna still can't seem to separate the love from the hate. She doubts she ever will.

"I'm sorry she's dead," Anna says, leaving the rest unspoken.

Done shaving, Seamus rinses the razor and closes it with a sharp snap. "It's almost two. Want me to take the next watch?"

Anna knows that would be the wise thing to do. Let Seamus check on the others. Put her feet up. Allow herself a rare moment of relaxation. But she's too restless for that. She needs to keep moving.

"No, I'll do it," she says. "You can get the next round."

She returns to the corridor, closing the door to Seamus's room behind her. She's in the process of turning away from it when she catches movement on the edge of her vision.

Someone is leaving the car.

Anna faces the door to the lounge, which is just starting to creak shut. All she can see of the person who passed through it is a bit of their shadow slipping along the floor.

"Tommy?" she says.

Anna follows the shadow, knowing it's not her brother and wanting it to be her brother and feeling foolish for even entertaining the idea that it could be him. The lounge is still dark, which only adds to her sense of foolishness.

She shouldn't be here.

Not alone.

Not with a killer on the train.

But, as far as Anna can tell, the lounge is empty. She moves through the car, sensing no one through the darkness. The lack of light sharpens her hearing, making the rattle-clack of the train sound even louder. When she passes the piano, the motion of the Phoenix jostles the keys just enough for a single note to ring out in the otherwise silent car. And when she nears the bar, Anna can hear the shivery tinkle of shuddering bottles.

Anna gives them a glance, wondering if that always happens and she's just never noticed it until now or if the train is moving more frantically than usual. She's about to turn and look out the window to gauge their speed when she spots something in the darkness behind the bar.

A shadow.

Slowly peeling itself away from the unyielding black.

No, not a shadow.

A man.

Anna tries to bolt back through the car but the man latches onto her shoulder and, with a single rough yank, pulls her against him. When she attempts a scream, a hand clamps over her mouth, stifling the sound. Still, she tries again, her lips barely moving against the meaty flesh of her attacker's palm.

Instantly, Anna starts to flail, all her limbs in motion. Arms swat. Legs kick. The man locks an arm around her, pinning Anna's own arms to her sides. She attempts another kick but misses as the man drags her into the dining car.

Unlike the lounge, it remains brightly lit, the tablecloths gleaming white, the silverware glinting. Anna twists her neck to get a good look at the man continuing to drag her down through the car. All she can manage is a glimpse of hairy knuckles as the man snatches something off one of the tables.

A steak knife, which immediately goes to her neck.

Anna gives a single, terrified swallow, during which she can feel the cold blade scrape against her throat. A horrible sensation. One that would make her cry out if she could. But the hand remains over her mouth while the serrated edge of the knife digs farther into her flesh. She feels breath against her ear, hot and foul-smelling. Words ride the air. A desperate whisper.

"I don't want to hurt you, but I will if I have to."

Anna knows the voice.

Herb Pulaski.

She tries to shout for help beneath his palm, even though that's impossible. Not when she's basically muzzled. Not when the knife stays against her neck, feeling like thorns jabbing her throat and sinking so deep that Anna assumes they've pierced the skin.

The thought sets off a fresh round of terror. Her body stills, searching for the sensation of blood being spilled, the telltale trickle. All Anna can feel is fear sweat spreading along her collarbone as Herb says, "I need to get out of here. There's no way I'm staying on this train. So you're gonna find some way to stop it and let me off—or else I'm going to slit your throat."

2 A.M.

SIX HOURS TO CHICAGO

TWENTY-SEVEN

"IF WE'RE GOING to do this, you need to learn how to fight like a man."

So said Seamus after he and Anna had formed a plan to bring the people who killed their brothers to justice. His assumption was that if things got out of hand, Anna wouldn't know how to defend herself.

She let him believe that.

Their first lesson in self-defense took place in the backyard on a sunny June morning. Within two minutes, Anna had brought Seamus to the ground three times.

"Maybe you need to learn how to fight like a woman," she said as he writhed in pain on the grass.

Her secret, Anna later told him, was that Aunt Retta insisted she learn how to fight. One of the many ways her aunt had tried to toughen her up. For years, she was coached by a former boxer who, on a set of used wrestling mats placed on the ballroom floor in Aunt Retta's mansion, taught her how to punch, to kick, to knock a gun from a man's hands into her own. And when Anna once accidentally kicked her instructor between the legs, she learned the number one rule of self-defense.

If all else fails, go for the groin.

Now, in the perfectly appointed first-class dining room of the Philadelphia Phoenix, Anna does just that. Lifting her right leg, she kicks backward. And as her foot slams into Herb Pulaski's crotch, Anna allows herself a single twinge of satisfaction. Those heels came in handy after all.

Behind her, Herb howls in pain and his arms go slack. Suddenly free, Anna springs away before whirling around to face him. She tries to reach for the knife at her thigh but realizes there's not enough time. Herb is lunging toward her, pained but angry.

Frantic, Anna grabs the closest object within reach. A plate, which she uses as a makeshift shield when Herb thrusts the knife toward her. The blade clinks off the china before Herb charges at her again.

Watching his ape-like approach, Anna thinks fast. She can't kill Herb. Not even in self-defense. She can only attempt to disarm him, which she does by flinging the plate at his head. It sails past him and hits the wall, shattering. Still, it makes him duck out of the way, which gives Anna enough time to reach under her dress, wrap her fingers around the hilt of her knife, and yank it from its sheath.

"I don't want to fight you," she says, wielding the knife at waist height. "Let's just talk this through."

"There's nothing to talk about. I *need* to get off this train."

There's a desperate edge to Herb's voice. He's scared, Anna realizes. As he should be.

"You know that's not possible," she says.

Herb takes a half lunge forward, which Anna counters with a full step backward, slicing the air with her knife.

"I'm begging you," he says. "I don't want to be next. That's the plan, you know."

Anna takes a backward step, caught off guard. "Plan?"

Herb tries to lunge at her again, but it's more of a stumble, the knife trembling in his hand. A thick sheen of sweat has broken out across his brow. He swipes at it with his free hand, the motion unsteady.

"Can't you see what's happening? The killer is making his way up the train, taking us out room by room. First Judd and then Edith. That means I'm next." Herb sounds more than scared now. He sounds crazed. "I'm not going to let that happen."

"And I'm not stopping this train," Anna says.

She shuffles backward as Herb surges forward, ungainly but powerful. He catches up to her in the middle of the car and thrusts his knife toward her in a series of quick jabs.

"Please," he says, his wheedling voice a far cry from his combative stance. "If you're worried about me running away, I won't. I swear. Just stop the train and the police can come and take me straight to the slammer. Just don't let me die on this train."

Just like with Edith, a strange sensation comes over Anna. An urge to do harm. She eyes Herb's throat, wondering how much effort it would take to drive the knife right through it.

"The way you let my brother die on a train?" she says. "The way you let dozens of others do the same?"

Herb gulps, guilty as charged.

"You could have prevented it from happening," Anna says as they continue to circle each other in the middle of the dining car. "You could have saved his life. All of their lives. But you didn't."

"I'm sorry," Herb says, his voice as weightless as a balloon, like even he knows it's too late for apologies.

"So you admit you could have stopped it?"

"Yes. And I'll tell the cops the same thing. Just help me off this train."

Anna comes closer, less afraid than she was earlier, although fear still very much exists. Now, though, she's scared not of Herb but of what she might do to him. That violent urge remains, coursing through her. Her grip tightens around the knife as she pictures driving it into his stomach.

"Why'd you let it happen? You knew men would die."

"I didn't know that for sure," Herb says. "And I didn't know who."

His breath has turned ragged. His whole body shakes. When he tries to charge one last time, Anna reaches for the nearest table and grabs another plate.

She swings.

Not at Herb's head, but the hand holding the knife.

The plate makes a chiming sound as it connects with his knuckles. Herb yelps and lets go of the knife, which hits the floor. He stumbles for it, but Anna's upon him.

Leaping onto his back.

Knocking him to the floor.

Landing with him in a writhing thud.

Anger seethes through Anna's body, sparked by the physical exertion. She straddles Herb's back as he attempts to rise and forces him back down against the floor.

"Tell me why you did it," she says, hissing into his ear. "Was it just for the money?"

"Yes." The word is half whisper, half croak, muted by the fact that his face is now pushed against the dining car's worn carpet. But it doesn't keep Herb from saying more. The words continue to flow in a panicked rasp. "I wasn't rich like you. I couldn't buy my way out of trouble. But I knew the trouble would go away if I let that engine get built. So that's what I did. If you wanted a confession, there it is. I'll tell the same thing to the police and a judge and whoever else you want."

"What about the others? They also did it for the money?"

"Not everyone," Herb says. "For Judd, it was payback. He was mad that your father never gave him enough credit. For me, it was the money. I think it was the same with Sal."

Even though Anna had long suspected greed was the motivation behind it all, having confirmation unleashes a fresh wave of anger. Her left hand goes to Herb's necktie, sliding it behind his head and tugging upward until his neck is exposed. Her right hand holds the knife against Herb's throat.

It feels good in her grip.

Too good.

Like an extension of herself.

Anna knows she's reached a precipice. A point of no return that she can either back away from or leap off into the abyss. With Edith, she managed to pull herself from the brink, mostly because of their shared history. She has no such ties to Herb, a man she barely knew and who twelve years ago decided her brother and thirty-six others should die on a greed-based whim. If she slit his throat, the exact thing he had threatened to do to her, it would be completely justified.

"Please," Herb says from beneath her. "Please don't kill me."

Seamus's voice rises from the doorway. "Anna, stop!"

Anna looks up to see him standing at the back of the dining car, no doubt drawn by the noise of the fight. Behind him are all the others. Dante and Reggie, Sal and Lapsford. All wear similar expressions of shock.

The knife goes slack in Anna's hand as the violence that had only seconds earlier coursed through her suddenly departs. It leaves her feeling empty, hollow, and slightly confused. Was that her who'd just held a blade to a man's throat? Would she have gone through with it if Seamus hadn't stopped her? The very thought shakes Anna to her core.

"He attacked me first," she says. "He threatened to slit my throat."

Only Seamus appears unsurprised. Of all of them, certainly he saw something like this coming—and trained her accordingly. "Is that why your neck is bleeding?"

Anna touches her throat, feeling a small patch of moisture. A shudder passes through her as she realizes how close Herb had been to following through with his threat—and how close she'd come to doing the same.

"Yeah," Anna says as she slides off Herb's back.

"Have you had that this whole time?" Seamus says, eyeing the knife.

Anna slides it back into its sheath. "Also yes."

"But Agent Davis searched you," Sal says as she glances Reggie's way.

"Guess I missed it," he says.

Anna grabs Herb's arm. "Get up."

Herb remains facedown on the floor, uncertain. "Where are we going?"

"Back to your room. Where you'll remain for the rest of this trip."

"I'm sure as hell not going back there," Herb says as he pushes himself into a kneeling position. "I told you, it's not safe."

"I'll protect you," Anna says. "It's not in my best interest to let you die."

She waits as Herb, also spent by their scuffle, climbs to his feet. Seamus grabs him by the arm and leads him away. "I'll stand guard outside his door," he says. "To make sure this doesn't happen again."

Reggie, Sal, and Lapsford follow behind them. Although they've all moved into the lounge and out of view, Anna can still hear their voices. "Are you afraid of him hurting her or her hurting him?" Sal asks.

Even Anna can see that it's a valid question. Especially now that everyone aboard the Philadelphia Phoenix knows she has a knife.

"Both," Seamus says.

TWENTY-EIGHT

ONLY DANTE REMAINS in the lounge, looking at Anna with a combination of fear and concern. "Are you okay?" he says.

Anna stretches, her limbs tight. When she rotates her neck, it lets out a sharp crack. "I can take care of myself."

"That's not what I asked."

"I'm fine," Anna says. "Really."

"You sure about that?" Dante's gaze drops to her neck. "Because you're still bleeding."

"Am I?" Anna says, touching her throat and finding a speck of blood on her fingers.

"Here. Come with me."

Dante grabs Anna by the hand. Before she can protest, he pulls her behind the bar. He then grabs a cloth napkin, dips it into a nearby ice bucket with an inch of water in the bottom, and places it against Anna's neck.

She snatches the napkin from his hand. "I can do it myself."

"Of course you can," Dante says.

Anna places it against her throat, the damp napkin blessedly cool against her skin. She didn't realize how hot she'd become, flush from both exertion and rage. Even now her blood continues to boil. She can feel her pulse thrumming at the side of her neck.

"Do you think Herb Pulaski really intended to kill you?" Dante says.

"I don't know. He's desperate to get off this train, that's for sure. He's convinced the killer is going room by room and that he's next."

"Maybe that was a ruse. Maybe he's the killer."

"I doubt it."

"Innocent men don't threaten women at knifepoint."

"Well, none of these people are innocent," Anna says, lowering the napkin. "But he seemed genuinely afraid."

"And are you afraid, Annie? Because I'm starting to think you should be. By the way, you missed a spot."

Dante takes the napkin and gently tilts Anna's head back. She reluctantly allows it.

"I've been scared since before we left Philadelphia."

Dante starts cleaning the spot she missed, standing so close that Anna can smell his aftershave. It's the same scent she remembers after all these years. A mix of cedar and citrus.

"But things have gotten out of hand," he says. "Two people are dead. And it's all my fault."

Anna goes still beneath his touch. "What does that mean?"

Suspicion storms her thoughts. Understandable, considering that they're in the same car where Judd Dodge died, standing at the very bar in which he accepted the drink that killed him. A drink that Dante had mixed. Anna thinks about the two of them in the galley. Had Dante been there earlier on the voyage, finding the poison beneath the sink? If so, had he already decided to use it to kill Judd?

Then there's Edith to consider. In the fifteen or so minutes Anna was gone from the observation car, Dante could have slipped

inside and killed Edith before returning to his room right before
Anna knocked on his door. While she has no way of knowing if
any of that really happened, it's entirely plausible.

"You didn't . . ."

Anna can't finish the accusation, leaving Dante to complete the
thought.

"Kill them? Of course not. But I am the reason you're here."

"Your father is the reason I'm here," Anna says, pulling away
from him.

Dante drops the napkin onto the bar. "And you wouldn't know
that without the evidence your aunt acquired. Do you know how
she got her hands on it?"

"No. She died before she could tell me."

"Maybe you should have asked me." Dante pauses. "Because
I'm the one who sent it to her."

It takes Anna a moment to fully comprehend what he's saying.
When it does finally hit her, she feels an unwieldy mix of awe,
confusion, and gratitude.

"*You* gave it her? Why?"

"Do you want the long answer or the longer one?" Dante says.

"Both."

"The long answer is because my father doesn't care one bit about
me. He never has. I spent my entire childhood trying to make him
love me. Something, it should go without saying, no child should
ever have to do. Their parents should love them unconditionally.
And my mother did. She wasn't always the best at showing it, but
at least she tried, which is more than I can say for my father."
Dante edges around the bar and starts pacing the area in front of
it. "For as long as I can remember, he treated me like a disappointment. Nothing I did seemed to please him. So I made it my mis-
sion to prove him wrong. I joined the family business. I worked

hard. I tried to impress him. And when that didn't work, I returned to the tactic I used as a teenager."

"Rebellion," Anna says.

Dante gives an enthusiastic nod. "Which meant digging through his dirt."

"But why did you pretend to be surprised when I told you about the evidence?"

"I didn't want the others to suspect I had anything to do with it," Dante says. "Rightly so, it turns out. You saw what happened to Judd. He all but confessed in this very car, and someone poisoned him because of it. If word gets out that I provided that evidence, whoever killed him and Edith might come for me next."

"Yet when we were alone, you continued to act like you didn't know."

"Because I didn't want *you* to know I was involved. That's why I started sending everything I'd gathered anonymously to your aunt. I didn't want you learning that I was helping to prove your father was innocent while I implicated my own."

Anna slides closer, filling the empty space between them. "Why not?"

"Because you hate me."

"*Hated* you," Anna says, the past tense surprising even her.

Dante flashes his famous crooked smile. "I didn't know that then. But I never forgot you, Annie. I know it was such a long time ago, that this might sound strange. But it's the truth."

Anna doesn't find it strange at all. She never forgot Dante. In many aspects of her life, he was the first. First boyfriend. First love. First heartbreak.

"Anyway, that's the longer reason," Dante says. "I never forgot you and I always wondered why my father forbade me from seeing you. Just like I always had doubts that your father did everything he was accused of. I know what everyone said about him being a German sympathizer, but it never made any sense to me that he would sacrifice his own son for what was clearly becoming a lost cause. Then there's the way my father bought your father's company so quickly—and for so little money. Because it all struck me as suspicious, I started investigating."

Anna leans against the bar top. "To clear my father's name—or to ruin yours?"

"My father's doing that well enough on his own," Dante says. "I learned, for example, that he's a tax cheat. In addition to being a different kind of cheater. He's had multiple mistresses over the years. No surprise there. He always treated my mother with the same disdain he shows to me. And I learned that his mighty railroad company has been losing money for years now. Train travel isn't what it used to be. People nowadays prefer cars, and soon they'll be preferring airplanes. Trains are the past. The future is in the sky. You didn't need to buy up every seat on this train, Annie. There would have been plenty of empty space."

"So your father's company is failing," Anna says, eager for him to get to the point.

"It would have already gone belly-up if he hadn't been able to swoop in and buy your father's railroad for dirt cheap."

"You discovered his motive."

"Trust me, that wasn't his motive," Dante says with a grim set of his jaw. "I found it out, eventually. After years of searching. My father hid things well, I'll give him that. A file here. A document there. Then there's the safe in his study, which had a combination that took me months to figure out. That's where the bulk of the incriminating evidence had been hidden."

Anna knows what he found. The memos and forgeries and bank records. All of it enough to arrest, try, and convict everyone responsible.

"How did it feel to learn all the horrible things your father did?"

"I was furious," Dante says. "And unbearably sad. And betrayed. Most of all, though, I just wanted to know why he did it."

"Greed," Anna says.

"But it's not, Annie. It's . . . worse."

The word wedges into her ribs like a dagger made of ice, shivery and ominous. Part of her doesn't want to learn what Dante discovered, even as another part of her needs to know. And even though she's certain she'll regret it in a minute or so, Anna can't help but ask, "What was his reason?"

"I think," Dante says, "it was heartbreak."

"That makes no sense."

"It does once you realize it was your mother who broke it."

The icy jab in Anna's chest grows sharper, colder. "My mother and your father were—"

"In love, yes." Dante gives her a weary look, as if he can't believe it, either. "A long time ago. Before you and I were ever born. They were even engaged for a time, although it didn't last very long."

"How did you find this out?"

"The safe in my father's study also contained letters," Dante says. "From your mother to my father."

"Love letters?"

He nods, and Anna's cheeks begin to burn. She remembers writing her own florid declarations of love to Dante.

Her whole life, she'd been told that she took after her father, and she believed it. After all, it was Tommy who got their mother's good looks, her vivaciousness. Yet Anna now knows that she was wrong. She's more like her mother than she ever imagined.

"Except for the last one," Dante says. "That was a breakup letter. Your mother wrote to my dad telling him that she was sorry, but she was ending things. She'd met someone else and fell head over heels in love."

"Did she say who it was?" Anna asks, even though she already knows. It's clear from the way her heart throbs and her body quivers and her head spins. Her body preparing her for news both shocking and so obvious in hindsight she's stunned she never thought of it before.

"Arthur Matheson," Dante says.

Anna sighs, for it all makes sense. Her parents married quickly. Only two weeks after meeting. To Kenneth Wentworth, that must have resulted in emotional whiplash. Loving someone. Thinking they love you. Then being left behind while they immediately find a new, permanent love.

Now Anna understands her mother's angry reaction when Dante and his father crashed that final Christmas party. She was worried Kenneth Wentworth was there to cause a scene. Anna also realizes why Mr. Wentworth forbade Dante from seeing her. He wanted a Matheson to experience the same heartbreak he did. Finally, it explains why Kenneth Wentworth ultimately targeted her father.

"I had it wrong," Anna says. "The whole thing."

This wasn't about making money. Maybe it was to Lapsford and Herb Pulaski and all the others. But for Dante's father, it was personal. And what he did wasn't merely an act of sabotage.

It was revenge.

TWENTY-NINE

ANNA THOUGHT NOTHING would top the jolt of surprise she experienced when Dante admitted he was the one who sent the evidence to Aunt Retta. She was wrong. Her legs go numb beneath her, and she finds herself leaning against the bar just to remain upright.

"Are you okay?" Dante says.

Anna responds with a weak shake of her head.

Yet she also should have known there was more to it than mere greed. Kenneth Wentworth planned something unthinkable, in the process damaging dozens of families. Only someone damaged in their own way could have gone through with it. And now that Anna knows why, just one more question remains.

Who else knew about it?

"I need to go," Anna says.

Dante grabs her arm. "We should really talk about this."

"No." Anna breaks free of his grip. "Not now. Please."

She flees the car, hurrying farther back on the train. In Car 12, she stops at the door of Room A and starts knocking. Sal, already annoyed as she opens the door, appears doubly so when she sees Anna.

"Did you know about my mother and Kenneth Wentworth?" Anna says.

Sal gives a noncommittal shrug. "I'd heard a few things here and there."

"Did you also know that's the reason he targeted my father?"

Sal leaves the door open as she retreats into the room, giving Anna the choice to enter or not. She does, stepping gingerly inside and closing the door behind her. The room, while large for a train, feels too small for the two women. In addition to physical baggage, in the form of Sal's multiple suitcases, the room is also filled by their shared past. Anna can feel it pushing against her and straining at the walls. A history too fraught to be contained in such a tight space.

"I didn't know that for sure," Sal says. "Ken Wentworth never explained why he was doing it. Just that it was going to happen and he needed me to be a part of it."

"Why'd *you* do it, Sal?" Anna winces at the way she sounds. So young. So vulnerable. She sounds, she realizes, like the girl she used to be. The girl who, in her mind, no longer exists. She's gone. Dead. A ghost. "I understand why the others took part. Even Edith. But all this time, I never figured out your reasons. Why did you betray my father like that? Why did you betray all of us?"

Sal drops into the chair by the window, her fancy clothes and bleached hair doing nothing to keep her from looking weary and old. A startling change from when Anna knew her. Back then, Sal had seemed not much older than Anna herself. Now no trace of that youthful woman exists. Gone, too, is the wry moxie that had made such an impression on young Anna. Present-day Sal strikes her as bitter and exhausted.

"It's complicated," she says, reaching for her handbag. "In ways you won't understand."

But Anna thinks she already does. She remembers how eager Sal was to please, constantly at her father's side, attending to his needs even outside the office. That's one of the reasons Anna had come to think of her as an older sister. Sal was always around, often joining the family in ways that went beyond being a devoted employee.

"You were secretly in love with my father," Anna says, amazed she'd never considered the possibility. "And you knew he'd never love you back."

Sal scoffs as she takes the lipstick and nail polish from her handbag. "That's an insult. Not just to me, but to our entire sex. Women can be motivated by things other than unrequited love."

"Then what motivated you? Greed?"

"Unlike some of the others, the money was secondary."

"Then why?" Anna says, still sounding childlike and wounded. "What made you do it?"

Sal opens the nail polish and, left hand splayed, begins to paint her nails the same crimson shade as her lips. "Shame," she says. "That and fear."

"I don't buy that. People died, Sal. *Tommy* died. All because of what Kenneth Wentworth did. And you helped him cover it up. What could possibly be more shameful than that? What was it you were so afraid of?"

Anna waits for an answer that doesn't arrive. As Sal continues painting her nails, stubbornly silent, it dawns on Anna that she's on the right track. It's clear another person was involved in her decision. If not her father, then someone else.

"Was it Kenneth Wentworth?" she says. "While he was still pining for my mother, were you in love with him?"

"I told you, I didn't do it because of a man." Sal spins the chair around to stare directly into Anna's eyes. "I did it because of a woman."

THIRTY

SALLY NEVER THOUGHT one night could destroy her life—and those of so many others. Yet one did. A night she will never forget and always regret. And it had started off simply. That's the strange part. There were no signs that something cataclysmic was on the horizon.

It was a Tuesday, and she'd been feeling particularly lonesome after another disastrous blind date with a rat-faced creep who'd tried to paw her within minutes of meeting. "You've got the wrong idea, pal," she'd said before ditching him.

But Sally hadn't felt like going home. Her date might have had the wrong idea, but the right one was very much on Sally's mind, leading her across the city to a basement bar beneath an intimates store. The mannequins in the shop window, dressed in silky slips and feathered robes, were a hint of what could be found below.

Inside, Sally went straight to the bar and ordered a drink. The bartender, the only man in the joint, obliged, making it fast and strong. Within minutes, the stool next to her was taken by a young redhead in a blue dress who looked so much like Rita Hayworth that Sally assumed she'd walked into the wrong kind of bar.

Thrumming her fingers on the bar top, she turned to Sally and said, "I never know what to order. What are you drinking?"

"A Manhattan," Sally said.

Rita Hayworth widened her eyes. "A Manhattan in Philadelphia? Is that even legal?"

"In this city, probably not."

"I won't tell. Your secret's safe with me."

Then she winked, making Sally understand the redhead knew exactly what kind of place she'd wandered into.

One Manhattan became two, which eventually turned into three. By the time her glass was empty, Sally had her hand on one of the redhead's supple thighs, pushing ever so slightly up her skirt.

"Take me home with you," Rita Hayworth said, her voice husky with lust.

Sally never took women to her apartment. She'd learned that from her father. A world-class philanderer, he screwed around in half the hotels in the city. Until the one time he didn't. Sally's mother had taken her and her sister to Cape May for the weekend. When they got home, they found their father still asleep and a brunette drinking coffee topless in the kitchen.

"I don't live alone," Sally lied.

"My hotel, then."

She grabbed Sally's hand without waiting for an answer, leading her out of the bar, into a cab, and into her bed. Sally spent the rest of the night there, marveling at the beautiful young thing in her arms and wondering how she'd gotten so lucky.

It turned out luck had nothing to do with it. Sally learned that two days later, when Rita Hayworth phoned her at the office asking if she could meet for a drink at her hotel. Too excited by the prospect of another good time with the fiery redhead, Sally never stopped to wonder just how she knew where to call her. Only when she reached the bar and found Rita in a corner booth with a man did Sally realize something else was going on.

Because it wasn't just any man seated next to the woman she'd recently taken to bed. It was Kenneth Wentworth, her boss's chief competitor.

"Miss Lawrence, so glad you could join us," he said, adding with a wink, "I believe you two ladies already know each other."

Rita refused to make eye contact as Wentworth placed a manila envelope on the table and slid it toward Sally.

"What's this?" she asked.

"Open it and see," Wentworth said with an unctuous smirk.

Sally opened the envelope—and almost passed out. Inside were a dozen photographs snapped from inside the closet of Rita's hotel room, showing everything they had done that night. The two of them kissing, undressing, tumbling into bed. By the time she got to the picture of Rita's face buried between her legs, Sally wondered why she hadn't yet died from shame, anger, and fear.

"Can I go now?" Rita asked Wentworth.

He handed her an envelope filled with cash and said, "Good work, kid."

The woman still couldn't bring herself to look at Sally as she scurried away, whispering a rushed "I'm sorry" while she passed. Too shocked by what was in those photos, Sally barely heard it. By then, her blood ran so cold she was certain it had frozen in her veins.

"You have a choice, Miss Lawrence," Wentworth said. "I can send copies of these photos to your mother, your sister, your employer, everyone you know. Or I can give them—and the negatives—to you to destroy. I can make these go away. In exchange for a favor."

Sally, who'd already decided to accept the offer without knowing what it was, said, "Anything you want."

What it turned out to be didn't become clear until the day after

Tommy Matheson's funeral. That was when Sally learned she'd be forced to create a convincing paper trail that connected her boss to the act of sabotage that killed his son and a bunch of newly enlisted troops.

If she did it, the photos and negatives would be hers, along with more money than she ever dreamed of having.

If she refused, then the photos would be made public and she'd be implicated alongside her boss.

Sally made her choice.

When the job was done, the photos and negatives were delivered to her in a wrapped gift box. She burned them in the kitchen sink, swigging directly from a whiskey bottle as she watched the flames rise.

Now she tells Anna what she never told anyone. Her dirty secrets. Her hidden shame. The only thing she leaves out is the crushing guilt she's felt ever since that day, knowing that Anna—who suffered far more than she ever could—won't care. Nor does she mention how the reason she's never said anything until now is because, having already ruined so many lives, Sally saw no point in destroying her own. So she took the money, knowing it would only make her more miserable.

"I'm not going to beg you for forgiveness," Sally says, suddenly thirsting for the dregs of whiskey that remain in her flask. "I know you won't give it to me, and I know I don't deserve it."

"You're right on both counts," Anna says.

"But I swear to you, Anna, if I'd known Tommy's death was part of the plan, I never would have agreed to it, no matter the cost. But he was already gone when they dragged me into it. Nothing I could have done would have stopped that."

If looks could kill, Sally knows she'd be struck down by the one Anna gives as she says, "My father also died. You could have stopped that."

"You're wrong there," Sally says. "One way or another, Ken Wentworth would have made this plan happen. The only difference is that I also would have gone to prison—and I probably would have been killed the same way your father was."

Anna glares at her. "There's a chance that could still happen."

Sally nods, knowing that's likely in her future if she doesn't get off the train before it reaches Chicago. What she doesn't understand is why Anna insists on bothering with all of it. If their roles were reversed, she wouldn't lure Anna onto a train under false pretenses and escort her to a group of waiting feds.

That's because Anna would already be dead.

Sally would have made sure of it.

"Now that I've admitted everything," she says, "are you still going to pretend you don't intend to kill me?"

"I told you, I'm not a killer."

Sally finishes painting her nails. Eyes on the glistening crimson, she says, "And what about your Irish friend?"

"Seamus? He's not one, either."

"Please don't tell me you actually believe that."

"What do you mean?" Anna says, matching her in prickliness. The room suddenly feels smaller, filling quickly with mutual distrust.

"What I mean is that he clearly killed Judd. Probably offed Edith, too."

Anna shakes her head. "Seamus would never do that."

"You sure?" Sally says. "Think about it. He was never searched, was he? Not completely. Once Mr. Davis saw that gun, it was all over. If your pal Seamus had poison in his pocket, none of us would know."

She watches Anna open her mouth, about to tell her she's wrong. That of course Seamus was searched. That all of them watched it happen. But when her lips suddenly press together again, it's clear Anna understands that Sally's right.

"He still wouldn't do it. Not without my approval. We came up with this plan together. We agreed not to hurt any of you." Anna pauses, making sure Sal is paying attention to what comes next. "Even though it's what all of you deserve."

"That might have been the plan, but things change when you're in the moment," Sally says. "Maybe the sight of all of us together made him so mad he couldn't help himself. Maybe he just snapped. It's certainly possible. Under the right circumstances, a person is capable of anything. I'm living proof."

"Seamus is better than you," Anna says, and Sally can't argue with that. Most people are.

"I'm not judging him. I've come to terms with the fact that all of us deserve whatever is coming our way." Sally turns her gaze to the window and the snowbound landscape passing beyond it. A kind of freedom she knows she'll never experience again. "All I'm saying is that if I were you, I'd make sure Seamus hasn't gone rogue."

THIRTY-ONE

ANNA MOVES THROUGH Car 12 in a daze. Although she's tried not to let Sal's words rattle her, they've prompted an earthquake. She feels as unsteady as the train car rattling down the tracks, swaying from one side of the hall to the other.

Seamus isn't the killer.

Anna knows this deep in her bones, just as she knows that Sal could be pointing the blame at Seamus to cast doubt away from herself. She could have killed Judd and Edith just as easily as Seamus. After all, she was one of three people to choose a martini before Judd, giving her an opportunity to slip poison into his glass unnoticed. And she had just as much access to Edith in the observation car as Seamus did.

What Sal didn't have, though, was good reason to kill Judd or Edith.

Seamus did.

And now that a thin ribbon of doubt has curled into her thoughts, Anna can't resist giving it a tug to test its strength. For instance, she knows Sal was right about Seamus not being fully searched. Only the coat of his uniform had been examined before the presence of the gun ended things. Maybe Seamus had poison waiting in a trouser pocket, still unknown to the rest of them.

As for Edith, it's clear she was murdered immediately after Anna left the observation car. As she searched the train, looking for the man she saw roaming the corridors, Seamus had just enough time to smother Edith to death before returning to his room.

Anna knows she shouldn't be thinking such things. She and Seamus are in this together. He'd never do something without first discussing it with her.

Would he?

She enters Car 13, finding it unnervingly quiet. Yes, the sound of the wheels rumbling over the tracks continues. It's the noises on top of it that are missing. Signs of life that indicate others are on-board. Coughs and conversations and footfalls on hallways carpets. Without those, the car seems as quiet as a tomb.

Standing in that strange silence is Seamus, still posted outside Herb Pulaski's room. He leans against the window across from the door, staring into the middle distance, stoic as always.

"Is Mr. Pulaski behaving himself?" Anna says.

"Haven't heard a peep out of him for fifteen minutes. What have you been up to?"

"I had a chat with Sal that was a long time coming."

"How'd that go?" Seamus says.

"It was enlightening." Anna pauses. "She said she thinks you're the killer."

Seamus gives her a questioning look. "And what do you think?"

"Was it you?" Anna says, her voice barely a whisper, as if that will make it any less of a betrayal. "Did you do it, Seamus?"

He's hurt by the question. Anna sees it in his big brown eyes, which reveal his every emotion. She's long wondered if Seamus knows how expressive his eyes can be. How she can look into them and know exactly what he's feeling.

"It's okay if you did," she says. "Well, it's not. Clearly. But I'd understand. You, of all people, have a right to vengeance."

"Where's this coming from?" Seamus asks. "It's got to be more than just something Sally Lawrence said."

"You haven't answered my question."

"I didn't kill Judd Dodge or Edith Gerhardt," Seamus says, clearly annoyed that it needs to be said. "I wanted to. I'll admit that. I want to kill the whole lot of them with my bare hands. But I haven't—and I won't. Because I know that isn't what you want."

Anna searches for the faintest hint that he's lying, but all she sees is the same grief-stricken expression that greets her every time she looks in a mirror.

"You believe me, right?" Seamus says.

"Yes," Anna says, because she does believe him. More than that, she trusts him. She has no choice. They're on an empty train with the same sworn enemies, one of whom is a killer. Seamus is the only person she can trust.

"Who do *you* think is the killer?" she says.

"My money's still on Dante Wentworth."

"I already told you, it's not him."

"You have something to back that up? Or are you just saying that because you're in love with him?"

"Was," Anna says. "I *was* in love with him."

Seamus swats away her comment with a skeptical "Whatever you say."

"I just don't think Dante's capable of something like that. Especially because he has no reason to do it. He didn't do anything wrong."

"He broke your heart," Seamus says.

Anna gazes out the window, barely able to see black sky peeking through white snow. "He did. But he's making up for it now. He's the one who gathered the proof and sent it to Aunt Retta. He admitted it to me. Apparently, he hates his father as much as we do."

"I highly doubt that," Seamus says.

Anna considers telling him what else she learned from Dante. That her mother and Kenneth Wentworth had once been engaged. That the main reason all of this happened is a longtime grudge held by a bitter, heartbroken man. She ultimately decides not to. Since it makes her feel worse, she can only imagine what it will be like for Seamus to learn that his brother was just an innocent bystander in all of it.

"Dante is on our side," she says. "Without him, we wouldn't be here."

Seamus rolls his eyes. "I'll be sure to thank him next time I see him. If we live to see Chicago, that is."

"You're worried that we won't?"

"Yes," Seamus says. "And if we do make it, I'm worried about what comes after."

Anna understands, for she feels the same. They've spent years grieving and raging, seething and plotting. All of it leading to this night, this train, this moment. And in a few hours—five, by Anna's schedule—it will all be over. Justice will be served, the guilty will pay, and they'll no longer have any need to rage, seethe, or plot.

It will be a life that Anna has no idea how to live. For so long, her entire existence has revolved around retribution. She can't imagine a future in which that isn't the case. How sad that is, she realizes. How utterly pathetic that this has been her only focus in life.

"What are you going to do when it's all over?" she asks Seamus, hoping that he's not like her, that he has at least one other thing to build a life around.

"No clue," Seamus says. "Whenever I think about the future, all I see is a black nothingness. No matter how much I try to envision one, that's all I can picture. Nothing. Just a void."

"You'll figure it out. We both will."

For Anna, that involves getting a job. This trip has cost her everything. There's nothing left of her aunt's inheritance. And while Anna likes the thought of working, she also knows she has zero marketable skills. Unless someone wants to hire a full-time revenge-trip coordinator, she's going to have to start at the bottom.

"*You* will," Seamus says. "Me? Not so much. I mean, will we even see each other again after this?"

"Of course," Anna says, even though she has her doubts. She can't think of a single reason why she and Seamus would continue to interact once the night is over. They have nothing in common. Only this. And while it's been enough to get them through the past year, she's uncertain it can sustain any form of friendship beyond it.

"Right," Seamus says, pretending to believe her.

A silence settles between them, but it's not the companionable kind that Anna has grown accustomed to. Those evenings when, after a long day of plotting, they shared a hushed dinner or a quiet hour of reading in the vast expanse of Aunt Retta's library. This silence brings with it a tension born of emotions unexpressed and words unspoken.

"Anna," Seamus says, shattering the quiet.

He points to the floor, where a thin line of red has started to roll beneath the door to Room A.

Blood.

A single rivulet oozing along the carpet.

Anna rushes to the door and knocks, the sound echoing through the car. "Mr. Pulaski? Are you okay in there?"

When no response comes, she tries again. "Herb?"

Anna twists the doorknob. It doesn't budge. The door is still locked.

"I'm getting Agent Davis," Seamus says before sprinting from the car.

Anna remains at the door, pounding on it, shouting Herb's name, pleading for a response even though deep down she already understands that one won't arrive. When knocking doesn't work, she tries the handle again, panic making her think that this time it will open, that she'd just done it wrong on her prior attempt.

By then, Seamus has returned with Reggie. He's removed his tie since Anna last saw him, the top button of his white shirt undone.

"He's locked in," she says in a panic. "I think he's hurt."

Reggie pushes her out of the way before throwing his full weight against the door, using his shoulder as a battering ram. The door rattles but doesn't open, forcing him to make a second attempt. When that one also fails, Seamus joins in. Together they crash against the door, to no avail. The only door that opens is the one to their direct left, which leads to the previous car. Peering through it are Dante, Sally, and Lapsford, lured there by the commotion.

"Go back to your rooms," Anna barks at them.

"What the hell is going on?" Lapsford says.

Behind him, Sally's face goes pale. "What's happened to Herb?"

Anna doesn't yet know, but whatever it is, it's not good. If it were, they'd be inside the room by now and there wouldn't be blood on the carpet, now smeared by Seamus's and Reggie's shoes as they stumble away from the door.

With twin grunts, both throw themselves at it one last time. The door finally gives way, splintering at the frame with a deafening crack. Anna pushes between them, peering into the newly opened room.

The first thing she sees is more blood.

A dark pool of it sits just inside the door, spinning off additional rivulets that threaten to join the one in the hallway. The motion of the train makes the blood shudder sickeningly, like a puddle in an earthquake.

Anna wills herself to look beyond it, moving her gaze deeper into the room.

Past the pool of blood.

To the stream of it that runs to the chair by the window.

Then to the chair itself, where Herb Pulaski sits, obviously dead. Somehow, his corpse remains upright, as if it has been waiting for them. There's an air of calm patience to the way his head tilts against the back of the chair and how his hands lightly grip the armrests.

The relaxed state of Herb's body stands in stark counterpoint to the look of utter horror on his face. A terror that transfers from him to Anna. Deep down, she knew Herb was dead before the door had been smashed open. Only it's worse than she ever could have imagined. Because Herb wasn't murdered in the same hands-free way that Judd was. Nor was his death as clean as Edith's. This was a different kind of end. A violent one.

Beneath his chin, a gash runs across his neck. It's slightly curved, like a second mouth that's spitting blood. Herb's eyes are wide with fear and his mouth remains open, as if emitting a silent scream.

And Anna, woozy from the horror of it all, can't keep from screaming along with it.

3 A.M.

FIVE HOURS
TO CHICAGO

THIRTY-TWO

NOISE FLOODS ANNA'S skull as she stares at the corpse of Herb Pulaski. Not her screaming, which ends as abruptly as it began, but a loud clanging that reminds her of when she was a girl visiting her father's manufacturing plant. All that pounding and thundering as men shaped stainless steel into what would eventually become a train. She covers her ears, just as she did as a child, but it does nothing to mute the sound jackhammering inside her skull.

Trapped in the noise, Anna can't tear her gaze from Herb and the blood and the slit across his throat, that sick smile. She's grateful when Reggie edges into the room, steps gingerly over the blood, and grabs the sheet from the bed to drape over the corpse.

Having Herb out of sight dulls the clanging in Anna's head enough for a dreadful thought to emerge.

He was right.

Someone is indeed moving up the train, killing them room by room.

Herb knew this and had warned her, but Anna didn't truly believe him. Instead, she thought a promise to keep him safe was all that was needed. Now he's dead in the most horrific of ways.

And just like with the previous two victims, Anna can't be satisfied with this particular brand of justice. Their suffering is at an end, over too quickly, which might be the point of all three murders.

The killer didn't do this to silence Judd, Edith, and Herb.

They did it to deny Anna the satisfaction of bringing them to justice.

She looks to Sally and Lapsford, who along with Dante approach the door to Room A, willing themselves to peek inside, regretting it once they do. Sally and Lapsford look especially stricken. It's clear they realize their number is dwindling. Normally, Anna would have taken satisfaction from that. She wanted them afraid, the anxiety ratcheting higher as they got inexorably closer to Chicago.

But not like this.

She wanted them to be afraid by her actions, on her terms. This is something else entirely, and she feels a quiver of fear herself when she considers that one of them is most likely responsible for this change of events.

Lt. Col. Jack Lapsford.

"You monster," Anna says, staring him down as he backs away from the door. "I know you did this."

Lapsford's eyes widen. "Me? We all know it was you. You're the only one carrying a knife."

Anna falters. A wobbling half step that brings her to the cusp of the room, blood-soaked carpet squishing beneath her shoes. "No, I—"

"Where have *you* been for the past hour?" Lapsford says.

"With me for most of it," Reggie says, still by Herb's corpse.

"And with me," Seamus adds. "Right up until we saw blood trickling under the door."

"In between, I was in Sally's room."

Sal doesn't immediately speak up to confirm her claim. The

silence, combined with the hesitant expression she wears, makes Anna realize nothing between them has changed since their conversation. She still hates Sal for what she did, and Sal still suspects her of being a killer. Knowing that, Anna sees no reason for Sal to speak up in her defense. That's why it's a complete surprise when Sal, slowly and grudgingly, says, "And she was with me before that. She's not lying, Jack."

"Well, I didn't kill him," Lapsford says.

"I'm not sure any of you could have done it," Reggie says as he rotates slowly, eyeing the entire room. "The door was locked, including the dead bolt." He points to the solid nub of metal jutting from the splintered door. "Which can only be engaged from inside the room."

Anna looks to the doorframe, where a chunk roughly the same size as the dead bolt is missing, presumably broken off when Seamus and Reggie smashed the door open. While it's easy to assume someone gained access to the room because Herb let them in, despite Anna telling him not to, the presence of the dead bolt complicates matters.

"How did the killer get out?" Dante says.

"Maybe Herb did it to himself," Sal suggests with a shrug. "He locked himself inside and committed suicide."

"Then where's the knife?" Reggie gestures around the blood-spattered room. "There's nothing here. If Herb slit his own throat, the knife he used would still be around, most likely in his hands."

Anna's gaze drifts to the sheet-covered corpse, her stomach churning as she recalls the sight of what's beneath it. Herb's wide, lifeless eyes. The gash across his neck. The glistening blood.

This, she thinks, isn't the corpse of a man who slit his own throat and then somehow managed to discard the knife before settling back into a chair. It's the corpse of someone who was killed by surprise.

Likely by someone Herb knew.

Someone he trusted and willingly let enter the room, perhaps locking the door behind him. Or maybe the killer locked it after swiping the blade across Herb's neck. Either way, the locked door left them no means of escape.

Anna takes a halting step into the room and looks around. She can't shake the feeling that she's missing something. A key detail that might not only provide an idea of who the killer could be but how they left the room.

Then she sees it.

"They used the window," she says.

Reggie turns to face her, surprised and impressed. "How do you know that?"

"The blood."

Herb's corpse sits at a spot where the wall and window meet behind him. To the left of the body, the wall is speckled red by arterial spray from when his throat was slit. So, too, are the curtains to his right.

But the glass of the window is free of such gore. There's not a speck of blood on it. That means the window had been open when Herb's throat was slit. And while the killer might have entered through the door, that window was their only way out.

Reggie nods to her, and they wordlessly approach the window.

"What do you think?" Anna says.

Reggie touches the glass, his fingers spread. "I'd say there's no chance someone could do it—if it wasn't the only other way out of this room. Is the window even big enough?"

Tilting her head, Anna sizes it up, estimating the window to be about three feet tall and just as wide. Big enough for Sally, Dante, Reggie, and even Seamus to fit through. The only person it would seem to rule out is Lapsford. She can't imagine him squeezing his considerable girth through such a tight space.

"When they left the room, they likely climbed onto the roof to get to another part of the train," Reggie says.

Under different circumstances, Anna would think it impossible. The Phoenix seems like it's going too fast for such a feat. The motion would make keeping one's balance on the roof very difficult. That is, if they weren't immediately blown off the train first.

An even bigger problem is manipulating the window. The ones on the Phoenix open and close by sliding up and down. Since Herb's window was already partially open, getting inside would have been, if not simple, at least relatively manageable. A quick lowering followed by a legs-first entry that, if done right, would catch anyone by surprise.

But climbing out the window and closing it behind them? That's a greater degree of difficulty. It would have required the killer to clamber out the open window and then close it while clinging to the side of the train. During a blizzard, no less.

To see if it's possible, Anna moves to the window by the bed and opens it in a single, smooth motion. Immediately, wind and snow blast into the room. Along with the noise of the train wheels, it's an assault on her senses that makes Anna plant her feet to keep from being blown onto the bed.

Using the sill as support, she pushes through the window until her entire upper body is outside. Immediately, she understands how strange it is to be on the outside of a moving train. How utterly wrong. Especially a train moving as fast as the Phoenix. Its speed whips up both wind and chill, which work in tandem. The cold instantly brings a bone-deep shiver. Making it worse is the torrent of snow. Each flake that hits her skin feels like a needle prick, while the wind acts as a large, invisible hand that's constantly shoving.

As she remains jutting outside the window, Anna notices how everything that's insulated and silent when tucked into a rail car becomes dangerously loud and real. Wheels churn mere feet beneath her, their metallic rattle-crunch sounding eager to chew her to bits if she should fall.

And how easy it would be to fall.

All someone would need to do is sneak up behind her and give her a shove. That fact makes Anna tighten her grip on the windowsill as she leans farther out of the train and looks to the room's other window. The one next to Herb's body that the killer slipped through.

A flat metal frame runs along the top edge of the glass, overhanging it by half an inch. There's a similar overhang inside the train, there to allow passengers to easily open and close the window. All someone needs to do is jam their fingertips beneath the jutting sliver of metal and either push or pull, both inside and outside the train.

But can it be done while clinging to the train's side? So far, it doesn't look like it.

Still hanging outside the train, battered by wind and snow and cold, Anna maneuvers herself into a sitting position on the windowsill, facing inside. With a death grip on the window frame, she leans as far outside as possible to examine the top of the train.

A mistake, she immediately realizes. The cold feels like a deep plunge into ice water and the wind is so strong she fears it'll yank her right out of the train. Snow streams past her face, obscuring her vision. Anna peers through it, noticing a ridge of metal on the edge of the roof that runs the length of the car. Although thick enough for someone to grab onto, Anna doubts a person could close the window while dangling from that alone. They would also need somewhere to plant their feet.

She wrangles back to her original position, searching the side of the train for such a place. In both directions, the Phoenix's exterior appears to be a flat expanse of stainless steel now flecked by ice and snow. It's only when Anna looks down that she notices something on which a person outside the train could find purchase.

The orange stripe that runs along the side of the car.

Situated just beneath the window, the colored stripe isn't paint but a panel affixed to the train's side. Above and below, it is a narrow metal strip on which someone could place their toes. While one couldn't stay there indefinitely, clinging spiderlike to the side of the train, Anna assumes it would give a person gripping the ridge along the roofline with one hand enough time and support to quickly close the window with the other.

Satisfied, Anna slips back inside the train and pushes the window shut. The wind and snow and noise instantly cease, yet their effect on Anna lingers. Flakes of snow stick to her windswept hair, and she can't shake the chill running through her body. Rubbing her arms for warmth, she turns back to the room.

Reggie is no longer there.

Instead, he's just outside it, joining the others in the cramped corridor.

"The killer definitely escaped through the window," Anna says. "Likely used the roof to get back into their own room."

She pauses, noting the odd way everyone stares at her. Even Seamus, who looks at her as if she's a stranger.

"What's wrong?" she says.

"How long were you with Sal before you came to see me?" Seamus asks.

He stands with his arms at his sides, his right hand balled into a fist. Anna suddenly feels uneasy. She doesn't like how he's acting, from his stance to his tone to the flash of suspicion currently in his eyes.

"Fifteen minutes," she says.

Standing next to Seamus, Reggie gives her a curious look. "Are you certain of that?"

"Of course."

"Then how did this get inside Herb's room?"

Seamus opens his fist. As he reveals what he's holding, Anna's heart halts. Not a skip, nor a stutter, but a full-on stoppage.

Because nestled in his palm is a tiny train engine, its surface silvery and glinting.

Her father's pin.

Anna looks down at her dress, where the pin had been at the start of the night—and should be right now. That it's not hits her with a sense of loss. A hole in her heart that's quickly being filled with confusion. When, how, and why did it go missing?

"I found it on the floor," Seamus says, making no effort to return the pin. "While you were at the window."

"Clearly it fell off on my way there. Or earlier while we were interviewing Herb."

"You were still wearing it then," Reggie says. "Can you remember the last time you noticed it was still pinned to your dress?"

Anna can. It was right next door, in the observation car, while she was confronting Edith. "A few hours ago," she says. "The pin could have fallen off anytime between then and now."

"That still doesn't explain how it ended up on the floor of a room where a man was just murdered."

Seamus says it, speaking with a gentle weariness. Even though his tone is more disappointed than accusatory, Anna knows that's what he's doing. Accusing her. Or at least considering the possibility that she's a killer. Ironic, seeing how thirty minutes ago Anna did the same with him. That both of them are doubting each other shows how much their plan has unraveled.

"There are a hundred ways it could have gotten there," she says, even though it's a struggle to think of a single one. Anna's mind spins, searching for logical reasons. "Herb could have stepped on it, and it stuck to his shoe. Or maybe it stuck to one of our shoes."

She stops, realizing how desperate she sounds. Filling the silence is Lapsford, who says, "More likely it fell off as you were sneaking out of the room."

"If I killed Herb, do you honestly think I would have told you how I did it?"

"Yes," Lapsford says. "To make you appear innocent. Even though we all know you're carrying a knife under your dress."

The hallway seems to close in around Anna. Her heart jumps back to life, thundering in her chest. "I've spent the past hour talking to all of you, with only minutes in between. If I had killed Mr. Pulaski, climbed out of the train, and crawled along the roof to my own room, it would have been so fast that I wouldn't have had time to close my own window, let alone the one in his room."

The words spark an idea in Lapsford's head. Anna sees it happen—a brightening of his eyes as the connection is made—and immediately regrets saying anything at all. Even though she has no idea what he's thinking, it can't be good.

"Then we'll just have to check your room and see," he says as he turns to leave the car.

"Be my guest," Anna says. "In fact, I'll lead the way."

She squeezes past him and all the others, starting off a parade of people marching to her room. One by one they go, moving into Car 12 and then Car 11.

As they move, another train going the opposite direction rumbles past. Because of the late hour, most of its windows are dark. A long row of oil-black mirrors reflecting the Phoenix itself. Behind them are regular passengers on a regular journey long ago lulled to sleep by the train's gentle rocking.

That's what this train is. A dream on wheels.

While that might be true of most trains, Anna knows it's not the case with the Philadelphia Phoenix. There's no dreaming on this journey. Only nightmares. A fitting sentiment, for Anna feels like she's in a nightmare when she opens the door to her room.

Inside, one of the windows sits wide open.

A window that had been closed the last time Anna was there.

Now it gapes open, letting in blasts of snow and frigid wind that jostles the drapes. One in particular flaps furiously. Anna reaches for it, realizing immediately why it's so loose.

The cord that had once been attached to it is now gone.

The same type of cord that had been wrapped around Edith's neck.

Anna has no idea who opened the window and removed the cord. Nor does she know when it happened. All she understands as the wind blows and the drape flaps is that she was wrong about the motive behind the murders. It wasn't to keep the others from talking. Nor was it a way to ruin her plan of seeking justice for all of them.

No, there's an entirely different reason for the killings—and Anna knows exactly what it is.

THIRTY-THREE

"HE'S TRYING TO frame me," Anna says as she shuts the window with an angry slam. It's just her and Reggie in the room now, Seamus having left to shoo the others back to their own quarters. "Just like they framed my father."

She thinks about not just who's been murdered and when, but how. Judd, poisoned because he was the first person to admit a role in the scheme that killed Anna's family, not to mention the first person to suggest she'd gathered everyone there to kill them. Edith, actually suffocated but made to look like she was strangled because that was what Anna had almost done when she lost control in the lounge. Herb, his throat slit after everyone onboard learned that she's carrying a knife—and after predicting he'd be the next victim.

Add in the missing drapery cord found around Edith's neck, the open window in her room, her father's pin, and the fact that she had good reason to murder all of them, and it makes Anna look guilty as sin.

"Let's say you're right," Reggie says. "Who do you think is doing it?"

"Lapsford," Anna says. "Because it serves two purposes at once.

It eliminates those who might implicate him while also making me look guilty, casting doubt on my mental state and the idea that my father was innocent."

"Do you really think he's capable of that?"

"He plotted worse before. There's no reason to think he wouldn't try it again."

Reggie shakes his head. "I meant physically capable. Killing Judd and Edith, yes. He's even capable of slitting Herb's throat. But then climbing out the window onto the roof of the train? You think someone Jack Lapsford's age and condition can do that?"

No, Anna doesn't. When examining the window, she wasn't even sure Lapsford could fit through it.

"Maybe there's a different way out of the room. Something we missed. Or maybe it *is* possible to latch the dead bolt from the outside. Open my door and check."

Reggie, who had closed the door after Seamus left, doesn't budge. "Or maybe you should just stay in this room and not come out until we reach Chicago."

Anna drops into the chair beside the window.

Reggie thinks she's guilty.

He doesn't outright say that. He doesn't need to. She sees it in his eyes, on his face, in the coiled tightness of his body. He thinks she's killed not just Herb, but Judd and Edith as well.

"You don't believe me, do you?" she says. "You think I'm the killer."

"I don't," Reggie says.

"Then why are you treating me like I am?"

"Because it's what everyone else thinks. And I'm worried there'll be a mutiny on our hands if I don't defuse the situation."

"By forcing me to stay in this room."

Under normal circumstances, Anna wouldn't mind that. She's quite used to being alone, having spent years living in isolation with her aunt. Home confinement born less out of choice than necessity. They were outcasts in a world that thought her father a man so cold-blooded he would slaughter his own son. KILLER SPAWN read one of the notes wrapped around the rocks that occasionally crashed through their front windows. Aunt Retta would burn the paper and use the rocks as a border in her garden.

Even after Seamus entered the picture, Anna spent more time than not by herself. So solitude should make her comfortable now. It doesn't. Because now she knows the killer can move from room to room *outside* the train. Not that anywhere was safe. Judd Dodge, after all, was murdered in a room full of people. Which, now that she thinks about it, seems like more of an outlier than the other deaths.

"Something doesn't add up," she says. "Judd died right in front of us. But Edith and Herb were killed in isolated places where no one could see it happening. Why?"

Reggie eases himself onto the bed. "If your theory is correct, it's to frame you."

"But that wasn't the case with Judd. I didn't make the drinks. I wasn't even near him."

"Do you think there's a reason for that?" Reggie says. "Judd Dodge was killed first. Was he worse than the others? Did he play a bigger role in what happened?"

"Yes," Anna says. "Even though it's impossible to rank the six of them from worst to least awful, some had more to do with what happened than others. And Judd Dodge, who built a locomotive designed to explode, is at the top of that list. But I don't think any of the others actively hated him."

"Did you?"

Anna turns, as if taken aback by the unnecessary question. "I hate all of them. Far too much to kill them."

"And you're certain Mr. Dodge didn't kill himself?"

"Certain? No. But I doubt it. Then again, I have no idea how it happened in the first place. There was a lot going on at the time."

She spends the next ten minutes relating all of it to Reggie, from her arrival in the lounge to everyone marching to the front of the train and back to Dante ending up behind the bar, mixing martinis.

"Do you think he could have poisoned Judd's drink?" Reggie says.

Anna doesn't—and not just because she's certain of Dante's innocence. "He mixed all four martinis in the same shaker."

"What about after he poured them?"

That's another no. Anna clearly remembers Dante pouring the drinks into four glasses before spreading his arms wide and saying, "Come and get 'em." After that, he stood back as the others approached the bar and grabbed a martini of their choice. Sal first, then Herb, Lapsford, and, finally, Judd.

"There you go," Reggie says. "One of them must have slipped the poison into his glass while they were choosing."

"But I was watching," Anna says. "We all were."

She closes her eyes, replaying the scene in her memory. In her mind's eye, it looks like a movie. Bright and flickering. She watches it like a movie, too. One she's seen before. Instead of getting caught up in the plot, she scans the background for details whose importance she missed in the moment. She sees Sal take her glass and Herb grab his. She watches Lapsford reach for one of the remaining glasses, decide against it, pick up the other. Judd takes what's left.

Anna sits up as a forgotten detail emerges. Lapsford brushing against Judd as he leaves the bar. That touch, while brief, could have been the moment Lapsford dropped poison into Judd's glass before moving smoothly away.

But it wasn't, Anna quickly realizes. The contact occurred while Judd was still on his way to the bar, meaning there was no glass in his hand when Lapsford passed. And no one was near Judd after he carried his drink to the center of the car.

Anna keeps mentally replaying the moment, telling Reggie what she sees in her memory. Sal gulping from her drink, her lipstick staining the rim of the glass. Herb taking tiny, nervous sips. Lapsford glaring at her over his glass, probably at that very moment finalizing his plan to fake a heart attack. Judd, off on his own, seemingly so uninterested in his drink that he yawns.

Things get blurry after that. There was so much activity going on in the lounge. First the train that clattered past, followed by Lapsford's fake emergency and Judd's sudden, surprising demise. While she might have missed plenty of details in those moments, Anna made sure to note where everyone was located during all of it. At no point while the glass was in Judd's hand did anyone get close enough to poison him.

But there *was* poison in his drink. She'd seen it with her own eyes. That gritty residue on the inside of the glass, bearing the same smell as the rat poison in the galley. It seems to her that the only person who could have put it there is Judd himself.

Anna gasps as it suddenly hits her.

A missing detail she'd only vaguely noticed, unaware of how important it would turn out to be. Not that she could have known. After all, how can something be considered important if it never even happened?

"He didn't drink it," Anna says to Reggie now. "The whole time that martini was in Judd's hand, he never once took a sip."

Reggie perks up. "Are you sure?"

Rather than answer, Anna springs to her feet. A signal that she's certain. Not just about Judd never taking a sip of his martini, but the fact that he wasn't poisoned at all.

The thought that Judd has been playing dead this whole time rattles through her head, louder than the train itself. And as she rushes to the door, Anna can only think of one reason why he'd do such a thing.

She pushes out of the room, leaving Reggie with no choice but to follow her. Seamus hears them and peeks out from his own room, confused.

"What's going on?" he says.

"I'll explain later," Anna tells him as she moves to the next car. Seamus trails after her, getting in line right behind Reggie. Over her shoulder, Anna says, "When you checked Judd's pulse, are you sure you didn't feel one?"

"Yes," Seamus says. "I'm sure. There was nothing."

Reggie gives him a brief backward glance. "Do you know the proper way to check someone's pulse?"

"There's a proper way?"

"So that's a no," Reggie mutters.

Seamus scowls at the back of his head. "Who are you to judge? And where are we going?"

"Judd's room," Anna says between cars.

"Why?"

"Because he might be the killer."

Anna slows once they enter the train's second-to-last car. An unconscious calming. As if she doesn't want to wake the dead now resting in its rooms. One of whom, it turns out, might not be dead at all. Another reason Anna remains quiet. If Judd is still alive, she doesn't want him to know they're coming.

Outside the door to Room C, she presses an index finger to her lips, signaling to Reggie and Seamus that they also need to be quiet. Because the man inside is assumed to be dead, Anna knows the door is unlocked. She reaches out, slowly grasping the handle. Then, without warning, she flings the door open.

Reggie enters first, storming in before Anna even gets a chance to move. Seamus is next, shoving into the room right behind him.

Anna, unceremoniously shoved aside, pushes in behind them, their sturdy backs blocking her view inside the room. In the sliver of space between their bodies, she gets glimpses of the window, the chair next to it, the door to the bathroom.

Reggie and Seamus are still in her way as they turn the corner to the bed dominating the other half of the room. Again, Anna sees only slivers. A strip of sheet. A glimpse of headboard.

What she doesn't see is Judd Dodge.

With good reason.

When Seamus and Reggie part, finally allowing Anna a clear view of the room, all she sees is an empty bed and a tossed-aside sheet that once covered what they all had thought was a dead body.

Judd himself, though, is gone.

THIRTY-FOUR

JUDD DODGE SITS in darkness, relieved to no longer be playing dead. He'd spent almost six hours doing exactly that. First for an interminable length of time in the lounge, during which he was certain he'd be found out, then for hours in the last room of the train's second-to-last car.

Other than a few brief trips elsewhere, he remained exactly where he'd been placed on the bed in Room C. His fear was that if he moved too far, for too long, someone would notice. So he stayed completely still beneath the sheet while his brain churned at full speed. What if someone *did* look in on him and notice his chest rising and falling? What if they *did* check his pulse? Correctly this time, and not like Seamus, who unwittingly—and, for Judd, luckily—missed the mark by an inch or two.

He eventually got tired of such restrictions, becoming so antsy that the urge to move was uncontrollable. It got even worse once he heard the racket two rooms away. Pretending to be dead was one thing when he was mostly alone in the car. Doing it with everyone nearby was a different story.

So he fled, even though it wasn't part of the plan. Judd doesn't care about that. For him, the biggest question running through his thoughts is this: What if the rest of the plan fails?

There's no reason to suggest it will, especially after he played his part so perfectly. All it took was a little unplanned distraction in the form of Jack Lapsford's temporary heart trouble and some old-fashioned sleight of hand.

Once he realized the train had left the station empty, Judd suspected Art Matheson's daughter was behind the journey—and that she had revenge on her mind. His hunch was confirmed when he saw who else had been invited. By then, a plan had already been formed.

And Judd was prepared.

While everyone was arguing in the lounge, he remained focused on the small amount of white powder hidden inside his pocket watch. Rat poison. Found beneath the sink as he passed through the galley after learning the rest of the train was empty.

When he opened his watch to check the time, Judd poured the powder into his martini glass, letting most—but not all—melt into the cocktail. After all, the others needed some way to know he'd been "poisoned."

To sell the illusion, he made sure that red-flecked foam also appeared on his lips. An impromptu bit of trickery that makes him exceedingly proud. It might well be the greatest trick Judd ever pulled off, for it made everyone think for a time that he was dead. Now he's certain they know he's not. Just as they now know what he's done.

Judd looks down at his hands, grateful for how the darkness hides them from view, keeping him from dwelling on the death they've brought.

Until twelve years ago, he never thought he'd be a killer. Even after he could be labeled as one, Judd still felt slightly removed from the act. Something he designed did the killing. Not him. Not directly. At least that's what he told himself during those long, sleepless nights in which guilt was his only emotion.

Now he can no longer lie to himself.

He is a murderer.

And he'll do it again if he has to.

If that's what it takes to escape his fate, he'll kill every single person on this train.

4 A.M.

FOUR HOURS
TO CHICAGO

THIRTY-FIVE

WHILE ONE OF the seven remaining living people aboard the Philadelphia Phoenix waits in darkness, the other six have gathered in the first-class lounge at the insistence of Agent Reggie Davis. Whether it's intentional or not, none of them sit near the windows. Instead, they remain clustered together in the middle of the car, all eyes on Reggie as he stands beside the baby grand piano.

"Now that we know Judd Dodge is alive, well, and hiding somewhere on this train," he says, "we can also assume he's the murderer."

"You think he killed Edith and Herb?" Lapsford says, his voice now missing some of his usual bluster. He's scared, Anna thinks. At least, he should be. She certainly is.

Yes, she's been a sparking jumble of nerves since before the Phoenix pulled out of the station. But that was from worry about the voyage not going according to plan. Now that it's gone completely off the rails, her anxiety has sharpened into something more primal.

She could die in the next few hours.

That prospect has always been present, Anna knows, rattling in the background as steadily as the train's wheels. Now that it's too loud and too shrill to ignore, she has trouble focusing on anything else. She's only vaguely aware of Reggie answering Lapsford's question.

"I do," he says.

"Why would he do that?" Sal says.

Anna's been asking herself that same question. Why would someone like Judd, one, fake his own death, and two, spend that time of deception moving through the train killing people while framing her in the process? That last part, Anna vaguely understands. By making it look like she murdered Edith and Herb, Judd hopes to take her down with the rest of them.

While she's relieved to at least be cleared of that suspicion, Anna can't help but worry about the rest of Judd's motives. What, exactly, is his endgame? Even if he'd managed to play dead until the end of the trip, the ruse will be over the moment authorities step onto the train in Chicago. He'll still be arrested right alongside everyone else.

Her gut instinct is that there's a different reason for Judd's actions. One far scarier than trying to frame her. Maybe he plans to kill them all and attempt to escape at the last second. Or maybe he simply snapped—the only motivation for his actions being insanity. If that's the case, all of them have reason to be concerned.

"*How* did he do it?" Dante says.

Anna has a better idea about that, and it involves Judd's deft sleight of hand. Of course the same man who made candy canes appear out of thin air could make it seem like he was poisoned to death. It helped that Seamus, who's no medical expert, already admitted to not quite knowing how to check for a pulse.

"Since I wasn't here to witness it, I don't know," Reggie tells Dante. "But it's my understanding that you and Mr. Callahan carried his body to his room. *My* question is how did the two of you miss the fact that he was still alive?"

That's something Anna hadn't thought about, even after they'd stormed into Judd's empty room and confirmed that he was still alive. But the way Seamus and Dante stiffen on either side of her makes Anna consider if one of them knows more than they're letting on. She hopes not. More important, she doubts it. In all the shock and confusion following Judd's apparent death, it was easy to miss how he wasn't really dead at all. Anna certainly had when she was collapsed on the floor beside him.

Then again, she didn't have as much contact with Judd as Seamus and Dante did. She hadn't lifted him off the floor by his legs and shoulders, carried him across three train cars to his room, lowered him onto a bed. Is it possible someone could do all of that without realizing the man they carried was still alive? Especially Seamus, who'd been the one gripping Judd's shoulders?

The only answer Anna can come up with is: maybe. After all, Judd's body was covered with a tablecloth the entire time, preventing Seamus from seeing a flutter of eyelids or the slight rise and fall of Judd's chest as he took a surreptitious breath.

Anna casts a sidelong glance his way, searching Seamus's features as he says, "What do you think I should have done? Perform an autopsy? The man looked dead, so I assumed he was."

"He's right," Dante says, in a rare moment of agreement between them. "We all thought that. Especially since we all assumed we'd just watched him die. Then again, I'm not the one who checked his pulse."

And just like that, the truce between Dante and Seamus ends. They glare at each other, Anna caught in the cross fire of their mutual contempt. Bearing his most dour scowl of the night so far, Seamus says, "What are you implying? That I helped Judd fake his death?"

"Maybe," Dante says.

Seamus lurches toward him. "And maybe I should punch you in your rich-boy face."

"Stop it," Anna says, thrusting her arms in front of them to block what she fears could become a full-on fistfight. "Both of you. Right now, we need to focus on the fact that a killer has been roaming this train all night."

She now has no doubt that it was Judd Dodge she saw earlier in the night, moving through the train. Not a figment of her imagination. And certainly not her brother. Just Judd, a living ghost, on his way to murder Edith. Anna assumes their paths never crossed because Judd had ducked into her room to cut the drapery cord they later found wrapped around Edith's neck.

Only two questions remain: Where is Judd now—and who does he plan to kill next?

That he intends to murder again is, in Anna's view, a given. He didn't go to all this trouble just to stop at two. She fears it's all or nothing.

"What are the odds that Judd, suspecting we'd eventually be on to him, simply jumped from the train?" Reggie says.

"Slim to none. He knows it'll probably kill him. If the fall doesn't, the storm will." Anna jerks her head to the window, where the blizzard continues to rage. "I don't think he'd go to such great lengths to fake his own death just to risk his life for real several hours later."

"Then let's assume he's still on this train," Reggie says. "Does anyone have any idea where he might be now?"

Anna shakes her head. "Judd Dodge helped design the Phoenix. He knows it like the back of his hand. Every nook. Every cranny. And, as we now know, he's capable of using the roof to get from place to place. Honestly, he could be anywhere."

"So we need to search the entire train," Reggie says.

"Or we can stay right here," Lapsford says. "It's doubtful Judd would try to kill one of us if we're all together."

"The train won't be reaching Chicago for—" Reggie looks to Anna for the answer.

"Four hours."

"That's too long to stay here hoping Judd won't strike again," Reggie says. "We need to find him before he finds us. That's the only way we'll survive until the end of the trip."

"But don't you think that's exactly what Judd wants?" Seamus counters. "For us to split up so he can pick one of us off?"

"Probably," Anna says. "But Reggie's right. We can't just assume Judd will stay hidden until this train gets to Chicago."

Reggie steps from the piano to the middle of the car. "I propose we search the train in two groups of two. One pair in the front half, the other in the back."

"Who's with who?" Seamus says.

"You and I should be in separate groups," Reggie says, wisely choosing not to elaborate why. It's not a good idea to remind everyone else that he and Seamus are both armed. "Anna, you'll go with me."

"I guess I'm with Seamus," Dante says.

Seamus scowls. "I'll go by myself, if you don't mind."

"Don't you trust me?"

"No," Seamus says. "For all I know you're in on it. Your father caused all this, remember."

"And I'm not my father."

Anna shifts as Seamus and Dante stare each other down. "Now is not the time for squabbling. Get along until Judd is found. After that, you two can go back to hating each other."

She gives Seamus a look that says *Do I make myself clear?* He responds with a grudging nod. With that settled, it's agreed upon that Anna and Reggie will search the front half of the train and Seamus and Dante the back.

"Do you think Judd is armed?" Dante asks.

"Probably," Reggie says. "And, as we now know, dangerous. Stay together. Look high and low. And do not let your guard down."

Seamus nods. "What should we do if we find him?"

"Shoot him," Reggie says. "One clean shot in the leg. It'll stop him in his tracks without causing loss of life."

"And what about us?" Lapsford says, rising to his feet. "You expect us to just sit here and wait?"

"I do," Reggie says.

Sal also stands, so eager to leave the lounge that her body subconsciously tilts in the direction of the door. "I'm not going to hang around waiting for Judd to kill me."

"Or me," Lapsford adds.

"Would you rather lock yourselves in your rooms and hope he doesn't come through the window and attack?" Anna says.

"No." Sal straightens her body and takes a decisive step. "I'd rather help you find that bastard."

Anna stares at her, wondering if Sal can really be trusted. Likely not. So far, she has proven herself to be anything but trustworthy. Yet Anna also understands she has little choice in the matter. Present circumstances require taking all the help they can get.

"What if I don't want to search?" Lapsford says.

Sal moves behind the bar and grabs two magnums of champagne. "Tough shit," she says, handing one of the bottles to Lapsford. The other she grips by the neck, wielding it like a club. "We need to stick together and we need to find Judd before he finds us. Where do you want us to start?"

"You two can patrol this car and the dining room," Reggie says.

That makes it official.

Like it or not, they're all in this together.

THIRTY-SIX

WITH SEAMUS AND Dante setting off for the rear of the train, Reggie and Anna begin their search of the front, starting with the baggage car. A single glance shows it to be empty.

They move into the first coach car, where there are very few places to look. Just beneath the seats and in the open luggage racks running the length of the car above them. In both, if Judd were there, they'd see him immediately.

The only true hiding place in the car is the lavatory crammed into a back corner, as small as a utility closet. Reggie takes a position in the middle of the aisle, his gun aimed at the lavatory door as he gestures for Anna to open it.

She approaches the door slowly, knowing Judd Dodge could be on the other side, clutching the same blade he used to slit Herb Pulaski's throat. That thought—that he could do the same thing to her—makes Anna's hand tremble as she grips the door's latch.

She lifts it, slowly, as her entire body now trembles. The whole time, Anna's careful not to make a sound, because if she does, Judd might know she's there. He might already know, she realizes, and be poised and ready to strike.

Latch released, Anna opens the door a crack. It creates a slit of darkness through which she sees nothing. Just a thick, ominous black. She tilts an ear toward the open space, listening for the sound of movement or someone breathing. All she hears is her own breath, which grows harder and more ragged by the second. She looks to Reggie, who gives a nod urging her to open the door all the way.

Anna does, flinging it wide open and leaping backward before Judd can come at her with his knife.

But Judd isn't there.

The lavatory is empty.

Anna, however, continues to tremble.

"Cold?" Reggie says.

Anna nods, although she's not sure if it's the temperature or the fear humming through her.

Reggie takes off his jacket and hands it to Anna.

"You're doing great," Reggie says as she gratefully slips it on.

They repeat the same search process in the second coach car, Anna willing her body to tremble less as she approaches the lavatory, lifts the latch, opens the door. It's also empty.

"Is that where you were hiding earlier?" Anna says as they move into the sleeper car.

"Yeah," Reggie says, visibly impressed.

"Why didn't you make your presence known then?"

"Because I was worried I'd be stepping into a battle zone." Reggie grunts as he looks around the car. "Turns out I was right."

"As the inadvertent creator of that battle zone, I apologize," Anna says.

After searching the lavatory at the rear of the sleeper car and finding nothing, they head to the coach lounge. There are even fewer places to hide here. Just chairs and side tables under which only children can squeeze. Anna knows because she and Tommy had done just that when they were young and the Philadelphia Phoenix had felt like a second home.

Their pace slows in the adjacent club car, which contains multiple places to hide. In addition to the counter where food is served, there's the janitor's closet at the front of the car. Once a place where Anna thought the poison that had killed Judd might be kept, it's now the most likely spot where a very much alive Judd could be hiding.

Reggie and Anna assume their positions. Him facing the door, gun drawn, her slowly beginning to pull it open. This time, when a crack appears between door and frame, there's no anxious pause allowing Anna to peek through it. The door immediately flies open on its own.

Anna leaps out of the way.

Reggie flexes his finger against the trigger of his gun.

But instead of Judd Dodge, what emerges from the darkness of the closet is nothing but a mop, two brooms, and a metal pail, all of which clatter to the floor.

"Well," Reggie says with a chuckle of relief. "I can honestly say that's the first time I've been attacked by a mop."

"Not a regular hazard of the job, eh?" Anna says.

"No. Usually the bad guys are a little more animated."

"How does it feel when you catch one of them?" Anna asks.

Reggie strokes his chin, deep in thought. "Satisfying. Knowing you're helping the greater good. You ever think of doing something like that?"

"Every day for the past year."

"I meant after this. What do you plan on doing once this is all over?"

Anna had asked Seamus the very same thing a little over an hour ago. Her answer now is the same as his then. "No clue."

"Well, in my humble opinion, I think you'd make one hell of an FBI agent."

"Are there women agents?"

"Not yet," Reggie slyly replies.

"I do enjoy a challenge." Anna kneels and reaches for the mop. "Permission to throw these guys back in the slammer?"

"Permission granted," Reggie says, allowing the faintest of smiles. "I'll start searching the galley."

He disappears into the next car while Anna continues gathering the cleaning supplies. She stuffs them all back into the closet and closes the door. On her way to the door at the back of the car, Anna looks to the windows. Outside, the blizzard still rages all around them. A full whiteout. She stands still a moment, trying to gauge if the Phoenix has slowed at all in the storm. Anna's train legs tell her no. It's still going full speed.

With a relieved sigh, she moves to join Reggie in the galley. It's dim inside, the only light coming from above the stovetop. In that wan glow, Anna spots something lying in a heap in the middle of the floor. As her eyes adjust to the gloom, she realizes what it is.

Not something.

Someone.

Anna moves closer to see Reggie on the floor, surrounded by a widening circle of blood. She drops to his side as he stares up at her through pupils dilated by pain.

He's still alive, thank God.

For now.

The amount of blood on the floor isn't a good sign. Neither is the knife sitting a few feet away, blood dripping from the blade.

"The bastard stabbed me," Reggie says, sucking in air through his teeth.

Anna doesn't ask him who. She fears that if she speaks, Reggie

will be able to tell how scared she is right now. How utterly terrified.

Because her worst fear has come to fruition.

Judd Dodge has struck again.

And this time he's no longer targeting the guilty.

THIRTY-SEVEN

ANNA LOOKS AROUND the galley, knowing there must be a first-aid kit somewhere. She spots one on the wall and lunges for it. The kit cracks open in her hands and its contents rain onto the floor. She falls to her knees, sorting through tubes of burn ointment, a bottle of mercurochrome, and small tins of rattling pills until she finds what she needs. Gauze pads. Adhesive tape. Scissors to cut them.

Before Anna can use them, she needs to check the wound. She lifts Reggie's shirt, noting but not dwelling on the two-inch slice in the fabric. It's the similarly sized gash in the bottom left side of his stomach that commands her attention. While not particularly wide, it looks alarmingly deep. Blood continues to gush through the puckered flesh.

She unwraps a gauze pad and presses it over the wound. Blood instantly soaks through it, bubbling out the other side. Anna covers it with more gauze and tapes everything into place.

A temporary fix.

Reggie clearly needs stitches. If Anna can't find some way to close his wound, it's likely he'll bleed out in the next hour or two.

She stands and starts searching every drawer, tossing aside

their contents, frantically looking for needle and thread. There's nothing. With time of the essence, Anna decides it's more likely to find what she needs in a different part of the train. But she can't leave Reggie by himself. Not when Judd is possibly still nearby.

"Can you stand?" she says.

Reggie shoots her a wary look. "Do I have a choice?"

"I'm afraid not."

"Take this," Reggie says, handing her the gun still gripped in his hand. Overwhelmed by the sight of the knife and the blood, Anna hadn't noticed it. Now she's takes it into her blood-slicked hands and shoves it into the pocket of Reggie's borrowed jacket.

He exhales, nods, then tries to rise off the floor. Anna swoops in to support him, ducking so that his arm is across her shoulders, transferring much of his weight onto her. Together they move through the galley, every step prompting a pained hiss from Reggie.

"It happened so fast," he says. "I turned my back for one second and the next he's sticking a knife in me."

"Judd?"

"Yeah."

The knowledge that Judd might still be nearby—ready to strike again—makes Anna quicken their pace. They push into the dining car, where Lapsford and Sal are simultaneously entering from the other end.

"What the hell happened?" Lapsford says upon seeing Anna and Reggie hobbling across the room.

"Judd attacked him. Have you seen anyone?"

"No," Sal says. "No one has come through here or the lounge."

"But he came this way," Anna insists. "Where did he go?"

A tense silence falls over the car as all four of them lift their eyes to the ceiling.

"The roof," Reggie mutters. "He's on the goddamn roof."

"We need to go," Anna says. "All of us. Right now."

Moving in a pack, they make their way into the lounge, where Anna veers behind the bar just long enough to grab a bottle of vodka. She's going to need something to clean the wound. After that, it's into Car 11, where Anna and Reggie stop at the door to his room.

"Do you have a sewing kit?" she asks Sal. "I need to stitch him up."

Sal nods. "I'll be right back."

Anna drags Reggie into his room. When she lowers him onto the bed, blood instantly starts to seep into the sheets. By then, Sal is back, thrusting a tin sewing kit into her hands. Anna opens it, seeing needles, scissors, and several spools of thread. It's not ideal— the needles aren't sterilized, and the thread is a far cry from sutures—but it'll have to do.

"Go back to your room," she tells Sal. "Lock the door. Stay away from the windows."

Anna follows the same protocol in Reggie's room. In the bathroom, she washes her hands, threads the needle, and pours vodka over its tip. She then grabs a washcloth and returns to Reggie's side. Anna peels away the blood-soaked gauze, douses the washcloth with vodka, and starts cleaning the wound. The first touch brings an agonized gasp from Reggie.

"Give me that," he says, reaching for the bottle.

Anna hands it over, and he takes several long, sloppy gulps. Properly fortified, he carefully shifts onto his uninjured side, giving her better access to the wound. Anna stares at it, dumbfounded. Of all the ways she'd pictured the trip going—and the various scenarios she'd come up with were many—this wasn't one of them.

Reggie takes another swig of vodka. "Have you ever stitched someone up before?"

"Oh, I do it all the time."

Reggie drinks half a swallow more. "Then you already know that you start by pinching the skin together at one end and looping the thread through it at least twice before tying it off."

"Of course," Anna says, keeping up the ruse because it's easier for both of them to ignore the truth that she has no idea what she's doing. Despite the vodka, Reggie's body tenses when she pinches the bottom end of the cut as instructed and prepares to slide the needle through the skin. He nods for Anna to keep going, so she does, piercing both edges of flesh and pulling them together with the thread.

Reggie winces, takes another drink. "Other than stitching up strangers, what else do you do for fun?"

"Fun?" Anna says.

"Yeah, you know. Hobbies. Amusing yourself."

Anna, having looped the thread through the wound's edge three times, ties it off. "I know what fun is."

"Yet your answer tells me you don't have any."

"I go to the movies sometimes," Anna says, now working her way upward, slowly sewing the wound like it's a piece of mending. She tries to pretend that's exactly what she's doing. Mending a dress and not sewing up flesh, blood slick on her fingertips.

"That's it?" Reggie says through gritted teeth, also pretending that this is just an ordinary conversation and not an emergency procedure that might possibly save his life. "An occasional movie? What about musicals?"

The question catches Anna so off guard that her hand almost slips. "Musicals?"

"Come on, you've heard of them. People onstage singing and dancing. They're very popular."

"I'm sure they are," Anna says, now at the halfway point, the wound closing tighter with each subsequent pull of the thread. "I assume you're a fan."

"Love them," Reggie says, his voice taking on a dreamy tone. Anna guesses it's either from the vodka or blood loss. She prays it's the former. "Give me an interesting plot and some hummable tunes, and I'm in heaven. Once this is all over, you should let me take you to one."

Anna looks up from the half-stitched wound. "Are you asking me on a date as I'm giving you stitches?"

"Maybe," Reggie says, hitting the bottle once more. "It doesn't have to be a date. We could go as friends."

"Friends?"

"I guess you don't have much of those, either."

"I've been busy," Anna says quietly.

"Plotting vengeance."

"Yes," Anna says. "For the past year, every thought, every action, every damn minute has been spent preparing for this night. And now it's all gone to hell."

"It seems I've hit a nerve," Reggie says.

Anna gives the needle an overzealous tug, making sure Reggie can feel the spiraled thread tightening through his flesh. "And I can hit several," she says.

"I'm sorry," he says, his voice distant and shrinking by the second. "It's just such a sad way to go through life."

"What else should I have done?"

"I told you that earlier—let the authorities handle it."

"But these people destroyed my family," Anna says. "Not yours."

Reggie grows quiet. So much that Anna assumes he's passed out, either from the pain or the vodka. It's a surprise when, after a minute of silence, he speaks again, his voice a gruff whisper.

"My family was destroyed, too. When my father died."

A sense of guilt settles over Anna. Of course everyone has their losses that are just as painful. "What happened to him?" she asks.

"He was murdered."

Anna's hand stills. "I'm so sorry. Did they catch who did it?"

"No," Reggie says.

"Is that why you joined the FBI?"

Reggie turns his head to look at her through glazed eyes. "Yes. Because I don't want anyone to experience what my family did."

"You want justice," Anna says, finally understanding why he'd been so annoyed with her earlier. By taking matters into her own hands tonight, she denied him—and the many men like him—the chance to right a terrible wrong.

"I do," Reggie says, his voice so far away he might as well be in outer space.

Anna says nothing, focusing instead on finishing the stitch job with a triple loop at the opposite end of the gash. She ties it off and lets out a deep, shaky breath.

"All done," she says, although Reggie can't hear her, having fallen into a vodka-and-pain-induced slumber. Anna knows that's for the best. He needs rest. She only hopes he doesn't toss around in his sleep and break her makeshift stitches. To lessen the chances of that happening, she gently rolls him onto his back.

In the bathroom, she washes the blood from her hands, which tremble uncontrollably. A delayed reaction not just to all the stress of the past hour, but the hours preceding it, and the days preceding them, and the year preceding those.

All of it has taken a toll, as her appearance in the mirror above the sink can attest. Anna thinks she looks positively frightful. There's blood on her dress, her hair remains a windswept tangle, and stress and sleep deprivation have turned her face pale gray. Her exhaustion is underscored by bruise-black circles under her eyes, which give her a spectral appearance. Simultaneously haunting and haunted.

Exhaustion clings to her as she shushes out of the room. She knows she shouldn't. It's safer inside with Reggie. But she also knows she'll go mad if she doesn't escape the chaos, just for a minute. In the corridor, she drifts to the middle of the car and stares out the window. The snow outside has slowed. Anna can again see the sky as it begins to fade from black to the hazy gray of dawn.

Just a few more hours, she tells herself. Then this will all be over.

If any of them live that long.

Every rattle of the train and every clatter of the wheels has her convinced Judd is right behind her, knife raised, ready to slash. It doesn't help that the lights have started to flicker again. While Anna doesn't know if it's just this car or the entire train, she doesn't like it. The blinking lights seem to her like a portent of something bad—a feeling that gets worse when they give up the ghost and flash out entirely.

Plunged into darkness, Anna's about to return to Reggie's room when a man appears in the doorway at the back of the car. What little Anna can see of him is bathed in the tepid light coming through the window. The meager glow falls in a slant across his face.

As he gets closer, Anna can make out only individual features. A nose. An eye. Half of a mouth. Just enough for her to piece together the man's identity. Shock vibrates through Anna like she's a bell that's just been struck.

"Tommy?" she says.

She's proven right when her brother—her thought-to-be-dead brother—steps into a patch of predawn light. Anna doesn't know whether to laugh or cry or scream, especially when Tommy says, "It's really me, Annie. Gosh, I've missed you."

He flashes that matinee-idol smile she had loved so much, opening his mouth wide to reveal two rows of rotting teeth and blood trickling between them. He lurches closer and Anna sees that his body isn't a body at all. Just a mass of blood and bone and sinew.

When Tommy tries to hug her, Anna finally knows how to react.

She screams.

THIRTY-EIGHT

"ANNIE?"

Anna jolts awake, unaware of where she is, why she's there, what's happening to her. A storm-cloud haze crowds the edge of her vision, making everything blurry and indistinct. She's hit with a memory from several years earlier. She and Aunt Retta turning on the newfangled television they'd just purchased, trying to make out images through the black-and-white fuzz. That's what this feels like.

Through the buzzing flicker, she sees a man kneeling beside her.

Not Tommy.

Dante.

"What happened?" Anna says.

"You tell me. I just found you lying here."

Anna looks around, seeing the fully lit corridor of Car 11. "The lights. They started blinking on and off and then went out."

"They've been on the whole time," Dante says.

"Really?"

"I think you must have fainted."

"But what I saw, it seemed so real."

"What else did you see?"

"Nothing," Anna says, choosing the lie over telling Dante that she swore she saw her mutilated brother. Again. "I think I'm just tired."

An understatement. Not counting her nightmare in the observation car, it's been twenty-four hours since she last slept. When she adds in fear and stress, Anna thinks it's a wonder she can remain conscious.

"When did you last eat?" Dante says.

The last thing she can remember is forcing down some toast and coffee at breakfast. After that she was too anxious to eat. Once she and Seamus boarded the Phoenix, food was the furthest thing from her mind.

"Twenty hours ago."

Dante lets out a low whistle. "See? I knew you should have had a sandwich. Food is fuel. That's why I went back and got mine."

"After we gathered everyone in the observation car?"

"Yeah," Dante says. "I went back to the galley, grabbed what was left of my sandwich, and took it to my room."

Anna sighs. It was Dante this whole time. Not Judd or her tired mind conjuring a stranger or Tommy back from the dead. Yet Anna had so wanted it to be Tommy. She realizes that now.

The old Tommy.

The brother who'd loved her so much and whom she had adored in return.

Anna wanted to see him and hug him and hear his voice so much that, now that it's confirmed it wasn't him, she's left with a shimmering feeling she can't quite identify. An inchoate ache.

"I miss him," she says as tears sting her eyes. "I miss Tommy. I miss my parents."

And she misses the person she used to be.

When her family died, Anna's world shrank to practically

nothing. Life with Aunt Retta was as isolated as could be. They went nowhere, saw no one. When her aunt died, Anna spent all her time plotting and planning, not because she wanted to do it, but because she felt like she had to. That she'd be a terrible daughter and sister if she didn't try to enact some form of vengeance.

But it's come at great cost. Not just financially but emotionally. She's denied herself so many of the things other women her age get to experience. Happiness. Fun. And, yes, love. Reggie was right. It is a sad way to go through life.

The realization shakes loose one of the tears, which rolls down Anna's face. Dante wipes it away, his touch a gentle caress. When he pulls Anna to his chest, she goes willingly, longing for some small moment of comfort in an otherwise brutal night.

Dante looks at her, lowering his mouth to hers, attempting a kiss. Anna remembers how good it felt to be kissed by Dante. She recalls it so well that it feels like they've traveled a dozen years into the past. That she's sixteen and he's eighteen and her family is still alive and so they're kissing beneath the willow on the edge of her childhood yard because they know they won't be seen there.

Unable to resist the pull of the past any longer, Anna lifts her face to meet his. But before she can reach Dante and fall under the spell of his kiss, she becomes aware of someone else in the corridor.

Seamus.

He looks at them, half-dazed. Like he's just seen a ghost. The only thing that snaps him out of it is the sight of Anna and Dante pressed together.

"What's going on here?" he says.

Anna backs away from Dante. "I was looking for you."

"And I was searching the back of the train," Seamus says, finally noticing her bedraggled state. "What happened?"

"She fainted," Dante says.

"After I stitched up Agent Davis," Anna adds. "Judd stabbed him."

"He did?" Seamus says. "Where?"

"The galley."

Dante goes wide-eyed. "When?"

Anna's no longer sure. Time has gotten blurrier the longer the voyage goes on. It could have been an hour ago or it could have been mere minutes. Anna decides to split the difference. "A half hour ago."

"I don't think that's possible," Seamus says.

"Why not?"

Seamus grabs her by the hand and pulls her away. Anna, in turn, reaches for Dante. He clasps her hand, his palm warm, his grip tight. They move first into Car 12 and then Car 13, with Anna caught between the two men, pulled along by one, pulling the other. In this awkward manner, they head to the middle of the corridor. There, Seamus gestures to the open door of Room B.

Edith's room.

"That's why not," Seamus says.

Anna lets go of both men and enters the room, tiptoeing deeper inside until she sees what he's referring to.

There, crammed into the tiny bathroom, is the corpse of Judd Dodge.

5 A.M.
___

THREE HOURS
TO CHICAGO

THIRTY-NINE

"IS THIS SOME kind of sick joke?" Dante says, blinking in disbelief at the body in front of them.

"If it is, I didn't do it," Seamus says.

"I wasn't accusing you."

Seamus gives a disdainful sniff. "Sounded like you were to me."

Anna tunes out the bickering and steps into the bathroom, standing over Judd Dodge. He's slumped across the toilet seat, one arm trapped beneath his head, the hand dangling limply. The other arm is flopped in front of him, fingertips scraping the floor. His legs are curled beneath him, bent like a contortionist. An undignified pose for a man who abandoned all sense of dignity a dozen years ago.

"Maybe he's been dead the entire time," Dante suggests. "And someone moved the body?"

"Or maybe he's still alive," Anna says, lowering herself until her gaze is level with Judd's wide-open eyes. Staring into them, she looks for a flicker of life. There's nothing. His pupils are empty pools.

Just to make sure, she presses two fingers against his neck, almost recoiling at the sensation. Although his skin still retains some warmth, there's no pulse behind it.

"Nothing," she announces.

"So he's really dead?" Seamus says.

"Yes, but for how long? Just because he's dead now doesn't mean he was earlier."

Anna continues to study the body, convinced she's missing something. Once again, she replays Judd's presumed last moments in her head. Yawning, checking the time, *not* drinking. Revisiting those seconds makes something click in her brain.

She shoves a hand into Judd's coat pocket, finding his watch. Opening the lid, she takes a long, close look. There, gathered in the rim of the watch face, are several small crystals of powder. She leans in, sniffs, detects the same sharp, chemical smell she'd noticed both in Judd's martini glass and the box of rat poison in the galley.

"It's poison," she says.

"I'll be damned," Seamus says. "You think he killed himself?"

"Not quite."

Anna tilts her head until she's face-to-face with Judd's body. Then she pulls down his bottom jaw and peers into his gaping mouth.

"What the hell are you doing?" Dante says, aghast.

Ignoring him, Anna shoves the same fingers she'd earlier held against Judd's neck into his mouth. This time, she *does* recoil. Her stomach enacts a nauseated somersault as she wills herself to probe the inside of Judd's mouth. His teeth are covered in a warm, sticky slime that gathers on her fingertips, and each touch of his gums sends a foul stench wafting from between his lips.

It is, Anna realizes, the smell of death.

Closing her watery eyes and taking short, quick breaths through her nose, she continues to run her fingers along Judd's teeth until at last she finds a sliver of something wedged between his upper molars.

Getting it out requires Anna to shove most of her hand into

Judd's mouth. She does—slowly—feeling a shudder of revulsion as his wormlike lips slide over her knuckles. Working blind, she pinches the sliver between her fingernails and tugs it loose.

Anna holds the sliver up to the light, making sure Seamus and Dante can also see. It's a shard of thin plastic, still dripping saliva. Anna holds it to the light, noticing how it's transparent and tinted pink.

"What is that?" Seamus says.

"I think it's Saran wrap," Anna says, remembering how she saw some in the galley, along with other ingredients that, when combined, could create the blood-flecked foam that has bubbled over Judd's lips. Red food coloring. Vinegar and baking soda.

Quickly, she explains how Judd could have kept small amounts of all three in individual bits of plastic wrap, creating makeshift capsules that he popped into his mouth. One strong bite would break the Saran wrap and mix the ingredients, creating the bloody-looking foam that gave the appearance he'd been poisoned. To complete the illusion, he spiked his drink with the rat poison hidden inside his watch.

"Then how did he really die?" Dante says.

"And when?" Anna adds, thinking about Reggie currently recovering two cars away after being stabbed by Judd. Based on the time of the attack and the residual warmth on Judd's skin, she concludes that he died within the past half hour.

All three of them crowd the bathroom doorway, searching for something that points to the manner of death. Yes, there's still a smear of bloody foam on the corner of his mouth, but Anna knows that's not real. Just one of the illusions Judd had been so fond of. She lets her gaze slide away from his mouth and down to the side of his neck.

"There," she says, pointing to a crimson patch of skin inches below his ear. "He was strangled."

Anna backs away from the bathroom door, her mind racing as the situation she'd thought she understood shifts into something heretofore inconceivable. To make sense of it all, she goes through what she knows. The certainties of the night, of which there are few.

She's certain, for instance, that Judd faked his own death. The spit-slicked bit of plastic wrap in her hand proves it.

The part that remains unclear is why. For the past hour, she'd become convinced it was so he could murder his co-conspirators one by one, getting rid of those who might implicate him while in the process framing her for their deaths.

But what if that wasn't his true goal?

And what if that wasn't what really happened?

Anna has no idea how long Judd was missing from his room, back when they all assumed he was dead. No one thought to look in on him until she realized he hadn't sipped his martini, giving him plenty of time to sneak through the train and start murdering people.

While it's easy to picture him killing Edith, Herb's murder is less plausible. Judd's clothes look clean and completely dry. If he had indeed slit Herb's throat and escaped out the window into a blizzard, there'd likely be both blood spatter and wetness from the snow.

Then there's the fact that it's unclear how long Judd's been dead. Anna's no doctor, so she could be wrong about that. Yes, it's likely that in the past hour or so, someone discovered his hiding spot and murdered him. But it's equally possible that he's been dead since long before that—including while Herb Pulaski was still alive.

If that's the case, then someone else knew all along that Judd was alive.

Because they'd been in on it with him.

Anna bolts from the room, stumbling into the corridor and backing against the window on the other side. All this time, she'd assumed only one killer was at work aboard the train. A single, silent entity trying to foil her attempt to bring them to justice by picking people off one by one. Now she understands the truth.

There's a second killer on the train.

And Anna thinks she knows who it is.

FORTY

SEAMUS REMAINS INSIDE Room B, which now suddenly contains two bodies. Hovering by the door to the bathroom, he watches Anna start off down the car. He chases after her, catching up in three long strides and tugging her to a halt.

"Where are you going?"

"To see Sal and Lapsford," Anna says. "Because one of them is the killer."

Seamus turns Anna around to face him. "Let's just think about this for a second."

"We don't have that much time. Look who's been targeted so far. Edith. Herb. Judd himself. He was working with someone to take the others out. I suspect he then planned to kill them last. But whoever it is got to him first."

"Then explain what happened to Agent Davis," Seamus says. "You said Judd just tried to kill him in the galley."

Anna edges down the corridor, forcing Seamus to follow along. "That's what he thought, but it might not have been Judd. And since you and Dante were back here, that leaves only two people. Sal and Lapsford."

Even though Reggie Davis has nothing to do with what happened twelve years ago, Seamus understands why someone would target him. He's with the FBI. Of course they'd go after the person who plans to arrest them the moment they reach Chicago.

"Which one do you think did it?" Seamus says.

"Lapsford."

That's Seamus's guess, too. Throughout the whole journey, he's been the most vocal about getting off the train. He even faked having a heart attack to do it. Then there's the fact that Lapsford was the only one seemingly uninterested in searching for Judd. While Seamus chalked it up to a selfish act from an equally selfish man, maybe the real reason Lapsford wasn't concerned is that he already knew Judd was dead.

"Let's say you're right," Seamus says. "What's your plan? If he knows you're on to him, he might do the same thing he did to Reggie."

"I'll pretend to check in on them. Ask a few questions, see if I can trip him up."

"I'll go with you."

"No," Anna says. "That'll make him suspicious. Let me do it alone. I'll yell if I need you."

"What if you can't?"

Anna pats the pocket of the jacket she's wearing. Reggie's jacket, Seamus realizes. "I assume you also have his gun."

"Of course," she says.

Seamus says no more. He's fully aware that Anna knows how to use one. He taught her himself.

"Be careful," he says as she sets off for the preceding car. When she's gone, he turns to Dante, still hovering on the edges of the room. "Roll up your sleeves. It's time to move Judd's corpse back to his room. Again."

The second time proves easier than the first, if only because there's less distance to travel. Instead of several cars, they only need to carry him to the next room. As they do, Seamus thinks about the first time they hauled Judd's body to his room, wondering how he missed all the signs that he was still alive. Surely he should have noticed Judd breathing, felt a pulse, or seen some form of movement. But Judd dead feels as lifeless and heavy as he did when he was merely playing dead.

Seamus's hands start to tremble as they lower the body onto the bed in Room C. The tremor is so bad that he's forced to let go early, making the corpse land with an ungainly flop.

"Everything okay?" Dante says.

Seamus grabs the sheet and covers the body. "Yeah. Just a hand cramp."

But it's more than that. To keep Dante from seeing his shaking hands, he shoves them into his pockets and leaves the room. His destination is the observation car, where he can have a moment alone. After the past hour, he needs it.

Outside, the sky has lightened to a muddy gray. Not yet night, not yet morning, but still storming. Surrounded by the observation car's windows, Seamus feels like he's trapped inside a snow globe. An unappealing thought that nonetheless summons a long-forgotten memory of being lost in a blizzard on his way home from school.

He was six or so when it happened. The whiteout conditions made everything unrecognizable, turning familiar streets into strangers. One wrong turn led to another and soon he was stumbling through knee-high snow with no idea where he was. The whole time he only got colder and more panicked while the snow fell harder and faster. Just when he was about to give up and let the storm take him, a figure appeared through the wintry haze.

His brother, Sean.

Seamus, hungry, shivering, and borderline hypothermic, ran to him. "I thought I was going to be lost forever!" he cried.

"You'll never be lost as long as I'm around," Sean said.

It wasn't a lie. When his brother was alive, Seamus always knew he'd be found. But now Sean's gone and Seamus feels forever lost.

He yanks his hands from his pockets. The tremor's gotten worse.

Seamus retrieves the pillbox, which he's carried with him all night. Now it shakes in his hand so much that the remaining five pills inside rattle together. Seamus lifts the lid and stares at them. He didn't plan on using another one. Not this soon. But his hands, moving as if they have minds of their own, insist on it.

As Seamus plucks a single pill from the box, he hears Anna calling his name. Faint and far away at first, it grows louder with each passing second. Seamus drops the pill back into the box, which is returned to his pocket. Then he's out of the observation car and quickly moving through the train.

He meets Anna at the front of Car 13. She's in a full-fledged panic, grabbing his arm and dragging him forward. "It's Lapsford," she says. "He's having a heart attack."

Seamus hesitates. "For real this time?"

"I think so."

Anna keeps tugging, eventually getting him into the previous car. Dante is already there, helping Sal prop Lapsford up as they guide him back to his room. Despite the frenzy, Seamus assumes Lapsford is again faking illness. One last desperate attempt to stop the train now that Chicago is less than three hours away.

Seamus follows them into the room. "Get him onto the bed."

This proves more difficult than expected. The others crowd around Lapsford, all jostling limbs and bumping elbows. It doesn't help that Lapsford is an unruly patient, writhing when he should be lying still, fighting them off instead of letting them help. After heaving him onto the bed, they face their next big task—figuring out what to do next.

Lapsford opens and closes his mouth like a fish on dry land, gasping for air. The effort turns his face beet red, making Seamus fear he has only minutes, if not seconds, before he passes out.

"Tell me what's wrong," he demands.

Lapsford clutches his chest. "My heart."

With Anna, Sal, and Dante huddled around him, Seamus takes Lapsford's wrist and checks his pulse. It taps out like Morse code, irregular and unintelligible. Anna was right. This is real.

"What do we do?" she says, panicked.

Seamus pulls the pillbox from his jacket and retrieves one of the chalky white tablets. He holds it out to Anna with a trembling hand. "Give him this."

Anna eyes the pill with suspicion.

"It's a muscle relaxant," Seamus says, reading her mind. "It might slow his heartbeat enough to keep him alive until we reach Chicago."

When Anna takes the pill, Seamus notices the way Lapsford eyes its transfer from his fingers to hers. He licks his lips and swallows, as if rehearsing how to get the pill down his throat as fast as possible.

Lapsford, Seamus understands, *wants* it.

Anna knows it, too, and dangles the pill over Lapsford's mouth, which yawns open.

"Can you talk?" she says.

Lapsford's voice is a desperate rasp. "Yes."

"Then tell me why you did it. Was it just for the money?"

Lapsford stares at the pill, eyes wide and begging. Anna pulls it farther away from his mouth.

"Answer me," she says. "Did you destroy my family just for the money?"

Seamus looks across the bed to her, startled. "Jesus, Anna. Just give it to him."

"Not before he answers," she says.

"Yes," Lapsford hisses.

Anna keeps the pill away from his mouth, silently taunting him with it. "Do you ever think about my family? Do you think about what you did to them?"

Lapsford, no longer able to speak, gives the smallest of nods.

"Anna," Seamus says. "The man is *dying*. Give him the pill."

"One more minute."

"He doesn't have that long!"

To Seamus, Lapsford seems to be fading fast. His breathing has shallowed to nothingness, and his eyes go dim. The last flicker of a candle before it goes out.

"What about those soldiers who died?" Anna quickly says. "Men like Seamus's brother. Do you think of them?"

This time, Seamus waits for an answer. He watches, breathless himself, as Lapsford nods almost imperceptibly. The faint motion releases an anger that Seamus tries hard to keep hidden. Lapsford helped plan the murder of his brother. And Sal, standing in a corner of the room wringing her hands, then helped to cover it up. In that moment, Seamus would kill them both if he knew he could get away with it.

Since he can't, Anna's plan is the next best option.

Making them suffer.

For the rest of their days.

But Lapsford's suffering might be at an end. He can no longer seem to move his head. His breath, if it exists at all, is undetectable. The only reason Seamus knows he remains alive is that his pupils continue to zero in on the pill still pinched between Anna's fingers.

"I bet you try hard not to think about them," she tells Lapsford. "But they force their way into your mind. All those boys you decided to sacrifice. I think they haunt your nightmares. Just like you're haunted by the fear that everyone is going to find out what horrible things you've done. And, trust me, everyone *will* find out. Even if you die a minute from now, I'll make sure they know."

It might be less than a minute, Seamus thinks. Sensing there's no time left, he reaches out and snatches the pill from Anna's fingers. He then shoves it into Lapsford's gaping mouth, his fingers sliding over his tongue as it's pushed to the back of his throat. There's a glass of water by the bed, which Seamus brings to Lapsford's lips and tips back.

A violent, choking cough rattles through Lapsford. For a moment, Seamus thinks it's too late and that the man is in the throes of death. He braces himself for that sad, final breath. But soon the coughing and rattling cease. They're followed by a disquieting pause in which Seamus is visited by warring emotions. He wants Lapsford to live and he wants him to die and he hates himself for feeling both of those things.

Lapsford begins to breathe again, the sound ending the fraught silence. When Lapsford looks at Seamus, he sees a light in the other man's eyes that hadn't been present mere seconds before. Seamus checks Lapsford's pulse again, feeling it greatly calmed. The pill seems to be working. Whether that's a good or bad thing remains unclear. Especially once Lapsford finds his voice again.

"You should have let me die," he murmurs.

FORTY-ONE

WHEN IT BECOMES clear that Lapsford will live for at least another hour, Anna backs away from the bed. She feels the others watching as she stands. Sal and Dante and Seamus, whose gaze is particularly unreadable.

In Car 11, Anna takes a quick look inside Reggie's room, finding him fast asleep. The lucky bastard. Anna's been awake so long her whole body aches, including her head.

Inside her own room, she collapses on the bed and stares up at the ceiling. Even if she did try to sleep, she knows it won't happen. She remains too upset by the stress of stitching up Reggie, Judd's murder, and the situation with Lapsford.

"Do you want to talk about what just happened back there?" Seamus says as he enters her room and drops into the chair by the window.

Anna keeps her eyes on the ceiling. "I needed answers."

"No, you needed to save him. The answers you could have gotten later."

"Not if he was dead," Anna says.

"I just wish you had talked to me about it first. We can't keep things from each other."

Anna props herself up on her elbows. "Like why you're carrying around a stash of muscle relaxants?"

"That's different," Seamus says.

"Is it? A man was poisoned—"

"He faked being poisoned."

"We didn't know that at the time," Anna says. "Yet you didn't think to mention how you were carrying around a box of mysterious pills."

"Because it doesn't concern you."

Anna scoots forward until she's sitting on the edge of the bed. "But it does. If it's on this train, it concerns me. Now tell me, why do you have them?"

"They were prescribed to me," Seamus says, the usual boom of his voice replaced by something so vulnerable, so small.

"Why?"

"Because I have an affliction." Seamus lets out a bitter chuckle, as if he finds the word ridiculous.

"What kind of affliction?"

"My nerves," Seamus says. "My brain has trouble controlling them, so I get tremors. And occasional spasms. And sometimes, I just can't move the way I want to. It's like I'm being grabbed by an invisible force, and it's shaking me. The pills numb my nerves just enough to give me back control. But only for a little bit."

Anna thinks about the way his hands shook as he gave her the pill. Looking back on it, there must have been a hundred instances in which she'd noticed a tremor but thought nothing of it.

"How long has this been going on?"

"A few years."

Seamus says it with such forced nonchalance that Anna suspects it's been longer. She edges closer to him, a newfound concern simmering in the pit of her stomach. "So, before we met?"

"Yeah."

"After this, we'll find you a doctor. A good one."

Seamus levels his gaze at her. "With what money?"

"That doesn't matter. We'll find the money. And then we'll get you the best doctor and he'll be able to cure you."

"There is no cure."

"But there has to be," Anna says.

"You think I haven't looked? I've been to all the doctors, Anna. I've tried all the treatments. Some of them helped, for a little while, at least, but then soon I'm right back to where I was." Seamus also moves to the edge of his seat, reaching a hand out to Anna. She takes it, alarmed by the way it trembles between both of hers. "That's why, when your aunt wrote to me, I wrote back. And that's why it was important for us to do this now. I'm running out of time to bring justice to the people who killed my brother."

"Of course there's time," Anna says.

Seamus lets out a long, frustrated sigh. "You don't understand."

"But I do! Yes, you're sick—"

"Anna, I'm dying."

The rest of what Anna intended to say dries up, leaving her momentarily speechless.

"The last doctor I saw gave me five years at the most," Seamus says. "Probably less. Soon the pills won't be enough to stop it. I'll need help walking. Then I'll be in a wheelchair. Then it's just a matter of time before the illness takes over completely." Seamus turns to gaze out the window. The sun has cracked the horizon, painting his face in shades of pink and gold. "I meant it when I told you my future is just a swath of black. It's the truth, Anna. There is no future for me. Not much of one."

Tears well up in Anna's eyes. She quickly wipes them away, trying to be strong for Seamus's sake. But it's hard to be strong in the face of so much loss. Her brother. Her parents. Aunt Retta. She can't lose Seamus, too.

"I'm not going to give up," she says. "And I'm not going to leave your side."

Seamus shakes his head. "You say that now—"

"Because I mean it. We're bound together by what happened to our brothers. And that bond will remain long after this trip ends."

Seamus stands, lifts Anna off the bed, and pulls her to him. When he kisses her, the act is so sudden and unexpected that it makes Anna seize up. Feeling her tense, Seamus lets go.

"I'm sorry," he says, backing away.

"Don't be," Anna says. In truth, she's the one who's sorry. She wishes she could bring herself to reciprocate Seamus's feelings. But he was right after their lone, misguided night together. It's all too sad. "I wish—"

Seamus stops her with a raised hand. "Don't say anything more. Please."

Anna nods and returns to the edge of the bed, giving Seamus the space to regain his composure. He takes a deep breath and stretches, his face emotionless.

"I should check on our patients," he says before dipping a hand into his uniform pocket.

Anna watches his hand move inside the pocket, the fabric bulging then retracting. Seamus checks his other pocket before moving on to the one on the inside of his jacket. Soon he's patting himself down like he's both cop and criminal.

"What's wrong?" Anna asks.

"My gun," Seamus says. "It's gone."

Anna bolts from the bed, instantly on alert. "Do you think it fell out of your pocket?"

"I don't know," Seamus says.

"When was the last time you noticed it?"

He continues to pat his pockets, as if it's possible he's mistaken and the gun isn't really gone. "An hour ago. When we were all in the lounge after finding out Judd really wasn't dead."

"So it could be anywhere," Anna says.

"Or with anyone," Seamus adds. "We need to check the lounge."

They bolt from the room, spilling into the corridor of Car 11 before rushing to the first-class lounge. Inside, Seamus immediately begins overturning chairs and cocktail tables, desperately searching for his missing revolver. Anna joins him, crawling across the floor on her hands and knees.

"Keep looking," Seamus says as she reaches the piano. "I'm going to check the observation car."

He hurries out of the lounge, leaving Anna to continue the search on her own. She continues along the floor for thirty more seconds before confirming there's no gun here. The only place left to look is the bar. She climbs to her feet, about to approach it, when her attention is caught by strange sounds in the next car.

A bang.

A shatter.

Another bang.

Hearing them, Anna goes statue-still. The mirrored shelves behind the bar capture her motionless reflection, splitting and distorting her shocked face into dozens of pieces. Wide eyes. Opened mouths. Flared nostrils. Anna stares at those broken bits of herself as she slowly identifies the noises she'd just heard.

They were gunshots.

Two of them.

FORTY-TWO

LEAVING THE LOUNGE, Anna stares down the empty corridor of Car 11, amazed by how long it appears. It stretches before her, seemingly endless, making her feel like a child again. So tiny, and the Philadelphia Phoenix impossibly huge.

Anna runs through the car, although to her the pace feels glacial. A long, slow slog to the other end in which she becomes aware of everything around her. The rocking of the train. The hum-rattle of the wheels. The world outside the window, passing in a blur.

At the last room of the car, she peers through the open door and spots Reggie on his feet, clutching his side. When their eyes meet, Anna shakes her head, silently answering the question in Reggie's gaze.

No, I don't know what's happening.

He takes an unsteady step toward the door and Anna offers another head shake, its message clear. *Stay here. Stay safe.*

She continues into Car 12, almost colliding with Seamus as he hovers just beyond the door. "Stay back," he says.

Anna doesn't.

She can't.

Not when she sees Dante at the other end of the car. Another person still present and accounted for.

"Lapsford?" Anna says.

Slowly, nervously, Dante slips through the open door of Lapsford's room. He returns a second later, visibly shaken. "He's alive."

A knot of fear forms in the pit of Anna's stomach, getting tighter when she looks to the door of Sal's room. It sits ajar, creaking in time to the rocking of the train.

Anna surges to the door, even as Seamus yells for her to stop. "Anna, wait!"

She ignores him and gives the door a push. It swings open, agonizingly slow, revealing a sliver of room that widens into a full view. The first thing Anna sees is Seamus's revolver. It sits in the middle of the floor, bathed in muted light coming through the window.

That's where Anna's eye is drawn next, seeing that the glass has been blown out, likely by the first bullet. She heard the shatter that accompanied the initial gunshot. Now only a few shards cling to the window frame, sharp and glinting. Wind howls through the empty space, whipping the curtains as snow gusts across the room.

Sitting in the swivel chair in front of the blown-out window is Sal. Silhouetted by the gray light of dawn, she looks like a shadow. One somehow discarded by its owner, so it now sits limp and motionless. Because of the way Sal's situated in the chair—head thrown back, closed eyes aimed at the ceiling—Anna is forced to take a step into the room to fully make out her face.

It's expressionless. A blank.

The last thing Anna sees is the red-black hole in the center of Sal's forehead. A single rivulet of crimson rolls down the bridge of her nose.

Looking down at Sal, Anna feels nothing. A surprise. She

thought some kind of emotion would roar forth. It turns out she's too numb for that now. Instead, she stands there, speechless, only vaguely aware of Seamus swooping into the room behind her. He picks his gun up off the floor, shoves it into his jacket pocket, then takes a sheet from the bed.

"No," Anna says, her voice hard as steel. "I'll do it."

Seamus hands her the sheet and Anna, quietly and reverently, drapes it over Sal's body. She leaves the room without another word, waiting until Seamus closes the door behind them before whirling around to face Dante.

"You," she says, the word a rasp that scrapes the back of her throat. "It was you."

"Me? I didn't do anything."

Anna approaches him, trembling and rage filled. "Quit lying to me! You're the only person here who could have done it. Reggie's got a stab wound in his stomach and Lapsford's heart is barely beating."

"What about him?" Dante says, pointing to Seamus at the other end of the corridor.

"He was with me."

"I didn't do anything wrong, Annie. I swear."

"You were working with Judd," Anna says. "You knew he wasn't dead. The two of you planned this whole thing out. I should've seen it the moment you asked him to pick his poison."

"I didn't mean anything by it. It's just an innocent phrase."

"Normally, yes. But in this instance, it was a signal to Judd to get ready to fake his own death. Then you started to kill the others one by one."

Dante takes a stumbling backward step, its awkwardness standing in stark contrast to the easy walk Anna witnessed earlier in the night. That swift glide through the corridors had made her think it was Tommy. A ridiculous notion in hindsight, but one Anna longed to believe.

"You were roaming the train," she tells Dante now, hurling the accusation at him. "Right before Edith died. You're the one who killed her. You're the one who snuck into my room and cut the cord to the drapes."

Anna touches the bodice of her dress, absently seeking comfort in the silver locomotive pin that had once belonged to her father. It takes a second for her to remember it's no longer there. Seamus now has the pin, after it was found on the floor of Herb Pulaski's room.

"You're also the one who took my pin," she says. "When we were in the lounge after Herb attacked me. You took it and planted it in Herb's room. You and Judd were trying to frame me. But then Judd left his room, proving he wasn't dead. So you decided to kill him. Did you do that before or after you stabbed Reggie?"

Dante stands in the middle of the corridor, swaying from shock. "How could I have done that? Sal and Lapsford were in the middle cars. They would have seen me pass."

"Not if you used a window," Anna says. "Which we know you can. It's how you escaped Herb's room after you slit his throat."

"Annie, I have no idea what you're talking about."

"I thought you were helping me," Anna says. "I thought you were different from your father."

"I am!" Dante stares at her, a dark, desperate look in his eyes. "I don't know what's going on, but I think we all need to calm down and just talk about it."

"We're done talking. I was so stupid to trust you."

"Please, Annie. Please just hear me out."

Dante tries to come toward her but is blocked by Seamus.

"She doesn't want that," he says, shoving Dante toward the open door to his room. Dante pushes back, but it's not an even match. Seamus is clearly the stronger of the two. The best Dante can manage is to nudge him back a step.

"I didn't do anything wrong!" Dante shouts from the other end of the car before ramming into Seamus again. All it takes is a few grunting shoves for Seamus to get Dante to the door of his room.

"You're going to get inside and stay there until we reach Chicago."

"What if I refuse?" Dante says.

"Then I'll shoot you."

Dante raises his hands and allows Seamus to back him across the threshold to his room. Anna follows them inside, visibly furious.

"Did your father send you?" she says. "Is that why you're here?"

"No! Of course not." Dante, still moving backward deeper into the room, reaches the chair by the window. When it hits the backs of his legs, he drops into it. "I have nothing to do with this and I have nothing to do with him."

"You still work for him."

"Only because I have no other choice," Dante says. "Believe me, if I could get out from under his thumb, I would."

Anna sighs. "I wish I could believe you. It would make this betrayal hurt less."

"What should we do with him?" Seamus asks.

"Tie him to the chair," Anna says. "Then we close the door and stand guard outside until we reach Chicago."

With trembling hands, Seamus undoes his necktie, sliding it free of his collar. He then leans forward and removes Dante's tie in a few rough, shaky tugs. Holding it out to Anna, he says, "Help me with this."

Anna takes the tie and approaches the chair. As Seamus lashes Dante's left wrist to the arm of the chair, Anna does the same with his right, avoiding eye contact.

"Annie, you don't need to do this," Dante whispers in her ear. "This is all a huge misunderstanding. You know me. You know I would never kill anyone."

Anna makes one more loop of the tie, topping it off with the tightest knot she can muster.

"That's the thing, Dante," she says. "I don't think I ever really knew you at all."

She turns and exits the room, refusing to look back, even as Dante continues to shout.

"Annie, please! Don't leave me like this!"

In the hallway, Anna looks to the window, surveying the snow-covered landscape passing outside the train. The fields, forests, and small towns in the distance look peaceful in the brightening dawn. A far cry from the chaos of the Philadelphia Phoenix.

Behind her, Seamus exits Dante's room and closes the door before joining her at the window.

"Here to say I told you so?" Anna says.

"No. I'm here to say I'm sorry. I know how hard this must be for you."

"You have no idea."

"Is there anything I can do?" Seamus says.

"Yes. Leave me alone. Just for a little bit."

Anna walks away, hurrying toward the back of the train, glancing over her shoulder to make sure certain Seamus isn't following her. In the observation car, she drops into the nearest seat. Only then do all the emotions she's kept at bay for the past hour rise to the surface. The grief. The fear. The guilt. All of them swirl around her in a churning flood. And Anna—too tired to fight them— allows herself to drown.

FORTY-THREE

SHE CRIES FOR exactly five minutes.

There isn't time for more.

Not when the real killer is still running free on the train.

Anna doesn't think Dante had anything to do with the murders. Everything regarding that, from her emphatic accusation to restraining him in his room, was just for show—and his own safety. Too many people have died or been hurt on this journey. Anna hopes forcing Dante into his room will help him avoid a similar fate.

As for the true killer, Anna assumes he'll be making a move very shortly. So she dries her tears and leaves the observation car, her body humming with anxiety and second thoughts. What if she made a mistake? What if she's wrong?

She assures herself that she's not.

She can't be.

Anna moves quickly through Car 13, unnerved by the silence. It's a potent reminder than only the dead inhabit this section of the train. She tries not to picture them as she passes their doors. It's useless. The lifeless faces of Judd, Edith, and Herb are all she sees.

It's just as quiet in Car 12, even though she knows this one is

still home to the living. The doors to Sal's and Dante's rooms remain closed, with Lapsford's door about to join them. Anna stops
at the back of the car, watching the once-open door now slowly
and quietly close. Someone has just entered and doesn't want anyone else to know.

Her timing, for better or worse, is perfect.

The moment the door is completely shut, Anna flies down the
hall, needing to hear what's happening inside the room. But she
can't press her ear to the door, no matter how much she wants to. It
could open at any moment, exposing her presence. She needs to
listen in secret, in a spot where she won't be discovered.

And the closest place to do that is the one she least wants to enter.

Sal's room.

Anna cracks open the door and slips inside, vowing not to look
at Sal's sheet-covered form because she has no idea how she'll react
if she gazes at it for even a second. Still, she comes close to looking.
A half glance Sal's way. An almost glance. Anna stops herself
when she sees the edge of the sheet covering her.

Facing the other way, she presses her ear to the wall between
this room and the one next door. Through it, she hears Lapsford's
familiar bellow.

"What are *you* doing here?"

Anna freezes, listening, waiting for a response that never arrives.

Lapsford speaks again. "Answer me, dammit!"

This time, Anna doesn't try to hear a reply. She knows there
won't be one. Because the other person in Lapsford's room isn't
there to talk.

They're there to kill him.

Just as she expected.

Catch them in the act. That's what Reggie told her had to
be done.

Now she's about to do exactly that.

Anna bursts out of Sal's room and into Lapsford's, not thinking about the danger lying in wait there. All she can think about is Tommy and her parents and how she needs to make sure at least one of the people who took them from her is brought to justice. If she can do that, even if it means dying herself, it will be worth it.

It's dark inside Lapsford's room. The curtains have been drawn across the windows and the lights turned off. The only things Anna can see as she moves deeper inside are the shadow-obscured body of Lapsford on the bed and an equally inscrutable person standing in front of it.

A man, Anna realizes. One with a pillow in his hands, which he presses over Lapsford's face.

Anna slams into him, sending them both tumbling to the floor.

She hits it first—a hard landing that shoots pain through her left arm and shoulder. More pain follows as the man lands on top of her. Momentarily crushed under his weight, Anna sees nothing but floor and carpet and the shadow under the bed. A fathomless darkness.

Then the man rolls off her and stands, allowing Anna a full view of the face she most expected to see—and most hoped it wouldn't be.

"I'm sorry," Seamus says, bending toward her and offering his hand. "You were never supposed to know."

6 A.M.

TWO HOURS
TO CHICAGO

FORTY-FOUR

ANNA KNEW.

Not all night.

Just recently.

When she realized Judd had been murdered, she suspected Seamus was behind it. Unlike Dante, he not only had the ability and opportunity to strangle Judd to death but also the motive. And when Seamus admitted his affliction, Anna realized the one thing he didn't have was time.

If he wanted to see justice be served, it would have to be now.

But the fact that Anna assumed Seamus was the killer doesn't keep her legs from feeling like they're about to give out beneath her. Or maybe it's the floor that's collapsing. Or the train itself.

"Why?"

The word comes out more plaintive and despairing than Anna intends. She can't help it, for even though she suspected it was Seamus, she is indeed in despair. Betrayal burns through her, so hot she's shocked she's still alive. She should be dead now, she thinks. Surely this will kill her.

Yet somehow, she remains stubbornly alive, swatting away Seamus's hand and crab-crawling out of the room. In the corridor, she leaps to her feet and attempts to run, but Seamus is quickly upon her, clamping a hand over her mouth and dragging her to the front of the car.

That he can do it so easily doesn't surprise Anna. He's strong. She's always known that. Which is why she also realized that Seamus is the only person on this train strong enough to kill the others. Anna easily pictures him smothering the life out of Edith Gerhardt and slitting Herb Pulaski's throat before squeezing out the window and climbing onto the roof to reach his own room.

She vividly remembers Seamus's words after they first sorted through those boxes of proof.

All of them need to die. And I want to be the one to do it.

And so he had.

Now Anna expects him to do the same to her, especially as they continue through Car 11 toward the lounge. An appropriate place for her to die, she thinks. The car where this whole cursed journey began.

But once they're inside, Seamus guides her into a chair and kneels before her, his hands on her legs. He slips one beneath her dress, the sudden violation making her inhale sharply. Seamus continues to slide his hand up her thigh until he reaches the knife.

"You won't be needing this," Seamus says as he yanks it from the sheath and tosses it across the lounge. "Even without it, I know you can flatten me to the ground. I assure you, there's no need to try. I won't fight back. I won't ever hurt you, Anna."

Too late for that, Anna thinks. Already he's hurt her more than she could have imagined. A cut so deep she doubts it will ever heal. As a result, she has no energy to fight Seamus. Grief and disappointment have depleted her.

"You knew Judd wasn't dead," she says, her voice flat.

"I knew."

"When?"

"The same time you found out."

"But only you found his hiding spot."

Seamus settles into the chair beside her. Anna, refusing to look at him, focuses on the view outside the lounge windows. The Phoenix has reached another river, running parallel to it, the snow on its banks blinding in the early-morning light.

"Yes," Seamus says.

Anna doesn't need him to explain what came next. How Seamus then strangled Judd. To make it seem like he had nothing to do with it, he led her and Dante to the scene of the crime.

"That's not what we agreed to," she says. "We wanted them all alive."

"No, Anna. *You* wanted that. I wanted vengeance, in whatever form it could come in. And if that meant all of them rotting in prison, I pretended to be okay with it, because it was better than nothing. But the truth is, I thought they deserved to die. Every last one of them."

"Then why did you go along with my plan?"

"Because I love you," Seamus says wearily, making it sound not like a declaration but a confession. A deep, dark secret he's only now being forced to reveal. "I know you don't feel the same way, and I've made peace with that. But I knew I'd never make peace with what they did, what they took from us. I needed to make at least one of them pay."

"Even though you knew it was wrong?"

Seamus jerks his head toward the row of cars behind them. "What *they* did was wrong, Anna. They murdered our brothers, along with dozens of other people. They framed your father. Your mother went insane because of it. Don't you dare sit here and pretend they don't deserve exactly the same treatment."

"They deserve worse," Anna says. "But not at our hands. We're better than that."

"You might be," Seamus says. "But I'm not. When I got the opportunity to murder one of those bastards, I took it."

Still unable to look at him, Anna keeps her gaze on the river outside. Despite going in the same direction, both train and water are gradually splitting away from each other in elevation. As the river dips lower, flowing through a snow-filled valley it carved millennia ago, the train climbs higher, following the gentle rise of the valley's edge.

"The opportunity was there without resorting to murder," she says. "You thought Lapsford was going to die. You even pleaded with me to give him the pill before it was too late."

"Because I didn't just want him dead. I wanted to be the one to kill him."

Yet Lapsford is still alive, thanks to Anna. Ironic, considering that, other than Kenneth Wentworth, he's the one she despises the most.

"Now that I know, are you still going to try?"

"No," Seamus says. "I've killed enough."

Anna wishes she still had her knife, because she longs to stab him in the heart. Not to fight him, and certainly not to kill him. She just wants Seamus to feel as much pain there as she does. Without the knife, all she can do is say, "I'll never forgive you."

Seamus nods. "I don't expect you to."

"They're going to arrest you, you know. Once we reach Chicago, you'll be rounded up along with the rest of them."

"You don't have to tell," Seamus says, even as his eyes—those windows to his soul—make it clear he knows she will.

Anna's own eyes well with tears. She might not reciprocate his romantic feelings, but she does love Seamus, in her own wounded way. Even now. Theirs is a more intimate bond than love, in which people sand down their rough edges for each other. She and Seamus sharpened theirs to brittle points.

Anna always knew one of them would draw blood. She just assumed it would be her.

"I wish you had trusted me." Anna shakes her head, the motion unleashing a single tear that rolls down her cheek. "I wish you had stuck to the plan."

"I couldn't," Seamus says.

Anna finally looks his way, overcome with curiosity. "How did it feel?"

"It was—" Seamus pauses, searching for the right word. "Beautiful. The sweetest release I've ever felt."

"Even though it also meant dooming yourself?"

"You're forgetting I'm already doomed."

Seamus removes her father's silver locomotive pin from his pocket. With extreme gentleness, he leans over and attaches it to the front of Anna's dress.

"This belongs to you," he says.

Seamus then kisses her on the cheek, stands, and, without another word, exits the front of the car. Anna remains seated a few more seconds. Just long enough for her to understand what he's about to do. When she does, she leaps from the chair and follows Seamus into the dining car. He's already on the other side, moving into the galley, the door swinging shut behind him.

And so it goes for the next several cars. Through the club car, the coach lounge, the sleeper car. Anna, quickening her pace in each one, doesn't fully catch up to Seamus until they've reached the baggage car. By then, he's already at the double doors in the side of the car, pulling one of them open.

"Seamus, stop!" Anna yells, her voice clanging off the walls.

He ignores her, moving to the second door and forcing it open, letting in the chaos of the outside world. The gusting snow. The whipping wind. The clattering wheels. It all makes Anna wince, even as she takes several steps toward the open doors.

"What are you doing?" she says, when deep down she already knows.

Seamus inches closer to the yawning opening, stopping only when he's on the precipice. The rush of air lifts his hair and flutters his jacket, which makes a flapping noise. Like a bird taking flight. Behind him, the snow-swept landscape passes in a blur of whites and grays. They're high above the river now, approaching a trestle bridge that crosses it.

"I'm leaving," he says.

Another tear cascades down Anna's cheek. She's not ready to say good-bye, in spite of what he's done. For the past year, he's been the only constant presence in her life. His absence will leave a void she'll never be able to fill.

"You don't need to do this," she says, resisting the urge to grab him and pull him away from the door. But he's so close to the edge that she fears one wrong move will send him tumbling off the train.

Anna knows what will happen to him after that.

"I already told you, I don't have a future."

"It doesn't have to be that way. You'll figure it out."

"I already have," Seamus says.

He turns to face the open door as the train reaches the bridge. A moment passes in which he takes in the gray billow of sky above, the ice-covered river below, the white line of the distant horizon. Anna holds her breath as Seamus remains framed in the doorway, perched on its edge. He turns back around to look at her, and her heart skips. She knows it means he's changing his mind.

Sure enough, Seamus pushes away from the door, running toward Anna, wrapping his big arms around her. She hugs him back, relieved that he's chosen to live.

But then he presses the revolver into her hand—and Anna realizes something else is happening.

"Take it," Seamus says.

Anna shakes her head, jarring loose more tears. "Please don't do this."

"You know what to do," Seamus whispers as he closes her fingers around the gun. "You can end this."

He breaks away from her, leaving Anna holding the gun in one hand and grasping for him with the other. But Seamus is already out of reach, on his way to the door. When he gets there, he doesn't pause or look back or even say good-bye.

He simply steps off the train and drops out of sight.

FORTY-FIVE

ANNA SCREAMS.

A pointless act.

Seamus is gone. She knows that. She watched the rag-doll flailing of his limbs as he fell, noted the sickening bend of his body as he hit the icy water below. Before she could see if he resurfaced unscathed, the train had reached the other side of the bridge and the river quickly slipped out of view.

Still, she screams, the rush of snowy air from the open doors ripping the sound from her lungs so she barely hears it. Even so, she doesn't stop. Because she needs to scream.

At Seamus.

For Seamus.

Grieving him and hating him and missing him although it's only been seconds.

The sheer act of screaming unleashes something in her. A startling, snarling pain she's kept locked down for a dozen years. Now that it's out, though, she has no idea how to stop it.

Nor does she know what to do next, despite what Seamus said.

You know what to do. You can end this.

The memory of those words finally makes Anna stop screaming. When Seamus first said them, she'd been too stung by betrayal and despair for them to register. They were like embers in a roaring fire, lost amid the blaze. Now, though, with Seamus gone and the scream dying in her lungs, they're all Anna thinks about.

He told her that for a reason, all while forcing the gun into her hand. At first, Anna thinks he wanted her to finish what he started. Kill Lapsford. Experience the beauty and sweet release of vengeance fulfilled.

But something else he'd said nudges into her thoughts.

When I got the opportunity to murder one of those bastards, I took it.

A single word in particular stands out from the rest.

One.

Anna slams the doors shut and collapses to the floor beside them. Pain tears through her now-silent throat, raw and throbbing. She gulps, winces, weeps, all the while trying to untangle her thoughts.

Of all the murders on this train, Seamus only admitted to one of them.

Anna gasps, the sudden intake of air making her wince a second time. Seamus never admitted to killing any of the others. Only Judd. And she can think of just one reason why he didn't confess to the other murders.

They were committed by someone else.

FORTY-SIX

THOSE REMAINING ALIVE in Car 12 of the Philadelphia Phoenix hear Anna's screams all the way in the rear third of the train. More mournful than pained, as soon as the sound reaches their ears, they know something bad has happened.

Not to Anna, but to Seamus.

The sound makes each respond in different ways.

In Room C, Dante Wentworth strains at the ties that bind his arms to the chair. He's been at it ever since Anna and Seamus left him here, and now that he suspects Seamus is gone, he pushes against them even harder. Body tensed and muscles straining, he grits his teeth and makes one final attempt, not easing until he feels one of the restraints give by a millimeter.

It does the trick, creating just enough space for Dante's left hand to slither loose of the tie. He uses it to quickly free his right hand, tugging at the knot in the fabric until it falls away.

A sense of triumph sings through his body. Despite their best efforts, he's managed to escape.

Next door, in Room B, Jack Lapsford's heart pounds out a staccato beat as he paces the room. It still hasn't settled down since he was ambushed by Seamus Callahan. He can't stop thinking about how big Seamus looked towering over the bed, gripping that pillow.

If Anna hadn't interrupted when she did, Lapsford might now be dead. A fact that causes his heartbeat to increase another notch. It now reverberates in his rib cage. Like an echo in a cave.

He hopes he's not having a heart attack. That would be rich, coming after he faked two of them in the span of twelve hours. Unlike his first failed attempt, the second had been an overwhelming success.

Physical exertion.

That was the key.

To get his heart pumping and his face flushed, Lapsford endured a series of calisthenics he hadn't attempted since boot camp. By the end, even he thought he was about to die.

But it worked. Seamus was certain he was having a heart attack.

Now left to his own devices, he lumbers from door to bed and back again. He does his best thinking like this. And right now he needs to come up with another way to get off this train.

In Room A, the body of Sally Lawrence remains exactly how Anna had left it—in the chair by the window, covered with a sheet.

The only change that's occurred in the hour or so since it was discovered is with the sheet itself, which has been jostled by the wind pouring through the open window. It's been happening for as long as Dante Wentworth struggled against his binds two rooms away. A constant motion that moves the covering millimeter by millimeter until, after one last nudge, it drops away.

When it does, another change occurs.

Sally opens her eyes.

FORTY-SEVEN

THE KILLER WAITS until almost seven A.M. to make their move, gliding through Car 12, trying not to make a sound. While silence probably isn't necessary anymore, it strikes them as being the smartest move. Having the people they intend to kill know they're about to do it makes things . . . difficult.

Especially the next victim, who will likely put up a fight. And this kill needs to be quick and quiet. A secret. Because the moment Anna finds out about it, she'll go into battle mode.

In the middle of the car, the killer pauses, listening. There's nothing to indicate anyone is nearby. Hopefully it remains that way. Not willing to risk it, they approach the door of the next person to die.

Jack Lapsford.

The last conspirator left.

After he's gone, only Kenneth Wentworth will remain. And while it would be nice to murder him, too, it'll be up to the courts to decide his fate. That should make Anna happy. She deserves at least one victory.

The killer is now right outside Lapsford's door, twisting the handle until it opens just a crack. They nudge it wider with a foot.

A light creaking of agitated hinges. And when the killer looks inside, they see someone seated in the chair by the window.

Not Jack Lapsford.

Anna.

She smiles, like she's been waiting for hours. Like she's known all this time what they had planned.

"Hello, Agent Davis," she says. "Feeling better, I see."

7 A.M.

ONE HOUR
TO CHICAGO

FORTY-EIGHT

AGENT REGGIE DAVIS leans against the doorframe, honestly relieved to be found out. It's been exhausting pretending to be helping Anna, when in truth he was doing the opposite. All this time, he's had only one goal in mind—kill the people who killed his father.

He was fifteen when it happened. A terrible age to lose your dad.

Unlike Anna's brother, Reggie's father wasn't a soldier being shipped off to basic training. At forty-five, his fighting days were long over. No, his father worked the railroad. An engineer. One unlucky enough to volunteer to drive a brand-new troop train carrying a group of U.S. servicemen to an Army base in Georgia.

"I'm doing my part," he told Reggie before he left that morning. "When you get to be old enough, I expect you to do the same."

The war was all but over by the time Reggie could enlist, so he did the next best thing and joined the FBI. For a time, it felt like he was doing right by his late father. He was one of the good guys, catching bad guys, making sure the scales of justice tipped in the right direction.

What he never, ever expected was the opportunity to avenge

his father. After all, the man everyone thought was responsible had been dead for a dozen years. But Reggie knew that had Arthur Matheson still been alive, he would have killed him with his bare hands if given the chance.

Then, miracle of miracles, he got it.

Reggie couldn't believe his luck when he learned not just who really killed his father but that all of them had been gathered together by Art Matheson's daughter. He didn't know what he was going to do about it. Not even once he'd boarded the train. But as everyone else—the porters, the conductors, even the other passengers—quickly disembarked, he realized something else was going on.

"I thought you brought them here to kill them," he tells Anna.

"That must have been a surprise when you realized I didn't," she says. "Is that when you decided to do it yourself?"

Yes. Although he wasn't in the lounge when Judd Dodge allegedly died, Reggie knew he hadn't been poisoned to death. Unlike what they show in the movies, poisoning is nasty business. Depending on the dose, there's vomiting, thrashing, spitting up blood. Reggie detected none of that beneath the tablecloth that covered Judd's supposed corpse. So the first chance he got, he snuck into Room C of Car 13 to see for himself.

"Are you going to tell everyone?" Judd asked in a panic when he'd been caught.

"Not if you agree to do everything I say," Reggie told him.

What that entailed was to pick the others off one by one. Edith and Herb, Jack Lapsford and Sally Lawrence. The order didn't matter. Just as long as they all died.

"How'd you put it together?" he asks Anna now.

"Piece by piece. Starting with your shirt." She eyes it now, the part not soaked with his blood a stark white. "When you first surprised us in the lounge, the one you were wearing was light blue."

Reggie had hoped no one would notice. His fault for not bringing along a matching shirt. Then again, there wasn't time to stop by his place to grab a different one. The white one at the bottom of his desk, kept there for sudden assignments like this, had to do.

"Did it get splattered with blood when you slit Herb's throat?" Anna says. "Or was it simply wet with snow after you exited through the window?"

"Both," Reggie says, thinking about the damp, blood-flecked shirt now sitting at the bottom of his suitcase. "When did you realize I'd changed?"

"While checking your wound. How is it, by the way?"

Reggie pats the side of his stomach. The wound still hurts. A lot. But at least he can move, thanks to Anna.

"The stitches are holding up nicely. You did a good job."

"An unnecessary one," Anna says. "When you stabbed yourself, you made sure the wound looked worse than it is."

"What makes you think I'm the one who did it?"

"The location. It's on the left side of your stomach. But Judd Dodge, the man you claimed to have stabbed you, was right-handed. If he had really snuck up from behind, as you said he did, the stab wound would have been on the right side of your abdomen."

Reggie can't help but be impressed. So far, he's been unable to get much past her.

"I couldn't risk the right side," he says. "Too many vital organs."

Anna cocks her head, curious. "Is that something they teach you in the FBI? The exact place to stab yourself that causes a lot of bleeding but not major injury?"

"It's surprising how much you learn on the job."

"Such as wounding yourself to make it appear like you're not a murderer?" Anna asks. "Did you kill Edith, too? Or was that Judd?"

"He did the killing, but at my suggestion. The cord from your drapes was also my idea."

"To make it look like I'd done it. It was the same with the open window and my father's pin. When did you take it?"

"In the observation car," Reggie says, recalling how easy it was to pluck from her dress as he pointed out Edith's smeared lipstick.

"I couldn't understand why I was being framed, even after I realized you were the killer." Anna places a finger to her chin, as if putting it together on the spot. "But now it's starting to make sense. By framing me, you were really framing Judd Dodge."

"I thought it would look more plausible that way," Reggie admits. "Judd fakes his death, kills those who could implicate him, then frames you for the crimes. He seemed to think it was a good idea."

"But in reality, once you murdered the others, you planned to kill him, claiming self-defense. You'd have a scapegoat, no one would be any wiser, and you'd be hailed a hero."

It was, Reggie thinks, a perfect plan. Practically foolproof. And it would have worked except for one key detail. Anna, of course, knows what it is.

"But then I figured out Judd wasn't dead. It didn't help matters that he left his room." Anna's voice gets quieter, distant. "And then Seamus killed him."

"Not part of the plan. At no time did he know what I was up to."

Sympathy compels Reggie to say it. He doesn't want Anna to think less of Seamus than she already does. Despite everything, he still admires her. She's plucky, determined. Very few of his fellow agents would have been able to pull off some of the things Anna accomplished during the night.

"Still, by then, your plan had fully unraveled," she says.

Reggie steps deeper into the room. "I wouldn't go that far. It could still work—if you don't tell anyone. Think about it, Anna. All this time, you've been craving vengeance. So have I. Now's our chance to get it."

"And we have very different ideas about what that looks like," Anna says.

"But we don't have to. They're bad people, Anna. They took everything from you. You deserve to do the same to them."

Anna shifts in the chair, uneasy. "Not all of them. Kenneth Wentworth isn't even on this train."

"That's the beauty of this. He'll suffer exactly the way you want him to. Humiliation. Prison. The most hated man in America. And those who helped him will be dead, which is what I want. We both get our way."

Anna wears a strange expression. A kind of hesitant doubt. Almost as if she wants to say yes but can't bring herself to do it.

"But what if I refuse to go along with it? Are you going to kill me?"

"Yes," Reggie says. "That is unfortunately the plan."

"But what if I kill you first?"

Anna uncrosses her arms, revealing Reggie's gun gripped in her right hand. The whole time she's been wearing his jacket, it's been right there, deep inside a pocket. Reggie doesn't know how long it took for her to remember it was there. It doesn't matter now that the gun is in her hand and aimed squarely at his chest.

He smiles at the sight. He can't help it.

"Before you shoot me, I have one question for you," he says. "Did you honestly think I'd give you a loaded gun?"

Anna's eyes dim. When she pulls the trigger, the action produces nothing but a sharp click.

"No, I didn't," she says, flicking her gaze to the hallway behind him. "And do you honestly think I'm the only one who knows you're the killer?"

Just then, Reggie senses someone at his back, followed by the wind of something fast and heavy rushing toward his head. When it connects with the base of his skull, pain explodes through his body, causing instant paralysis.

He drops to the floor, his vision distorted, like he's looking through smudged glass. As he flops onto his back, he sees Sally Lawrence step into the room. In her hand is the blunt object she'd just used to take him down.

The champagne bottle she'd picked up in the lounge. She now holds it by the neck, its base smacking against her open palm.

It's the last thing Reggie sees before his entire world goes dark.

FORTY-NINE

SAL DROPS THE bottle and wipes the crimson spot on her forehead, destroying the illusion of blood and a bullet hole. While it lasted, though, it was surprisingly effective. Anna was taken aback when she first saw it, even though she knew it was created by two items in Sal's handbag.

Lipstick and nail polish.

While not the most sophisticated way to fake a shooting death, their options had been limited. Anna knew it was a risk, but she hoped that Sal shooting out the window behind her would cover the lack of blood spatter, while keeping Seamus at a distance would hide the fact that she wasn't dead. Thank God, the risk paid off.

The entire ruse had been Anna's idea, thought up on the spot when she started to suspect Judd had been strangled to death by Seamus. Because she assumed he would target Sal and Lapsford next, she decided to make it look like one of them had been eliminated. The other would then be used as bait to lure Seamus and catch him in the act.

What Anna hadn't counted on was there being a third killer on the train.

"What will you do for us if we go along with this?" Sal asked after Anna presented her idea while Dante and Seamus were moving Judd's body for the second time.

Anna shook her head. "Nothing."

"Then why should we help you?" Lapsford said.

"Because both of you will die in the next three hours if you don't. He's after you, not me."

That was enough to convince them.

It was decided that Sal should fake being shot after Lapsford pretended to have a heart attack more convincing than his first attempt. The goal was to make him look more vulnerable to his would-be killer, thereby encouraging an attack. To sell the illusion of urgency, Anna angrily peppered Lapsford with real questions. That his answers might not have been true doesn't matter. It kept Seamus distracted enough to not realize Sal had stolen the gun from his jacket pocket.

"Can I trust you?" Anna had asked them before going ahead with the plan.

"No," Sal said. "But just like me, you don't have any other choice."

Anna didn't. But Sal ultimately did the right thing. Now the two of them move into the corridor, stepping over Reggie's unconscious form.

"Nice work back there," Anna tells Sal, who accepts the compliment with a nod.

"You're welcome."

"But it doesn't make us square," Anna adds. "Not by a long shot."

Sal nods again. "I know."

They burst into Sal's room, where Lapsford's been hiding. A last-minute decision made after his close call with Seamus. Stuffed into the room with the two of them, Anna still can't quite believe they're temporary allies. Sally Lawrence and Jack Lapsford are the last people she thought she'd be working with.

A truce that might not last much longer.

Anna can only trust them so far.

With that in mind, she sprints back into the corridor, on the way to Dante's room. One of the trip's other unlikely allies. She gets as far as the door when he opens it and peers outside. "Here to accuse me of murder again?"

"I'm sorry," Anna says. "I know you didn't do anything wrong. It was part of my plan to catch the real killer."

"You could have at least warned me," Dante says with a sniff.

"I'll explain everything later. Right now, I desperately need your help."

"What's happening?" he asks.

"Nothing good."

Dante slips out the door and follows her down the hall. At the door to Lapsford's room, he spots Reggie unconscious on the floor.

"You should tie him up."

"That's my next order of business," Anna says.

"Where's Seamus?"

"Gone."

Anna says nothing more than that. One, there's no time, and two, saying what happened out loud will make it real. And she's not ready for that. Certainly not now. Likely not ever. So she keeps moving, pulling Dante into the room with Lapsford and Sal.

"The three of you stay in this room, no matter what. Lock the door behind me. Open it only when this train comes to a stop in Chicago." Anna turns to Dante. "Can I trust you?"

Dante doesn't so much as blink. "Yes."

Anna presses Seamus's gun into his hands. "Guard them with your life."

She leaves the room, pausing in the corridor just long enough
to see Dante close the door behind her and to hear the lock being
turned. Then she's off again, racing to Reggie's room in the next
car. Inside, she spots his overnight case and flips it upside down,
spilling its contents onto the bed. A tie. A shirt flecked with Herb's
blood. A list of names with three crossed out.

And bullets.

A whole box of them.

Anna grabs it and with shaking hands loads six bullets into
Reggie's gun. Seamus was right. She can end this.

She's out the door a second later, bursting into the next car.
Halfway down the corridor, she skids to a stop and looks into
Lapsford's room.

The patch of floor where Reggie had been sprawled only two
minutes earlier is now empty.

The window on the other side of the room is wide open.

And Agent Reggie Davis is gone.

FIFTY

ANNA FOLLOWS REGGIE out the window, a decision made after only a second of thought. With him on the roof and her inside the train, there would be no way for her to tell where he was headed. He could appear anywhere, at any time. Even entering the train again through a window in the room where Dante, Sal, and Lapsford are barricaded. But if she's on the roof, Anna reasons, she'll be able to see exactly where Reggie is going.

Taking a deep breath, she kicks off her shoes and stands on the chair. She then squeezes through the window and sits on the window frame, her legs still inside but her upper half now fully out of the train and buffeted by wind and snow.

The sheer force of the elements feels like a physical assault. The cold is brutal and the snow smacking her face stinging. After only seconds outside, Anna begins to ache from the chill, even while wearing Reggie's jacket. It's enough to make her want to slide back into the room, which she almost does. The only thing keeping her in place is the idea, however misguided, that what she intends to do has been done before. Still unknown is if Anna herself is capable of it.

The train's vibrations, while noticeable on the inside, feel amplified when outside. The exterior of the car hums with movement—a constant shimmying that would bother Anna more if she wasn't distracted by the oversize presence of everything the train passes. Each tree and telephone pole feels terrifyingly close. Every object zipping by contains a gravity, a weight. Everything— from the wind to the snow to the objects running alongside the rails—feels like they're grasping at Anna, threatening to rip her from the train.

With her arms spread wide, she hugs the side of the train and slowly starts to stand on the windowsill, moving first one foot, then the other. While ditching her heels was the right move, Anna wishes she had an alternative to bare feet. The cold edge of the windowsill presses like a razor blade against her soles. She dreads finding out how the roof of the train will feel.

Speaking of the roof, it becomes eye level with Anna once she reaches a standing position. Through a veil of falling snow, she takes in the expanse of the roof in front of her, noting its pros and cons. On the plus side, it's wide—a little more than ten feet—and not completely smooth. A series of evenly placed ridges run the length of the roof, giving her something to grip when she attempts to climb onto the top of the train.

The downside is that the roof is far from flat. It bears a slight curve that, when combined with the scattered patches of ice and packed snow, might weaken her grip and make her movements unsteady once atop it.

If she even reaches the roof.

Anna has her doubts as she places her palms flat against it, finding it shockingly cold. Like touching a sheet of ice. The pads of her fingers stick to the metal, requiring her to carefully pry each one off the frigid surface lest they freeze there. Definitely not the kind of grip she wants or needs.

Not that she has a choice in the matter. It's either keep climbing or go back inside. She can't remain outside the train indefinitely. The longer she's out here, the more intense things become. The air seems colder, the push of the wind stronger, the objects along the tracks ever closer. When the train crosses a road, the warning signal—a fuming cacophony of red lights and a clanging alarm—gets so close that Anna swears she feels it brush her back even as she flattens herself against the train's side.

Once it's cleared, Anna takes a deep breath that she fears could be among her last. Then she begins her ascent. Simultaneously pushing off the windowsill and pulling on the metal ridge along the roof's edge, she clambers as fast as she can. The snow is so thick she can hardly see. Her bare feet slap against the freezing steel. Her fingers claw at the equally cold roof. Through some combination of miracle and might, she makes it to the top of the train in ten seconds flat.

After rolling to the center of the roof, Anna struggles to stand. For as weird as it was to be clinging to the side of the train, it's even stranger to be on top of it. More dangerous, too. Up here, she's exposed on all sides, surrounded by the cold and hammered by snow-specked wind that makes her feel like she's pushing against a locked door. In these conditions, Anna swears the only thing keeping her upright is the metal roof beneath her feet, the soles of which seem to be frozen to it.

Then there's the ice, circles of which dot the roof's surface like land mines. One wrong step could send her tumbling from the train.

She knows what will happen after that.

When she first reached the roof, Anna was more worried about staying upright than which direction she faced. Which is why she now gazes upon the last two cars of the train, including the observation car with its window in the roof. Unsticking her feet, she rotates slowly until she's looking down the length of the train.

Through the snow, she spots the dark shape of Reggie two cars away, on the roof of the first-class lounge.

"Reggie!" she yells as she pulls the gun from her jacket pocket and thrusts it in front of her. "Stop!"

He turns around, looking dazed from the blow to his head, the climb to the roof, the wound at his stomach. Reggie clutches it as he shouts back, making sure she can hear him over the roar of the wind.

"You're not going to shoot me, Anna!"

He's right about that. Anna knows that even a superficial wound would likely send him toppling off the train to certain death. Something she definitely doesn't want. Reggie has now joined the ranks of Sal, Lapsford, and Kenneth Wentworth. People she wants to see punished for as long as possible, in as many ways as possible. Reggie's death, quite simply, would be too unsatisfying for her.

Reggie knows this, because instead of scrambling away, he starts walking toward her.

Anna shuffles backward, unwilling to fire the gun. Reggie keeps moving, crossing onto the roof of Car 11 in broad steps. Anna continues to back up, cautious, her gaze constantly snapping from Reggie to her feet to the space behind her. By the time Reggie reaches Car 12, she's still moving off it.

"Don't come any closer," Anna warns as she steps atop Car 13 and takes in their surroundings. They're approaching the outskirts of Chicago now, the scrubby, snow-covered fields ceding ground to brick-front factories, warehouses, row homes. She imagines people inside them looking through grimy windows and seeing the two of them atop the Philadelphia Phoenix. Reggie reaching the end of Car 12, Anna merely in the middle of Car 13, still carefully backing across the roof.

"We don't need to do this, you know," Reggie says, close enough now that he no longer has to raise his voice. So close that Anna can see fresh blood oozing from the wound at his side.

"We don't," she says. "So turn yourself in."

"Or you can drop the gun."

Anna shakes her head. "Not a chance."

"There's always the option of joining me," Reggie says. "Did Seamus tell you how it felt to kill one of them?"

"He did." Anna pauses, unsure if she should share it. "He said it was beautiful."

"It was. You can experience it for yourself, you know."

"I'd rather see you in prison along with the others."

"You know as well as I do that they had it coming," Reggie says. "Judd. Edith. Herb. As do Sally and Lapsford."

"What about Dante?" Anna asks. "To get away with this, you'll have to kill him, too. And he didn't do anything."

Reggie steps onto the roof of Car 13, forcing Anna to continue her backward shuffle.

"He's a Wentworth," he says. "His father caused all this. Think about that, Anna. Your brother and my father are dead, but the Wentworth men still have each other. That doesn't seem fair, does it?"

Anna's at the end of the car, quickening her pace as Reggie draws closer. Not that it will do her any good. When she crosses to the next car, she suddenly realizes what Reggie has known all along.

She's reached the observation car.

The last one on the train.

There's nowhere left for her to go.

"Stop!" Anna says, pointing the revolver at Reggie's chest, her index finger dancing along the trigger.

Reggie keeps walking, joining her atop the last car, halting only when the barrel of the gun is pressed again his chest. "Just admit that you're not going to shoot me," he says. "Not up here."

"No," Anna says. "Down there."

Pure panic shines in Reggie's eyes as they flick from Anna's face to the gun to their feet. Anna follows his gaze, making sure they're standing exactly where she wants them to be.

Directly atop the observation car's skylight.

Anna points the gun toward the glass and, without hesitation, pulls the trigger.

FIFTY-ONE

THE SKYLIGHT GIVES way in an instant. Anna and Reggie both drop through it, glass raining down around them as they fall.

They land at the same time, the impact with the floor below knocking the air out of Anna and replacing it with all-consuming pain. She can tell it's the same for Reggie, who writhes in agony against her, their limbs tangled.

Still, both of them survived the fall mostly unscathed. No broken bones, as far as Anna can tell. Just intense pain and a few small cuts from the shattered glass. Reggie sports a gash on his cheek, weeping blood. Anna has one on the back of her hand, in addition to a splinter of glass in the side of her neck. She plucks it out, the shard's tip bright red.

Anna tries to sit up but is stopped by pain pulsing through her shoulder and hip. That leaves Reggie on his feet first, limping around the car in search of the gun that got lost in the fall.

Spotting it in a nearby pool of glass, Anna lunges for it. Reggie sees her do it and goes after it, too. Their bodies again collide—a breathless fight for the gun. Although Reggie's arms are longer, Anna is faster, and she latches onto the gun's handle before swinging it in his direction.

Reggie slowly climbs to his feet, hands raised. Anna remains on the floor, sitting up just enough to grip the gun with both hands and aim it at his chest.

"Don't move a goddamn muscle," she says.

"You're still not going to shoot me," Reggie says. "I know you, Anna Matheson. You act all tough, but deep down you're the same scared girl you were when your family was killed."

Yes, Anna's scared.

Terrified, really.

Of dying, of course, but also of failing. That more than anything. To not bring at least one of the people who destroyed her life to justice would be a disservice to her brother, her parents, her aunt. If that happens, then Reggie might as well also kill her, because Anna knows she won't be able to live with herself.

That absolute terror of failure pulses through her, as rapid as her heartbeat. Still, she keeps the gun aimed at Reggie as she stands on legs shaky from the fear, the fall, the entire night.

"Are you certain of that, Agent Davis?" she says.

"Positive."

Anna fixes him with a steely gaze. "You're wrong."

She doesn't plan on killing Reggie. Just a single shot to the leg is all it will take to disable him. He said so himself. Anna's aim drifts lower, the gun now pointed at Reggie's upper thigh as her index finger stutters against the trigger.

She steadies it.

Begins to pull.

Prepares to shoot.

Beneath her feet, the train starts to lurch. Anna moves with it. Reggie, too. Both tilt forward, unsteady, tugged by forward momentum as their surroundings suddenly slow down.

Anna locks eyes with Reggie as both realize what just happened.

After twelve hours of constant motion, the Philadelphia Phoenix has come to a stop.

FIFTY-TWO

A MOMENT PASSES in which nothing moves.

Not Anna.

Not Reggie.

Not even the train itself, which sits motionless on the tracks even as its engine continues to hum.

Then Reggie breaks into a limping jog, heading out of the observation car. Anna gives chase, hobbled by pain and panic and the bite of glass shards beneath her bare feet. She sways, her train legs useless now that the Phoenix has stopped. By the time she enters Car 13, Reggie is already gone, moving slowly but surely toward the front of the train.

Anna goes after him, limping as fast as she can through the first-class passenger cars, the gun still in her grip. She slows down when she reaches the lounge, where there are more places to hide. She learned that the hard way with Herb Pulaski. Now she cautiously checks the car, expecting Reggie to attack at any second.

But he's not in the lounge, crouched behind the bar.

Nor is he in the dining car, huddled beneath a table.

Instead, Anna finds Reggie in the galley, leaning against the counter to catch his breath. When Anna pushes through the door at the back of the car, Reggie ducks through the one at the front of the galley, into the club car.

Anna runs after him, leaping over the puddle of his blood still in the middle of the floor before crashing into the club car.

She doesn't see Reggie just inside the car, pressed against the wall.

It's only when he grabs Anna's arm as she's streaking past that she realizes he's there at all. Reggie wrenches her arm behind her back and shoves her against the club car's counter.

The surprise of it all sends Anna into fighting mode as Reggie tries to wrest the gun from her grip. She cocks her leg and lifts her foot, preparing to do what she did to Herb and go for Reggie's groin. He leaps away before she can do it, her foot missing him entirely. As she readies another attempt, he swoops in and steals the gun.

Anna kicks again. Hard. This time, she makes contact. The blow sends Reggie staggering backward against the window, rattling the blinds and creating undulating bars of shadow on the opposite wall.

He thrusts the gun in front of him, pointing it at Anna. Staring down the barrel, she runs her arm across the counter, searching for something she can use to defend herself. The only thing within reach is a stack of empty coffee cups.

She grabs one and flings it at Reggie's head. It sails past his ear, into the window behind him, spiderwebbing the glass with cracks.

Anna keeps throwing them. One cup. Two. Three.

The first misses entirely.

The second hits Reggie's chest.

The third lands square in his face, his nose crunching beneath it in a spray of blood.

Reggie howls in pain, one hand covering his crushed nose while the other continues to hold the gun.

Now it's Anna's turn to run.

She sprints to the front of the car before streaking into the adjoining coach lounge, not pausing to see if Reggie is after her. She's certain he is. If not now, then soon. So she keeps running, through the sleeper car and the coach cars, pain screaming through every inch of her body.

In the baggage car, Anna's footfalls echo loudly in the emptiness all around her. There's no place left to run, nowhere left to hide. Her final option is to somehow get into the locomotive. Only there will she be safe.

Anna runs to the steel-reinforced door that leads to the locomotive. She pounds on it, praying that Burt Chapman, the train's sole engineer for the entire journey, will ultimately ignore her earlier instructions.

"Open up!" she yells. "Please!"

Behind her, Reggie enters the baggage car. Anna can hear his footsteps, slow but steady. There's no need for him to hurry. After all, he has the gun.

She whirls to face him, her back against the door. The center of Reggie's face is a bruised, bloody pulp. His nose bends at an unnatural angle, dripping blood. More blood oozes through the side of his shirt, where his stitches have no doubt come undone.

Fear closes around Anna like a fist, squeezing tight, holding her in place. Its grip is so tight that she's barely aware of the sounds coming from the other side of the door.

A sigh.

A twist.

A creak.

Then the door suddenly drops away. What once supported her is now just a void that Anna would fall right through if not for someone else filling the space. Relief floods her body as she turns to the open door.

But it's not Burt Chapman standing on the threshold, preparing to pull her to the safety of the locomotive. It's someone else entirely. Someone who's been on this train the whole night without her knowing it.

Kenneth Wentworth.

FIFTY-THREE

ANNA SEIZES UP at the sight of him. In the past year, not a day has gone by in which she didn't think about everything Kenneth Wentworth took from her. He's haunted her nightmares—and her waking hours, too. Now, standing right in front of her, is the man who instigated everything. Nothing any of the others had done would have happened without him, the puppeteer pulling all the strings.

He's the reason her brother is dead, along with thirty-six others, including Seamus's brother and Reggie's father.

He's the person most responsible for framing her own father.

He's the man whose horrific actions drove her mother to suicide.

Anna's both fantasized about and feared this moment, wondering how she'd react. Would she scream? Would she weep? Or would she simply kill him in a way that inflicted the most pain? Right now, Anna feels capable of all three. The sensation is overwhelming, all-encompassing, and, ultimately, crippling. In the end, all she can do is stare into the eyes of Kenneth Wentworth so he can see how much he's destroyed her life.

He stares back, as if expecting her to flinch.

She doesn't.

"You know who I am," she says.

It's not a question.

"I do, Miss Matheson," Wentworth replies with disconcerting calmness. "I also know why you're here."

Anna takes in his clothes, a surreal combination of white shirt and necktie worn beneath gray engineer's overalls. Despite driving a train all night, he retains a distinguished look accomplished only with lots of money. His silver hair is neatly combed, his face enviably tan. White teeth sparkle behind his Cary Grant smile.

"Where's Burt Chapman?" Anna asks. "He's supposed to be the engineer."

"I fired him back in Philadelphia," Wentworth says, his smile remaining even as his voice hardens. "Did you really think I wouldn't be aware of what's going on with my own train? Or that when someone pays my employees to skip work I wouldn't be told about it? Most of all, when I get invited to ride a train I own, did you not think I'd find out who sent it?"

Anna had considered all of that when planning the trip with Seamus. She'd decided it was worth the risk.

"Why didn't you stop the train earlier?" she says. "In fact, why did it leave at all?"

"Because it's been a long time since I took the Phoenix out for a spin. It's a hobby of mine, you know. I enjoy it very much. Also, I was curious to see where the journey took us. Care to enlighten me?"

Anna gets his meaning. He wants to know who's dead. She's not about to tell him.

"You thought I was going to kill them," she says.

"I assumed you were entertaining the idea, yes."

"Because you *wanted* me to kill them."

Wentworth keeps smiling. "It certainly would have made things easier for me."

"They're about to get harder," Anna says. "Because there's proof of what you've done. It shows who did what and how all of it was your idea. Don't ask me how I got it, because I won't ever tell you. What I will say is that it's now in the hands of the FBI. They're waiting for us in Chicago. And if this train is even five minutes late, I'm certain they'll start looking for it. If they haven't already."

Anna thought it would feel good to say all that to Kenneth Wentworth. But what should be a moment of victory is undercut by rage, grief, exhaustion, and the knowledge that not everyone who wronged her will experience true justice.

Or maybe she doesn't feel triumphant because Wentworth doesn't look defeated. His smile never wavers, even as it flickers into outright bemusement.

"I always wondered what my son saw in you," he says. "All those years ago, when he mistakenly thought he was in love with you. You take after your father in that regard. Utterly unimpressive."

Anna touches the pin on her dress. Wentworth was wrong about her father. Just like he's wrong about her.

"I know that's why you did it," she says. "I know it's because you hated my father."

"I didn't hate him," Wentworth says. "I just wanted what was rightfully mine."

"You mean my mother."

Anna touches the pin again, thinking of the real Margaret Matheson. The resplendent woman with the irrepressible sparkle that lit up every room.

"I know you were in love with her," Anna says. "I don't think you ever stopped loving her. Not even after she left you for my father."

Wentworth's smiling façade melts away, revealing something sadder and meaner underneath. "She didn't leave. He took her."

"He *loved* her," Anna says, thinking about the way her father had looked at her mother. That beam of adoration. "And she loved him in return. Far more than she ever loved you. That's why she chose him over you."

"No, he stole her," Wentworth seethes. "He stole the life I was supposed to have with her. The family I was supposed to have with her. The son that should have been mine."

"Dante? He's been yours the whole time."

"I meant my other son," Wentworth says.

Anna goes still with shock. She thinks about her parents' whirlwind courtship, speedy marriage, early bundle of joy that should have caused a scandal. It didn't because Anna's father was respected and her mother was beautiful and they were so happy together that it didn't matter to people when their first child was born.

The only person who cared was that child's real father.

"Tommy," she says, unable to keep herself from searching Wentworth's face for hints of her brother. They're everywhere. The smile. The eyes. The easygoing grace.

Dante shares many of those traits, which is why Anna thought it was her brother she saw roaming the Phoenix. But it wasn't Tommy she kept seeing.

It was his half brother.

"I guess you didn't know everything after all," Wentworth says.

Anna stares at him, shaking. From shock or anger, she has no idea. "How long did you know?"

"I had my suspicions. Maggie never told me she was pregnant, but the timing always struck me as odd. Your father pretended Tommy was his son, even though anyone could see, if they looked long enough, that he bore no resemblance to plain Arthur Matheson. I certainly noticed it the one and only time I was allowed to meet my son."

Anna knows exactly when that was. Her family's final Christmas party. The same one where she had met Dante. While the two of them bantered, fueled by undeniable attraction, Kenneth Wentworth was speaking to his other son for the very first time.

Pain presses against Anna's temples. A headache brought on by both surprise and rage. Kenneth Wentworth took her brother from her once. She refuses to let him do the same to his memory.

"Tommy was the son of Arthur Matheson. Maybe not biologically, but in all the ways that matter. And he was my brother. I loved him, and you took him from me."

"I loved him, too," Wentworth says. "But I wasn't allowed to act like he was mine. I wasn't even allowed to speak to him. And when *my* son died, I wasn't even allowed to mourn him."

Anna recoils. An instinct she can't control. Nor can she stop the tears that are forming. Angry ones so hot they sting her eyes. "You caused his death! You didn't deserve to mourn him!"

"I didn't know he'd be on that train," Wentworth says, his own eyes now glistening. "And he shouldn't have been. Your father should have kept him from going. He should have kept him out of the war entirely. But he didn't and my son died and that's why I had to kill him."

"He was killed in prison."

"Yes," Wentworth says. "At my instruction. The family of the man who did it was rewarded handsomely."

Anna recoils further as more boiling tears emerge. Her father never got a chance to defend himself. It didn't matter that no one might have believed him but her and Aunt Retta. He still would have had the opportunity to lay out his case, prove his innocence, be set free. If that had happened, perhaps her mother's grief could have been contained. At least enough to preserve her sanity, to give her the will to keep living.

If all of that had happened, Anna might still have her parents.

But Kenneth Wentworth took them, too, and now she can only keep backing away, putting as much distance between them as possible. Anna's certain that if the gap closes by an inch, the urge to rip him apart with her bare hands will be too strong to resist.

But after two more backward steps, Anna collides with someone standing behind her.

Reggie.

She forgot he was there, listening, a witness to Kenneth Wentworth's confession. Making no move to harm her, he says, "Still think they all deserve to live?"

Anna can no longer answer that. She honestly doesn't know.

"This whole time, you've been spouting all these noble declarations about justice and honor and not sinking to their level," Reggie says. "But I know you, Anna Matheson. Deep down, you're just like me. You want something more satisfying than justice. You want revenge."

Yes, Anna wants revenge. She's always wanted it. But more than that, she wants her old life back. Twelve years ago, the existence she'd imagined for herself was snatched from her. She was like a derailed train, thrown off the tracks, broken apart.

Killing Kenneth Wentworth, she realizes, would be a way of putting herself back together and following the course she'd always planned. It won't be completely the same. Her family is still gone, and nothing will change that. Anna will always carry their absence with her.

"Think about what they did," Reggie says, still behind her, his voice a hiss slithering into her ear. "To your family. To you. Think about Seamus. And his brother. And all those other innocent men who died. I guarantee, if they were in your position right now, none of them would hesitate. Not for a second. Not even Seamus. But you're the one who's suffered the most. Out of everyone, you deserve this."

He reaches around, offering the gun. Anna accepts it with hands so numb she can barely feel it.

"You want to kill him, don't you?" Reggie says. "You've wanted to kill all of them all night. And you have every right to feel that way."

Anna takes a faltering half step toward Kenneth Wentworth, who eyes the gun now in her hands. He looks scared, and it thrills her. At last, a feeling of triumph.

"Please don't shoot," he says. "Please, Anna."

She aims the gun squarely at his heaving chest. Her index finger trembles against the trigger.

"Admit what you did," she says. "Admit that you destroyed my family."

Wentworth's mouth drops open, but no words come out. In that fraught silence, Anna steps closer, her aim never wavering.

"Admit it!"

"I did it," Wentworth says.

Anna takes another step. Point-blank range.

"Did what?" she says.

"Destroyed your family." Wentworth gulps after he says it, as if he's trying to take the words back. But then, he pushes out more. "I destroyed so many families. And I forced others to do it, too."

"How does that make you feel?" Reggie asks Anna.

She releases a long, drawn-out sigh. "Angry."

"And aren't you tired of holding in all that anger?"

"Yes," she says. "So tired."

She's spent the past year of her life in a state of perpetual rage. Before that were years of sorrow preceded by grief. Raw and cutting. The kind of grief she can't ever forget, because it won't let her. It left scars on her soul.

"I just want it to end," she says as tears continue to burn her eyes.

Reggie nods in both sympathy and understanding. "You know how to make that happen."

Anna spares a thought for Seamus, the man who embarked on this journey knowing he likely wouldn't reach the end. His final words now sound loud in her thoughts.

You know what to do. You can end this.

Anna can.

And, with one sudden pull of the trigger, she does.

ARRIVAL

MORE THAN TWO dozen FBI agents are waiting on the platform when the Philadelphia Phoenix slides into Chicago's Union Station. Although ten minutes late, the train pulls up with such ease that anyone passing by would think it had just finished another regularly scheduled overnight journey.

But there are no passersby present. The station was cleared an hour ago, leaving only cops in the concourse and FBI agents shifting nervously on the platform.

When the train comes to a stop, they force open the door to Car 13 and pour inside. With weapons drawn and hearts pounding in anticipation, they storm the Phoenix, moving from car to car, room to room.

The first discovery they make, in Car 13, is the dead bodies of Judd Dodge, Edith Gerhardt, and Herb Pulaski, each one tucked away in their individual rooms.

They find three more people in a single room of Car 12. Sally Lawrence, Lt. Col. Jack Lapsford, and Dante Wentworth. All remain very much alive, although there's some initial concern when they see that one of them is holding the other two at gunpoint.

Dante drops the gun and raises his hands. "They're all yours, boys."

The agents making their way to the front of the train don't encounter another soul until they reach the baggage car just behind the locomotive. That's where they find one of their own—Agent Reggie Davis.

He sits on the floor, a bloody hand clamped over a fresh bullet wound. One shot to the leg took him out.

Jerking his head toward the open locomotive door, he says, "They're in there."

Sure enough, the agents find Anna Matheson and Kenneth Wentworth at the front of the train. Wentworth stands at the controls while Anna remains slightly behind him, pressing an FBI-issued gun against his lower back.

She raises her hands when the agents swarm the front of the train and says, "My name is Anna Matheson. Beside me is Kenneth Wentworth. He is directly responsible for the deaths of thirty-eight people, including my father and brother, and indirectly responsible for one more—my mother."

The team's lead agent gingerly takes the gun from Anna and, with equal gentleness, places a hand on her shoulder. "Miss Matheson, we've scoured the evidence you provided and know what he did. We're deeply sorry for your loss."

Other than Seamus, no one had ever said they were sorry for her loss. That simple, basic kindness almost causes her to break down. Under such circumstances, not even Aunt Retta could disapprove. But the tears will have to wait just a little bit longer.

There's one more thing Anna needs to do.

After getting her various cuts and bruises tended to, she stands outside Union Station, watching the guilty be carted away. Lt. Col. Jack Lapsford is first. He limps handcuffed toward a black sedan, guided by two federal agents who ignore his protests that he's done nothing wrong, that Anna Matheson is a liar and murderer just like her father. The bellowing stops once Lapsford is shoved into the back of the car.

That's when he begins to bawl, as a photographer from the *Chicago Tribune* swoops in for a picture.

Sally Lawrence is far more mannered as she's taken into custody. No sniveling tears for her. Instead, she walks briskly, head held high. When she passes Anna, she asks the agents to stop.

"Anna," she says.

And that's all she can say, the words she intended to speak seemingly gone. Anna understands, for she also finds herself at a loss for words. There's so much that needs to be said. But as they face each other, Anna and the woman she'll always know as Sal settle for silence. It's not an apology, and it's certainly not forgiveness. But it's close. Enough for Anna to know that it might be all the closure she's going to get with Sal. If that's the case, she'll take it.

Kenneth Wentworth offers no such satisfaction. The man who caused Anna so much pain can't bring himself to look at her as he's taken away, not even after she spared his life. Wentworth is too busy badgering the FBI agents escorting him.

"What's this evidence you keep talking about? Have you even looked at it?"

"We have," one of the agents says.

"And what does it show?"

"That you're going to die in prison."

That's satisfaction enough for Anna. She doesn't need Kenneth Wentworth to look her in the eyes. Besides, there'll be plenty of time for that in the future. She's certain she'll be seeing him in court.

Dante sidles up next to her as his father is driven away. Watching the car recede down the street, he says, "I didn't know he was on the train, Annie. I swear to God. If I did, I would have told you."

"I believe you."

"And I didn't know about Tommy, either. Not until my father told me as they were arresting him."

Anna believes that, too. It's obvious to her that Dante Wentworth isn't the heartless cad she thought him to be. The heartless one in his family is the man now in FBI custody.

"I wish things were different," he says. "We would have been good together."

Dante's word choice tells Anna he now understands what she realized when talking to his father. There was a good reason for keeping them apart all those years ago. One that remains today. She and Dante can only be friends, and Anna welcomes the idea. She literally has no friends—and Dante will soon need one. He has a hard few years ahead of him.

"You and your mother need to brace yourselves for the hate that's about to come your way," Anna says. "Things will be said about you. Horrible things you don't deserve. All you can do is hold on to what you know to be true. And if it ever feels like it's too much to bear, write to me. I promise to write back."

"Can I also write to you about my brother?" Dante asks, the quiver in his voice reminding Anna that Tommy's memory no longer belongs just to her. Dante has just as much claim to it as she does.

"Of course."

Dante nods, grateful. "Good. Because I have a lot of questions."

"I already know the answer to one of them," Anna says. "You would have loved him."

Satisfied, Dante bows before offering one last crooked grin. "I look forward to our correspondence, Annie."

Once he's gone, Anna closes her eyes and exhales. There's a shakiness to the air rushing from her lungs. Grief. At last bubbling up. She's about to let it pour out of her when she spies Reggie

Davis being led away. Instead of handcuffs, he's been relegated to a wheelchair pushed by one of his fellow agents. Although his nose has been bandaged, the skin around it remains puffy and bruised. At Reggie's request, they come to a stop in front of Anna.

"Give us a minute, will ya?" he tells the agent, who gets the hint and backs out of earshot.

Anna inhales, uncertain if she wants to be alone with a murderer. Especially one who almost convinced her to kill as well. She'd been a millisecond away from shooting Kenneth Wentworth in the heart. The only thing that stopped her was a faint flicker of mercy.

"I want you to know that I confessed," Reggie says. "I told them exactly what happened. That Judd Dodge murdered Edith Gerhardt and that I killed Herb Pulaski—and then strangled Judd to death."

Anna releases the breath she'd been holding in. "You don't need to do that."

"And no one needs to know what Seamus did," Reggie says.

"I'll still know."

"Try to forget. And try to forgive him. Hopefully me taking the fall for it will help with that. Seeing how I'm about to be locked up for God knows how long, it's the least I can do."

Anna looks away, feeling a lump in her throat that she forces back down. "Thank you. I appreciate it."

Reggie shrugs it off. "You seriously wanted them all to live, didn't you?"

"Very much so."

"Why? And don't say it's because you're better than they are. That would have been true even if you'd killed them all."

"I don't know why," Anna says with a sigh.

She really doesn't. Because she also wanted them dead. And just like Seamus, she wanted to be the one to do it. Now that it's all over, she can admit this to herself. The reason she couldn't on the train is that she might have acted on those feelings—and she would have lost her own humanity in the process.

"Good-bye, Anna Matheson," Reggie says as he starts to be wheeled away again. Looking past her, he adds, "My boss is coming. I suspect he'll want a word with you."

Anna turns to see a gruff bulldog of a man in a black suit and matching fedora walking her way. "Miss Matheson?" he says, holding out his hand. "Ed Vesper. Head of the Philadelphia bureau. I just wanted to congratulate you. You got them."

"Not all of them," Anna replies.

"You got enough. You should be proud of yourself."

Of all the things Anna's feeling, pride isn't one of them. In some ways, she feels like a failure for not keeping everyone alive. In others, she feels like a coward for allowing a few of them to live. She suspects that the tug-of-war between the two will always be with her.

"What are you going to do now?" Vesper says.

Anna had asked Seamus the same thing back on the Phoenix. Now she can't help but wonder if he survived that fall from the trestle bridge. She hopes he did. She prefers to think that he broke through the icy water, crawled onto shore, and started walking toward some bright future in which he can find a cure for his affliction, find someone who loves him, and find forgiveness for his misdeeds. Anna holds on to that image, understanding that it's likely she'll never know.

When it comes to Seamus, the only certainty is that, contrary to what she said on the Phoenix, she's already forgiven him. He—and his memory—deserve that much.

As for Anna's own future, it stretches out before her like railroad tracks pointing to a distant horizon, the destination unclear.

"I don't know," she says, thinking about Aunt Retta's mansion, a place that, despite living there for so long, she's never thought of as home. A good thing, it turns out, because she'll need to sell it. It's literally the only asset she has left, having spent the rest of her inheritance on this single rail journey. "I guess I'll need to get a job."

Vesper nods. "May I make a suggestion? Come work for me in the Philly bureau."

"I'm not secretary material."

"Who said anything about being a secretary? I'm talking about becoming an agent."

Anna scoffs. "With the FBI?"

"Yes," Vesper says. "Agent Davis told me all about you. He said you're smart, got great instincts, and can handle yourself in a fight. Also, it's clear you're not afraid to shoot a fellow if needed."

"And you believed him? After what he did?"

Vesper cocks his head. "Was he lying?"

"No," Anna says. "All of that is true."

"Then I encourage you to put those skills to good use in a more official capacity."

Anna says nothing, mulling the possibility. She's already brought three of the people who destroyed her family—plus an unexpected additional killer—to justice. But there's no need to stop there. Plenty of other criminals remain free. Ones who've done bad things, destroyed other families. They also deserve punishment. Why should Anna deny herself the chance to help make that happen?

"Is that something you'd be interested in?" Vesper says.

Anna nods. "I think it is."

"If you'll allow me to escort you home, I can tell you more about the job."

Anna prepares to head back into Union Station but is stopped by Ed Vesper, who says, "I thought you'd have your fill of trains. If you don't mind, we'll be flying back to Philadelphia."

No, Anna doesn't mind at all. Trains are the past. Dante told her that. The future, he said, is in the sky. So Anna willingly follows Ed Vesper to the car that will whisk them to the airport.

Her own future awaits.

ACKNOWLEDGMENTS

EVERY BOOK IS a team effort, and this one wouldn't exist without the hard work and dedication of many people. First and foremost, I'm in debt to my amazing editor, Maya Ziv, and my equally amazing agent, Michelle Brower. Their suggestions and advice helped make *With a Vengeance* the book I always thought it could be.

Thank you to everyone at Dutton and Penguin Random House, especially Ivan Held, John Parsley, Emily Canders, Caroline Payne, Stephanie Cooper, Ella Kurki, Amanda Walker, and Ben Lee.

At Trellis Literary Management, I need to thank Allison Malecha, Tori Clayton, and Elizabeth Pratt.

Thank you to Sarah Dutton, who is not only the world's best first reader but who also suggested the title *Trainemies*, which still makes me giggle more than a year later.

To my friends and family, thank you for always believing in me and understanding when I must vanish for months at a time to toil away in my writing cave.

Finally, all the thanks in the world go to Michael Livio. None of my books would be possible without your patience and understanding.

ABOUT THE AUTHOR

Riley Sager is the *New York Times* bestselling author of nine novels, most recently *Middle of the Night* and *The Only One Left*. A native of Pennsylvania, he now lives in Princeton, New Jersey.